T0131529

BEAUTIFUL SINNER

A Morgan Montgomery Series

AAVENA **SMITH**

BEAUTIFUL SINNER
A MORGAN MONTGOMERY SERIES

Copyright © 2019 Aavena Smith.

All rights reserved. No part of this book may be used or reproduced by any means, graphic, electronic, or mechanical, including photocopying, recording, taping or by any information storage retrieval system without the written permission of the author except in the case of brief quotations embodied in critical articles and reviews.

This is a work of fiction. All of the characters, names, incidents, organizations, and dialogue in this novel are either the products of the author's imagination or are used fictitiously.

iUniverse books may be ordered through booksellers or by contacting:

iUniverse
1663 Liberty Drive
Bloomington, IN 47403
www.iuniverse.com
1-800-Authors (1-800-288-4677)

Because of the dynamic nature of the Internet, any web addresses or links contained in this book may have changed since publication and may no longer be valid. The views expressed in this work are solely those of the author and do not necessarily reflect the views of the publisher, and the publisher hereby disclaims any responsibility for them.

Any people depicted in stock imagery provided by Getty Images are models, and such images are being used for illustrative purposes only.
Certain stock imagery © Getty Images.

ISBN: 978-1-5320-7745-6 (sc)
ISBN: 978-1-5320-7746-3 (e)

Library of Congress Control Number: 2019909039

Print information available on the last page.

iUniverse rev. date: 07/08/2019

For my mom, who has always believed in me.
This one is for you.

Prologue

Thunder cracked as lightning flashed brightly through my bedroom window. I pulled the blanket up closer to my chin, my eyes wide and frightened. I was nine and I'd always been scared of storms for as long as I could remember. I don't know what it was about them, maybe it was just a small child thing. You know, scared of the closet, always making your mom or dad check under the bed for monsters.

So maybe I was just going through some nine-year-old drama.

Or maybe not.

Thunder boomed and lightning flashed as a tall figure appeared in my window. It had horns on top of its head and long sharp claws extended from its fingertips. I screamed bloody murder. It didn't take long for my bedroom door to burst open and my mom and Stefan ran in like they were ready for a fight. They probably were, given the fact that they were both holding small daggers in their hands.

They looked around my room, their chests heaving with each breath. But there was nothing there and the tall scary figure in my window was now gone.

My mom crossed the room to me and sat down on my bed and wrapped her arms around me. "It's okay." she soothed. "There's nothing here."

I was crying now, and my chest shook with every sob. "It was in my window." I cried.

"What was in your window?" My mother asked.

"A monster."

"What did it look like?"

"It had horns and claws."

Stefan walked over to my window and peered out. "I don't see anything. Whoever it was is gone now." he said with a frown. "I'll go out and check, just to make sure. Stay in the house." And he left the room as Nate walked in all sleepy eyed.

"What's going on?" he asked. "Why was she screaming?"

"Morgan saw someone in her window." My mom said. "But they're gone. Your father went down to make sure."

Nate nodded as he walked to the window and looked out. "I don't see anyone. All I see is rain and lightning."

A few minutes later Stefan was back. "I checked everything. I didn't see anyone." He looked at me. "Is she okay?"

My mom nodded. "Yes, she's fine."

My crying had stopped, and my heartbeat had slowed. The monster was gone. Okay, it hadn't been a monster, it had been a demon. But to a nine-year-old it might as well have been.

Stefan put a hand on Nate's shoulder. "Okay, let's all go back to bed and get some sleep." He and Nate turned and left the room.

My mom stayed behind for a few minutes, long enough to tuck me in again, reassure me that everything was going to be alright, and kiss me on the forehead. Then she left.

I never saw my mother again.

CHAPTER ONE

I *was having a bad week, and* by the looks of things it wasn't going to get any better.

First, I'd been suspended from my job for the next two weeks. It wasn't my fault, but I was the one being accused of lying. Go figure. Second, I had been dumped by my boyfriend and I was now homeless. And third, I had gotten a phone call saying that my stepfather had been injured.

Okay, he wasn't my stepfather, he and my mother had never gotten married. But he'd been the man who raised me since I was nine. Since the night my mother disappeared.

My name is Morgan Montgomery, I'm an agent for the PCU. Paranormal Crime Unit. It's a branch off the FBI. We deal with crimes of the supernatural world. The branch is nationwide, but there aren't very many teams. So, when a case pops up, the team closest to it gets it. But there have been those rare occasions when we work together.

But back to my bad week which was about to get worse. I was now on a plane to Seattle, to see my stepfather and friends I hadn't seen in years. Two and a half years, in fact.

I wouldn't say I was nervous, but I wasn't exactly not freaking out either. And for good reason. I wasn't sure how everyone was going to react. It had been two and a half years since I saw Stefan. He was the father I always wanted and in some ways, he was my father. He'd always been there for me whenever I needed him. No matter what.

I'd never known who my real father was. My mom had never told me, and Stefan would always talk around it whenever I asked. There were days when it drove me crazy. I knew there were things he wasn't telling me. Things about why my mom left and where she'd gone. I knew he knew who my father was. He just wouldn't tell me.

But over the years I'd grown up and out of asking him questions I knew did no good.

But it wasn't just Stefan I was worried about seeing. I had friends that I hadn't seen in years either. I talked to them on the phone, but it wasn't the same as seeing them. And then there was Nate. He'd never liked me and never hid the fact that he did. He was Stefan's son and hated me to his core. I was like the devil from where he was concerned.

My plane landed and I winced. I was so not looking forward to this. To all the looks and all the questions, about my job and my now ex. Which they didn't know about either. Yet.

I got off the plane and decided none of that mattered. I was on vacation. Granted it wasn't a tropical island with umbrella drinks. But hey, it was still sunny, and Seattle had a beach. And if I played my cards right, I might meet a nice guy and have wild revenge sex.

Okay, okay, maybe not the sex, but I was sure to find at least one nice guy. And it just so happened I was walking toward one right now.

Julian Kincaid was the nicest and sweetest guy I knew. He might have been one of Nate's best friends, but you really couldn't hold that against him. He was tall with shoulder length black hair that was pulled back into a low ponytail, dark coffee brown eyes that sparkled, and a personality that was sure to make anyone smile no matter what mood they were in. He wore faded jeans low on his hips, white sneakers, and a red T-shirt that said, Warning: May cause staring and hot flashes from the opposite sex, on the front of it.

And yeah, he was getting stares from the opposite sex. Whether that was because of his shirt or just because he was downright sexy, I didn't know.

He stood there holding a sign that said, Special Agent Sexy. I smiled when I saw it.

"Hey sexy." Julian said and pulled me into a hug.

I hugged him back. "Hey." I said.

He kissed me on the cheek. "How was your flight?"

"Okay. I have three bags."

Julian raised an eyebrow. "Planning on staying long, huh?"

I shrugged, trying to stay nonchalant. "Never know what I might need. I'm a cop, remember? I'm always on call." It was only a half lie. I was a cop, but at the moment, I wasn't exactly on call. I'd been suspended over something that wasn't entirely my fault. But I wasn't about to say any of that. At least not right now.

Julian nodded, not questioning me. He got my bags and we made our way to the car.

"So, how's Stefan?" I asked as he drove.

"Better. He's sore, but he's up and walking. Of course, Nate throws a fit every time he comes home and finds Stefan up and moving around. But you know how he is. He's stubborn."

I nodded and smiled. I did know. Stefan Williams was an angel. No, I'm not making a joke or saying he was that pure of heart. No, he was an actual angel. He was born that way two hundred and forty-eight years ago. And he had the white wings to prove it. Not to mention the power. He was from a long line of angels. So with that said, I knew exactly how stubborn he was.

Then there's the demons, the not so good guys who only want chaos. There are four different kinds of demons. The first are the vampires, they drink blood. And forget everything you've heard about them. They can come out during the day, they can still eat normal food, and unless they give you their blood in return, you won't become like them if they bite or feed from you.

The second are the werewolves. And it's pretty much the same about them. They don't turn furry and howl at the moon when it's full. They can shift whenever they want. And it only takes one scratch or bite from them for you to turn. But they have to be in wolf form. The third have the ability to turn themselves into something not romantic or cuddly. Into something with horns and claws. And the forth, well, they're less. They're like the first three. They look normal. They look human. And unless you know what they are, you'll never know they were something beyond it.

The angels and demons have one thing in common. They can procreate. And I along with all of my friends, are proof of that.

Yes, my mother was an angel, and therefore, so am I. And like I said before, I never knew my father, but even at that it wasn't exactly true. I have long black hair, dark teal eyes, and Italian features. Which tells me one thing. My father was Italian. How do I know this? Well, my mom has long black hair, bright blue eyes, and no Italian features. Which means I got my inhuman green eyes and olive skin from my father. Whoever he is.

But there are more than just angels and demons in the world. There are also other things, like fairy's and warlocks and mutants and other things that go bump in the night or bump in the day depending on the monster and its motives.

"Well," I said. "I'm glad he's doing better." I frowned as I thought of something. "Do you know what happened?"

Julian nodded. "Yeah."

"And?"

He sighed. "He went out on a bounty. The demon jumped him and got the better of him, tore him up really bad. And honestly, it looked worse than it actually was."

Stefan runs a P.I firm and does some bounty hunting on the side.

"And the demon?" I asked, already knowing.

"Dead. Stefan managed to kill him before he blacked out."

I'd known that.

"So, how's work?" Julian asked.

This had been one of the questions I'd been dreading. "Okay."

"And Daniel?"

And that had been the second. "I don't want to talk about him." I said.

Julian gave a knowing smile. "Okay." And he left it at that.

I sighed in relief. I didn't feel like going into detail about how the man I'd loved had dumped me and then thrown me out of the house we'd shared for over a year and a half. No, I didn't want to talk about that. And honestly, I'm not a hundred percent sure I really even loved him. I mean, I think I did, and God knows I said it often enough. But I'm not sure what we'd had was love.

Not even close.

We'd had sex, but not as often as he thought we should. And I knew that right there was the big problem, but not the entire one. There had been something else and it had come between us like a brick wall. We both had a job where we never knew when we were going to get called away. There had never been time for sex. We were both cops. Both PCU agents. Always being called away. And when I'd been the one accused of lying, he dumped me.

Yeah, talk about a buzz kill.

"Morgan." I heard Julian say. "We're here."

I blinked and sure enough he was right. I peered out the side window at the mansion. It was still as big as I remembered it. The house was white with pink and red rose bushes planted by the door. White tiger lilies were planted in the yard and the green grass was freshly cut. This had been my home as a child. The last place I ever saw my mother.

I got out of the car as Julian grabbed my bags from the back. We walked to the door and made our way inside. The inside of the house was still as I remembered too. There were ten bedrooms with their own bathroom, Stefan's office, Nate's music room, a few rooms that held weapons, a dining room, kitchen, and a sitting room. And let's not forget the pool in the back.

I walked into the sitting room and was surprised to see just how much everything looked the same. The walls were still painted red, there was a fireplace and above it was a mantel with pictures of Nate and I when we were younger. In the center of the room there was a long black leather sofa, with two matching armchairs. On each side of the sofa there were two small side tables with a lamp and a picture frame on each. In front of the sofa there was a long coffee table. On the wall across from the sofa and chairs, there was a large wide screen TV and a few shelves with DVDs. The titles were arranged in alphabetical order from action, fantasy, and the few chick flicks that were there.

Sitting on the sofa wearing blue PJ bottoms and a white T-shirt was Stefan. He still looked the same too. Short wavy blond hair, bright blue eyes, and a warm smile. And despite his age, he didn't look a day over thirty. The only change in him I could see was how weak and pale he looked.

But then again, he'd taken one hell of a beating.

Sitting on the sofa with him was Alec Messer and Dylan Ryan. They were friends of Nate's. They were both tall with short brown hair and green eyes. Cam Kincaid—Julian's father, sat in one of the chairs. He had short black hair and dark coffee brown eyes like his son. And a personality I was sure Julian had inherited from his father.

They were all talking when Julian and I walked in. Stefan saw me and smiled wide. "There's my favorite girl." he said getting up from the sofa and wincing at the pain.

"Don't get up." I said walking toward him. "You need to rest."

He didn't listen. He got up and met me halfway. "Now don't you start.

I'm two hundred and forty-eight years old. I'm as healthy as a horse. It's going to take more than a wise ass demon to put me into the ground."

I smiled and nodded. He was probably right.

"Okay." I said and hugged him.

He hugged me back. "How was your flight?"

"It was fine." I said as I heard the front door shut. I pulled back just as a tall man walked in. He like Stefan, had short wavy blond hair and bright blue eyes. Unlike Stefan, he didn't have a warm smile or if he did, he'd never shown it to me.

Nate.

He stood there with a glare as his eyes fell on me. "What the hell are you doing here?" he snapped.

"Hi, Nate." I said and smiled, knowing it would get under his skin. "It's nice to see you too."

"Yeah well, I can't say the same."

"Nathaniel." Stefan scolded. "Be nice. Morgan is here to visit. We don't see her that much as it is."

Nate rolled his eyes and muttered something under his breath.

Stefan turned his attention back to me. "So, where's Daniel? I've been looking forward to meeting him. Will he be coming later?"

I winced as Julian chuckled. "She's not talking about him."

Stefan raised an eyebrow. "Oh?"

I sighed. I might as well get it over with. Everyone would find out sooner or later. "He dumped me." I said and pushed back the tears.

"Why?"

"Because of some stuff at work. I've been suspended for two weeks."

"I'm sorry." Stefan said hugging me again. "What are you going to do?"

I shrugged. "I don't know. I guess I'll just wait and see what happens at work and find another place to live."

"That's why you brought so many bags." Julian said putting everything together.

I nodded. "He threw me out."

"Wow." Nate said. "Sounds like he came to his senses."

"Nathaniel." Stefan scolded again.

He shrugged and leveled his gaze on his father. "What are you doing up? The doctor said for you to take it easy."

Stefan waved him off. "I am taking it easy. And besides, I'm tired of laying in that bed and doing nothing." He walked over and grabbed one of my bags and started for the stairs.

"Dad." Nate said, an unhappiness in his voice.

"I'll be fine. Most of everything is healed. Now stop parenting me like I'm some kind of child."

Julian laughed. "You've got to admire his enthusiasm." he said grabbing the other two bags and following Stefan up the stairs.

I stood there and tried not to laugh.

Arms wrapped around me and I smiled. "Hello cupcake." Cam said and pressed a kiss to my temple. "I've missed you."

I turned in his arms and hugged him. "I've missed you too." I pulled back and smiled at him. "So, how's he really doing?"

"Not sure. He's put on a brave face and so far, it hasn't cracked."

"Do you know why he was attacked?" I asked.

"No clue."

"There has to be a reason."

"They're demons Morgan, they don't need a reason." Alec said getting up. He walked over and kissed me on the cheek and five seconds later, Dylan did the same.

"I know." I said. "I'm just being a cop about this. You know, the whole motive thing."

Cam nodded. "Yeah. And if you want my opinion, I think the demons are planning something. Something big and it worries me not knowing what the hell is coming."

He had a point. Sure, demons didn't really need a reason to attack anyone. But Stefan wasn't just another human. He was an angel. And the demon would have sensed that. Or at the very least known who he was. It was out of character for a demon to attack an angel like that. An angel was more likely to fight back and win than a human. And I had no doubt Stefan was mostly healed. Our ability to heal ourselves was remarkable.

I walked over to the sofa and sat down. A small yawn escaped me. "You must be exhausted." Stefan said coming down the stairs.

"I'm a little tired, but I'll be fine." I said.

"Nonsense. It's still early. Go lay down for a few hours and when you get up, we'll get a pizza."

I laughed. "Shouldn't you be taking your own advice?"

Stefan smiled. "Probably. Now go get some rest. Everyone will want to see you and you should be at your best."

"Everyone?"

He nodded. "Yes."

Great. I guess I wasn't going to get out of seeing everyone tonight. "Okay." I said getting up. "I'll go lay down for an hour." I kissed him on the cheek and made my way up the stairs.

Once I got to my room, I shut the door, walked over to the bed, turned on the lamp and sat down. I looked around the room and sighed. This had been my room growing up. Like the rest of the house, it too looked the same as when I'd left. The walls were painted a dark teal, the same color as my eyes. There were white curtains over the window, a white dresser, and a closet. The comforter on the bed matched the paint on the walls. To the right of the bed there was a door that led to a bathroom.

I pulled out my cell and set it on the bed side table and tossed my purse on the floor. I kicked off my shoes and laid back on the bed. I closed my eyes and sighed. Everything was going to be alright. I had to believe that. In two weeks, I'd go back to Boston and back to my job. That is, if I even had a job to go back to. And if not, I'd figure something else out.

And honestly, I wasn't entirely sure I wanted to go back to Boston. He'd be there and I didn't think I was ready for his attitude. For all the accusing stares. And I knew it wouldn't just be Daniel, but everyone on the team. I'd known better than to date someone I worked with, but did that stop me? No. I gave into his charm and my hormones.

I laid there and tried to turn off my brain. And surprisingly it wasn't that hard, because within minutes I fell asleep.

CHAPTER TWO

I was awakened by the sound of my cell phone ringing. I sleepily grabbed for it and answered. "Montgomery."

"Is this Special Agent Morgan Montgomery?" A strong male voice asked on the other end.

"Yes." I said, turning over and looking at the clock. It read 9:30 pm. I'd slept for over two and a half hours.

"This is Special Agent Elliott Bronson. I'm with the Seattle PCU team. I'm sorry to bother you this evening agent Montgomery, but there's been a murder."

I sat up in bed. "Um . . . okay, but . . . I've been suspended. I don't think I'm allowed on a case."

"I'm aware of that agent." he said. "I've called for backup and I've been told you're the closest." He paused. "Listen, I'm a few men down and I'd appreciate it if you'd give me a hand."

I wasn't sure I should say yes. I'd been suspended for the next two weeks. If word got back to my superiors in Boston, I could get in a lot of trouble. But the cop in me was curious.

"Agent Montgomery?" Bronson said.

"Okay, give me the address." I said.

I got up and slipped on my shoes, then grabbed one of my bags. Opening it, I pulled out my black shoulder holster and put it on and then checked my gun before sliding it back in and grabbing for my purse and cell phone. I headed downstairs where I found everyone talking and I was greeted with smiles when they all saw me.

"Hey there sleepy head." Julian said. "Have a good nap?"

"Yeah." I said. "Hey, can I borrow your car?"

"Sure. Planning a joyride?" He reached into his jeans pocket and pulled out his keys and handed them to me.

I took them. "No. Just got a call. There's been a murder and the local PCU team needs some backup." I kissed him on the cheek. "Thanks."

"Be careful." Stefan said as I turned and started walking out.

"I always am." I said.

I walked out of the house and got into Julian's red Porsche. It wasn't what I'd normally drive to a crime scene, but it would have to do.

Twenty minutes later I arrived at the crime scene. Red and blue police lights flashed; yellow crime scene tape blocked off an alley by a bar. The word INSIDIOUS glowed blood red above the building. Really? The owner named his bar after a word that meant treacherous and seductive? Okay, whoever this guy was I was sure he must have been a trip.

I grabbed my badge and made my way toward the yellow crime scene tape. There was a young police officer who stopped me. I flashed him my badge and he let me through.

I made my way slowly down the long alley way. There were two men at the bottom of it. One was standing and taking pictures, he had short brown hair and mocha skin. The other man was kneeling down. He had short blond hair.

I walked up and it only took me about a second before I saw the body. It was a woman, no more than twenty. She had long blond hair, her makeup was clean giving her a natural look. She wore a short jean skirt and a pink silk top. She had one black heal on her right foot, the other heal was a few feet away. This girl looked too pretty and young to be found at a place like this.

"May I help you?" The man with the mocha skin asked.

I showed him my badge. "Special Agent Montgomery."

"About time." said the man kneeling down by the body. "Tell me agent, what do you see?"

At first, I was confused, but then I realized this was a test. So, I looked at the body and tried to see what would win him over. On the girl's neck there were two small fang marks, blood was running out of them. But not enough to prove she bled to death. I looked closer and that's when I saw it. Her neck was bent at an odd angle.

Someone had broken her neck.

"Her necks been broken." I said. "Which means, it's not necessarily a vampire."

"Are you sure?" The man asked.

"Yes."

"How sure? How do you know she wasn't drained?"

"Because vampires don't drain their feeders. It's impossible. So, whoever killed her did it after she gave blood."

"Very good, agent Montgomery." The man got up and smiled at me. "I'm agent Bronson, we spoke on the phone." He offered me his hand. I took it.

The other man smiled at me. "Hi, I'm Special Agent Rafe Carlos. It's nice to meet you."

"So, what did you need me to do?" I asked.

"I need you to talk to a couple of men." Bronson said. "Their names are Kyriss and Constantine. We told them we needed to speak with the manager or the owner, but they say he's busy." He paused. "I don't want this to come out wrong, but I don't think they're human. Which would explain why they won't talk. So, I was hoping . . ."

"That since I wasn't human, I could get them to talk?" I finished for him. I wanted to ask him how he knew that I wasn't human, but I already knew. Word had travelled fast in only a few days.

"Yeah."

It made sense. Most supernatural beings didn't take too kindly to talking to humans. And if these men were demons . . . well, that explained everything right there.

"Okay." I said. "I'll talk to them." I looked down at the victim. "What's her name?"

Bronson flipped through his notebook. "Delisa Shaylee. Twenty. One of the bar staff found her when he came out to take out the trash."

Why did that name sound so familiar? I looked around the alley. "I don't see a dumpster or any trash cans."

"Yeah, we caught that too." Carlos said. "Sounds fishy."

It did. I continued surveying the alley and that's when my eyes fell on the stairs leading up to a door on the side of the bar. "What about those stairs?" I asked. "What's up there?"

"Hard to say." Bronson said. "We asked, but no one would tell us."

I frowned at that. "Okay, well, I'll go talk to the two men." I turned and walked off, pulling out a small notebook and pen. It took me about a minute to locate the men, but once I finally found them it wasn't hard to miss them.

They were both tall and gave off that supernatural vibe. One had shoulder length blond hair that was pulled back into a low ponytail. He wore dark jeans low on his hips, a dark T-shirt, and boots. When I got closer, I saw he had blue eyes. The other man had short brown hair, bright glowing green eyes, and mocha skin. He wore black leather pants, a black T-shirt, and boots.

Yes, these men were definitely demons.

I walked up to them and smiled as I showed them my badge. "Hi, I'm Special Agent Morgan Montgomery, from the PCU. I would like to ask you a few questions about Delisa Shaylee."

"Are you for real?" The blond guy said.

"Um, yeah. Why?"

"You look too cute to be a cop." he said and flashed me a breathtaking smile I was sure was meant to melt me into a million pieces and was sure had other women.

I ignored it. I was here to do a job, not flirt. "Save the flattery for someone else, Mr. . . . ."

"Kyriss." he said. "I'm Kyriss."

"Kyriss." I said, my voice stern. "I'm here to do a job. And the sooner you let me do it, the sooner we can all go home."

He still smiled at me all the same, still looked me up and down like I was a piece of cake or a machine he'd liked to take out on a test drive.

"My apologies." The other man said. "I'm Constantine. My friend is an idiot who only thinks with his manhood. I assure you he meant no disrespect, agent Montgomery." He turned his head to glare at his friend. "It won't happen again."

Kyriss rolled his eyes. "Yeah, sure."

Constantine turned back to me and smiled. "We would like to help with the woman, but I'm afraid we can't."

I ignored that. "Did either of you know Delisa Shaylee or see her with anyone?" I asked.

Constantine shook his head. "No."

I looked toward Kyriss. "How about you? Did you know her or see anything?"

"Nope." Kyriss said and smiled.

"Look," I said. "this girl has fresh bite marks on her neck. Now you or someone else had to see something."

"There are a lot of girls . . . humans, who find getting marked by a vampire exciting. Do you know how many girls I see every night with fresh bite marks on their necks?" Constantine asked. I didn't say anything. "It's not illegal, agent. And it's not just human women either. I've seen demon and angel women alike with bite marks."

"Have you ever bitten anyone?"

"No, I'm a werewolf. I don't do that."

I looked at Kyriss and he shook his head. "Not really. I prefer my blood from a glass. Once you drink from a source it's hard to . . . keep things non-intimate."

I nodded. I'd heard stories. It was like sex for a vampire. "Okay. Is there any way I could talk with the manager or the owner?"

"No." said Constantine. "He's a very busy man."

So, the manager and the owner were the same person. "Okay, well, is there any way I could speak with him at a later date? He does have a cell phone, right?"

"I am afraid that that will be impossible. Like I said, he's a very busy man."

"Yes, but surely he'd take some time out of his busy schedule to speak with the police. I mean, this is his business and she was found in the alley beside it. A murders got to be bad for business."

Constantine smiled, and I knew he was about to lie to me. "I'm sorry, but like I've been saying, he's very busy."

I doubted that, but I didn't push. I had a feeling it wouldn't do me any good, so I moved on. "What about the stairs on the side of the building? Where does the door lead to?"

"Nowhere you need to worry about." Kyriss said.

I raised an eyebrow. There was something going on here. "Why don't you let me decide that?"

"It's just storage space." Constantine said flashing Kyriss a look. There was a moment of silence between them, before Kyriss nodded. Constantine turned back to me and that's when I knew. They'd just used mind-speak to communicate between each other.

"Well," I said. "are you sure there's nothing you're not telling me?"

"Yes, we are sure." Constantine said. "We know nothing that can help you."

I nodded. "Okay. If you think of anything call me." I handed him my card.

He took it. "Of course, agent Montgomery."

I turned to walk back to where Bronson was waiting and that's when it happened. The air began to shift, and I was no longer standing outside the bar. I was now standing in a dark room. It was so dark I could barely make out anything in the room. There was a faint glow of light coming from small torches throughout the room and I could smell dampness and dust.

I tried to move but found I couldn't. My arms were shackled over my head and I could feel that my strength was fading fast. I looked on either side of me, because I could sense someone standing there, but I couldn't see who they were. It was too dark to make out their faces. But my vision-self knew exactly who they were, and she hated them to her core.

In the far corner, there were two men talking. Only it didn't look so much like talking as it did arguing. One was tall with wavy black hair and dark blue eyes that reminded me of the sky at night. The other man was also tall, with short black hair and . . . dark teal eyes. Eyes like mine.

My vision-self knew both of these men too. One, she hated almost as much as the men standing next to her. The other she . . . loved. And it broke her heart to know there was nothing either of them could do to stop this. She hated that it had come to the one thing she'd feared most.

Her death.

His loss.

Their love being cause for a madman to go even madder. And then, as if nothing had happened, the air began to shift, and I was now back to reality. I was kneeling on the ground, my hands gripped two strong arms. My breathing was coming in waves and my heart was pounding.

God, I hated when that happened.

"Montgomery?" Someone was saying. "Agent Montgomery?" It took me a moment to realize it was Bronson.

I blinked. "I'm . . . I'm okay." I stuttered.

"You don't look okay." Bronson said. "You look like you've seen a ghost."

I swallowed hard, taking in deep breaths. "I'm okay. This happens all the time. I just need a minute." I knelt there for a few more moments and then stood.

"What was that?" asked Carlos.

"It's called premonition. It's one of my powers."

"What?"

"She can see the future." Constantine said. I hadn't realized he and Kyriss was there. "A very rare ability. Only those from pure bloodlines inherit it."

"Cool." Carlos said.

Actually, it wasn't cool. It was annoying and had a tendency to be painful at times. I'd had that vision ever since I was a teenager. It was always the same.

Constantine stared into my eyes for a long time. He tilted his head to one side as if in thought. And then, very slowly, he smiled. "Ah, I see. Interesting."

"What?" asked Kyriss. He was silent for a heartbeat before his eyes widened. "Oh, shit."

"Yeah." said Constantine. "Oh, shit indeed."

I was suddenly feeling confused. They were looking at me like they were waiting for something. "Um, am I missing something?"

They didn't answer.

"Okay then." I looked at Bronson. "If you're done with me, I'll go."

"Yeah. I'll walk you to your car." Bronson said with a nod.

We made our way back to the car and the whole time I could feel eyes watching. I looked around but saw no one. Maybe I was just being paranoid.

When we got to the car Bronson whistled. "Nice."

"Thanks. It's not mine. It belongs to a friend."

"Must be some friend. What's his name?"

I frowned. "What makes you think it's a guy?"

He shrugged. "This is a guy's car."

I rolled my eyes. "His name is Julian." I said as Bronson nodded. "And he's only a friend. Nothing more. I'm home visiting my family and friends. And I don't have a car, so he let me borrow his."

"Oh. Well, sorry. I just assumed—"

"That since he let me drive his car, I was sleeping with him." I said cutting him off.

"I didn't mean it that way."

"Then how did you mean it, agent Bronson?"

He winced. "I guess like that. Sorry. I didn't mean to offend you."

It was too late for that. "It's fine. And just so you know, they didn't know anything about the victim. But that doesn't mean they're not hiding anything." I tore out the piece of paper with my notes and handed it to him. "Here, I took some notes." I said and he took the piece of paper.

He nodded. "Okay. And thanks for your help. I really do appreciate it. Our last case was bad. It put one of my men in the ground and another in the hospital."

"I'm sorry." And I meant it. There were just as many risks with this job as there were with others. I'd been a PCU agent for over two and a half years. And I knew what it was like to lose someone you worked with. It was hard but you got through it. You got up every day and made sure they didn't die in vain. "Well," I said. "I should probably go."

Bronson nodded. "You have a safe drive. And thank you again." Then he turned and walked off.

I stood there and watched him cross the street. My gaze fell on Constantine and Kyriss. They were watching me with curiosity in their eyes. I could still feel someone watch me and somehow, I knew it wasn't them I was sensing. Although I could feel their gazes as well.

No, it wasn't the two men I'd just talked to only minutes earlier. It was someone else. Or something else.

For reasons unknown to me, I turned my gaze up. I don't know why I did it, I just did.

Insidious was a two-story building. The first level was the bar itself. The second . . . well, it looked like it was some kind of apartment loft. There were white lace curtains hanging in the window, a faint glow of light illuminated just enough for me to see inside. Yeah, storage space my ass. Someone was living there.

In the window was a shadow of a man. I couldn't see him very well to make out his features. But something inside of me registered who he was. No, there wasn't a name or a face, but a part of me deep down in my soul knew who he was.

I'd seen him somewhere before. Or well, I'd sensed him. And what I was sensing right now wasn't human. Not even a little bit.

The man peered out the window and I knew without a doubt he was looking at me. Watching. It was both an unsettling feeling and calming at the same time. He stood there and watched me watch him. And I might not have been able to see his face, but I knew he was smiling.

The man in the window stood there for a moment longer, then he backed away and he was gone. I stood there and tried to shake the familiarity I was feeling. My eyes locked with Constantine's and a knowing expression formed on his face. He knew I'd seen the man in the window. He smiled at me and slightly nodded his head.

I frowned and wondered if maybe I was seeing things. No, I'd seen him. But just shook everything off. I was on vacation and trying to get over my ex. I didn't need anything else to add to my already shitty week.

So instead of questioning everything, I just got into the car and drove away.

CHAPTER THREE

I got home to find the driveway full of cars. Great. I guess Stefan wasn't going to give me one night. Now I was going to have to do my best to act like I was happy to see everyone. Not that I wasn't. I couldn't wait to see my best friends Sabine and Piper. I'd missed them. So yeah, I was looking forward to seeing them. I'd just would have liked to have tonight to get my head around being home, before I was bombarded by everyone and their questions.

Oh well. I might as well go inside and get this over with.

I got out of the car and made my way inside where I found a house full of people I hadn't seen for a very long time. And as soon as I walked in, I was jumped by my best friend Sabine. She saw me, gave a little squeal, and ran over and wrapped her arms around me. Sabine Kincaid was a few inches shorter than me with long black hair, dark coffee brown eyes, and an attitude that could cut glass. Yeah, she could make you laugh, but she also wasn't afraid to speak her mind either.

"I've missed you so much." she said, squeezing me.

"I've missed you too." I said, hugging her back.

"My turn." Piper said walking up. Sabine pulled back and let Piper hug me. My other best friend, Piper Ryan, was a tall red head with dark emerald green eyes. She was one of the kindest people I knew. She cared about everyone. But I guess when you have the ability to feel other people's pain and the power to heal, it kind of makes you sensitive. "I heard about Daniel. I'm sorry."

"It's okay." I said. "I'm trying to get over it."

She pulled back and smiled at me. "I heard that too."

I just smiled. I could only imagine what else she and everyone else had heard. I had no doubt Stefan had given everyone the full 411 on my personal life.

Piper stepped back just in time for me to lock eyes with one of the people I was dreading to see. Kaydan Lewis stood there and just smiled at me. He was tall with short sandy blond hair and pale baby blue eyes. He wasn't what I'd call sexy, but he did have that cute boy next door look that made him adorable at times. He was one of my best friends and my somewhat ex.

We'd had a thing back when we were kids. Okay, when we were sixteen. We'd been each other's first. In more ways than one. I could still remember the day Sabine and Piper were laughing their asses off as I told them about me and Kaydan having sex for the first time. How everything was fine until it was time for the condom. He couldn't get it open, and then after he did, he had trouble getting it on.

Hey, we were both virgins. We had no idea what we were supposed to do.

After we relieved each other of our virginity, we became . . . obsessed with each other and, well, sex. I could still remember the night Stefan caught us on the sofa, almost naked and really going at it. He'd yelled and gave a big speech about birth control and teen pregnancy and how we were too young to have a baby. I remember taking Kaydan's hand and taking him up to my room where we'd continued where we'd left off.

And yeah, Stefan had been pissed. I had been mad too. I'd been angry because he and Nate had brought girls home all the time. Nate had had one night stands at least twice a week or more. Stefan had dated a few women after my mom, but most of the women he brought home were only there for the night and never seen again. So yeah, I was mad that they had sex all the time with different people, and I was getting shit for only having sex with one.

Can someone say double standard?

I stood there and just stared at Kaydan. We'd ended things on a good note and had managed to stay friends all this time without getting mad or jealous when we saw the other with someone else. He smiled at me. "Hey stranger." he said. He walked over and gave me a hug and kissed me on top of the head. I inhaled and God he smelled good.

I silently scolded myself for that. I was not here to play ride the pole with Kaydan.

I pulled away and took a step back. I didn't trust myself. I knew me. Just because I was telling myself to not jump his bones didn't mean I would listen to myself either.

"You look good." I said. "Been working out?"

He nodded. "Yeah."

An awkward silence fell between us. Great. Now what?

"Well, I'm hungry. Let's eat." I turned to see Matt. He was Kaydan's older brother. He had the same short sandy blond hair and pale baby blue eyes. I smiled when I saw him. Matt had always considered me his little sister and had always treated me as such. He was very protective of me and so was Julian. Between the two of them, no one had even dared to treat me badly. At least when they were around. He walked over and gave me a hug. "Hey babe. Welcome home."

Home? Did he just say welcome home? I winced as I realized I might be moving back home and finding a new job. It was kind of depressing.

"Thanks." I said, my voice not sure.

Matt laughed. "It's not the end of the world."

That was what he thought. To me, my life was pretty much over. I liked what I did. I liked helping people and putting bad guys behind bars. But if I was fired, I wasn't sure what I was going to do. I guessed I could move back home and work at the firm, but I didn't really like that option.

"Oh, and by the way," Matt said. "I'm sorry about Daniel. He's stupid and deserves to be thrown into a pit with hungry lions and eaten."

I giggled. "Thanks."

"Come on, let's go get some food."

We all went to the kitchen. As I walked in, I smiled. The kitchen was the same too. The walls were an olive green with burgundy cabinets. There were stainless steel appliances and a small island was in the center of the room with four stainless steel stools on each side. Sitting on the island were five boxes of pizza and two things of breadsticks. My stomach growled.

I walked over to the island and opened one of the boxes and smiled. Green peppers, mushrooms, and light sauce was the perfect pizza in my opinion. And I knew no one else would eat it. No one understood how I could eat a pizza without pepperoni on it. Easy. I didn't like pepperoni, never had. I took a slice and bit into it and found myself moaning.

"Wow." Julian said. "It's like watching Food Network porn."

I smiled and just shook my head. Only Julian would think that.

"So, Nate, what have you been doing since I've been gone?" I asked around a bite of pizza.

He shrugged. "Nothing much. A little bit of this and that and some things in between."

"Is that your way of telling me it's none of my damn business?"

"Now what would make you think that?"

"Well, seeing as you hate my guts . . ." The truth was, I already knew what he'd been doing. Nate had been working at the firm. He did a lot of bounty hunting. He had a gun and a special badge to prove it. It wasn't like being a cop, but it was still important work. And my guess by the shiner he was sporting, had been from one of his pickups. Nate was one of the best. And if you tell him I said that, I'll deny ever saying it.

"What the hell do you want, Morgan?" Nate snapped. "For me to say that I'm happy to see you and glad that you're home? Well, I can't. I'm not happy to see you. And I wish you would find somewhere else to go."

That should have been my cue to go get my stuff and leave. Find somewhere else to go, but I didn't. No, I just stood there and stood my ground. Fighting with Nate wasn't anything new. And I was good at it. I'd been doing it for as long as I could remember.

"Nathaniel." Stefan scolded. "Enough. Stop trying to pick a fight with Morgan. And she's not going anywhere. This is her home too. So, stop."

"Whatever." Nate snipped. He grabbed his beer and took a big gulp. Yeah, I could use one of those myself.

"Okay, changing the subject." Stefan said and then smiled as he addressed me. "So, Morgan, how did it go at the crime scene?"

I shrugged. "It was fine. Probably some lovers quarrel." I hadn't thought about that, but it did make sense. It could be the girl's boyfriend. I mean, maybe he found her at the bar and saw the bite marks on her neck. Yeah, that would probably cause some jealousy and maybe a bit of rage. I wouldn't want my lover allowing some bloodsucker to take blood like that.

Bloodletting was like sex to vampires. So, if a woman allowed a vampire to bite her and suck out her blood . . . well, she wasn't looked upon greatly. Blood whore wasn't a word of endearment.

So yeah, if Delisa Shaylee had a boyfriend I'd be looking at him.

"I was wondering how did you get your gun past airport security?" Julian asked.

"I have a special permit." I said. I handed him back his keys.

"Hey guys, sorry I'm late." A tall guy said walking into the kitchen. I looked up to see Alexi Messer. He was Kaydan's best friend. We'd hung out, but only because of Kaydan and I'd suspected he'd had a thing for Piper. He wasn't my friend, but he'd always been nice to me when I saw him. He had short brown hair that I knew if left to its own devices, would stay curly. He had dark green eyes that sparkled when he saw Piper and he smiled.

She smiled back as a light blush tented her cheeks.

I flashed Sabine a look and she gave me a look back that said she'd explain later.

Alexi walked over to the island and smiled at me. "Hey, welcome home. And I'm sorry about Daniel. I was looking forward to meeting him."

Really? Wasn't there anyone who didn't know about Daniel?

"Thanks." I said. I looked around the kitchen. Everyone was here. Well, everyone but two people. "Where's Willow?"

Julian paled but smiled as he said. "I don't want to talk about her."

I knew what that meant. And it explained why he hadn't pressed me about Daniel. "I'm sorry."

"Don't be. I'm over it."

I nodded. "What about Kelsey?"

"She's at a friend's house. She wanted to be here, but she has an English paper do." Cam said.

Kelsey was the baby sister of Julian and Sabine. She was fifteen now. I silently wondered if her 'friend' was a boy or a girl.

We all talked and ate for about an hour until I'd decided I'd had enough. I said good night to Stefan and gave him a kiss on the cheek. Sofia Kincaid and Tamsin Ryan smiled at me and wished me good night. They along with their husbands, Cam and Donavan were the only ones out of Stefan's friends who liked me. Sheldon and Daphne Lewis and Luke and

Natasha Messer weren't exactly big fans of mine. I never understood why. Nor did I care.

I went up to my room, grabbed my PJ's and took a shower. After I was done, I got dressed. I stepped out of the bathroom into my bedroom and stopped in my tracks. Laying back on my bed and acting as if he did it every day, was Kaydan. His shoes were off, and he was stretched out.

"What are you doing in here?" I asked, already knowing the answer and hoping I was way off.

Kaydan smiled and patted the spot next to him. "Come here and find out." There was a sexy edge that filled his voice as he said the words.

I didn't want to find out. I wanted him to leave so I could go to bed. Alone. I was not in the mood for a booty call. I was tired and wanted to go to sleep and . . . and I was trying my best to stay away from men. Kaydan included.

But unfortunately, my feet didn't listen. I walked over and crawled in next to him. He smiled. He draped an arm over my waist, and I felt myself stiffen.

"Relax." he said, pulling me closer. But I couldn't. What the hell was I doing? He leaned in and kissed me and for one second, I allowed myself to like it.

That is, until there was a knock on my door, and it opened. Stefan stuck his head in as I jerked away from Kaydan. But it was no use. Stefan still got an eye full. Still saw Kaydan's hand under my shirt, still heard the small moan that escaped my throat.

Stefan's eyes widened as I tried to sit up. "Oh, sorry." he said. "I didn't mean to interrupt. I was just coming to make sure you were okay and see if you needed anything. But I can see that Kaydan's already got that covered." There was a smile on his face, and I knew once he left he'd go downstairs and tell everyone about me and Kaydan.

Kaydan gave a small chuckle and I resisted the urge to hit him.

"No, that's okay. We were just talking." I lied.

"Right." Stefan said. "Well, I'll leave and let you two get back . . . to your conversation." He shut the door and I was horrified.

Kaydan gave a bark of laughter. "Nice. Now that everyone will be listening—I mean Julian, where were we? Oh, I remember." He pulled me back down and kissed my neck, his hand going back under my shirt and returning to my breast.

"Kaydan." I said. "Stop. We can't do this."

"Why not? You're single. I'm single. We're both adults. So why not?"

"Because I'm not going to be your fuck-buddy."

Kaydan pulled back. "Wow, that's harsh. And besides, I'd never think of you as my fuck-buddy."

"Then what would you call it?" I asked sitting up. "We're friends and we've had sex. So, what would you call it?"

"Not that."

I exhaled. "I'm sorry, but I can't do this. I just got out of a relationship and I'm not in a hurry to get into a new one. And even if I did go out with someone, it wouldn't be you. God, Kaydan, you're my best friend. I'm not going to jeopardize our friendship for a quick screw."

"It wouldn't be quick." Kaydan quipped. "But okay, I see your point. I love you and next to Alexi, you're my best friend. And I guess sex would complicate that."

Yeah, it would. Which was why I was stopping it now, before we did something that would get us both hurt.

"Okay, so do you want to talk about what happened at work and with Daniel?"

I shook my head. "Not tonight." I wasn't ready to tell anyone about that.

"Okay. Well, I guess I should go and let you get some sleep." He gave me a quick kiss and left.

I sat there and frowned. I loved Kaydan and he was a good friend. And right now, that was all I wanted. It hadn't been all that long since the breakup and I wasn't ready to jump into bed with someone else. I mean sure, I had an unhealthy sex drive, but I was still able to control it. A little.

I laid back and the man in the window at Insidious popped into my mind. Who was he and why had I felt as if I knew him? I didn't have a clue. But there was just something about him that so familiar. I shook my head. I didn't have time for this. My life was complicated enough without adding a man I never even seen get to me.

My mind went to the girl in the alley. I needed to give Bronson my theory. I grabbed my cell and found his number in my recent received calls list. I pushed redial. His phone rang but went to voice mail. So, I left him a quick message about how I thought maybe a jealous and enraged boyfriend might be worth checking into.

After, I tossed my cell on the bed side table. I reached up and turned my lamp off. I was tired despite the fact I'd had a two-and-a-half-hour nap. I closed my eyes and allowed sleep to take me under.

CHAPTER FOUR

woke up the next morning fresh and ready for anything. No, I wasn't ready to tell my friends and family about my job and about Daniel, but I was ready to face all the looks.

I got out of bed and padded to my bathroom and just stared at myself in the mirror. I might have felt okay, but I sure as hell didn't look it. I looked worn and a bit rough around the edges. There were dark rings around my eyes, and they were a bit bloodshot, but I didn't remember crying. I put a hand over my stomach and rubbed it. I felt the first of unshed tears threaten to sting my eyes and cursed myself when a few of them escaped.

I brushed them away and just told myself to breathe. But it was hard. I still felt so empty inside, like something was missing. I mentally slapped myself. *Snap out of it.* I thought. I didn't need this shit, not now. Not while I was home. I wasn't ready to tell my family. I knew I'd have to eventually, and I knew when I told them, they'd give even more looks of sympathy. And honestly, I wasn't sure I could handle any more of that.

I shook my head and told myself it didn't matter. They didn't know. So, I turned and made my way downstairs and into the kitchen where I found Nate and Stefan sitting at the island, their heads over a bowl of cereal.

"Good morning, babe." Stefan said with a smile.

"Morning." I grabbed a bowl and spoon and sat down at the island. I poured cereal and milk into it and started eating. I could feel someone watching me. I looked up and sure enough, Stefan was looking at me like he was waiting for me to disappear. "What?"

He shook his head. "Nothing." But we both knew it was not nothing. "So, what do you have planned for today?"

I shrugged. "Nothing really. I thought I'd go see my mom's family—let them know I'm home."

"That sounds nice."

I doubted it would be nice, but they were my mom's family and mine too. My uncle Asher was a nice man and I liked my cousins Avery, Cristabel, and Grayson. I'd missed them too. And really, it wasn't them I was worried about seeing. It was my grandparents. Or better yet, my grandmother. She was a hard woman, always had been. She hadn't approved of my job or my lifestyle and had made no secret about it. But at the end of the day I was her granddaughter and she loved me. She may not have liked me having a dangerous job, but she loved me.

"Maybe." I finished my breakfast and did a quick scan of the fridge and cabinets. I had been right, there was no food in them. "How do you guys stay alive?"

"Fast food." Nate said. "Not that it really matters. You're only going to be here a few weeks, then you'll be gone. So why do you care?"

I rolled my eyes. "I'll pick up some stuff while I'm out."

"Don't bother. We won't eat it."

"Nathaniel." Stefan scolded. He smiled at me. "That would be great. Thanks. We could use a home cooked meal."

I nodded. "Okay. Well, I'm going to get ready and go. Mind if I borrow the Mazda?"

"No. I'll put the keys on the coffee table."

"Thanks." I kissed him on the cheek and headed up stairs.

When I was showered and dressed, I grabbed the keys from the coffee table and drove to the Montgomery home. It was just as big if not bigger than Stefan's house. But then again, there were nine people living here. My grandmother Camille wanted an unified family. Which meant the family lived together? When my mom moved out because she wanted to be independent, my grandmother had gone postal.

When my mom had disappeared, Camille had demanded that I come and live with her and the family. I could still remember the day she came to get me, still hear the hint of tears in Stefan's voice as he begged her to not take me.

"Please Camille, please don't take her away from me." Stefan had begged. I was in his arms, clinging onto him in a death grip.

"You're not her father." Camille had snapped, her voice cold.

"Yes I am. I am her father in every way that matters. I love her and it doesn't matter that she's not mine by blood. But Morgan is my daughter."

Camille had never liked Stefan and had never kept that a secret either. And this whole situation hadn't made her like him anymore or hate him any less. And we all knew she was only doing this because she was upset about my mom just up and leaving in the middle of the night with no explanation. So therefore, she was taking it out on Stefan like it was his fault my mom had abandoned her daughter.

When it was all said and done though, I had stayed with Stefan, but only because my uncle Asher had sided with Stefan, by saying, *"This isn't going to solve anything. Her mother has already abandoned her and taking her away from him is only going to cause more damage."* Camille hadn't liked that but had stopped arguing. But I think if she could have gotten away with it, she'd dragged me out of there kicking and screaming. But she hadn't. Not because she didn't want to, but because she would've had to deal with Asher and the others.

There would have been no way he would've allowed her to do that. Asher knew how important Stefan was in my life. He knew I couldn't handle losing the only other parent I'd ever known. I never met my real father. I don't even know his name. No one talks about him, even though I'm sure they all know who he is. I've never understood why they've felt the need to keep the knowledge of who he is a secret. But I guess they have their reasons.

I sat in the car and just stared at the house. It was a white two-story house with blue shutters and a wraparound porch. On the porch there was a porch swing and a few hanging plants. In the yard there were rosebushes and cherry blossoms. The grass was freshly cut.

I just sat there and didn't move. I didn't want to go in there and have to explain why I was home. Why I hadn't called them to let them know I was coming home. I had been somewhat relieved when I hadn't seen them at the house last night. Maybe Stefan had done that on purpose, knowing it would have been too much. It had been one thing to see Sabine and the rest of my friends, but the family I barely acknowledged, well, that was something different. There would have been a scene and questions demanded to be answered.

I sighed as I got out of the car. I might as well get this over with. I had to see them sooner or later. I couldn't ignore them forever. And if I had lost my job and had to move back here, well, they'd find out and they wouldn't be happy to be out of the loop. Especially Camille.

I walked up to the house and rang the doorbell. I stood there for about thirty seconds before the door opened. Asher stood there wearing dark jeans and a blue T-shirt and dark shoes. He had short black hair and bright blue eyes, and there was a dumbfounded expression on his face.

"Morgan?" he said, mouth gapping. After about two seconds he grabbed me and pulled me into a hug.

I hugged him back. "Hi."

Asher pulled back and smiled. "Come in. This is sure to make everyone's day." He stepped back and I walked in as he closed the door. I followed him into the sitting room. "Look who's in town."

Everyone in the room looked up from what they were doing and the five pairs of eyes that were looking at me turned their lips up into a smile.

Okay, here's something you need to know about my mom's family. Everyone has black hair and bright blue eyes. Even the ones who married in.

My aunt Ember jumped up from her seat and ran over to me. "Ahhh!" She hugged me tight and I hugged her back. This was going to be a repeat of last night. Only difference, Stefan had known I was coming home, and these people hadn't. "You're home. How long are you here?"

"A few weeks." I said.

Ember was my mom's older sister and the middle child of the three. Asher was the oldest child and my mom was the youngest.

And here's something else you should know about them. No one in this family looked a day over thirty. Actually, no supernatural creature looked a day over thirty. Immortality had its perks. Although, you were never really immortal. If the wound was severe enough or if your neck was broke, you died. Just like everyone else.

Ember let me go and the hugging started. My grandfather James was the first to hug me followed by my other uncle, Jonathan. My aunt Isabel was after him. The last was my cousin Grayson. He smiled as he wrapped his arms around me. "Welcome home." he said as two women came down the stairs.

It was my other two cousins, Avery and Cristabel. They took one look at me and screamed like excited little girls. "Morgan!" I was enveloped in two sets of arms.

"What's with all the screaming?" A female voice asked. Avery and Cristabel stepped back to reveal a tall woman with long black hair that was pulled tightly into a bun. Her bright blue eyes shined not with sparkles, but with suspicion. Camille, my grandmother, was always suspicious. About everyone and everything. She was a hard woman. She crossed the room, her gaze fixed on me. It was hard to tell if she was happy to see me or if she wasn't. But whichever it was didn't matter. She pulled me into a hug. "Welcome home Morgan. How long are you here?"

"A few weeks." I said.

"When did you get here?" asked Avery.

I swallowed hard. No one was going to like my answer. "I got in last night."

There were looks of betrayal, mostly from Camille. "I see." she said, a hint of anger in her voice. "I bet Stefan just loved that. Having you all to himself."

"Mother." Asher said. "Don't." He looked at me and smiled. "Morgan is here and that's all that matters. I understand why she waited."

I winced. "I'm sorry. I just needed a bit of time before I came here." Yeah, this was going exactly how I thought it would.

"I understand." Asher repeated.

"Well, I don't." Camille snapped. "We are your family. Your blood. You shouldn't need time before coming and seeing us."

Grayson snorted. "What family have you been in? We're crazy. Or at least most of you are." Camille glared at him, but he didn't pale. He just smiled.

Camille started to say something, but Ember cut her off. "So, Morgan, when do we get to meet Daniel?"

I sighed. "Daniel and I aren't together anymore."

"Why not?" Cristabel asked.

"Because of some stuff at work. I've been suspended for two weeks."

Everyone looked down. "I'm sorry." Jonathan said. "What are you going to do?"

I shrugged. "I don't know. I guess I'll wait and see if I still have a job in two weeks and go from there." That was all I really could do wasn't it? All because I was being accused of lying. And I hadn't. I hadn't made it a secret.

"Well, maybe you could find a more suitable job." Camille said. "One that doesn't involve a gun and dangerous situations."

"I like being a cop and I'm good at it." I said stubbornly.

"I know." And she didn't sound pleased.

I stayed a bit longer and promised Avery and Cristabel that we'd hang out and catch up. After I left the doom and gloom of the Montgomery house, I went to the grocery store. If I was going to be staying here for the next two weeks, I might as well give Stefan and Nate a decent meal.

I tossed food into the cart and when I was done, I went to the checkout. After I paid for the groceries, I made my way to the car. As I put the bags into the back seat, the feeling I was being watched washed over me like a wave. I stopped and looked around but saw nothing. But still the feeling was there, so I turned around. I saw nothing and no one.

And then I saw him.

Standing across the street was a tall man. He had shoulder length blond hair and a good build. It was my guess that it had taken him hours in the gym to get it. I couldn't see his eyes, but if I had to make a guess, I'd guess they were blue. Although, I couldn't be sure of that. He wore faded looking jeans low on his hips with a black T-shirt and tan work boots.

He stood there and watched me like a lion watches its prey. It was kind of chilling and only freaked me out when he smiled. It was a slow, taunting smile that promised only pain and danger. I shivered. I didn't like the way he was looking at me. I suddenly wanted my gun. Maybe when I got home, I'd put it on, so I'd feel safer. Yeah, that's what I'd do. I'd go home and carry my gun around as I made dinner. That way, if this psychopath showed up, I'd just shoot him.

Okay, I wouldn't shoot him. But I'd scare the shit out of him.

But by the look he was giving me I doubted that would happen either. He didn't seem like the scared off type. He seemed more like the one who did the scaring instead of being scared himself. So maybe I would shoot him after all.

I stood there and watched as a semi drove passed and the man disappeared into thin air. I blinked. More chills ran up my spine, but not out of fear, but out of knowledge. The man was a demon. Great. Just fucking great.

I shook my head. It was probably nothing and I was probably just over thinking this. I pushed the cart over to the cart holder thing and made my way back to the car. Yeah, it was probably nothing. Just because a demon was watching me didn't mean he was out to get me.

Or maybe I was wrong. When I reached the car and was just about to unlock the car door, I felt an uneasy presence. I looked up to see the man from across the street standing next to the car. He stood there and just watched me. That made me uneasy. Who was this guy and what did he want? I'd heard of stalkers. I do read and watch TV. But this wasn't one of my books. I wasn't a badass heroine who lived for danger and could kick someone's ass without much thought. I did not have wicked fighting skills and quick reflexes or witty lines.

Okay, maybe I did.

I was a cop after all and an angel. I did have wicked fighting skills and quick reflexes. And maybe a few witty lines.

"What, decided to come say hi instead of stalking me? Or did you just realize how much of a douche you were for staring?"

He gave a bark of laughter. Yeah, I so could use my gun right now. I had a bad feeling about this guy. And I had been right. He was a demon. His eyes were his tell, they were glowing red.

"What do you want?" I asked, deciding maybe being stern was the way to go, instead of smart-ass jokes.

His face sobered, but only a little. It was mixed with humor and a bit of seniority. Like he thought he was better than me. Or maybe he'd just been up on the pedestal for so long his power went to his head. "To warn you." he said. There was a hint of an accent I couldn't place. Swedish maybe? Yeah, that's what it was. He was Swedish.

"To warn me about what?"

"That he is coming for you."

"Who's coming for me?"

He smiled. "Oh, no. If I told you it would ruin the surprise." There was a note in his voice that said I wouldn't like it.

"Then why tell me?" I was getting the feeling that this was a prank or something.

"Because it will be fun watching you squirm while you are being taunted." Yeah, this asshole was definitely a demon. They liked doing that. Taunting and torturing things. It's how they got their kicks. And this dickhead wasn't any different.

"Look asshole, I don't know who you are, but it's against the law to threaten a police officer. Especially one who is more than willing and very capable of kicking your ass. I'm a PCU agent and I have a gun and I'm not afraid to use it. So whatever sick and twisted game you're playing, I advise you to stop."

I don't think I scared him. There was no fear in his eyes or any other part of his body. If anything, I think I amused him. He wasn't scared of me or the fact I was a cop. And that, in some ways, scared me. I've been on this job for two and a half years. And in those years, I've seen and dealt with a lot of things. Lots of situations that involved psychopaths and delusional beings. And in most of those situations, I knew what I was dealing with and how to handle it. But this guy . . .

This guy seemed off on so many levels it wasn't even funny. He was composed and calm. Too calm to be reassuring to me. I knew guys . . . demons like this. They were unpredictable and always gave off a vibe that said they were bigger and meaner than you. Nine times out of ten they were. And they were dangerous.

This guy screamed danger and pain.

My eyes flicked down toward his arms and that's when I saw it, knew I was in deep shit. On his left forearm was a tattoo. It was a skull with a sword through it. Hilt pressed to top of skull, sword tip pointing down from what would have been neck. Yeah, this guy was dangerous alright. And that explained why he was so calm.

He knew there was no way in hell I would attack him. I knew better.

He smiled again. "You are going to be fun. I look forward to playing with you." And with that, he turned and walked away.

I stood there; my mouth gapped open as I watched him walk away. What the hell? What was going on? Why was this demon warning me about someone coming for me? Better question, why was one of Samael's men warning me? It didn't make any sense.

And I know what you're thinking. Who the hell is Samael? Well, let me tell you. Samael is a demon, but not just any demon. He's the demon. He's the right hand of Lucifer as Michael is of God. Samael is a greater demon and so powerful, that even his own allies fear him, let alone his enemy's.

I've never met him personally, but I've heard stories. And none of them are very pretty.

A thought ran through my head. Was Samael the one coming for me? And if so, why? Why would I be important to a man like that? And with what I'd heard about him, I was sure it wasn't going to be anything good.

Perfect. Just fucking perfect. This is all I needed. It wasn't enough that I had been dumped and thrown out of my house or might lose my job and have to move back home. But now I might have one of the most psychopathic demons after me.

Yeah, this really puts the fucking icing on what was already a shitty week.

CHAPTER FIVE

I got home sometime later, my mind still running like a racehorse as I tried to decipher what the demon had been talking about. Someone was coming for me. Okay, so did that mean there had been a hit put out on me? I wasn't sure. It was possible. There had been that PCU agent in New York who'd had a hit put on him, after he put away a warlock for soliciting young girls on the black market. He hadn't liked his 'business' being shut down.

So, if there was a hit put out on me, then who? I didn't have an answer to that either. There'd been too many bad guys to count. Too many pissed off criminals who'd gotten caught and put behind bars. So, it could be anyone.

Better question was, was Samael somewhere behind it? To my knowledge, I hadn't killed or put anyone away who had been connected to him.

I sighed and leaned my head against the steering wheel. I did not need this shit. I had enough going on in my screwed-up life to worry about, let alone a psychotic greater demon putting a hit out on me. Yeah, this week just kept getting better and better.

I got out of the car and grabbed the bags and made my way to the front door. I raised an eyebrow as I realized that there was a red Honda in the driveway. I didn't recognize the car. I made it inside and walked into the sitting room to find Stefan sitting on the sofa. But he wasn't alone. There was a woman sitting on the sofa with him. She was wearing a short red skirt, white silk blouse, and black pumps.

I stood there in complete shock and horror. Because well, they were kissing and touching and . . . rubbing. Oh my God! Stefan was making out with some girl on the sofa. One hand was under her shirt and the other was . . . in a place I rather not say.

After a few seconds I found my voice. "Really? You're really making out on the sofa like you're two horny teenagers?"

The woman gasped as she and Stefan jerked away. There was a sheepish grin on his face, but the woman looked horrified. I couldn't blame her. If I'd been on the sofa with some guy practically doing the deed and his child came in and caught us? I'd be horrified too.

Stefan smiled wide, not seeming bothered at all. "It's my sofa."

"Yeah, but I sit on it. And . . . and you're old. Shouldn't you be tired or something?"

He just laughed. "Morgan, I would like for you to meet someone. This is Mariska Spencer, my girlfriend. Mariska, this is Morgan, my daughter."

Mariska got up, straightened her skirt, smiled and offered me her hand. "Hi, it's nice to finally meet you. Your father has told me so much about you."

I just stared at her hand. "Funny, I never heard anything about you." My voice came out colder than I'd attended. Since when did Stefan have a girlfriend? And why hadn't he told me? Okay, I really had no room to talk when it came to not telling anyone about what was going on in one's life.

She dropped her hand and frowned. It was clear this wasn't going as they'd thought it would. Stefan sighed. "Morgan, I figured out of you and Nate, you'd be the more understanding."

"How long? How long have you been seeing her?"

"Six months."

Wow, six months and he hadn't even felt the need to tell me. "Right." I said. I went into the kitchen and set the bags down on the countertop. I grabbed some paper towel and disinfectant and went back into the sitting room. "Move." I said.

Stefan got up and moved over to stand by his new girlfriend and wrapped an arm around her. I sprayed the sofa down and wiped it down with the paper towel.

"Morgan." Stefan said. "Why are you so mad about this?"

"I'm not mad." I snapped. Okay, maybe I was mad. I sat down on the sofa and just stared him and Mariska down.

Stefan sighed and rubbed a hand over his cheek. "Morgan." He began. It seemed as if he was having trouble trying to find the right words. And finally, after a minute of consideration, he spoke, voice low. "It's been a really long time since yours and Nate's mother's and . . . and I think it's time. I'm ready to settle down."

"What, now you're planning on marrying her?" There was venom in my voice.

"Wow." Stefan said amazed. "Now you're sounding like Nate."

Maybe I was being selfish—and I probably was—but I didn't want Stefan to be with this woman. I mean, okay, she seemed nice and all that. But if he'd really been that serious about her, why hadn't he told me about her? I talked to him on the phone all the time.

Why didn't you tell Stefan about you know what? A small voice in the back of my mind asked. I wanted to say it was different. But was it really? No. But still . . .

I started to answer, to say that I was nothing like Nate, when the doorbell rang. "I'll get it." I said getting up.

I walked through the foyer toward the door and silently cursed myself for not getting my gun first. If it was the guy from the store or an assassin coming to kill me, then I was screwed.

But thankfully, it was neither. Instead, it was a tall man with black wavy hair and piercing dark blue eyes that reminded me of the sky at night, and a heart pounding smile.

"Hello." he said with a hint of a Russian accent. "I am looking for Special Agent Morgan Montgomery."

Okay, maybe he was an assassin after all.

"I'm agent Montgomery." I said.

His face lit up as I said my name and he very slowly looked me up and down, and then he smiled. "It is nice to finally meet you agent Montgomery. I have heard so much about you." He extended his hand. "I am Balian Ivanski." There was something about him that I just couldn't put my finger on. It was starting to drive me crazy.

I took his hand and shook it. "Hi. It's nice to meet you. Can I help you with something?"

He nodded. "Yes. I want to apologize for Kyriss and Constantine, for how they acted last night. I know it must have seemed as if they were hiding something. And I wanted to assure you, they were not." His voice was matter of fact.

This was new. I looked at him with suspicion. "What's it to you, Mr. Ivanski?"

He smiled a bit nervously, like he hadn't expected me to call him out on it. Then he recovered. "I was informed of the situation, and I just wanted to reassure you that Kyriss and Constantine told you everything. And . . . offer you my services. If there is any way I can assist you, I would be glad to help."

Yeah, I just bet he would.

"Thanks. But uh, I'm not the active agent on the case."

"Oh. I am sorry. I just assumed you were since you were there."

"No, I'm on . . . vacation. I'm visiting my family." There was no way in hell I was telling him about my being suspended. "Agent Bronson needed help, so I gave him assistance. And this . . . this is inappropriate Mr. Ivanski." I used my cop voice, the one I used when I interrogated a suspect.

Balian's lips twitched, like he thought this was funny but was trying his best to hold back a laugh. "My apologies agent Montgomery. I meant no disrespect."

I wasn't so sure about that. This guy was coming off as a man who always got what he wanted and did what he wanted, even if that meant disrespecting a police officer. I highly doubted he came here to ask me politely to back off. No, he came here hoping I'd just believe that the men I talked to last night was telling the truth about not knowing Delisa Shaylee.

"Mr. Ivanski—"

"Balian." he said. "Please, call me Balian."

"Balian." I said. "I don't know who the hell you are, or who you think you are. And honestly, I don't give a shit. But it's illegal to bribe a cop."

"I am not bribing you." He said it as if it was ridiculous. But he was smiling, which told me I was right on the money.

I nodded. "Yeah, yeah you are. That's why you're here. Because you think I'll back down if you just kindly explain that Kyriss and Constantine was just doing their job. But let me tell you something, this isn't my first rodeo. And if I find out that they were lying to me or knew something . . . or if you knew something and are keeping it from the police? I will arrest you. All of you. And it will not be all rainbows and blue skies. Trust me, you do not want me to be the one who interrogates you. Do I make myself clear, Mr. Ivanski?"

Yeah, I was being a cop about this.

A slow taunting smile curved his lips. "Ah, but you do not have any jurisdiction."

"That's where you're wrong. I'm PCU. I have jurisdiction everywhere inside the US."

"Yes, but I thought you were suspended?"

My mouth gapped open as my breath caught in my throat. How in the hell did he know that? It was impossible. But still, somehow, he knew. I opened my mouth, closed it, then started again. "Suspension or not, if I find out that you were somehow involved? I will take you down."

I put as much power behind my voice as I could muster without it sounding as if I were being cocky. Because I wasn't. I had no idea who this guy was or what he was actually capable of. So, it did me no good to threaten him with any more than I could deliver.

It would have been stupid on my part to taunt the big bad demon with nothing to back it up.

The bastard actually laughed. A full out, head back, gut retching laugh. And when he spoke, that smooth and sensual sound of his Russian accent wrapped around me like a sheet of seduction and desire. "Oh . . . oh, I am sorry. But you just . . . you must be so much fun when you are angry." His laughter died down. "Oh, you are just simply precious."

"Tell that to my ex. I'm sure he'd beg to differ."

He nodded. "Yes, I am sure. But any man who willingly let you go or gave you up, would not be much of a man in my book."

For a moment everything stopped. I gazed into his unusually looking dark blue eyes that for some reason made me think of the sky at night. The feeling that I knew him washed over me like a wave. "Have . . . have we met before?" I asked feeling as if I should have known him.

"Not to my knowledge."

"Oh, I'm sorry. It's just . . . I feel like I know you from somewhere." Great, now he probably thought I was an idiot.

Balian smiled wide. "That is quite alright, love. But I can assure you, if we had met before, you would have remembered it."

"Right." I said as a blue Nissan drove up the driveway.

Sabine and Piper got out and made their way toward us. "Hey." Sabine said. She looked at Balian and frowned. "Hi Balian."

"Hello Sabine. Piper." he said with a nod at both.

I raised an eyebrow. "You know him?"

"Everyone knows him." Sabine said.

"Apparently not everyone." I muttered.

"You've been gone for over two and a half years. So of course, you wouldn't know him. And besides, you haven't been missing much from where he's concerned."

Balian gave a small chuckle. Apparently, there was no love lost between them. "I should be going. It was nice meeting you agent Montgomery. Thank you for your time and . . . understanding." He started walking toward his car but stopped and turned. "Agent Montgomery?" he said. "There is one more thing." He gave a half grin that was both seductive and menacing at the same time. "Thy dark prince has found thy dark beauty."

There were chills that went up my spine, as I watched Balian turn around and walk away. I watched as he climbed into his black BMW and drove away fast, like the devil himself was after him. Maybe he was.

"That wasn't creepy." Sabine said.

I couldn't have agreed with her more.

We went inside and I shut the door. I followed Sabine and Piper into the sitting room. I couldn't shake this feeling of familiarity. Something deep down inside my soul said that I knew Balian. And that his words had meant something. But what?

I walked into the room and resisted the urge to smart off. I was the only person I knew who was quick to anger. It didn't take much to piss me off. So, when I walked into the room and saw Mariska in Stefan's arms and consoling her—and let's not forget Sabine and Piper standing next to them and patting Mariska on the back—it kind of struck a nerve.

Stefan looked up at me and I rolled my eyes. I knew what he was about to do, and I needed to stop him before he did it. "Don't." I said, voice sharp. "Don't you dare start. I do not need this shit right now." I didn't stop walking until I got to the kitchen.

I didn't trust myself to not say more.

So, leaving the room was the safer option.

I put the groceries away and kept out what I needed for dinner. I was in the middle of chopping green peppers when Sabine and Piper walked in. I knew by the expressions on their faces that they knew what I had said and how I'd handled meeting Mariska. They didn't look happy.

They sat down and I waited.

"So, you don't like Mariska." Sabine said, voice tight.

"I don't know Mariska." I said.

"Then why are you acting like this?"

I stopped chopping and looked up to meet her eyes. I could feel anger boiling up to the surface. "Why didn't he tell me?"

"Why do you think? Because he was afraid how you were going to take it. And besides, it wasn't like you were here." That was Sabine. Blunt and straight to the point.

"I know that. But I'm just frustrated because he kept her from me. I'm his daughter. I'm supposed to know if he's seeing someone and if it's getting serious."

Like he was supposed to know what was going on with you?

I hated it when my inner voice was right.

"Just give Mariska a chance. She's really nice." Piper said. Of course, she thought Mariska was nice. She liked everyone and had the kindest soul of anyone I knew. Piper had the ability to sense other people's pain. Literally. She even had the ability of healing. It—they were both a blessing and a curse.

I shook my head. "I don't know if I can."

Sabine sighed. "Morgan, they're soul mates."

"What?"

"Their souls are bonded together."

"I know what that means. Are you sure?"

She nodded. "Afraid so." That was Sabine's gift. She had the ability to see people's souls and their auras. She could tell if someone was meant to be together just by seeing if their souls were bonded—if they each carried a small piece of someone's soul in theirs.

Stefan came into the kitchen and I could see the disappointment in his eyes. He'd really wanted me to accept her with open arms. He went to the fridge and grabbed a bottle of water. "So, who was at the door?" he asked not looking at me.

"Balian." Sabine said before I could open my mouth.

Stefan raised an eyebrow. "What did he want?"

"To bribe me." I said putting the green peppers and mushrooms into the skillet. "But I set him straight. I told him if he was hiding anything, I'd arrest his ass faster than lightning."

Stefan barked out a laugh. "You told him that? Wow. No one talks to him like that. Most are scared of him."

"I'm not."

"Well, you should be. Be very careful, Morgan. Balian Ivanski isn't a nice man. There have been rumors about him and the circle he hangs with. Rumor has it, he's dangerous."

I could see that. There had been that vibe that said he wasn't one to mess around with. But was he dangerous? I didn't know and I didn't want to take a chance and find out.

"Okay. I'll stay away from him." I said. Stefan turned to walk out. "Stefan." He stopped and turned. "I'm sorry. For how I acted about Mariska. I'll give her a chance. And if she wants to, she can stay for dinner."

The smile that stretched across his face was breathtaking. He crossed the room and hugged me and kissed the top of my head. "Thank you. This means so much to me." Then he walked out of the room smiling.

"Well, aren't you full of surprises." Sabine said.

I shrugged. "So, Piper, what's the deal with you and Alexi?" I said changing the subject.

I turn around long enough to see her squirm, before going back to cooking.

"Tell her." said Sabine.

There was a sigh. "We . . . had sex." Piper stammered.

I was shocked but yet not. I had seen the way Alexi had looked at her growing up. And I'd seen the way he looked at her last night. There had been something there. "When?"

"New Years. We were drinking and one thing led to another . . . and we had sex."

"So, are you guys like together now?"

"No. I think he wants more, but he hasn't said anything. We haven't really talked about it."

I turned off the stove. I drained the Pasta, put it into a large bowl along with the green peppers and mushrooms, and went to mixing it together. "Do you want more?"

"I think so. I really like him." Piper smiled. "But I'm not the only one with something to tell." She looked at Sabine.

Sabine rolled her eyes. "Okay fine. Three months ago, Matt and I kissed. That's all. No sex. Just one hot kiss."

I stopped what I was doing. Piper and Alexi hadn't surprised me all that much, but Sabine and Matt? That one I had not expected. "What? You and Matt?"

"Yeah, and I think there's something there. And before you ask, yes, yes, I think I'm in love with him. But I'm not sure what to do about it. There's just so much to consider before going into a relationship with him. He's Julian's best friend. And if he finds out, he's going to explode."

No doubt about that. Julian might talk a big game, but at the end of the day, Sabine was his baby sister. And best friend or not, there was no man good enough for her.

"I understand." I said. "Are you guys staying for dinner?"

Sabine checked the clock on her phone. "Yeah. I have an hour and a half before I have to go home and get ready for work."

I nodded and grabbed some plates. Sabine was a nurse. Which was no surprise since her father was a doctor. Piper was a realtor. Her profession was probably going to come in handy if I got fired and had to move back to Seattle.

I put the Pasta onto the plates and a piece of garlic toast from the oven and pushed the plates toward them with a fork. "So, how's work been?"

"Good." Piper said. "I'm just about to close on a house for a couple expecting their first child."

"Hmm."

Nate walked in at that moment and glared at me as he went to the fridge and pulled out a can of coke.

"Hey, are you staying for dinner?" I asked.

"No. Just got a lead on an FTA. So, I gotta bounce." he said.

"Okay. Well, let me give you something to go. If you're going to be staking out all night, then you can at least have a decent meal."

Nate sat down as I went and got a small Tupperware bowl with a lid. I put some of the Pasta into it with some parmesan cheese and fastened the lid. I wrapped a piece of garlic toast in aluminum foil and handed them to him with a fork.

"Thanks." Nate said. He looked down and sighed. "So, dad told you about Mariska."

I nodded. "Yeah. I didn't take it very well."

"Yeah, me neither. We actually got into a really big fight."

"You did?"

"Yeah."

I sat down and stared at the counter. So maybe I was more like Nate than I wanted to be. "So, you're okay with them together now?"

Nate thought about it. "Yeah, I guess so. I mean, I'm not happy about it, but I understand. It's been over twenty-one years since my mom and Elizabeth died. And what, fifteen years since your mom disappeared? So yeah, I understand that he's lonely and ready for a family again. Dad's just not cut out for casual sex."

I winced a little. Nate's mom Charlotte had been murdered when he was six, her throat slit. She had been six months pregnant with her and Stefan's second child at the time. A baby girl, who they were going to name Elizabeth Grace. Stefan had come home from work to fine his pregnant wife dead and his six-year-old son laying next to his mother, screaming his head off. They'd never found who'd done it.

Nate had witnessed the whole thing but refused to talk about it. And Stefan respected that. I understood to a point, but sometimes felt like maybe he needed to talk to someone about it.

"Why didn't he tell me?" I asked, my voice low.

"I don't know." Nate said, and I believed him. "Maybe it's because you closed yourself off from everyone when you left." He paused and seemed to be considering something. "Do you want to know why I'm mad that you're home?"

I raised an eyebrow. "Why?"

"Because, the prodigal daughter has returned."

"I don't understand . . ."

He blew out a breath. "Morgan, dad has three children. He has me, his oldest. There's Elizabeth, the child who died. And then there's you. You may not be his biologically, but you are his daughter. He loves you and I'm not sure there's anything you could do that would make him hate you. That's why I'm mad that you're home. Because you are his favorite."

I didn't know what to say. I'd always known that Stefan considered me as his daughter. I'd been seven when my mom and him got together and had been nine when she up and disappeared. He'd been the only father I ever knew and the only parent I'd had for over seventeen years. He'd raised me.

"I'm sorry." I said finally. "I didn't know it was that bad. So, I'm sorry."

Nate shrugged. "Don't worry about it."

I frowned. "So, you and Stefan's been fighting?"

"A little. He's pretty much let me know, that what he does, is none of my business." There was a hint of hurt in his voice. He got up, grabbed his stuff and walked to the doorway and stopped and turned. "Morgan?"

"Yeah?"

"Just so you know, Daniel doesn't deserve you. And if any of you repeat that, I will deny I ever said it." And then he walked out.

I smiled a little at that.

"So, I'm off tomorrow and there's this club called Illusions. Do you want to go?" Sabine asked.

I nodded. "Yeah, that would be okay."

"Good. I'll let Kaydan and Alexi know."

"Okay. Let's meet up here and I'll drive. Someone needs to be a designated driver. And out of the five of us, I'm the more responsible one."

Sabine snorted. "You, responsible? When?"

"When I moved away. Being a cop taught me a lot. And responsibility was one of them."

Yeah, in more ways than one. When my mom had disappeared, I'd closed myself off. I became hard and tough. I inherited an attitude and because of that, it had drove the people around me crazy. I snapped at everyone and got mad at the simplest thing.

So, it was safe to say, that when I got older and became a PCU agent, I took the first job outside of Seattle. I didn't like snapping at my friends and family over every little thing. So, I left. I left because I didn't want to hurt the people I loved. And if I'd stayed, my reckless behavior would have gotten someone I cared about hurt.

I fixed more plates and called Stefan and Mariska into the kitchen to eat. We all sat there and ate and talked and I got to know a little about the woman who stole Stefan's heart. Sabine and Piper left shortly after and I went up to my room and went to bed early. It had been another long day. And I was tired and just wanted to sleep.

I changed into my PJ's and crawled into bed and went to sleep. All thoughts of assassins and Russian men lost to a dreamless sleep.

CHAPTER SIX

The next morning, I woke up early and went for my morning run. I hadn't been on one since getting back and my being restless was proof that I needed one. I ran hard and fast as my mind raced even faster. I just couldn't seem to be able to get Balian out of my head. And his words. *Thy dark prince has found thy dark beauty.* What did that even mean? Was it some kind of riddle or threat? Had I been right, was there a hit out there for me?

But why? I hadn't done anything. Okay, that wasn't exactly true. I had done something. Just ask my ex and the board of the PCU. They'd tell you.

I finished my run and made my way inside the house. I went to the kitchen and started breakfast. It was seven, and Stefan and Nate would be getting up for work soon. And sure enough, five minutes later, Stefan padded into the kitchen followed by Mariska. Yeah, I'd forgotten that she'd spent the night last night. I guess he really was feeling better.

I gave a forced smile and poured them both a cup of coffee.

"Thanks." Mariska said.

Nate walked in with a big smile on his face. I knew all too well what that meant and ten seconds later, a blond-haired girl walked in. She was pretty, but it was hard to believe that he'd slept with her and if it hadn't been for the fact that I'd heard it . . . well, you get my drift.

Last night had been a house full of moans and screaming orgasms. And none of them had been from me. It was depressing.

"Can I get you some coffee or cook you some eggs?" I asked the blond.

"No." she said. "I don't eat carbs."

I raised an eyebrow. "Eggs are protein, not carbs."

She looked at me and blinked as if she'd just realized I was there and smiled. "Aw, you didn't tell me you had a little sister. She's cute."

I saw Stefan smirk and just shake his head. I knew what he was thinking. "I'm not his sister."

She shrugged as if she could really care less. "Oh, my mistake." She turned to Nate and smiled. "It was fun. I'll see you around." She kissed him and then turned and left.

I stared at Nate. "So, no exchanging of numbers or anything?"

"We exchanged." Nate said.

"What, body fluids?"

Stefan choked on his coffee and coughed. "She kind of has a point, Nate."

"Not true. We shared a special moment together. Nothing I expect either of you to understand."

"Oh, I understand." Stefan said.

"Me too." I said. "You shared a special moment in your bed."

"You sound jealous." Nate said with a smile.

"I am not." I lied. "I'm just stating a simple fact. The only thing you two shared was sex and nothing more."

"We shared more than just sex."

"Really? Did you two talk?"

"No."

"Are you planning on seeing her again?"

"Well, no. It was just—"

"A one-night stand." I finished for him.

Nate didn't say anything, and Stefan was laughing his ass off. He knew I was right.

"So," I said. "How do you want your eggs?"

There was a hint of a smile that played on his lips as he said. "The same way I like my women. Soft and easy."

"You are such a man-whore."

"Who's a man-whore?" Julian asked as he walked into the kitchen, followed by Alec, Dylan, and Matt.

"Nate." I said. "His latest conquest just left."

"The blond from the bar last night?"

Nate nodded.

Julian whistled. "Nice."

"How did you manage to tap that?" Alec asked. "She turned at least three other men down."

"It really wasn't that hard." Nate said and smiled. "She just needed a gentleman."

"Oh, and doing what you two did last night was you being a gentleman?" I asked with amazement.

"Yes. Because, well, I was gentle. Ow!"

I threw my spatula at him. I couldn't believe he said that. Okay, maybe I could. He was in fact a man after all. I shook my head. "How can you say that?"

"Easy." Nate said. "She just wanted a nice guy and I'm a nice guy. We talked a little and came back here and had some fun. No one got hurt."

"How do you know that? How do you know she didn't wake up feeling dirty and used? I mean, she was basically your sex toy last night."

"Clearly someone needs to get laid." Matt muttered under his breath.

Nate narrowed his eyes at me. "Like you have any room to talk. I seem to remember a string of guys from high school. Kaydan included. You were like some kind of sex kitten on over drive or something."

I winced. "I was young and stupid. And I was going through puberty. My hormones were going through the roof."

"Tell me about it." Stefan said. "I don't think anyone could have as much sex as you did as a teenager. Seriously, where did the energy come from?"

I didn't have an answer for him, because I didn't know. I had always been one of those people who were ready. If you know what I mean.

"So, how long has it been since you've been laid?" Julian asked.

I answered him before thinking. "Four and a half months."

Every head in the room snapped up. "How? How is that possible?"

I might as well tell them. If I didn't, they wouldn't stop asking until I did. I bit my lower lip and pushed back the tears. "Some stuff happened, and he refused to touch me." I looked down. This was starting to get painful. "It's funny, you know. He complained because we weren't having it enough, then complained because when we did, I didn't want to stop. Then some stuff happened, and he didn't want to touch me anymore."

"What kind of stuff?" Stefan asked. His voice sounded of a concerned father.

I shook my head. I wasn't ready to talk about it. And well, because I wasn't sure how they were going to take it. I had kept them all out of it and dealt with it alone. It was my private pain and I wanted it to stay that way until I was ready. "Just stuff. I don't want to talk about it." Yep, I was closing them all out again.

"Morgan . . ."

"Stefan please, don't. You can't fix this. You can't make it better. And talking about it isn't going to solve anything either. It just makes it worse."

"How do you know?" Stefan asked.

I closed my eyes and caught myself before putting my hand over my stomach. I opened my eyes. "Trust me. You can't fix this." I blinked back tears, but a few still escaped. I wiped at them. "Shit."

Stefan got up and walked around the island and pulled me into his arms. I didn't fight him and just relaxed. "I'm sorry. And whatever is going on . . . I'm here. I'll be right here when you're ready to talk."

I appreciated that. I knew when and if I was ready to talk, I could talk to Stefan. I mean, this had been the man who'd given me the whole sex talk. The one I went to the morning I woke up with my first period and had no idea what it was. That had been more embarrassing than the sex talk. But he'd dealt with it like a pro. He'd gone out and bought me a thing of Kotex and Midol, and then instructed me on how to put them on.

Hey, I didn't have a mother. She had disappeared and Stefan had been left to pick up the pieces and deal with all of that stuff. I suppose Sofia or Tamsin could have dealt with that part, but Stefan had never gone to them and I had never really minded.

Stefan had dealt with it all and never once complained about it. Not even the day I told him I'd had sex. He'd just taken me to the free clinic, gotten me a checkup and then bought me a box of condoms. Then said, "I expect you to use these. I want you to be safe and not stupid. You're too young for a baby. So, if you run out, buy more or ask me." There had been a pause and a cringe as he continued. "If you don't have any protection with you, there are some safe . . . sex things you could do." Then for the next hour, he'd gone over a list.

I pulled back and smiled. "I know."

Stefan kissed me on the forehead. He went back to his seat and sat down. "So, any plans for the day?" he asked.

I nodded. "Yeah. I'm going out with Sabine and the others tonight. We're going to this club called Illusions."

Stefan froze.

"What?"

He shook his head. "Nothing. It's just . . . be careful, okay?"

"Okay. Why?" I asked.

It was Nate who spoke. "Because Illusions isn't a very safe place. Trust me, when you walk in, you'll understand."

I guess I was going to have to just take his word for it.

I finished breakfast and then the men went to work. I talked to Mariska for a bit longer before she left to go to her own job. She was a ballet instructor. I spent the rest of my day checking on Stefan and cursing myself whenever Balian popped into my mind. I'd only met him once and I was already fascinated with him.

Maybe I could use my connections to check him out.

At six o'clock, Sabine and Piper showed up with a handful of clothes and makeup. By the time they were done, I looked like a stripper. I was wearing a short black leather skirt, a shiny sequence red top that was very low cut, and five-inch black leather knee high boots. My hair had been straightened, my makeup done light, and my body was covered in glitter.

Sabine had said the glitter was necessary, but I wasn't sure.

When we were done, we went downstairs to meet up with the boys. Stefan was sitting on the sofa and raised his eyebrows. "Sabine's doing." I said.

He put up his hands. "Hey, I didn't say anything."

"Yeah, but you were thinking it."

"I think you look hot." Kaydan said with lust in his eyes as Nate walked into the room.

Oh boy, that wasn't a good sign. I did not want to have to deal with Kaydan and his feelings tonight. Tonight, I just wanted to be the twenty-three year old I was, instead of the uptight cop I was almost every day. I just wanted a night of fun with my friends with no strings attached. Was that too much to ask for? I didn't think so.

"Of course, you do." Nate said with a hint of something I couldn't decipher.

"What's that supposed to mean?" Kaydan asked in a sharp tone.

Nate shook his head as he started undoing his gun holster. "Nothing. I'm not in the mood to try to explain unrequited love to you. You wouldn't understand anyway."

Kaydan narrowed his eyes at him. "And what would you know about it? It's not—" He stopped and looked at me then back at Nate.

"It's not what you think Kaydan. So, don't go getting your panties all bunched up in defensive mode."

"Then what the hell is it then?"

Nate set his gun and holster down on the coffee table and looked at Kaydan. "It's called observing." Something passed across his features and I wondered if there was more going on here then what met the eye. If maybe Nate had his own secret or maybe he really disliked Kaydan. Because the look he was giving him wasn't exactly friendly.

What was I missing?

"Okay," Sabine said rolling her eyes. "If you two are done peacocking, could we go now? I need a drink and a few dances." Her voice was sounded of that of a mother scolding her children with a hint of something that said she was so over it.

Kaydan stopped glaring at Nate and smiled. "Yeah, let's go." And with that, he draped an arm around my shoulders and led me out of the house and to the car.

We all got into the Mazda and Sabine gave me directions to the nightclub. Illusions was two blocks from Insidious. The nightclub was a tall building with a sign in the front in blue lights that said *Illusions*. It was a tad bit different than the other buildings on the block. It was taller and took up more space, whereas the other buildings were small and Illusions seemed to tower over them with its intimidating tallness.

We got in the long line and waited our turn to go inside. The bouncer at the door was built and looked like he could break us in half. I guessed werewolf. He never asked for ID, just took my left hand and put a red glowing stamp on the back.

The stamp was kind of cool. It was a red smiley face with two pointy fangs. It made me wonder what kind of club this was.

It didn't take us long to get onto the dance floor. I danced and danced and danced some more. Most of them with Kaydan. He'd pretty much claimed me since we'd arrived. He put his arms around me and pulled me closer, and I let him. I let him move his body with mine to the beat of the music. Because like I said, tonight I wasn't a cop. I was just here to have some harmless fun.

A new song came on when I felt the urge to look up towards the back of the room. In the back was a door, my guess it was to the office. The door opened and a man walked out. My heart stopped, then leaped with happiness. He was wearing a black suit; his wavy black hair was as messy as ever and his blue eyes shined with mischief.

Balian glided through the room like a dark angel—or maybe a fallen one. He seemed so captivating I couldn't look away. Not even when his gaze flicked up and met mine. It was so weird. It was almost like he knew I was there and exactly where I'd be standing. He smiled and it went all the way up to his eyes.

"Morgan? What's wrong?" Kaydan yelled over the loud music.

I hadn't realized until that moment, I'd stopped dancing. I blinked, then smiled. "Yeah, I'm fine. I think I'm going to go back to the table for a little while."

"Okay. I'll go with you." Kaydan took my hand and led me through the crowd of bodies to our table where the others were.

I sat down and Kaydan sat down next to me. I smiled because I was having too much fun to let what he was doing ruin it. I sat there and looked around the club. It was neat. There were red, blue, and purple strobe lights. The waitress's all wore short black leather skirts with either red, blue, or purple silk tops and black stiletto boots.

The waitress's moved from table to table, caring trays of drinks. Some of which confused me. In some of the glasses there was a red, almost like blood type substance. What confused me further, was that our waitress seemed to have fangs. Okay, that was different. She was a vampire. Although, I wasn't sure if the fangs were real or just some kind of cool prop. I'd heard of clubs like this. They were called underworld clubs. Most of them were underground. So, if this was one of those underworld clubs, the owner was very brave.

Yeah, very brave indeed. The underworld clubs were meant for supernaturals, humans weren't allowed in them. So, if all of this was real, well, then, this guy was breaking all the rules by allowing humans into his club.

"So, what do you think?" Sabine asked.

"It's cool." I said looking around.

"Yeah, it is cool." Kaydan said agreeing with me. I had a feeling by the smile he had, he'd agree with me on anything.

I smiled back as I heard Piper giggle. Yeah, it was apparent that everyone could see that Kaydan was trying to make his move on me. Although it wasn't exactly hard to guess, since he wasn't hiding it. Great, now I would have Sabine and Piper teasing me about Kaydan. But I guess it wasn't all that surprising. There had been a time when Kaydan and I couldn't seem to keep our hands off each other. And they had all teased me about him then too.

I looked at Kaydan and saw a need in his eyes. Okay, I needed an out. "Um, I'll be back. I need to use the ladies room." I said getting up and doing my best to not run away. I could hear Sabine and Piper's laughter behind me.

I went to the bathroom, did my business, and told myself to breathe. It wasn't the end of the world. So, what if Kaydan was into me and wanted to get physical? It didn't mean I had to marry him. Maybe I could just have some fun. We'd done that before. We'd had sex with no strings attached and it had been fun. And it had been a long time since a man had touched me. And if I was being honest with myself, my body was aching for a release.

So maybe Kaydan could help with that.

Snap out of it, Morgan! Get a grip. I told myself.

I took a deep breath and made my feet move. I opened the door and walked out, only to stop in my tracks. Leaning against the wall in the small hall was Balian.

"Hello agent Montgomery." he said. "I am surprised to see you here." His dark blue gaze swept down my body slowly, starting from my red silk top, to my black skirt, to my black knee-high boots, and all the way back up to my lips.

I opened my mouth to speak, closed it, and then tried again. "Hi."

I stammered. "I'm surprised to see you here too. I didn't peg you as the clubbing type."

His smile widened and seemed radiant. My lower body tightened. "Yes, I would ask you to dance, but . . . this is not my dance."

"Oh." I suddenly wondered what his type of dance was. "So, what are you doing here?"

"Checking up on some things. You?"

"Out with friends. And call me Morgan. I'm not on duty tonight."

"Ah, I see. You are on vacation, I remember. Are you having fun?"

The bastard was mocking me. "Yes." I said nodding. "This place is cool. I really like the vampire props. Whoever the owner is, he's a genius." I phrased it like that, because I wanted to see if I could get a reaction out of him.

Balian laughed, a full out laugh that curled around me like a silk sheet of seduction. "Oh, little orchid, you amuse me so, I find myself in ecstasy just being in your presence."

I swallowed hard as I felt my body tighten all over. "Um, thanks?"

He just smiled.

"Morgan, hey, everyone was worried." Kaydan said, walking up and stopping next to me. He saw Balian and his eyes narrowed. "You." he snipped. Kaydan turned to me. "Did he hurt you?"

"No." I shook my head. "We were just talking."

"Oh, okay." Kaydan said, but I could tell he wasn't happy. "Well, everyone is waiting. Sabine ordered more drinks."

"Okay." I said. "I'll be there in a sec."

Kaydan just stood there and didn't move. "I'll wait for you."

I frowned and resisted the urge to roll my eyes. I was starting to get the feeling there was no way to get rid of him. Great, just what I needed. An overprotective boyfriend. But Kaydan wasn't my boyfriend and I could take care of myself.

"What are you still doing here?" Balian asked. "Morgan has dismissed you."

Kaydan glared at Balian and I could tell he'd struck a nerve. "I am not some servant that you can order around."

Balian tilted his head to one side, as if in thought. "No, I cannot. But your behavior suggests otherwise. Perhaps you really are a lapdog. And frankly, I find it annoying."

"I don't give a shit what you think." Kaydan snapped. "You keep your hands off her."

That was it. I stepped in front of Kaydan. "Kaydan stop." I said. "Go back to the table with the others. I'll be there in a minute."

"But . . ."

"Your master has spoken." Balian quipped.

I ignored him. "It's okay. Go and I'll be there soon."

Kaydan gave me a look and then nodded. He turned and walked away, back to the table where the others were.

I heard Balian chuckle. I turned on him. "What was that?"

"What was what, darling?"

"You know what. And don't call me darling. We're not friendly enough for that."

Balian only smiled. "I thought you said you were out with friends?"

"I am. Kaydan is my friend."

"I am no expert, but should there be a 'boy' in front of friend?"

Damn. You know it's bad when even a stranger can see that a guy is into you. "No. Kaydan isn't my boyfriend. We're just friends."

Friends with benefits. A voice said in the back of my head.

"Does he know that?" Balian asked.

I stood there amazed. What the hell was I doing? "You know what, I don't know why I'm doing this. I don't owe you an explanation."

"Don't you?"

"No." I said, and started to turn and walk away, but Balian grabbed me by the wrist, stopping me. I looked at the hand that was clasping my arm. "Let me go."

Balian didn't listen, he just stepped forward making me step back until I was pressed against the wall. He let my arm go as he moved in, pressing his body to mine.

"What are you doing?" I asked, as panic set in and my heart began to race. "Don't tell me, you're looking for a quickie?"

Balian just laughed. "A quickie, you say?" His voice sounded amused. "Hmm, let me see. I do not mine quick interactions with the opposite sex. But with you . . . with you I would take my time." He leaned in closer. "Take my time exploring every curve . . ." His hand slid down my side, fingertips barely touching. "Every crevasse . . ." His hand moved down further. "Every inch of your skin, taking my time until I found that spot that left you withering in my arms."

There were no words. The only thing I could do was swallow hard, lick my lips, and listen to my heart go thump, thump, thump. My breathing came out in waves, as I tried to find my voice. I tried to speak but couldn't. He was too close. Way too close.

Balian moved in, his lips only mere inches away from mine, his manhood hard and pressed into me. "Do not say you do not wonder what it would feel like if I kissed you." he whispered.

Well, I hadn't until he mentioned it. Now it was stuck in the back of my brain and wouldn't leave. "I don't." I breathed; my voice shaky.

"No?"

I'm not sure what happened, but somehow, I found the will to push Balian back. I looked him in the eyes and said. "No, I don't wonder what it would feel like if you kissed me." Then I walked away with the sound of Balian's laughter behind me.

"Keep telling yourself that, love."

I walked back to the table where the others were. I did my best to smile and act as if everything was okay and Balian hadn't gotten to me. But the truth was, I wasn't okay and Balian had gotten to me. There was just something about him that just pulled me toward him. I couldn't explain it, so I didn't try. I just smiled and danced with Kaydan and let him put his hands on my hips.

A few hours later, it was time to go home. We all piled into the Mazda laughing and still high from the night's events. It was raining pretty hard, but not hard enough that I couldn't drive. It had been a fun night despite the Balian thing. But I had done my best to hide everything from my friends.

"You have got to be freaking kidding me." Sabine slurred just as Piper and Alexi's lips locked. "I am not sitting back here and watching them make out."

Kaydan and I were laughing so hard there were tears in our eyes. Piper and Alexi had started kissing back at the club and showed no sign in stopping anytime soon. I guess Alexi was making his move.

"Hey, you two." I said with a smile. "No tongue wrestling on the back seat."

Piper giggled and set back, but Alexi's lips moved to her neck.

"Well, at least someone's getting lucky tonight." Kaydan said and smiled at me.

Oh no. My laughter cut off. I looked forward and kept my eyes on the road and ignored what Kaydan was hinting at.

I dropped Piper and Alexi off at his house and watched them barely get inside the door before the first of their clothes came off. I took Sabine home and texted Sofia to come out and help her inside. After that, Kaydan and I went back to the house. I had no intentions in sleeping with him, but knew if given the chance, he wouldn't pass it up.

I pulled to a stop in the driveway and we got out of the car and made our way into the house. Kaydan had put an arm around my shoulders and pulled me close as we walked into the sitting room. Stefan and everyone were still here and looked up when we came in. There was a big round table in the room now with a stack of Uno cards on it.

There were smiles and a few grunts of hello.

"Hey guys." Stefan said. "Have fun?"

"Yeah." I said and fought not to frown. Stefan hadn't talked like that since I was a teenager.

Kaydan dropped his arm and slid his hand down my back and leaned in. "I'll see you upstairs." He kissed me and headed up the stairs. A few seconds later there was a sound of a door closing and I knew it was to my room. I guess Kaydan decided he was going to get lucky tonight after all. Great. Just perfect. How was I going to get out of this? Better question, did I want to get out of it? I didn't know.

I heard chuckles and turned to see Julian and Alec laughing.

"Something funny?" I asked.

"Yep." said Julian. "You should see your face. It's priceless."

I glared at him. "I'm happy you think it's funny."

"Come on, Morgan. It's just sex, not a marriage proposal. Go up there and screw his brains out."

"Julian!" Stefan said. "Don't be crude."

I shook my head. I wasn't going to comment on that. I was too tired. "I'm going to bed. Good night."

"Have fun." Julian said.

"Dude, you did not just say that." Matt said.

"What?"

"Man, he's my little brother and she's like my baby sister."

I didn't hear anymore after that, because I had made my way upstairs and went into my room and closed the door. I turned to face my bed and found Kaydan already there. He was laying on the bed on his back, the sheet pulled up enough to cover the lower half of his body, and he was naked. His clothes were in a pile on the floor and a silver square wrapper was laying on the bed side table on his side of the bed.

I didn't move. I just stood there and stared at him. I stood there and debated on what I should do. As I saw it, I had three options. My first was to get undressed and join him in the bed, let him ravish my body and take care of my little problem. The second was to grab some clothes and find a new room for the night and let him have mine. But that sounded like running away. My third option was to just change into some clothes and get in bed beside him, tell him I wasn't in the mood.

That option sounded better, but not by much. But I did it anyway. I grabbed my PJ's and started stripping out of my clothes. Kaydan's eyes had been closed but opened when he'd heard the sound of clothes coming off. I stood there for a half a minute in nothing but my undies. Kaydan's eyes filled with lust and need that said, yeah, take off your clothes and come let me play with you.

It would have been easy too. I could tell by the . . . bulge under the sheet that Kaydan was ready. All I had to do was remove my undies, mount him, and ride him like a racehorse. It would even be satisfying to a point. I would have my release and he would have me for a night. But I couldn't do it. Kaydan meant too much for me to use him like that.

He would not be my rebound.

I put on my PJ's and then crawled in next to him. My back was to him as I reached up and turned off the lamp and laid down. I laid on my side and stared into the darkness. Kaydan turned over and wrapped an arm around me, pulling me into his body. Yeah, he was ready alright.

His lips brushed my ear and his hand slid under the waistband of my shorts. "Why did you get dressed?" he whispered. His fingers brushed the inside of my thigh. I couldn't speak, which was bad because I couldn't tell him to stop.

"Kaydan." I breathed. "S-stop." Shit. "We can't do this."

"Why?"

"Because you're drunk." It wasn't the entire truth, but it was what I could come up with.

"I'm not that drunk." He nipped my ear and moved his hand from under my pants, to up under my shirt.

Now what?

Tell him the truth.

I didn't like the truth. But I went with it. It was all I had. "We can't sleep together because it would be like using you."

"Using me?"

I sighed. "Kaydan, I love you and you're my best friend. I don't want to hurt you."

"You wouldn't hurt me." he said.

"Yes, I would. And you know it." I pulled his hand out from under my shirt and laced our fingers together. "I just got out of a long relationship. Do you really want to be my rebound sex?"

He was quiet for a minute. "No, I guess not." He sounded sad as he pulled me closer. "You know, if I'd been smart, I would have never ended things with you. I would have tried to make things work. But I was a stupid kid who just wanted sex and you were willing. So, I thought, 'hey, she's my best friend and she wants to have sex. So, we could do it until we didn't anymore.' See, stupid kid."

"You weren't stupid. We both made the decision to have sex and then stop and just be friends."

"Yeah, but I think part of mine was we were getting close to College and we were both going to be leaving. So, I guess I thought it was time and a relationship wouldn't work. But if I'd been smart, I would have never let you go. And if I'd done that, you wouldn't be in pain right now over a man that doesn't deserve it. Instead, we'd be married and have a baby. Or at least with a baby on the way." I stiffened as he kissed my shoulder. I felt him smile. "I think I would have wanted a girl." His voice was soft, and I felt a tear slide down my cheek.

"Why a girl?" I asked trying my best to hide the tears.

"Because I would want a pretty little girl as beautiful as her mother."

His words brought back a memory I tried to forget. It had been the same conversation, but only Daniel had wanted a baby boy. *"Because I want a little boy, I can teach how to play football and how to pitch a baseball."* His voice had been soft and excited about the possibility.

"Morgan, are you okay?" Kaydan asked sounding concerned.

I wiped at my eyes. "Yeah, I'm fine."

"Then why are you crying?"

I shrugged. "I don't want to talk about it. I'm tired and just want to go to sleep."

"Okay. Let's go to sleep." He pressed his lips into my hair and kissed me. "I love you."

"I love you too."

"Night."

"Night." I said. And we went to sleep.

CHAPTER SEVEN

"**A**re you sure you and Kaydan** didn't do the nasty?" Julian asked for the hundredth time.

I rolled my eyes. "Yes, I'm sure. Kaydan and I just slept."

Julian gave a mock frown. "That's a bummer. I was looking forward to all the juicy details."

I laughed. He hadn't been the only one. I had gotten up this morning to find Stefan looking at me expectantly. He hadn't wanted details, but a conformation that I'd gotten lucky. But I hadn't and I'd said that much. Unfortunately, when Kaydan got up and came into the kitchen, his kiss on the side of my neck said something totally different. That had gotten me a knowing smile that said, liar.

Nate had walked in about that time, groaned, balled his hands into fists, but kept his mouth shut.

Now I was in the sitting room sitting on the sofa trying to explain myself to Julian. "He's my best friend, I would have only been using him. It would've been wrong."

"True. But still, you need to find a man and have a little fun."

"I don't need a man. I'm happy just being single for now." I said. It was true to a point.

"Okay. But when you're ready, I know a guy."

"No. No blind dates. No set ups."

Stefan smiled. "Yeah, Julian. Who knows who you'd set her up with."

"Exactly." I shivered just thinking about it. I looked at the clock and it read twelve. "I think I'm going to fix some lunch. Are you guy's hungry?"

"Yeah." Stefan said. And Julian nodded.

The doorbell rang. "I'll get it." I said getting up. "Meet you in the kitchen."

They nodded and I made my way to the door and opened it. Standing there was Bronson and Carlos. They were looking around at the big house. They turned and smiled.

"You didn't tell me you were rich." Bronson said.

"I'm not. My stepfather is." I said. "What are you guys doing here?"

"The victim's blood work came back. She's a supernatural."

I raised an eyebrow. "Really? What kind?" This was very interesting. She hadn't had a tell. Or at least not on her body.

Carlos smiled. "Fairy."

My heart stopped as I realized why her name had sounded so familiar to me. Delisa Shaylee was a fairy princess. Literally. Her parents were King and queen of the fairy court. Known as the royal court at times. "Shit." I said. "Shit. This is bad. Very, very bad."

"Why?" asked Bronson curiously.

"What is bad?" asked Carlos

I just looked at him. "Seriously? You don't recognize her name?" I was met with blank stares. I sighed. "Have you guys eaten?"

"No, we were just on our way to lunch." Carlos said.

I opened the door wider. "Come on. I'll feed you lunch while I explain why this is a very bad situation."

They walked in and I closed the door and led them into the kitchen. Stefan and Julian were sitting at the island. They looked up and smiled.

"Agent Bronson, it's nice to see you again." Stefan said.

"Likewise." said Bronson. "I'm happy to see you're doing better. The last time I saw you, you were in the hospital hooked up to an IV."

I winced at the mention of Stefan's attack. I grabbed some can chicken, mayo, and pickles and set them down on the counter with a bowl, spoon, and five plates. I put all the food contents into the bowl and mixed it together. I spread it onto some bread and handed everyone a sandwich with some chips. I pulled out some glasses and filled each one with iced tea.

We all sat there in silence for a long time, before Carlos said. "Wow, this sandwich is like heaven. Who knew, an agent that can cook. That's sexy."

"It's only can chicken, pickles, and mayo mixed together on two slices of bread. Anyone could do it." I said.

"Maybe so, but this is the best chicken salad sandwich I've ever had." Carlos said around a bite of his sandwich.

Bronson nodded. "I agree. How did you become such a good cook?"

I shrugged and looked at Stefan. He and I both knew the answer to that question. He smiled, but it was sad. "When I was nine," I began. "My mom ran off in the middle of the night. It was just me, Stefan, and Nate. Stefan wasn't really that good of a cook. So, I took over."

"You started cooking when you were nine years old?" Carlos asked.

"Yes, she did." Stefan said. "It is one of the parenting things I regret. Before I met Lauren, it was only me and my son and . . . even then I had struggled trying to feed him."

"What happened to his mother?" Bronson asked.

"She died . . . she was murdered." I could see the sadness in his eyes and heard it in his voice. I knew even after all these years it still got to him.

"I'm sorry." Bronson said. "I didn't mean to bring up bad memories."

Stefan gave a sad half grin. "It's alright. It is our way of life. We live and fight and die. That is just how it is."

Bronson and Carlos looked confused. But it was understandable. They were human and unless you were a supernatural, you wouldn't understand.

Bronson turned his gaze toward me. "Not to change the subject, but why is it a bad thing that Delisa Shaylee is dead?"

Stefan and Julian's heads snapped up. "Delisa Shaylee? As in Princess Delisa Shaylee? The daughter of King Androcles and Queen Cecily Shaylee?"

"Yep." I said.

"Damn." Julian said speaking for the first time. "This is bad."

"Why?" asked Carlos. Then it clicked. "Oh. She's a fairy princess."

"Yeah. And it looks like a vampire killed her." I said. "If she would have been a regular fairy, the court would have been apeshit. But she's royal. Apeshit isn't a strong enough word to explain how pissed they are right now. And this could cause a war between the fairy's and vampires. Which is bad."

"Why?" Bronson asked still looking confused.

"Because vampires are just another form of demons. And demons follow and take their orders from Samael. And Samael isn't going to allow the fairies to attack without consequences. Samael will wipe them out." Stefan said matter of fact.

I couldn't have said it any better myself. Samael was a madman. You would have to be out of your mind . . . maybe even crazy to attack him head on like that.

"Who's Samael?"

Seriously? "How much about supernaturals do you know?" I asked.

"Only what I learned in my classes. They're strong, fast, and don't like us that much. They have tells that give them away. Some are more noticeable than others."

And that was what was wrong with the PCU. It had been a good idea ten years ago, but now not so much. Supernaturals didn't like humans and humans were the only ones they'd hire to do the job. They put humans in classrooms and taught them how to handle the supernatural world, then put them out there expecting inhuman creatures to abide by the law and do what the puny humans told them to do. Yeah, that didn't go over so well.

The idea had been to crack down on supernatural crimes, but it had only made it worse. Cops had either ended up hurt or dead. The demons and other inhuman beings didn't respect the PCU or life for that matter, to care about the new law. Sadly, angels had been the only ones to abide by it. But then again, they'd hadn't even disobeyed it in the first place.

I told Bronson and Carlos about Lucifer and the fall from heaven. How he brought with him a fleet of angels and thus became demons.

"Okay, but doesn't that make you a demon too?" Bronson asked after I was done explaining the fall to him and Carlos.

"I am not a demon." Stefan said in a clipped tone.

"But she just said—"

Stefan cut him off. "My people were sent here by God himself to help police them. When they came to earth, they'd been here for so long that . . . like the demons, they learned they could procreate."

"Okay, but aren't all angels like men?" Carlos asked.

Stefan shook his head. "No. Well, in heaven they have no sexual orientation, like male or female. They are just simply angels. But when they came to the earth . . . they took on different forms such as female and male."

"But I thought that angels weren't allowed to have sex. Wouldn't that have made them fallen?"

"No. For one reason. It was forbidden to lay with the daughters of man, not with one of their kind. They did not sleep with human women or think themselves as Gods like the demons did. They simply procreated with each other for the simple fact of more warriors, more for the cause."

"Okay, I guess that makes sense. So, who's Samael again?" Bronson asked.

"A demon. A very powerful demon. Samael is as old as time itself. He was created with all the other angels in heaven and was one of the first to fall with Lucifer. He is the devil's right hand as Michael is of God." Stefan answered. I was so happy that he was here to help, because I wasn't sure I would have told everything right.

"I understand that." Carlos said and I believed him. "But what I don't understand is this. She was killed by a vampire. How does this demon have any say over them?"

"Well, there are technically four kinds of demons. There are the ones like Samael, who look normal and can blend in with humans. There are the ones who can make their body change into something hideous. Then there's the vampires and werewolves."

There were more blank stares.

"Vampires and werewolves are demons. There are no clans or packs. They do not follow an alpha or clan leader. They follow and take their orders from Samael, because they are his. They were angels at one time and fell from heaven. Or they were a human and were turned. But there haven't been very many cases of that happening. But they are demons. Even the few who were turned." I said.

"I get it now." Bronson said nodding. "This guy's got a power and controlling trip."

Julian laughed. "Yeah, you could say that."

"So why wipe out the fairies? Does he have that many men?" asked Carlos.

"Yes and no." Stefan said. "It's a bit more complicated than that. Have you heard of the Mark of Cain?"

They nodded.

"When Samael fell, he had a big army. But like us, if the wound was too serious it killed them. He lost a lot of powerful men, because they were killed. So, some time back, he found a way to assure he would not lose any more men."

"What does this have to do with the Mark of Cain?" Bronson asked.

"This was inspired by that. Samael found a way to create his own version of the mark. It's a tattoo placed on their left forearm. A skull with a sword through the top of it."

"How does it work?" I saw the wheels turning in Bronson's head.

"The skull is the curse and the sword is the seal. That's what makes it active." Stefan said. "It's sort of like a bomb or mine."

"Yeah." said Julian. "One wrong move and . . ." He spread out his arms and made a sound like something exploding. "You're in a million pieces and all the kings horses and all the kings men, won't be able to put your fried body back together again."

"So, it kills their enemies the moment they attack." Carlos said.

"Immediately." Stefan said.

"So, what do we need to do? How do we keep a war from happening?" Bronson asked.

"You need to talk to the king and queen—make them understand that you are doing everything you can to bring Delisa's killer to justice. That taking it into their own hands is against the law." I said.

"We've informed the court. But they won't let us in to ask them questions about Delisa."

Made sense, fairies didn't like humans any more than any other supernatural. "Fairies don't like humans or their laws. So, it's understandable that they won't let you inside the court or its community. Fairies are very private about their affairs and don't take too kindly to outside help."

"Do you think you could get them to talk to us?" Bronson asked.

"Maybe."

"Then I want you on this case starting now." And there was a note in his voice that said this wasn't up for discussion.

"I don't know if that's a good idea." I said. "I've been suspended, and I could get into a lot of trouble if my superiors find out. And I'm already in enough trouble as it is."

"You won't." Bronson said. "I won't let them. I'm a few men down and I need the help. I can't do this on my own. Carlos and I need you." He paused and considered something. "And it's stupid for them to punish you for . . .

this. You seem smart and know what you're doing. And if they fire you, you should sue the bastards."

I was honored that he felt that way. But not everyone thought I should be able to keep my badge. Daniel and my old team especially. But I appreciated his kindness. "Thank you. And yes, I'll help. Do you have any suspects?"

Bronson smiled wide. "Yep. Your boyfriend theory worked out. His name is Ivan. No last name." His smile only got wider as he said the next part. "And he's a vampire. I have a list of people who saw them together the night Delisa was killed."

That sparked my interest. "Do you have an address?"

"No. But I was told he'd be at this nightclub tonight. A club called Illusions."

Shoot me now. "Are you serious?"

"Yep." Carlos said. "Interesting name, huh? Rumor has it, it's run by a vampire. And it's said to have real vampires working there." He smiled. "And it's also said that he's the same owner of Insidious. Go figure."

Yeah, that was suspicious. "Okay. Let me get dressed and we'll head out. We'll go to the royal court first and talk to the king and his family. Providing they will let us in. Then we'll go see Mr. Vamp—see if he knows anything."

I ran upstairs and rummaged through my closet. I hadn't brought any work clothes with me, but luckily, I found a pair of black leather pants. I put them on with a black T-shirt and boots. I swept my hair up into a ponytail, so my hair would be out of my eyes and I wouldn't have any blind spots. I put on a pair of black leather fingerless gloves and my shoulder holster.

I looked badass.

I grabbed my badge and purse and headed downstairs. Everyone was in the sitting room.

"Damn, you look sexy." Julian said with a smile. "You're giving me all kinds of fantasies about handcuffs and interrogation rooms."

I laughed and rolled my eyes. Only Julian. I walked over to Stefan and kissed him on the cheek. "I'm going to head out."

"Okay." Stefan said. "Be careful. And I love you."

"I will and I love you too."

Bronson, Carlos, and I headed out and piled into his SUV. I drove since I knew where we were going and would be doing all of the talking once we got there.

I looked up into the review mirror and saw Carlos smiling. "What's so funny?" I asked.

"Nothing." he said and smiled wider. "It was just the way you said I love you to your dad. And his concern. It was . . . sweet. I'd got a lot of impressions from you the other night, but never sensed you as a daddy's girl."

"I'm not a daddy's girl."

"Yeah, you are. It's sweet." He laughed when I glared at him through the mirror.

CHAPTER EIGHT

There had been no more teasing about being a daddy's girl from Carlos. We'd all drawn silent for most of the drive to the fairy royal court. This had given my mind time to wonder off to dangerous places. Like Balian. I'd only met him twice and both times he had puzzled and captivated me to the point it was driving me crazy.

I knew somewhere deep down in my soul that I'd seen him before, but I just couldn't place him. But that didn't keep my mind from racing.

Last night Balian had been sexy and mysterious with a hint of a bad boy offering a good time. Yeah, I knew exactly where his good time would lead. To his bed. My mind suddenly wondered what it would feel like under him . . . or on top. I had a feeling one night with him and I'd be a goner. My lower body started to tighten with a needing ache just imagining it.

Damn it. I didn't need this distraction. I had enough on my plate as it was. I needed to get through these next few weeks and pray I had a job. I needed to help solve this case and bring Delisa Shaylee's killer to justice. Along with convincing Androcles that starting a war with Samael would solve nothing. That it would only bring more death. Probably his and his families. I didn't need a distraction like Balian Ivanski. Not to mention I didn't really need a man in my life right now anyway. I needed to get over Daniel first before either jumping into bed or starting another relationship with someone else.

"Is this it?" Bronson asked?

I blinked and looked around, slowing the SUV. There was what looked like a hidden drive with two stone sculptures of fairies with wings on either side of it. Unless you knew what to look for, you'd never know it was there for all the trees and wooded area. The fairy community was hidden by woods and by some small chance humans found it, they were stopped by two guards standing in front of a black medal gate connected to a nine-foot red brick wall.

I turned onto the hidden drive and drove down a gravel path. About a minute into driving down the small road, we were stopped by two fairy guards. They were both men and tall. One had short brown hair and the other had blond. By the looks of them, you didn't want to mess with them. They were big, well-toned and muscled.

I came to a stop and rolled down my window as one of the guards walked up. "This is private property." he said. "State your business."

"I'm Special Agent Morgan Montgomery." I said, showing him my badge. "These are my associates agent Bronson and agent Carlos. We're here to speak to king Androcles."

The fairy looked me over. "The king and his family are in mourning. You cannot see him."

"I'm aware of that." I was getting nowhere. "What's your name?"

"Amari. And he is Debythis."

"Okay, Amari, I need to talk to the king. It's about his daughter. I need to ask him and his family some questions about Delisa that might help me catch her killer. It won't take very long." It was a long shot, but I was hoping . . .

Amari narrowed his eyes at me. "You are a cop. You can do nothing to help."

"I'm not just a cop." Yeah, like I said before. Fairies didn't like humans any more than demons.

The other guard—Debythis, walked up and stared into my eyes. "She's not human. But she is one of them."

I had no idea what that meant. Maybe he was referring to the fact I was a cop. So therefore, I was human nonetheless.

Debythis gave me a disgusted looked and turned. "I will call and see if he will see her."

"Us." I corrected. "My team comes with me."

"Whatever." He stepped away and pulled out a small cell phone. After a few minutes he hung up and walked back over. "Let them in." He looked at me. "You will not be allowed to roam freely throughout the court. You will be met by two guards. Do not get out of your car until they arrive."

"Stiff asses much?" Bronson muttered.

I saw a look pass over Debythis's eyes and I knew it was time to get us out of here. "Okay." I said. "I understand." And I rolled up the window. I turned to Bronson who was smiling. His smile vanished when he saw my face. "Keep your opinions to yourself. Do not make smart ass comments. We are about to enter another world."

"They're in the same world as me." Bronson said with a frown. I could see that he was having trouble understand just how much shit we were about to enter.

I shook my head. "No. Not really. Their world may be on human soil, but don't kid yourself. The fairy community is another world. And they don't live by human laws. They live by fairy. If you show them disrespect, then you will pay for it. And you do not want to be put into a fairy prison."

"I'm a cop." Bronson said. "That should count for something."

"Not to them it won't. So, don't mouth off. And by the way, prepare yourselves. This might become a bit overwhelming."

I put the SUV in drive and slowly drove through the now open gate. I saw Bronson's and Carlos's mouths drop open and their eyes widen in awe as we drove down the small road and into open space. The word community is exactly what it is. A community. A town. It's a town within a town. If that makes any sense. One minute you're in Seattle and the next you're in Wonderland. Only you don't have to fall down a rabbit hole to get there.

There were gray cobblestone houses and huts. There were clothes on clothes lines drying in the breeze. Women walked the streets caring pails of water, the end of their long skirts held up by one hand. There were a few men leading some horses down the street. Everything was sort of surreal. Almost like you walked from the modern world to the medieval.

"Wow." Carlos said. "I feel like I walked into Beauty and the Beast. I wonder where Belle is? Do you think she's in that big castle down there with that talking candle stick?"

"Breathe Rafe." I said with a smile. "I told you it could become overwhelming."

"You sound like you've been here?" Bronson said.

"I have."

"When?"

"When I was younger." My smile widened when my gaze flick to his quickly. I knew what he was wondering. "Let's just say I allowed my hormones to rule my body when I was a teenager. And there was a fairy boy I was into."

"Oh." he said. "What was his name?"

"Esten."

"Do you think you'll see him while we're here?" asked Carlos.

"No." God help me if I did. We hadn't ended things on a good note.

I slowed to a stop at the big castle at the end. And it was everything a fairy castle should be. It looked like Buckingham Palace, but with some differences. There was a lot of walls that were made up from dark looking glass. There was gold and lilies carved into what marble was used to build the castle outlined by silver. Okay, it didn't look anything like Buckingham Palace.

"Really?" Bronson said. "Did they build that out of glass and marble?"

"And don't forget gold and silver." I said turning off the SUV. I looked up at the building. It was at least four or five stories high. I tried to picture Delisa growing up here and came up blank.

"Those must be the guards." Carlos said.

I turned my eyes toward the front of the castle. There were two men standing there looking impatient. "Yeah, that's our escort."

We got out of the SUV and made our way up the long steps to where the fairy men were waiting. One had short black hair and silver eyes, the other was blond with russet eyes.

I flashed them my badge. "I'm Special Agent—"

"We know who you are." The tall one with the silver eyes said cutting me off.

Okay, this guy was awfully cranky.

"I am Fierce." he said.

"Really?" Carlos said. "You don't look fierce."

I flashed him a look that said shut the hell up. I turned my gaze to Fierce and smiled. "It's nice to meet you. Who's your friend?"

"My name is Uraynus." The other fairy said.

"Say that ten times fast." Carlos muttered.

If looks could kill, Carlos would have been dead. Uraynus gave a look of death and I knew he was going to do something, because he stepped forward. I stepped in front of Carlos. "Back off." I said. Great, this was all I needed. A fist fight with a fairy.

"Move bitch." Uraynus snarled. He shoved me out of the way, and I stumbled. That was so the wrong thing for him to do. I effortlessly regained my balance and had him shoved up against the wall. His arm tightly bent behind his back and his face pushed into the wall.

"You ever touch me again; I will break off your arm and shove it up your ass." I said, my voice sounding cold and filled with promise.

"Enough!" A strong male voice yelled. "Release him and put down your weapons."

I turned my head to see a tall man standing just inside the door. He had wavy black hair and blue green eyes that seemed to be swirling. I looked behind me and saw that Bronson and Carlos had their guns out and pointed toward Fierce.

I sighed. This wasn't going the way I'd planned. I let Uraynus go and stepped back. He turned and swung his fist to hit me but stopped when the swirly eyed man yelled. "Don't!"

He stopped mid-swing. "But they insulted me."

"They are humans." The man said as if that was answer enough. Apparently, it was, because Uraynus nodded and stepped back. The man in the doorway walked forward and offered me his hand. "Special Agent Montgomery, the king has been waiting for you. I am Theophilius. I will escort you to the den. Follow me."

I followed him. Carlos walked next to me and I leaned in close and whispered into his ear. "Keep your fucking mouth shut. That stunt you pulled back there could have gotten you killed. These people don't play around, and they have no sense of humor. Just keep your mouth shut and take notes. Let me do all the talking."

Carlos nodded and we continued walking in silence. I only hoped he'd listen and do what I said. There'd been enough trouble as there was. The last thing I needed was to have to shoot my way out of here with Bronson and Carlos.

We walked down a very long hallway and made several turns. From what I could tell, the décor was pretty much the same. Lots of purple lilies with pale green leaves. We were taken through another corridor and entered a big room I guessed was the den. And like the rest of the place, there was a lot of purple and pale green. The walls were a light purple with pale green sheer curtains. There was a small love seat that was pale green with lilies embroidered in gold thread. There were also several other armchairs with the same design and small gold tables with clear crystal vases of purple lilies.

I guess they had a thing for purple, green, and lilies.

Sitting on the love seat was a tall man with long brown hair and dark green eyes that seemed to be radiating with anger. His green eyes were narrowed in a glare, his jaw set, and his hands were in tight fists. He was King Androcles Shaylee. Sitting next to him was his wife, Queen Cecily Shaylee. She was tall too, but not as tall as me. She had long white blond hair and pale green eyes that were blood shot from crying. She wore a pale green dress that reminded me of something they used to wear in ancient Greece. Looking at her, I couldn't help but think that Delisa had looked somewhat like her mother. And I wondered if her eyes had been the same shade of green.

Sitting in one of the chairs was a boy around my age. He had short brown hair and dark green eyes like his father. Zarek Shaylee sat there with accusation in his eyes. In the chair next to him sat a young girl who looked to be a few years younger than Delisa. She had the same long white blond hair and pale green eyes as her mother. Ila Shaylee looked at me with a pleading expression. I took it at that, that whatever her father was planning, even she knew it was wrong.

We walked in and Theophilius gave a small bow. Bronson and Carlos flashed me a look and I shook my head. We were not here to give politeness and bow like we were his servants.

"Your Highness." Theophilius said. "May I introduce Special Agents, Montgomery, Bronson, and Carlos."

Androcles did not smile or even thank us for coming. No, he just sat there and assessed us. He looked us over like we were roaches on his wall, and he was trying to figure out how to squish us without ruining the paint.

This guy was going to be a joy to talk to.

I walked forward two steps and gave a sad smile. "I'm agent Montgomery. I'm sorry for your loss."

"Thank you." Androcles said. "Please, call me Andros. And . . . no amount of sympathy is going to change anything. My child is still dead.

Murdered by a monster like you. Does he really believe sending you here is going to change my mind?" His voice was cold like ice, but not entirely void of emotion. There had been a harshness to his voice as he'd referred to me as a monster.

Okay, this wasn't the first time I'd been called a monster. To humans, every supernatural was a monster. Even the angels. We weren't human and it was unnatural. But being called a monster by a fairy was something new. As far as I knew, fairies didn't have a problem with angels. Granted, they didn't exactly like us, but they liked us better than demons and warlocks. So, I had no idea what Andros was talking about.

"What are you talking about?" I asked.

He got up and narrowed his eyes. "Don't act like you don't know what I'm talking about, you hell-breed."

Hell-breed? That definitely was a new one.

"Okay, whatever that means. Moving on. I would like to ask you a few questions about Delisa." Maybe if I just jumped right into why I was here, then maybe he'd stop insulting me.

Andros walked over to a table with assorted liquids and poured one into a glass. "What do you want to know?" His tone was mocking now.

"When was the last time you saw your daughter?"

"A year ago."

That was interesting. "I'm sorry."

He knocked the drink back and set the glass back onto the table. "Don't be. She wanted to leave." His shoulders slumped and he turned to face me. "I love my—" Pain shot through his eyes. "I loved my daughter and I wanted what was best for her. But sometimes she didn't make the best choices."

"Like Ivan?" I asked, wanting to see his reaction to the question. "Did you know she had a boyfriend?"

"Yes. Why do you think she left? She wanted to be with him. With a vampire. And now she's dead."

So, he knew about Ivan and that he was a vampire.

I looked toward Carlos and he was scribbling everything down onto a notebook.

"He killed her, didn't he?" It was Zarek who'd spoke. "That fucking vampire killed my sister." His voice was harsh sounding.

There was a small whimper that came from Cecily. "My poor baby girl." she cried.

Zarek got up and went to her. "Mother, I'm sorry." He pulled her into his arms, and she cried softly into her son's light gray suit.

"We don't know he's the killer." I said. I didn't want them jumping to conclusions.

"I know who the killer is. And he's going to pay for this." Andros snarled.

"Taking matters into your own hands isn't going to solve anything." I said. "It will only cause war with Samael."

"Then so be it."

"Samael didn't kill your daughter, Andros. A demon did."

"I don't give a shit! My child is dead and as far as I'm concerned, that bastard is responsible!" His voice boomed.

And that was what I'd been afraid of. Like I'd said before, if Delisa Shaylee would have been just a regular fairy girl, the royal court would have been apeshit. But . . . Delisa was a fairy princess. Androcles was not going to stand by and allow his daughter's killer to be set free. If he found who did it, he was going to kill them. Very publicly. And when Samael saw what happened to his demon? Well, let's just say there would be hell to pay.

"If you go after the demon who killed your daughter, Samael will kill you. And your family. He will kill every fairy he can find. He'll wipe you out and your race will become extinct."

Andros leveled his gaze to meet mine and when he spoke, there was pain and promise. "I want my daughter's killer found. Now!"

"And I will find him." I said. "But you have to be patient. Her murder cannot be solved overnight. But I promise, Andros, I will find him, and he will pay." And that was all I could promise him.

"That's not good enough." That came from Theophilius. "Delisa was a nice girl. She made some bad choices, but she was good. She didn't deserve to be killed like that and left in an alley. She deserved better." There was pain in his voice. Evidently the king and his family weren't the only ones crushed over Delisa's death.

"I'm sorry. I understand that you're all frustrated, but you have to trust me. Starting a war with Samael is just suicide."

"It may be, but we are who we are." Theophilius said.

I understood that.

"When can we bring Delisa home?" Andros asked.

I didn't have an answer for that, so I looked at Bronson who'd been quiet. "Soon." Bronson said. "The medical examiner still has some evidence he needs to collect."

Andros nodded, but didn't look all that happy about it. "Is there anything else you need to know, agents?"

I turned toward Ila sitting there as quiet as a mouse. She looked so young and so fragile. "Did Delisa ever say anything to you about Ivan or if they were having any problems?"

Ila looked down at her hands. "No." she said, her voice soft. "Delisa left a year ago and I've never spoken to her since."

"When she was here, did she ever talk about Ivan or about anyone else?" I asked hoping I wasn't going over the line. One quick glance toward Andros said I was close. That caught me by surprise. Was he keeping something from me?

Ila shook her head, but I got the feeling she was about to lie to me. "No. We never talked that much when she was home."

"You were sisters. Close in age. She must have confided in you about something."

She started to open her mouth to speak but was cut off by her father. "That is enough, agent Montgomery. You've asked your questions and we have answered them."

Actually, they hadn't really. But I wasn't about to push my luck. We were lucky he'd allowed us through the gate.

"Okay." I said and pulled out a card and handed it to him. "If you think of anything, call me."

Andros gave Theophilius a look and he took the card. Guess he was above taking work cards from cops. "Theophilius will escort you out."

Theophilius bowed before his king and made his way through the doorway. We followed him all the way back to the SUV. I couldn't help but wonder what they were keeping from me. Why had Androcles cut his daughter off from telling me something that might help find his other daughter's killer? Something wasn't adding up.

We got back to the SUV and Theophilius stood there and watched us get into it. I sat there for a moment and frowned. He walked around to the driver's side window and I rolled it down. "Is there a problem agent?"

Now that he'd mentioned it. "Why did Andros cut Ila off?" I asked. "If she knows something that could help, she should come forward." Okay, I was pushing my luck here. But hey, I was a cop, and I didn't like when people kept vital information from me.

Theophilius narrowed his eyes and I knew I was onto something. "There are some things that are no concern to you or the police. This is a family matter. No concern to you. Now you may be on your way agent. You're over doing your visit." Then he turned and walked away.

"Wow." Bronson said as I rolled up the window. "These people need to take a happy pill or something."

I nodded. "Yeah. So, why's the medical examiner still holding Delisa's body?"

"I told him to hold it. There's still some things you need to know before we talk to the boyfriend. I'm guessing you want to do most of the talking there too?"

"Yeah. He might talk to me."

"Hope so." said Carlos. "This guy's been almost arrested five times now."

"Why do you say almost?"

"Because every time we go in to get him, someone gets hurt. He's put a lot of cops in the hospital. He keeps saying we can't touch him, that he's under . . . protection." Carlos paused. "You know, now that I think about it, I believe he said he was under Samael's protection."

That caught my interest. "Has anyone been killed?"

"Nope. But cops won't try to arrest him anymore. I think they're scared."

Made sense. If this demon had caused harm to more than one human cop, then they would probably just leave him alone. I had seen it before. A supernatural proves too hard to arrest and the humans back off because they are too scared that someone is going to get killed. "Okay, let's go see the body, and then we'll go have a talk with Mr. Badass."

CHAPTER NINE

The morgue was like any other. It was white and smelled like bleach and disinfectant and still gave me the creeps. This was the part of being a cop I hated. I didn't like morgues and I doubted that would change anytime soon.

I stood in front of a slab, Delisa's body laid on it. Her eyes were closed, her pale skin looked even paler. She would have looked as if she were in a deep sleep if not for the fact that she was dead.

Dr. Quon Ming stood on the opposite side of the slab. He had short black hair and brown Asian eyes. He wore a white doctor coat over a white dress shirt and black slacks. He was in the middle of telling me what he'd found on the body.

"As you can see, there are two puncture wounds on the left side of her throat. I concluded that they were in fact fang marks. I believe she gave blood no more than thirty minutes before she was killed."

So Delisa had fed someone before she got her neck broke.

"But that wasn't the cause of death." Ming continued. "Her neck was broken. My findings concluded it was someone with superhuman strength."

"How so?" Bronson asked. "How do you know it was a supernatural?"

"I don't. But . . . she wasn't human. With humans, it doesn't take much to break their necks. But Delisa wasn't human. So that tells us she was harder to kill. Supernaturals don't die easily. In most cases around the world, they were killed by another supernatural. If she'd been attacked by a human, she would have been able to fight him off because she was ten times stronger. A supernaturals body is stronger, all the way into their bones. So no human would have been able to snap her neck."

I already knew this of course. I was a supernatural. The only way to kill me was to puncture my heart to the point it couldn't be repaired or break my neck. So Dr. Ming's findings were accurate. Delisa Shaylee's killer was a supernatural.

"I also found blood and semen between her thighs."

"She was raped?" God help us if she was. Androcles would go mad.

Ming shook his head. "No. I don't believe she was raped." He reached down and pulled up the white sheet covering her body enough to reveal her thighs. He spread them apart and there it was. Another set of fang marks.

"Kinky." Carlos said.

Yeah. Very. Taking blood from a source was like sex for a vampire. So if she gave blood and had sex . . . well, you do the math.

"I also found semen inside her. Your guy didn't use protection. I collected it and sent it to the lab. No hits yet. He may not be in the system."

That figured. We had a lead and our killer wasn't even in the system.

"What do you need?" I asked.

"DNA samples and fang mark impressions. I think if we had them we could at least find our biter and her lover of the night." He smiled then. "But I'm guessing whoever you have as a suspect won't be very forthcoming or willing to give you what we need."

"We have one suspect. And trust me, when I'm done with him, he'll be very willing."

Ming laughed. "I bet. You're probably stronger than you look." His eyes roamed my body and became warm. "You're not human are you?"

"No. What gave me away?'

"Your eyes. Never saw anyone with eyes like yours. They're breathtaking. Maybe a bit hypnotizing. And your bodies not bad either." His smile widened as he looked even younger than he was. Quon Ming was in his thirties, but right now he seemed younger.

"Never going to happen dude." I said shaking my head, but I was smiling.

"Never say never."

"When you two get done salivating, could we get back to the body on the slab?" Bronson asked sounding impatient.

"We're not salivating." I said.

"Sure." Bronson said.

"Speak for yourself." Ming said.

"Is there anything else you can tell us?" asked Carlos, changing the subject.

Ming nodded and put the sheet back over Delisa. "I found something interesting. I got some blood work back and she tested positive..." He trailed off and took a deep breath, his smiled gone. "Delisa Shaylee was pregnant."

My head snapped up. "What?" This changed everything.

"She was pregnant. About six to seven weeks. She probably didn't even know she was caring a child. She was that early along."

My heart sank and my world began to spin as gray spots blurred my vision.

"Are you going to be sick?" Carlos asked. "You don't look so good."

I didn't feel so good either. I felt like I was going to pass out. Who would do this? Did her killer know about the baby? Was that why she was killed? I thought about it for a moment. No, I didn't think so. Why would someone kill her for being pregnant? It didn't make any sense. And if Ivan was the killer, I doubted he did it because she was caring his child.

"Yeah, I'm fine. I just need a minute." I said. I took deep breaths and blew them out slowly. I would not pass out in the morgue. I took one last deep breath and stood up straight. I put on my cop face, hiding my true feelings. "Is there anything else?"

Ming shook his head. "No. Not really. I took a DNA sample of the fetus and sent it to the lab too. The DNA sample I collected from between her thighs didn't match the baby's. So he wasn't the father."

Okay. Either Ming was wrong about the rape or Delisa was seeing someone behind Ivan's back. That right there seemed to me to be more than enough motive. Ivan finding out his girlfriend is screwing around on him might have caused him to get angry enough to kill her.

Love and betrayal made a lot of people do a hell of a lot of things. Could you say lover's quarrel?

Yeah, I was betting fifty bucks that Ivan killed her.

"If we got you more DNA, could you try to match it?" I asked.

"Yep. Just get me a sample and I'll test it." Ming said.

I turned to Bronson. "I'm ready to go see Ivan now. You sure he's at Illusions?"

"Yeah, I'm sure." Bronson said. "Just remember what I said. This guy's dangerous."

I smiled wide. "Oh, I remember. And I'm hoping he does something stupid." Yeah, if Ivan was anything like I'd heard, he'd do something stupid alright. And tonight if he did? Well, he'd learn he wasn't as protected or a badass as much as he thought he was.

CHAPTER TEN

t was dark, the stars sparkled and the moon shined bright in the night sky. It was warm, but then again it was May after all. Bronson parked the SUV in front of Illusions. The blue glowing sign was on, but there were no bodies waiting in line to get in. The street was empty.

This was weird. Last night the place had been hopping with people wanting in and you could hear the music booming from inside. But there was no one.

We got out and I made sure I had my badge on me. I didn't need my purse for this so I left it in the car. I walked up toward the door and my eyes landed on a sign that said, Private party. Okay, something was going on. But I ignored it and continued walking, only to be stopped by the bouncer. He was at least six-foot-five and looked like he could break you in half with his hands. He probably could.

He stood there and glared at me and I hadn't even started talking yet. Great. I flashed him a smile hoping it would help. It didn't. He just continued to glare. He had dark orange eyes, his head had been shaved, he wore nothing but dark jeans and boots, showing off his hard abs and muscles and dark chocolate skin. And yes I know what I've said, but it was really hard to keep my eyes from looking him up and down in appreciation.

"There's a private party going on tonight. Invitation only." The bouncer said.

I flashed him my badge. "Is this invitation enough for you?" I asked. "Special Agent Montgomery. I need to speak to an Ivan."

"You have to come back later. No humans. No cops."

"That's not very nice." Carlos said. "I love a good party."

"I have my orders." The bouncer said. "No invitation, no entry. You have to leave and come back tomorrow night."

"Will Ivan be here tomorrow night?" I asked.

He shrugged. "Can't say. Maybe he will, maybe he won't."

He was giving me the run around. If he knew we were coming back tomorrow night, he'd tell Ivan and Ivan would disappear. "Listen, we really need to speak to Ivan. If we can't go in there, then maybe he could come out here?" Who said I couldn't compromise?

The bouncer narrowed his eyes. "Not going to happen."

Okay, so maybe asking nicely wasn't the way to go here. "Fine, have it your way." I said. "We're going in. You can either let us in or we can force our way in. You choose." I stood my ground and didn't flinch when a trickle of power tickled my skin. The bouncer was trying to do something to me with his power, but it wasn't going to work. One of my other powers was resistance. Which meant, others power didn't work on me. It just bounced off. So when whatever he was trying to do, wasn't going to do anything but cause him to use more energy trying to get it to work.

I stood there and smiled when I saw the fear fill his eyes. I pushed out with my own power then, and the bouncer looked like he wanted to wet himself.

"You can go in." he said, voice breathless with a hint of pain.

"Thank you . . . what's your name?"

"Chiron"

I nodded. "Well, thank you Chiron. You did the right thing."

He grunted. "Doubt that."

He was probably right.

I made my way inside the club with Bronson and Carlos behind me. There was music playing low and a few demons on the dance floor were dancing. Avril Lavigne was singing something about hello kitty. On the far end of the room there was a long black leather sofa and two armchairs with a glass coffee table in front of them.

This place certainly looked different when it was just occupied by demons.

I walked toward the sofa and chairs, and resisted an urge to roll my eyes. There was a man sitting in one of the chairs with a red head straddling his lap. Her tongue was down his throat. In the other chair was pretty much the same scene. Only the girl was blond. Sitting on the sofa was a man and a woman. The woman had long white blond hair and what looked like lavender eyes. The man . . .

My steps faltered a bit when my eyes locked with his. He had short black hair, dark teal eyes, and Italian features. He was the man from my vision.

Who was he and what was he doing here?

I wanted to ask, but right now his identity wasn't why I was here.

I stopped in front of the coffee table and pulled out my badge. "I'm looking for Ivan."

The man kissing the red head pushed her back. "I'm Ivan." His eyes widened and he smiled. "Well, hello." He pushed the girl off his lap and got up. Ivan wasn't what I'd pictured Delisa Shaylee's boyfriend looking like. He was five-eight in height. He had shoulder length pink hair and pale blue eyes. He wore black leather pants that looked one size too small, a black T-shirt, and black leather boots that went up to almost his thighs with silver pointy spikes. He wore black eyeliner. There was a ring in his left eyebrow and one in his lip. His cheekbones were sharp, his nose narrow, and his skin was powder white.

Either that was how he was created . . . or this guy was taking being a vampire way too serious. Not to mention, seeing as he was just tongue wrestling with a red head a few seconds ago, well, I guess he wasn't all that broken up about his girlfriend's death.

He gave me what I assume was supposed to have been his play-boy smile. "What can I do for you?" He raised a hand to brush it down my arm. "Want to sit down on my lap? Or if you want some privacy, we could go to the back. Have some fun there."

I gave an eye roll in my head. Was this guy for real? His girlfriend hadn't been dead more than two days, and he was already moving on?

I flicked my eyes toward the other man in the second chair. My heart stopped for a moment. It was the man from the parking lot. He smiled at me and gave a nod. Great.

"So how about it?" Ivan said, stroking my arm. "Want to go to the back and play?"

It was time to get down to business. I raised my badge. "Special Agent Morgan Montgomery. I'm from the PCU. I'd like to ask you a few questions about Delisa Shaylee."

His smile was gone so fast it was almost funny. He removed his hand and stepped back. "You're a cop?"

"Is that a problem?" I asked. He didn't answer. "Where were you two nights ago?" I might as well jump right in.

"None of your fucking business."

"Listen. We can do this one of two ways. You can answer my questions here or we can go to the police station. Take your pick."

"How about neither." he snarled. "How about I take you to the back and teach you how to kneel for a long time."

"Or how about I kick your ass and drag you to the station anyways." I said. This guy was out of his mind.

He smiled then. "You can't touch me. I'm under Samael's protection." he said defiantly.

I looked down at his left arm and it was blank. There was no tattoo. I laughed. "Really? You really think that empty threat is going to save you from me?"

He was starting to get mad. "It's not an empty threat. If you touch me, Samael will kill you."

"You want to know what I think about Samael and his protection and your empty threat? Bullshit. I'll kick his ass and then yours. You'll still go to jail and I'll still be alive." Okay, I was calling his bluff. I only hoped he was smart enough to tone down his macho shit. I looked at the man in the chair and his lips were turned up in a half grin. The man sitting on the sofa was glaring at me. I looked back at Ivan and saw his hands tighten into fists. I knew what he was about to do. "Don't do it." I said. "Don't be that stupid."

Apparently he was, because he didn't listen. He swung his fist at me and I ducked, shoving my own fist into his chest. He let out a breath and then came back at me. This time his fist connected with my face. I stumbled back, but regained my balance. I kicked him hard and he went down like a sack of potatoes. I punched him in the face for good measure, and then rolled him over onto his stomach. Bronson handed me a set of cuffs and I handcuffed Ivan.

"You bitch! I'm going to fucking kill you!" Ivan yelled.

"Yeah, yeah." I said.

"What is going on out here?" A man said with a Russian accent.

I looked up to see Balian. He didn't seem happy to see me. I looked around the room and saw that everyone had stopped dancing.

I got up and Bronson and Carlos helped Ivan get up off the floor. "I gave Ivan a choice and he chose the hard one." I quipped. Behind me I could hear Bronson reading Ivan his rights.

"And under what grounds may I ask are you arresting him?" Balian asked, voice cold.

"Well, for one, assaulting a police officer. And two, not giving cooperation in an ongoing investigation."

"I thought you were on vacation?"

"I was. But agent Bronson needs my help. So I'm helping."

Balian gave me a hard expression. "And how did you get in here?"

"I persuaded the bouncer." I said with a cocky smile. I saw a look cross his face. "Don't worry. I gave him a choice and he chose the easy one. He's not bleeding."

"That is a relief." He muttered. He leveled his now fiery gaze on me. "Ivan did nothing wrong."

"We'll see. I haven't talked to him yet."

Something filled his eyes as his nostrils flared. I saw something shift behind his eyes and knew this wasn't the sexy guy who'd come onto me the night before. No, the man standing in front of me right now was a demon. A very pissed off looking one.

"Look." I said. "I understand that you fill the need to defend your friend. But there's a dead girl whose killer needs to be found."

"But Ivan did not do it." Balian insisted. "He would never have hurt her or anyone."

I doubted that seeing as he'd threatened to rape me only minutes before. But Balian couldn't have known that. Maybe he didn't know his friend as well as he thought he did.

"Then tell me this, Mr. Ivanski." I used my cop voice. "If that's true, why didn't he just answer my questions when I asked him? Why was he tongue wrestling with a red head, instead of acting like a broken hearted man, whose girlfriend had just been killed? Answer me that."

Balian said nothing.

It was my turn to level my gaze with his. "I have a job to do. Interfere with it and I'll arrest you and everyone here. You can all spend the night in a cell. I could come back with a warrant and have this place searched. I'm betting there's at least one thing going on here tonight that's illegal. How would you like that Mr. Ivanski?"

Balian glared at me. "Fine." he said through clenched teeth. "Go. Take him. But I am telling you, he did not do what you are accusing him of."

"I'm not accusing him of anything. He's the one who's acting guilty." And with that, I turned and walked out. My body was screaming at me to go back, to go back to Balian and let him do whatever he wanted to do to me. I ignored my body and just kept walking, my hands in tight fists at my sides. The sooner I was out of here the sooner I could control my body.

Bronson and Carlos were already in the SUV with Ivan when I got in. Bronson just looked me over. "That looks like it hurts. You should have that checked out. You could have a concussion."

I shook my head. "No need. It's already healing." I leaned my head against the stirring wheel and told myself to breathe.

"You okay?"

"No."

"What's wrong?" asked Carlos.

Everything. I thought. "Just stuff." I said setting up. "Nothing I need to worry about right now." Oh man, my body was really screaming at me now. But it just really needed to get over itself. I wasn't in the mood for this right now. I was dealing with so much and my hormones trying to control my body was the last thing I needed.

No cookie for my libido. It was just going to have to deal.

CHAPTER ELEVEN

The interrogation room was a small, windowless room. There was a small stainless steel table in the middle of it with two chairs. One on each side. I sat in one and Ivan sat in the other, his face was screwed up into an angry expression as he stared me down. I guessed this was his way of trying to frighten me. It wasn't working.

Bronson and Carlos stood on the other side of the room, their backs leaning against the wall as they observed. I wanted them here to not only witness what was going on, but also to take part. I had told them if they had a question, then to ask it. Ivan would answer it one way or another.

Ivan just sat there and said nothing. There was a new cut on his forehead from where I'd banged his head into a desk after he'd given a perverted suggestion to a female officer. The whole Seattle police station had been in shock when they saw us dragging in Ivan. Their mouths had fell open and their eyes had widened. One cop had burst out laughing after I'd banged Ivan's head into the desk and said. "Ops. You should be more careful. You could cause brain damage doing that."

That had gotten me a few clapped hands. I knew why to. It had been a long time since the Seattle police department had made an arrest on a supernatural. And when I'd walked in with Ivan, they'd all looked at me like I was some kind of super hero. I wasn't however, just a supernatural myself who didn't take bullshit well.

Now I sat across from Ivan and watched him stare me down. He didn't want to be here and he was pissed that I'd gotten the better hand and kicked his ass. That happened a lot actually. There had been a lot of inhuman creatures who thought they were bigger and meaner than me and found out different. Several co-working men thought that since I was pretty and a girl, they could walk all over me or suggest I spend the night with them.

Being a PCU agent was hard sometimes. You never knew where you were going to be on a day by day bases. We didn't have our own station and we didn't have a desk. We used what accommodations were given to us in whatever state or town we were in. If we needed to interrogate a suspect we used their interrogation room like we were doing now.

I sat up straight in the chair and opened the file with all the information on this case we had. "So, where were you two nights ago?" I turned my eyes up to look at him. Ivan said nothing. "Okay, you don't have to talk. You can listen. I'll tell you what I think happened." I leaned back. "I think you found out Delisa was cheating . . . maybe you caught her. And in a fit of boiling rage, you killed her." I didn't mention her broken neck, because that hadn't been released to the public. And if Ivan had killed her, he already knew and maybe, just maybe he'd incriminate himself.

"I didn't kill her. I loved Delisa." Ivan said.

"Did you? Because it didn't seem that way back at the club."

"Yes. I loved her."

"Then help me out here, Ivan. Give me an alibi and help me catch Delisa's killer. Because right now everything's pointing toward you."

Ivan looked down and shook his head. "I can't help you."

"Why?" I asked.

He looked up at me with a hard expression. "Because I told you, you have no authority over me. You think just because you're a supernatural like me, that it gives you some kind of edge? Well, it doesn't. You're a cop and I don't talk to the cops."

"Really? You're talking now." Carlos said.

Ivan narrowed his eyes at him. "One day you humans will learn your place on the food chain."

"Is that a threat?" I asked. I leveled my gaze on him and replaced my cop voice with a voice I didn't quite recognize. It was frightening and cold. "You should be very careful what you say, Ivan. Remember, I can hold you for forty-eight hours. In which time, you are mine. And I might forget that I'm a cop and remember that I'm not human." There was power behind my words and I saw Ivan's eyes widen with something like fear.

He started to say something, but was cut off when the door to the interrogation room opened and Constantine walked in. He had on a black suit and was caring a briefcase. "I am Constantine Gonzales. I will be representing Ivan."

My mouth fell open. "You're a Lawyer?"

"Yes." he said and sat down. "I need a moment with my client." No one moved. "I am not asking. Either you give me a moment or my client and I are leaving."

Bronson and Carlos looked at me and I nodded. We left the room. I didn't like this, but there wasn't much I could do about it. Ivan was lawyering up. That was a bad sign. If he was innocent, then why did he need a Lawyer?

We stood outside the door for about five minutes before it opened and Constantine walked out.

"Okay." he said. "My client is willing to cooperate on one condition."

"And what is that?" I asked. I was getting a bad feeling.

"He will only talk to you. The humans have to stay outside."

"Are you shitting me?" He was out of his damn mind.

Constantine gave me a hard expression. "That is our offer. Take it or leave it. And I will be taking him with me regardless. So it really doesn't matter."

I hadn't expected this. But I wanted answers. And the only way I was going to get them was doing the one thing I didn't want to do. But if I didn't, then Ivan was going to walk and I'd never get another chance to question him. He'd disappear.

"Fine, but I'm letting it be known that I don't like this." I said. I went back into the room to see a smug looking Ivan. The bastard was smiling. I sat down as Constantine closed the door and took his own seat. I didn't like this. Something about this whole situation was wrong. "Okay, I'm listening. So talk."

Okay, let's see what story he and his Lawyer came up with.

"What do you want to know?" Ivan asked.

"Where were you two nights ago?"

"At a party." He looked at Constantine and Constantine nodded. "Samael has these parties. I . . . wouldn't call them orgies, but well . . ."

I raised an eyebrow. "Beg pardon? Orgies?"

He nodded. "Yeah."

Okay, this was unexpected. "So you were cheating on Delisa?"

"No. We had an arrangement."

"An arrangement? What kind?"

"We could see other people. Sometimes we brought other people to our bed. Sometimes I watched her with them, or she'd watch them with me. Sometimes it was another woman or another man. It really depended on what mood we were in."

Wow, talk about an over share. I knew there were people out in the world who liked doing that sort of thing. But I wasn't one of them. The thought of having two men in my bed at the same time made me cringe. I swallowed hard. "Okay, well, did any of your lovers act jealous, like they weren't as into sharing as they led on?"

"No. It was against the rules. Delisa and I were together and they were our guest. If they started acting out they couldn't play with us anymore." Ivan seemed to think about something. "There were some men I didn't know about. I mean, I knew she was sleeping with men outside our group, but I don't know their names. That was the other part of our arrangement."

Okay, this just kept getting better and better.

"Can you think of anyone who might have done this?" I asked.

He shook his head. "No, not really. I have no idea who would want to kill her. Everyone loved her."

"What about her parents?"

"What about them?"

"They hadn't seen her for over a year. Why was that?"

He frowned. "Because they couldn't deal."

"How so?"

"Well, for one, she was seeing me. I'm a vampire. They didn't like the idea of me corrupting their precious and pure royal fairy bloodline. They wanted her to stop seeing me and be with a nice pure blooded fairy, but she wouldn't. She loved me." Ivan looked down at the table. "And the other? Well, they found out something else they didn't exactly like."

"What was that?"

"Delisa didn't only like men, but she liked women too. She was bisexual."

My mouth almost dropped open. "She was what?" I couldn't believe this. Had I heard him right?

"Delisa was bisexual. And when her parents found out, they went postal. Me—a vampire, they could deal with. They figured it was just a phase. But when they found out that their precious daughter was also into girls, they couldn't handle that. So she left." He smiled then. "That part actually made our sex life so much better. Her being into men and women."

I was going to puke. Okay, maybe I wasn't, but this wasn't how I'd expected this to go. I hadn't expected to find out that Delisa was bisexual. I mean, it didn't bother me per say—it was their life. Their preference. Not mine. Just because I was into men—and one at a time, didn't mean it was wrong. It just meant I preferred a different sexual experience.

"Okay, let me get this straight. You're saying, that you were at an orgy having sex the night your girlfriend was murdered? That's your alibi?"

"Yes."

I sat back in the chair and crossed my arms over my chest. "Wow. I don't know if I should believe you or if I should be pissed off that you're lying to me."

"I'm not lying to you." Ivan said.

"Then I want a list of everyone at these . . . parties and I want a list of everyone in your bed. Men and women both."

"I don't think it would be a good idea to give you the list."

I raised an eye brow. "Why not?"

"Because Samael could get angry. You only go through invite, and most of the ones who go are higher ups. His main men."

"Well, Ivan, I can't help you there. I want that list."

"You will have it." Constantine said speaking for the first time.

"Good. Now, would you be willing to give me DNA and fang impressions?"

Ivan seemed confused. "Why do you need DNA?"

That caught me by surprise. "There was DNA found on her body . . . and inside."

"That's impossible. They weren't allowed to go inside her. That was against the rules."

"Well, I guess someone went against the rules." Or Ming was wrong and she was raped. I looked at him and saw pain in his eyes as he put everything together. And maybe that was why I did what I did next. "Did you know she was pregnant?"

Ivan's and Constantine's heads snapped up. "What?"

"Delisa was pregnant. About six to seven weeks. Did you know?"

He shook his head. "No. She never said anything about a baby." A tear slid down his cheek. "I was going to be a father."

Well, there went that theory.

I frowned and looked down. "I'm sorry. I thought you knew." I pulled out a few sheets a paper and a pen and slid them to Ivan. "I still need those names." I got up and left, giving him some privacy.

Ten minutes later, I had two lists in my hands and the lab had Ivan's DNA and fang impressions. I stood in the hall and watched him leave. Constantine was finishing some paper work on Ivan's release. When he was done he walked over to me and he didn't look happy.

"What the hell is going on? What kind of game are you playing?" I asked him.

"I'm not playing a game agent." he returned.

"Really? Why do I get the feeling you're lying to me?"

"Maybe because you're paranoid."

"You don't look like a Lawyer. Why didn't you mention that the other night?"

He shrugged. "It never came up. And besides, one could argue that you don't look like a cop either."

I snorted. "Yeah, well, they've tried." I leaned my back against the wall. "You know, just because Ivan shed a few tears back there doesn't mean he didn't do it or that I believe him."

"He didn't do it."

"How do you know?"

"Because I do." He gave me a hard look. "How do you know he did?"

I shrugged. "I don't know, maybe I'm being a cop about this, or maybe a woman. But a man who says he loves someone or is supposed to be in mourning, doesn't go out and shove his tongue down another girl's throat."

"He told you they had an arrangement." Constantine said.

"I get that, but why not show some sadness?"

"You think he's guilty."

I nodded. "I think he's guilty. I think he's lying. Maybe not about the arrangement, but about not being jealous. I think he found out that she was sleeping with someone that wasn't on the list and it made him angry. Angry enough to kill her."

Constantine nodded. "Yes, it would make sense, but there is one problem. Ivan has an alibi."

I smiled smugly. "Yes, that seems convenient. An orgy, huh? That was the best you two could come up with?"

He shook his head in exasperation. "I'm done. I have a feeling no matter what I say, it isn't going to change your mind." He narrowed his eyes. "Be careful how deep you dig, agent Montgomery. You may not like what you find or what might find you."

"Is that a threat?"

"No. It's a certainty. And for the record, you don't deserve him. He's too good for you." And with that he turned and walked away.

I stood there feeling confused. What did he mean I didn't deserve him? Didn't deserve who? The only man that came to mind was Daniel. That was weird considering he'd never mentioned having a friend in Seattle. Or a Lawyer friend who was a werewolf.

Yeah, that would be ironic. Especially considering the way he was doing me.

Bronson and Carlos walked up and stopped next to me. "Did you get what you needed?" Bronson asked.

I blinked. "Yeah, I got a list of all their lovers and a list of every one who attends the orgies."

Carlos whistled. "Damn, the demons have all the fun."

I smiled and scanned the first list. No one seemed to stand out at me, so I scanned the second list. The orgy list. A few names did stand out. But one stood out more than the others. I blinked and took a closer look, afraid I was looking at it wrong.

"What is it?" asked Bronson.

I shook my head. "Nothing. At least I don't think it's anything." But I couldn't be sure. Was this something? Was I looking at this from a cop's point of view or was I looking at this from another perspective? I wasn't sure.

"Okay." he said. "How about I buy you a burger and you tell us about the interrogation."

"Okay, that's fine." I took one last glance at the list and came to a conclusion. This was probably my best lead. Only problem was, I just had to figure out the best way to check it out.

CHAPTER TWELVE

"**S**o explain to me again *why* it would be bad if Androcles made war with Samael?" Carlos asked around a bite of his burger.

I took a sip of my coke. We were at a local diner and I'd just got done relaying everything back to Bronson and Carlos. Now they were asking a hundred and one questions. "Well," I began. "when I was a little girl, there was this old legend that said, whoever killed Samael would inherit a million enemies. And I've always heard Stefan say, 'You may have cut the head off the snake, but you'd still have to fight the body.' Meaning—"

"You'd have to fight Samael's allies." Bronson finished.

"Yeah. And well, I've always heard that there's a war coming. A war between the angels and demons. And if that's true, then God help us. It's not going to be very pretty."

"Do you believe that?" asked Carlos.

I thought about it. "Yeah, I do. One day Samael's going to snap and he's going to start a war."

"Do you think it'll be quiet or do you think humans will know?"

"I think there's going to be a lot of bloodshed. Humans included. Samael's not going to care if a few hundred humans get killed. To him, they'll be nothing but unfortunate casualties of war. A necessity for a higher cause. And nothing more."

It was a cruel reality no doubt. I had been raised to understand that one day I might be needed for something other than doing good. Today I took that understanding with me on the job. Just because I was a cop, didn't mean I stopped being an angel. If a war broke out I'd be expected to participate. To stand next to my family and friends and fight.

My school day hadn't ended when I came home. I had to train. Learn how to fight. Which was why when Ivan attacked me, I knew how to get the upper hand. Stefan had made sure I knew how to defend myself.

I looked at Bronson and Carlos, who were sitting across from me and saw a hint of fear in their eyes. They hadn't been raised like I had. They didn't understand the danger of this situation.

"That would be against the law." Carlos said after a moment.

"Samael doesn't care about the law." I said.

"So if Androcles kills whoever is responsible for his daughter's murder, then that will mean war in Samael's eyes?" Bronson asked.

"Yes."

"Well, that just bites. I guess we have no choice but to find the killer." Bronson looked at me sideways. "Do you really think Ivan killed her?"

"Well, let's look at the facts. He didn't exactly look all broken up about it when we found him at Illusions. He never showed any sadness until I told him about the baby. Maybe he was telling the truth, maybe he wasn't. All I know is, something's not adding up here. Why have a Lawyer? Why say he was at an orgy?"

"That bothers you. Why?"

"Which part?"

"The Lawyer."

I sighed. Why did Constantine bother me? That was a good question. "I'm not sure. I think part of it has to do with the fact he kept who he was from me. Why not tell us he was a Lawyer?"

"Because he's a supernatural Lawyer. Because like everyone else, he's hiding something." Carlos said. "I bet fifty bucks that most demons in the city know what happened to Delisa Shaylee and who did it and why. But they won't talk. Am I right?"

I blinked at Carlos and smiled. Talk about a fast learner.

"Well, look at you." Bronson teased. "Keep this up and you'll be an expert."

"Thanks." Carlos said with a smile.

"Yes." I said. "Yes, you're right. And by some chance I'm wrong and it isn't Ivan, we need to create a suspect list. I still think it was a lover's quarrel. So we should take a good long look at the lists." My eyes flicked down at the two sheets of paper. There were a lot of names on it. A lot of possible suspects. But all the names seemed to blur together except one.

Balian's name stuck out like a sore thumb. It taunted me to the point of possible insanity. For reasons beyond my comprehension it bothered me. But why? It wasn't like I knew him well enough to be jealous of him being with other people. But damn it, I was jealous. Pissed even. And I didn't understand why I felt that way. Balian wasn't mine, not even close.

I took my pen and crossed his name off. "He's mine." I said. "You can split the list however you like. But Balian Ivanski is mine."

"Why?" Bronson asked with a raised eyebrow.

"I sort of know him." There was another raised eyebrow with a smile from Bronson. "Not like that."

"Is he the guy you had words with back at the club?" asked Carlos.

I nodded.

Bronson picked up the list and frowned. "Do you think he'll talk to you?"

"Hard to say." I said, knowing that was an understatement. "I have to find a way to approach him about it."

"Why not just go see him and ask?"

I shrugged. "I can't explain it. But something is telling me to take this easy. To not rush this. If I just go up to him and ask . . . him questions about his involvement, he's going to elude me."

"I don't know about that." Carlos said. "I saw the way he looked at you. I think he likes you . . . a lot. I'm sure if you asked him nicely, he'd tell you anything."

I rolled my eyes. "Maybe. But a man is the last thing I need right now." No I certainly did not.

We finished eating and talking about the case, then Bronson drove me home. He pulled the SUV to a stop in the driveway and let it idle.

"Thanks for dinner tonight." I said sincerely. It had been a nice change from late night dinners with my old team.

"No problem." he said. "It was the least I could do since you were the one who got punched." He smiled then. "You really should get that looked at."

"I'll be fine. I don't really feel it anymore. It'll mostly be gone tomorrow."

"Okay. I'll come by in the morning and pick you up and we'll go check out some leads and see if we can piss off some demons."

I laughed. "Sounds good."

There were headlights from a car coming up the drive. "Anyone you know?" Bronson asked.

The car parked next to the passenger side of the SUV. I nodded. "It's just Nate."

"That's your brother?"

I shook my head. "He's not really my brother. I don't know why people think that. He's never even acted like my brother."

"Oh, I'm sorry. I didn't mean to—"

"No, it's okay." Nate got out of his car and looked the SUV over. He saw me and frowned. "Look, I'll see you tomorrow."

"Okay."

I got out and made my way to the front door where Nate was standing. "A friend of yours? Moving on already?"

"No. He's a PCU agent and he needs help with a case."

"I thought you were suspended." There was curiosity in Nate's voice, like he was looking forward to see how I answered his question.

"I am. But agent Bronson needs help, so I'm helping." I said. Why was I explaining myself to him? I didn't need his approval.

Nate gave me a hard look. "Oh, right. It's a cop thing." He moved closer and raised a hand and brushed it lightly across my face where it was now bruised. "That looks like it hurts."

I couldn't speak, because I was too focused on his fingers on my skin, warm and soft. His bright blue eyes locked with mine and something in them changed. They became softer . . . caressing even, maybe even warm. He took a small step forward and leaned in and I thought I was going to faint. What the hell was going on with Nate?

I tried to speak, but my throat closed up. Oh, my God! What was happening?

I swallowed hard and fought the sudden panic and found my voice. "Yeah, it did hurt. But it doesn't anymore."

Nate stared into my eyes and blinked. He stepped back and dropped his hand. "Did you get your man?"

"Yeah. He thought he was going to teach me a lesson, but found out different."

He smiled and opened the door. "That's a demon for you. Cocky as hell."

We made our way inside the house and into the sitting room where we found Stefan and Mariska cuddled together on the sofa. They were watching a movie and smiled when they saw us.

"Hey, there's two of my favorite people." Stefan said. "How was work?"

"The same." Nate said. "I found my FTA and had a scuffle, but I didn't end up punched like Morgan."

Stefan came to attention then. "Morgan got punched?"

"It was nothing." I said. "Just a badass demon who wasn't as badass as he thought."

"Your suspect?"

"Possible suspect. Actually, he's our only suspect. We have a few lists of possible bad guys, but I'm sure. We're going to go check them out tomorrow." I frowned. "Do you know a Lawyer by the name Constantine Gonzales?"

Stefan nodded. "Yeah. He's a werewolf and supposedly a friend of Balian's. But that's just a rumor. Why do you ask?"

"Because he showed up tonight at the police station as Ivan's Lawyer."

"Oh . . . Well, he's a pretty good Lawyer. As far as I know, he mainly does supernatural cases and always wins."

That was a nice thought. All my hard work to put Delisa's killer away and he gets off because he has a badass Lawyer who's just like him. A demon with bad intentions.

"Okay." I said around a yawn. "I'm beat. I think I'm going to go to bed."

"Okay babe." Stefan said. "Night."

"Night." I said and went upstairs.

I laid my gun and cell phone on my bedside table and changed out of my clothes. I laid there and let my mind run for a bit. It started with Androcles. What was he hiding and did it have anything to do with his daughter's death? Then it switched to Balian. Why was his name on that list and did he know who the killer was? Was he withholding vital information? And if so, how was I going to get him to talk? My mind ended with Ivan. He had showed no emotion tonight over Delisa's death. Not until I told him about the baby. Had he killed her? Or was there some bigger picture I was missing? Some bigger motive here than a lover jealous of another and lashing out and killing someone out of a fit of jealous rage? There were just too many unanswered questions.

My last thought before sleep took me under, was of Constantine and what he'd said about me not deserving someone. I had no idea who he was talking about, but regrettably I agreed with him. I was damaged and a train wreck waiting to happen. Any man in his right mind would be best to run away and not waste his time with me. I wasn't worth it.

Not even a little bit.

CHAPTER THIRTEEN

The next morning Bronson picked me up and we drove to a house in Wedgwood. It was a nice neighborhood with evergreens that hinted at the primeval forest that was once there. It seemed like a neighborhood to raise a family and I could actually picture children playing in the street. It was hard to believe that a vampire couple lived here in this neighborhood. I wondered if their neighbors even knew of their existence.

Kendra Farris and Flynn Garwood lived in a white one story house with pink rosebushes and white daisy's. It looked like a house for a family, not a house for a vampire couple. According to the list Ivan had given me, Kendra and Flynn were not the family type. They were into kinky sex with him and Delisa. Supposed lover's I guess.

Bronson pulled over to the side of the street with Carlos parking behind him. We all got out and stared at the house. There were two cars in the driveway. They were home.

"Okay, let's do this." Carlos said.

I nodded. "Yeah, let's do this."

We walked to the house and stepped onto the stoop. And that was when we saw it. The front door was half open. I looked at Bronson and Carlos and they shrugged. An opened door wasn't a good sign. I hardly thought Flynn and Kendra were the kind of people who left their door aloft.

I knocked on the door. "Mr. Garwood? This is Special Agent Morgan

Montgomery. I'm from the PCU. I need to ask you and Miss Farris some questions regarding Delisa Shaylee." There was no answer. Another bad sign.

"Excuse me?" A female voice said. We turned to see an older lady standing outside from the house next door. "Are you looking for the couple who live there?"

"Yes." Bronson said. "But they're not answering. Have you seen them?"

"I saw them last night. They were making some awful racket. Some kind of party I guess. I went over to tell them to keep it down. We have children in this neighborhood you know. They have school. Don't need to be waken up by nonsense."

"Did you talk to them?"

"No. Some other man opened the door. I'm surprised they even heard me ring the bell. Dang music was bleepin loud. I told him to turn down the music, but he just laughed at me and slammed the door in my face. I thought about calling the police, but I don't like being a busybody."

Bronson smiled. "I'm sure. When did the music stop?"

"Around four this morning."

"Did you see anyone leave?"

"No."

"What did this man look like?" I asked.

"He was tall and had dark hair and glowing green eyes. Other than that, I don't remember. I'm old and my memory isn't as young as it used to be." She lowered her voice a little. "Want to know what I think? I think they were doing that fornicating thing."

"Why's that?" I asked.

"They were making those fornicating sounds. I heard some screaming."

"Are you sure that's what you heard?" Carlos asked.

"I know fornicating sounds when I hear them. I'm not deaf you know. Just old."

I had to bite my lower lip to keep from smiling. One quick look at Bronson and Carlos showed they were doing their damnedest to not laugh. She was one of those adorable old ladies who always knew what was going on in the neighborhood because she was always looking out her windows. If angels could age, then this is what Camille would have looked like.

"Okay." I said. "Well, thank you." The old lady waved her hand and went back into her house. I turned to Bronson. "I'm not sure, maybe it's the half open door, but I don't think fornicating was going on last night."

He nodded. "Ring the bell again and if no one answers, we'll take a look."

I did what I was told. I rang the doorbell. "Mr. Garwood, it's the PCU. We need to ask you a few questions." Again, like before, there was no answer.

I looked at Bronson and he nodded. I pulled out my gun and took aim as I pushed the door the rest of the way open and stepped inside. The inside of the house looked normal for a vampire home. One would have pictured blood red walls and torture chambers. But instead of that, the walls were a light blue with daisy curtains. It looked and felt like any other home.

Bronson and Carlos took search through the house declaring each room they checked cleared. I was looking around the front room when I heard Carlos yell. "Dear God!"

"Outside now." Bronson said.

A few seconds later Carlos came running down the hall and had barely made it out the door when he emptied what I guessed was his breakfast in the rosebushes. I holstered my gun and headed for the hallway and found Bronson in a bedroom in the back. It was painted a light green and there was a huge bed in the center of one wall. But that wasn't what made Carlos empty his stomach in the rosebushes.

On the floor at the end of the bed was a body of a man, his chest was bare and there was blood all over his back. His hands had been bound behind his back and his mouth gagged. The way his body was bent gave the impression that he'd been kneeling when he was killed.

In the center of the bed was a woman, her arms and legs were tied to the bedposts and she was completely nude. Her mouth was also gagged. There was so much blood it was going to be hard to tell which wound inflected had killed her. Above her on the wall, were the words, 'Satan's whore' written in blood. Probably hers.

I stood there and stared at Kendra Farris and Flynn Garwood's bodies in amazement. Well, I guess it hadn't been screams of pleasure the old lady had heard. But screams of two people being tortured.

"I guess it would be wrong to assume that it's just a coincidence that they've been murdered, given the fact that they're on the list." Bronson said.

"Yeah," I said. "It would be wrong to assume that this is a coincidence."

"Damn." Bronson pulled out his cell phone. "I'll be back. I got to go call this in." And then disappeared out of the room.

I walked around the room slowly, so I wouldn't ruin any evidence or miss any clues. I knelt down beside Flynn's body, but didn't touch him. I didn't have any gloves on me. I looked at his back and by the looks of it, someone had sliced a blade down the length of it. I took notice of the carpet around his body. On the right side of the bed the carpet looked disturbed, like someone had been standing—or kneeling on one spot for a long time, then dragged away.

A picture I didn't want began to form in my brain. Someone had come here, tied Kendra and Flynn up, and then made Flynn watch them do whatever it was to Kendra. *Oh dear God.* I thought as I stood up and looked up the length of Kendra's body. Her thighs were spread open wide and there was blood between them.

Bronson walked in and tilted his head to the side. "You've thought of something."

I nodded. "He raped her." I whispered. "The bastard came here, tied them up, and then he raped her and made Flynn watch."

"Jesus." Bronson said.

"What?" Carlos said walking into the room and holding his stomach.

"Are you okay?" I asked. "You're not going to be sick again are you?"

Carlos shook his head. "No, I'm fine now. So what's going on?"

"Morgan think's he raped her and made her mate watch." Bronson said.

I saw Carlos start to drive heave. "Rafe, maybe you should go get some more fresh air. It's not a sign of weakness to need air."

He looked at me and smiled, his face still green. "I know. Bronson and I had this talk four years ago when I joined the team. But I promise I'm not staying to prove anything. I'm just trying to get past a fear. I've had this problem with blood for a while now. This is the first time I've been sick in six months. It's a working progress."

"Really?"

"Yeah." Bronson said. "He used to get sick at every crime scene that involved blood." He laughed. "I had to restrain myself once from punching a local cop for mouthing off at Rafe over getting sick."

I nodded. I knew where he was coming from. It had been the same way for me too when it came to my old team. The other female agent on the team had gotten a lot of shit from the other cops outside of the PCU for getting sick. Only difference, I hadn't restrained myself. Daniel had to pull me off the cop and I had been screamed at by the leader of our team for over an hour. But the screaming hadn't stopped when I got home. Daniel and I had gotten into a big fight over that. It had ended with him storming out of the house and not talking to me for the remainder of the case.

The case had taken us over a week to solve.

Carlos looked at the bodies. "Do you think they're connected to Delisa's murder?"

"Yeah." I said. "I do. I think whoever killed Delisa is cleaning house."

"Do you think it's Ivan?"

"Maybe."

"The old woman said the man had dark hair and green eyes. Ivan has pink hair." Bronson said.

He had a point. "True. But like with Delisa, Flynn and Kendra weren't human. And there were two of them. So if this is Ivan's work, then he brought help this time."

"So I guess we're now looking for more than one suspect?" he asked and I nodded. "Well, shit."

Yeah, my sentiments exactly.

CHAPTER FOURTEEN

The one thing I've learned as a cop, is that no matter how much people say they're not into gossip, they seem to be awfully nosey when shit like this happens. But hey, I guess you couldn't exactly blame these people. Wedgwood wasn't exactly the kind of place this shit happened in. It was a nice clean neighborhood where family's came to raise their children.

But now this nice quiet neighborhood was tainted by a gruesome murder of two vampire neighbors. Yeah, sure, they hadn't known they were living next to inhuman creatures, but the deaths had brought an impact on everyone who lived here.

A crowd had gathered and whispers had started floating through the air, as Kendra Farris and Flynn Garwood's bodies had been taken out of their home in black body bags. Crime scene photos and evidence had been taken. Everyone had been interviewed and questioned about what they may have seen or heard. Everyone's story had been the same. A party had gone on last night with loud music. No one had seen anything.

Same oh, same oh.

Now I was back at the morgue with Bronson and Carlos, waiting to see what Dr. Ming had found. We'd been waiting out in the hall for over two hours when the doors opened and Ming popped his head out. "Okay, I'm ready for you."

I pushed myself from the wall and headed inside with the boys behind me. Kendra and Flynn laid on two separate slabs, their skin pale and eyes closed. "So what did you find?"

"Nothing good. These two went through a lot of torture before they were killed." He walked over to Flynn's body first. "I found some lacerations on his back. Some were deep, others not so much. They were probably made by a blade of some sort."

"Cause of death?" asked Bronson.

"His neck was broken. But not before a lot of blood loss. And my guess is that it was slow." He moved to Kendra's body. "The torture done to her was more severe. She also has stab wounds on her body, but more toward her upper chest. I found lacerations under one breast, but none of them ever pierced her heart. And you were right about the rape. I found semen from multiple donors."

"Multiple?" I asked.

Ming nodded. "Yes. I've sent the DNA to the lab."

"Cause of death?" If I even dare ask.

"Well, it's hard to say. I found bruising around her neck that gives the indication that she was strangled. But her neck is broken."

I blinked. "What?"

"Your guy strangled her then broke her neck."

Well, I guess he wanted to make sure she was dead. I looked at Kendra and then at Flynn. Here were two people who died a horrible death. But why? What was the motive behind this? Why kill Delisa, then two of her lovers? A thought popped into my head. Were all the names on the lists possible victims? Did that mean Balian might be next on the serial killers list? Were we even dealing with a serial killer?

I thought about all three murders. All three had broken necks that gave a pattern of how he preferred to kill. Connection? They were all involved with each other. Sexually. So how many on the list had to die for this to be considered as a serial killing?

And if this was Ivan's doing? What had been his trigger? What had made him snap and start killing everyone he'd had sex with?

None of this made sense.

"Oh, before I forget. There was a hit from the DNA you collected yesterday." Ming said.

"From Ivan?" I asked.

He nodded and I braced myself.

"Is it from the semen?"

"Nope. Ivan's DNA matched the fetus. He's the father."

That didn't come as a surprise. "What about the fang marks?"

"No match."

So Ivan was the baby's father, but he hadn't been the one who'd bitten or had sex with Delisa. So maybe I'd been right after all. Perhaps Ivan didn't like sharing as much as he'd led on. Maybe he saw her with someone and that had been the fuse that started the fire.

I thanked Ming and we headed back upstairs. "This doesn't make any sense." Carlos said as we rode the elevator. "Why would Ivan kill all his lovers?"

"Well, for one." I said. "He's a demon. Demons don't really need a motive to do horrible things. That's why Lucifer has them. They're hardwired to do his bidding. So the fact that he snapped isn't really that big of a surprise. But the cause of it? Well, it could be anything."

Bronson nodded. "I think we need to go have another little talk with Ivan. See how he reacts to the murders."

"I agree. Have you found an address yet?"

"No. But we could go back to Illusions and see if he's there or if someone knows where he's at."

I snorted. "Good luck with that."

They both smiled.

We drove to Illusions and found it empty except for a few waitresses and of course Balian. He was standing at the bar looking over some papers. When he saw us walking toward him a frown formed on his face.

"Now what?" he snapped. "What do you need now?"

"We need to speak to Ivan." I said.

"Ivan is not here."

"Know where he is?"

"No. And even if I did, I would not tell you."

Well, at least he was being honest. "Wow. You demons sure stick together don't you?"

"Are you trying to be sarcastic?" Balian asked.

"What was your first clue?" I said with a smile that was mocking.

He tilted his head to the side. "It is not becoming of you. A lady who wants respect should never use sarcasm."

"What makes you think I'm a lady?" I asked.

"Clearly I assumed wrong." His gaze became warm. "But I guess I should have known. After all, you dress like that and carry a gun. So perhaps I was wrong. You are no lady at all."

Carlos snickered.

Balian gave him a look of disapproval, then turned back to me. "Why are you looking for Ivan?"

"There was another murder." I said.

"And you think he had something to do with it?"

"Well, given the fact he knew them, yeah."

Something crossed his face. "Who?"

"Kendra Farris and Flynn Garwood. They were found this morning. We think they were tortured before being killed."

Balian frowned. "I knew them. Nice couple. Who would do such a thing?" I just gave him a look. "Ivan would never hurt anyone. I know him."

"Or maybe you just think you do." I said. "I mean, sometimes we think we know someone, but in reality we don't. People we love hide their true self's from us, sometimes more because they know we love them." Yeah, I was going there. But hey, never in a million years would I have thought Daniel would have done what he did. And in truth, I felt so stupid for not seeing it when I did. But I guess if this stuff would have never happened, then I'd still be with a man who thought of me as a monster.

"I suppose so. But I know him and I am telling you, he did not do this."

"Maybe not, but we still need to talk to him."

"Do you know where he might go?" asked Bronson.

Balian shook his head. "No. Ivan never told me where he lived. That is how it is for a lot of us. We like having private quarters that no one knows about."

I suddenly found myself wondering where he lived and what it looked like. Bad, very bad. "If you see him, you should call me." I wrote my name and number down on a napkin that was laying on the bar. I slid it toward him. "Here's my number."

He looked at it as if it was the most fascinating thing he'd ever seen. "I will." There was a promise in his voice that said he'd call me, but not with information about Ivan's whereabouts.

"Listen, I probably shouldn't be telling you this, but well, Ivan gave us a list of all the people he'd slept with and another list . . . of people who attend a special party that Samael throws. And well, Kendra and Flynn were on the list. I think whoever is doing this, is killing people on those lists. So you should be careful."

Balian's lips twitched. "You are afraid for my wellbeing. How thoughtful of you, little orchid."

My heart went pitter patter. "Just be careful. I'd hate for your body to be the next one I find." Why the hell did I say that?

He smiled this time and my whole body melted. His Russian accent became rough. "Yes, I would hate for that out come as well. I have some plans for the future that do not involve my untimely demise. Plans that involve . . . a certain woman in my life." His dark blue eyes never left mine. "And I intend for these plans to pan out. If she will have me."

Holy crap! My lower body tightened and my mouth became dry. I don't know why, he probably wasn't even talking about me. Okay, okay, I knew he wasn't talking about me. But the only thing I could think was, *lucky bitch*. And the second thing was that if I found out who this woman was I was going to rip her hair out and scratch up her face.

I had no idea where these feelings were coming from. I didn't know Balian well enough for thoughts like that. Hell, this man wasn't even my type. He was too hard and rough around the edges and gave off this renegade vibe. I found it hard to believe that we'd have anything in common or have anything to talk about.

Why would you even need to talk? That voice inside my head asked.

Yeah right, like that's all I needed. Wild monkey sex with a sexy Russian demon who seemed to be doing me with his eyes right at this very moment.

Well, on second thought, that didn't exactly sound like a bad idea.

Damn it! I needed to pull it together.

Balian's smile became wider as if he were reading my thoughts. I bit my lower lip to keep from blushing, but that only made it worse and I ended up blushing anyway.

Carlos chuckled and that made me blink. I found my composer and cleared my throat. "Well, thank you for your cooperation, Mr. Ivanski."

That made him laugh a little. "Of course. It is my pleasure to help assist you in any way you need me to."

Oh, boy. I was so over my head with this one it wasn't even funny. But I stayed in control of my expression and just smiled slightly. I gave him a small nod and turned and walked away. There was no way I was even going to try to speak. My voice would have given everything away.

I could feel Balian's gaze on my backside like a hot iron. I knew he was watching me walk away with lust in his eyes. I knew I was doing the right thing by walking away, but my body still protested, my soul screamed for me to go back. But I didn't listen. I just kept walking and didn't stop until I was back inside the SUV and safe from myself.

"Wow." Bronson said. "If I hadn't known any better, I'd guess you just left him standing there with a hard on." He turned his head to look at me. "Do you always have that effect on men?"

I shook my head. "I don't know. I've never given it much thought." My voice was raspy.

"Well, maybe you should. It seemed to me, that if he could have gotten away with it, he would have set you on the bar and fucked you stupid." He paused. "Sorry for the phrasing."

"Don't be. You're right." Oh man was he ever. I had seen it in Balian's eyes. He wanted me and he didn't care if it was on the bar or somewhere else. I took a deep breath. "Now where do we go?"

"I want to check out a few more leads, then we'll call it a night and I'll take you home."

I nodded. "Sounds good." Yeah, anything that would get my mind off Balian was a good idea to me. Even if it was finding another dead body.

CHAPTER FIFTEEN

The rest of the day had gone by without much luck or anymore leads. We talked to a few more people who'd been on the lists and no one knew anything. They were probably lying, protecting Ivan. But thankfully we hadn't found anymore dead bodies. So I guess the whole day hadn't been a total bust.

Bronson dropped me off at home and I went inside to find Alec, Dylan, and Matt in the sitting room. They all smiled when I came in.

"Hey," Alec said. "Rough day? You look beat."

I flopped down on the sofa next to him and exhaled. "Not really. Just the same as always. You know, dead bodies and possible serial killers."

"Serial killers?" Matt asked with a raised eyebrow.

"Yep."

"I thought you were working on the Shaylee case?" said Dylan.

"I am." I said and sighed. I might as well tell them. It was going to be all over the news. "We found two more bodies this morning. They were killed the same way and they're connected . . . in a way."

"How were they killed?" asked Alec.

"That's privileged information."

He chuckled. "Yeah, that's what I figured."

"So where's Stefan?" I asked. "I thought he was staying home."

"Stefan went out and Nate's on a bounty. I'm not sure when they're supposed to be home." Matt said and smiled. "I think Stefan went to Mariska's, so I doubt he'll be home until morning."

I sighed. I guess I was going to be home alone after the guys left. That was a depressing reality, but it was my life. I'd spent the past four and a half months alone despite the fact that I'd lived with someone. Just because he's laying next to you in bed doesn't mean he's really there. I'd learned that and then some. I could barely remember what it felt like to be in someone's arms and sleep. To have someone look at you and not see or wish you were someone else. To not see resentment in their eyes. A lot had happened and I was learning to be on my own again.

And God was it hard. Part of me missed Daniel and part of me didn't. In some ways it was like losing my mom all over again. There had been days when I wondered if I'd run into her on a case. Would I even recognize her? Would she recognize me? I had no clue.

My cell phone rang and I dug it out of my pocket and answered. "Montgomery."

"Is this Special Agent Montgomery?" A female voice whispered.

"Yes."

"This is Ila Shaylee. You came and talked to me and my family yesterday about Delisa. You said if I thought of anything I should call you." She paused. "I think I know something that might help you catch her killer. Can I meet you somewhere private?"

"Yeah, sure. Where did you have in mind?"

"Could you meet me at the fairy statues at the front of the path to the gate?"

"Yeah, I can do that. I'll be there in an hour."

"Okay." she said. "Oh, turn your headlights off just before the path." And then she hung up.

I stared at my phone and blew out a breath. I had a bad feeling I wasn't going to like what Ila Shaylee had to tell me. I got up and put my cell back into my pocket. "Well, duty calls boys."

"Or do you mean booty calls?" Matt said and burst out laughing.

"Dude, you so need to stop hanging out with Julian. He's a bad influence." I said. "And just so you know, I'm meeting a girl."

"Kinky. Decided to bat for the other team now, huh? That's hot."

"Matt!"

That only made him laugh harder and Dylan and Alec joined in. I ignored them and made for the door. I got into the Mazda and took off toward fairy land. My mind had come up with over a dozen reasons why Ila would want to meet me and none of them were very good.

When I was close to my destination I turned off my headlights. When I was just about to the fairy statues I stopped and parked. I got out of the car and walked the rest of the way. I was happy that I was inhuman, because it was too dark for a human to be able to see. But since I wasn't I could see where I was going without any problems.

Up ahead I could see Ila Shaylee standing at the edge of the road that led to the gates and she wasn't alone. Zarek Shaylee was with her. They both seemed nervous about something which made me feel uneasy. What the hell was going on? What could they possibly tell me that could make them act like this? I had no idea, but knew I was about to find out.

When they saw me walking toward them relief filled their faces.

"You made it." Ila said. "I was afraid you weren't coming."

"You said you had information that could help find Delisa's killer." I said.

She nodded and looked up at her brother. "Tell her Ila." he said. "It's okay. You can trust her."

That was almost comical considering he'd accused me of not being able to do anything about his sister's death. But I wouldn't hold that against him. He was grieving. "Yes, your brother's right. You can trust me."

Ila looked down and didn't meet my eyes. "About a year ago, I went into the human world." she began, voice soft, barely a whisper. "Delisa invited me to a party that she and Ivan were throwing. Father didn't want me to go, but I promised him I would stay out of trouble and Delisa said she would watch me. Make sure I was safe."

I was getting a bad feeling about this party. Ivan had said that he and Delisa had gone to orgies thrown by Samael. Maybe it wasn't Samael throwing the orgy party's. Maybe it was Ivan.

"It's okay." Zarek said. "Go on." He placed a hand on his sister's shoulder.

Ila nodded and continued. "Everything was going as planned. No one bothered me. I sat on the sofa for most of it and watched everyone dance. Then Ivan came over and he sat down next to me. He draped an arm around me and asked if I was having fun. I said yes. Then he . . ." She trailed off and I saw . . . shame in her eyes. "He offered me this powder stuff. He called it

Pixie Dust—said it would make me feel really good. I told him no, but he said, 'Come on, it's only a little Pixie Dust. Just put it in your coke. You won't even taste it.' I didn't want it, but I didn't want to make Delisa upset."

There were tears in her eyes now. "So I gave in. I let him put the powder stuff in my drink. After that, everything became a blur and . . ." The tears came. "I woke up the next morning beside a vampire I didn't know. My clothes were not on my body and there were fang marks and blood between my thighs."

That bastard. I was going to kill him. The hell with locking him up behind bars. I was going to fucking kill the bastard. Wouldn't hurt a soul my ass. I knew what she was telling me. Ivan had slipped her a date-rape drug and had her raped.

"Did you tell anyone?" I asked.

"I told Delisa, but she wouldn't listen to me. She just accused me of lying. I told my father and he was outraged. He and Delisa had a big fight. After that, she left and never came back."

No doubt. This must have been what Theophilius had been talking about—why Androcles had stopped his daughter from talking any further. The king would not want many to know that his eldest daughter had allowed his youngest daughter to be raped. It would show a sign of weakness that he couldn't afford.

"I'm sorry." I said. And I know it was lame, but it was all I had. "And forgive me, but what does this have to do with Delisa's murder?"

"I'm not sure. But I feel as if you need to know this. That it may help." Ila said.

I looked over at Zarek. "What do you think?"

"I think the bastard deserves everything he gets." Zarek said. "It may not be death, but maybe death would be too easy. Perhaps rotting away in a cell for the rest of his miserable existence would be justice enough."

Well, at least he wasn't talking murder and war.

I left Ila and Zarek feeling hollow and numb. But I also felt like beating the shit out of someone. And when a memory came back to me? Well, I felt even more pissed.

"Be careful how deep you dig, agent Montgomery. You may not like what you find or what might find you." Constantine had said.

I got into the car and drove past the speed limit on a hunch and pure rage. When I got to Illusions, I parked the car and got out. I stormed past the bouncer and heard cries of protests from people waiting to get in. I stormed into the building for the second time today with one goal. Find Constantine Gonzales and beat the truth out of him one way or another.

I found him standing at the far side of the room. I crossed the space between us like a raging bull seeing red. I wouldn't have been surprised if steam was coming out of my ears.

There wasn't anyone on the dance floor. The club wasn't open yet, but it would be soon. So I needed to work fast. Constantine took one look at me and I saw him curse. I reached him and grabbed him by the collar of his shirt and slammed him against the wall.

"You bastard!" I yelled. "You knew. You knew he had her raped and you still defended him."

"What the fuck are you talking about?" he asked and winced when I punched him in the face.

"Don't play dumb with me. You know damn well what I'm talking about. Ila. You knew Ivan had her raped. But you still defended him. Why?"

I let go of his collar and he slid to the floor and stared up at me, his lips a bloody mess.

"Why do you think?" he said.

"Besides the fact that you're a demon and untrustworthy? I haven't a clue." I pulled out my gun and took aim at him. "Give me one reason why I shouldn't kill you."

"Because you have taken a vow to serve and protect, and killing me would be against your moral code?"

"Wrong answer. Strike one."

"Because I am unarmed and it is against the law to shoot an unarmed man?"

"Okay, fine, I'll give you that one. Now tell me about Ivan."

Constantine gave a bark of laughter. "Tell you what? That he is a sick and twisted bastard? That he gets off by drugging young girls and having them raped? Or that he enjoys watching them being raped? Or my favorite, he keeps them drugged up so he can have his very own personal sex doll? But I'm guessing you already figured most of that out."

Actually, I hadn't. But I wasn't about to tell him that.

"If he disgusts you so much, why are you his Lawyer?"

"Because he pays well. And . . . he's Samael's new little lap dog. Whatever Samael wants is what Samael gets. And he wanted Ivan out of jail."

"So what? He's got a thing for Ivan or something?"

He snorted and wiped at his lip. "Or something. His mate Lilith has a fancy for Ivan."

"Okay, so? That doesn't explain anything." I said.

"It should. There are two things Samael cannot stand. One is disobedience from his people. And the second is the bitch fits Lilith throws whenever she doesn't get her way."

I was starting to get a picture. Lilith finds out that her little toy is in jail and pitches a fit until Samael agrees to send Constantine to get him out.

"Was Ivan really at an orgy the night Delisa was murdered or was that just a lie to get him out of jail?" I asked already knowing the answer.

He shook his head. "Lawyer-client privilege."

"I'm the one with the gun, remember? So answer the question."

Constantine glared at me. "Fine. No, he wasn't at an orgy. But he didn't make it up. Samael really does have them. But yes, he lied. I have no idea where he was that night. I swear. I was just sent to get him out. That is all."

"You swear you're not lying to me?"

"I swear. All I know is, he and Delisa got into a fight that night and he left."

"What was it about?" As if I didn't already know.

"It was something about one of the men in her life. He was causing trouble and Ivan wanted him gone, but Delisa was having a hard time making the man leave."

"Was it someone she was sleeping with?"

"Probably. Most of the men in her life were in her bed."

I lowered my gun and returned it to its holster. This case just kept getting deeper and deeper into hardcore territory.

"Was there anything else you needed from me?" Constantine asked with a sigh.

"Just one." Before he knew what was coming, I kicked him in the chest. There was a crack and a whoosh as his breath escaped him. "That was for Ila. I'm sure you can deliver my message to Ivan." And then I walked away.

"Bitch." he muttered.

I got back into the car with a new clarity and a new mission. I was going to take Ivan down even if it killed me. Even if it cost me everything I had. But the joke would be on them. I didn't have all that much. I also made a mental note. The old lady had said the man who'd answered the door was tall with dark hair and glowing green eyes.

Suspect number two: Constantine Gonzales.

CHAPTER SIXTEEN

By the time I made it back home I was exhausted both mentally and physically. I parked the car next to Stefan's and frowned. I guess he decided to come home after all. I got out of the car and went inside. I stood in the sitting room and just stared at the stairs. I was so tired I didn't think I was going to be able to make the climb up to my room. So instead I kicked off my shoes, took off my holster, checked the safety on my gun, and laid them down on the coffee table along with my cell phone.

I laid down on the sofa and closed my eyes. It had been a very long day and all I wanted was sleep. I didn't want to deal with anymore crime scenes or suspects or any kind of drama. I just wanted a peaceful sleep. But my mind had other plans.

I thought about Ila and what she'd told me tonight. No wonder Androcles was looking at war with Samael. His youngest daughter had been raped by a demon and now his oldest daughter had been murdered by a demon. Yeah, he had a lot of cause for war. Honestly I was surprised he hadn't done anything about it. If it had been me raped, Stefan would have already killed the demon responsible and then some. So why hadn't Androcles made a move on the demon? Maybe he didn't know the demons name. Although, that wouldn't have mattered to Stefan. He would have killed them all so he'd knew he got the right one.

Then I thought about Delisa, about what Constantine had told me about

Ivan. I'd known he'd lied, but now I had conformation. But why would he lie unless he had something to hide or if he'd done it? Yeah, my money was on Ivan. There was just too many things pointing to him.

I laid there a bit longer and finally I drifted off to sleep.

I woke some time later to the feel of hands touching me. I opened my eyes to see Nate. He was sitting on the edge of the sofa next to me, his hand was hovering above my face, his fingers brushing my skin as they pushed back a strain of my hair out of my face. I moved a little to find I was now under a blanket.

"Nate, what are you doing?" I asked sleepily.

He blinked, eyes now wide and swallowed hard. "I...uh...I didn't mean to wake you. I just...I saw you asleep and thought you needed a blanket." He was talking fast in a hushed whisper. "I'm sorry. I shouldn't have...damn it." He turned away from me and rubbed his hands over his face.

I sat up and just stared at him. Nate was acting so weird. I wanted to ask him what was going on. But I didn't. I wasn't sure I really wanted to know the answer. So I asked him something else. "So what time is it?"

"Two." He looked down.

"Nate." I said and touched him on the arm. "What's going on?" There I said it. It was now out in the open.

Nate opened his mouth to answer me but stopped when we heard the sound of a door closing from upstairs. A few seconds later Stefan came down the stairs looking fresh from sleep.

He looked from me to Nate and back, then smiled. "Hey, I thought I heard voices. When did you two get home?"

"A few minutes ago." Nate said fast. I didn't even bother correcting him on when I'd gotten home. If Nate wanted to lie to Stefan and keep whatever this was from him, then that was fine. Frankly, I didn't quite understand it myself. So it did me no good to try to explain it to someone else.

"Well, you two should get to bed. It's late. And I know you both probably have a very busy day ahead of you tomorrow."

"Okay dad. We will in a few minutes."

Stefan just stared at us with a look that said 'get your asses to bed now.'

I smiled and got up. I knew that look all too well. He wasn't going to leave until we went to bed. So I grabbed my gun and cell and headed upstairs and into my room, but not before I stopped and kissed Stefan goodnight. I got to my room and set my stuff down on the bedside table.

I sighed. I was tired and finding out what was going on with Nate would have to wait until tomorrow. Or at least, day light. I stripped out of my clothes and crawled into bed in only my undies. I used to do that a lot when Daniel and I were together. Tonight it felt right. Granted, there wasn't going to be a warm body laying next to me, but hey, you can't have everything.

I laid there and closed my eyes and drifted off to sleep.

CHAPTER SEVENTEEN

The next day had been long and tiring with no luck in any new leads. Bronson, Carlos, and I had spent the day talking to more potential victims from the lists, but that had come up blank too. Everyone had said pretty much the same thing. Ivan was a nice guy who wouldn't hurt anyone. Yeah, tell that to Ila and his other rape victims.

Now we were back at the mansion. We were in the kitchen going over the last few names on the list. It was 5:30 and I was cooking dinner. Bronson and Carlos were sitting at the island looking discouraged. I knew the feeling. We had one suspect, who we were sure had done the crime, but as it was seeming, had no evidence that he actually done it, because no one was talking and there was no DNA matches on Delisa Shaylee's body but one.

But it hadn't been Ivan's DNA. The semen found in her body had matched one of the DNA samples from Kendra Farris's body. So whoever raped Kendra had been with Delisa sexually.

I was standing in front of the stove when Sabine and Piper came in. They eyed the men sitting at the island and gave a questioning look my way. "Hey." I said with a smile. "How's it going?"

"It's going okay." Sabine said as she and Piper sat down. "I have an hour before my shift starts, so I thought I'd come say hi." Which explained why she was wearing pink hospital scrubs. "So who's your friends?"

"Oh, that's Elliott Bronson and Rafe Carlos. They're from the PCU. I'm helping them on a case. Boys, this is Sabine Kincaid and Piper Ryan. We've been friends since we were like six." I said.

There was a chorus of hello.

"So, are you guys staying for dinner?" I asked.

"Yeah, and you should set two more plates." Sabine said.

I turned around to ask why, but came up short when a young girl around the age of fifteen came running in. "Morgan!" Kelsey yelled as she wrapped her arms around me.

I hugged her back. She was Julian and Sabine's baby sister. She had the same long black hair and dark brown eyes as her two older siblings. "Hey." I said.

She pulled back and smiled. "Hey. Sorry I haven't seen you since you got back. It's the end of the school year and I had some finals to study for."

"I understand. Are you excited about the summer?" I looked up to see another girl around Kelsey's age standing in the door way. She was tall for a human with long blond hair pulled up in a pony tail and baby blue eyes.

"Yeah." Kelsey turned toward the girl. "This is Jayce. She's my best friend. Jayce, this is Morgan. She's friends with my sister and brother. She's a cop."

Jayce stepped into the kitchen. "That's cool . . . Do you carry a gun?"

I smiled. "Yes."

"Do you ever shoot it?" she asked eyeing the gun in the shoulder holster.

"Only when I have to."

"Cool." she said and sat down. "Can I see it?"

"Um . . . no."

"Why not? I think guns are cool."

I just shook my head. "Not going to happen. They may be cool, but they are still dangerous. Especially to those who don't know how to use them."

She frowned, but took no for an answer.

I smiled. "Are you girls staying for dinner?" They both nodded. I sat a plate of food down in front of everyone. Tonight was chicken parmesan with garlic toast. I pulled out glasses and set them down on the counter with a picture of ice tea. I would have offered Bronson and Carlos a beer, but I didn't like drinking in front of Kelsey. And besides, we were still somewhat on duty. "Oh, and by the way." I said. "This is Elliott and Rafe. They're friends of mine from work."

Kelsey and Jayce eyed them with the curiosity of school girls going through puberty. Which meant that they scanned them from one end to the other. But who could blame them? Bronson and Carlos were nice looking guys for humans.

"So, what do you young ladies have planned for tonight?" Carlos asked with a smile.

"We're going to a party tonight." Kelsey said and then blushed.

I wonder. "So, what's his name?" I asked.

She looked horrified. "His name? Oh, right. His name. Greg. But it's not his party."

"But he is going to be there?"

"Yeah."

"Ah. So you know about . . . being careful?" I asked her, already knowing the answer, but wanting to hear it anyway.

She nodded.

"Mom and I had the sex talk with her a few weeks ago." Sabine said. "She knows all about it. Safety comes first. No condom, no cookie."

"Good." I remembered being her age and not understanding what the hell was going on with my body. I had been sixteen when I'd lost my virginity, but I knew there was girls who'd lost theirs even earlier. I was glad that Sofia was talking about this with Kelsey now, rather than later. "So tell me about this Greg."

"He's so nice and sweet. And he's cute. He's the one who asked me to the party." Kelsey said.

"And he's okay with Jayce coming along?" Piper asked around a bite of food.

"Yeah. He said it was cool."

Just then Nate walked in. My mind went back to last night and the way he'd been so nice to me. "So, what's on the menu?" he asked.

"Chicken parmesan." I said. "Want some?"

"Can it be takeout? I can't stay."

"Sure." I got up and grabbed a Tupperware bowl and filled it with food. I wrapped a piece of toast in aluminum foil and handed them to him with a fork. "Here."

He took it and smiled. It was warm and so unlike Nate. Especially when it came to me. "Thanks." he said and turned to walk out.

I looked down and bit my lower lip. "Nate?"

He stopped and turned. "Yeah?"

"Can we talk?"

Nate stared at me and swallowed hard. "Um . . . can this wait? I really need to go." There was a panicked note to his voice.

"Oh, yeah. That's fine. We can talk later."

He nodded. "Later then." Then he turned and left.

"Okay." Sabine said. "What the hell was that all about?"

I winced and walked back over and sat down. "Nothing."

"It sure as hell didn't look like nothing. Now explain before I beat it out of you."

I rolled my eyes. "It's nothing. Really. It's just . . . he's been acting kind of weird around me. That's all."

"How?" Piper said.

"Yeah." said Sabine. "I want details. How has Nate been acting around you?"

I sighed. "I don't know, he just has. He's been really nice to me. Kind of sweet."

"Yeah, that is weird." Sabine said.

"How's that weird?" Rafe asked. "Aren't brother's supposed to be nice to their sister's"

I nodded. "Yes, but Nate's never been nice to me. And he definitely hasn't ever treated me like a sister."

"Oh. Well, could have fooled me." he smiled. "But hey, I'm new to your life and all that."

I smiled. I hadn't known these men but for a few days, but at the same time I felt like I'd known them my whole life. I knew it would be a breeze working with them. I kind of liked them in a way. I had asked Bronson earlier when we had been alone about his other agent. Her name was Livea Greene. I hadn't met her yet and doubted I would. She was still recovering from her injuries.

There had been a rogue vampire on the loose and when they'd gone to arrest him, well, he'd gone apeshit and had attacked them. Since he was faster and stronger he'd gotten the upper hand. One agent had died and another had been seriously injured. That had been part of the reason why he'd wanted me on the case. Because he didn't want a repeat. I couldn't say I blamed him.

"You know." Kelsey said. "I think Nate's hot."

Jayce nodded in agreement.

I had never given it much thought. But now that it was out there, I realized she was right. Nate was good-looking. But then again, he looked like his father and Stefan wasn't exactly unnoticeable to women.

Sabine looked at her watch. "Well, I got to go." She looked at Piper. "Want me to drop you off?"

Piper shook her head. "No. Alexi said he was coming over here later. He can bring me home." Sabine and I gave her a knowing look and she blushed. "It's not like that."

"Uh-huh." Sabine said.

"Seriously it's not."

"Uh-huh." I echoed.

She gave us both a glare. "Hey, neither of you have any room to talk, since your love life's are in the dumpster." She pointed a finger at Sabine. "You are in love with a man who is your brother's best friend, and would be killed if Julian ever found out." She pointed her finger at me. "You have just been dumped. And you need to figure out what you're going to do about Kaydan and his feelings before you start a relationship with anyone. Right now you're damaged goods."

"Wow that was harsh." I said. "When did you start taking ass kicking lessons from Sabine?"

Sabine snorted. "Yeah, it was almost like I was kicking my own ass." She smiled. "Who knew our little Piper could be such a viper? It was almost scary."

"Hey, I can be tough when I need to be." Piper said. "You two can't be the tough bitches all the time."

I laughed. "Piper, honey, I hate to break this to you, but I'm not as tough as you think I am."

"I know, but you're tougher than I am. I could never do what you do. Not because I don't want to, but because I can't. I sense other people's pain and I can heal wounds and stuff. I could never work in a hospital or chase down a bad guy because it would be too painful. It would kill me or drive me mad."

I knew it was hard on Piper. Sometimes I thought she got the short end of the stick when it came to supernatural powers. Yeah, healing was a good ability to have, but the sense of a stranger's pain was more than anyone could bare. I'd thought my ability to see the future was annoying, I couldn't imagine going through what Piper did when she got too close to someone who was hurting.

"I'm sorry." Sabine said and hugged Piper. "I understand where you're coming from. Do you think it's easy for me too? It's not. I can see people's auras and see when two people are soul mates. And I hate it. I can see a part of my soul entwined with Matt's. And it scares me, because I don't know how he'd take it if I told him." She looked down and a sadness filled her face. "I hate telling people that they're soul mates. I've told them in the past and nothing happened. They're still a part."

"Julian and Willow?" I asked.

"Yeah. One minute they're happy, living together, talking marriage and babies, and the next thing I know, it's over. She left and he won't talk about it. Or at least he won't talk about it with me." She frowned. "I'm happy that you and Alexi are trying to be together. I really am."

Piper sighed. "Yeah, we're going to tell our family's soon." A horrified expression crossed her face. "Oh man, Luke and Natasha are going to love this."

I doubted that. Luke and Natasha were too much like Sheldon and Daphne. Up tight and with no humor. When they found out that Kaydan and I had slept together, they had gone postal. They'd accused me of introducing their son to sex and corrupting him. They'd pointed a finger at Stefan and blamed him, because it was his child who'd done it. Their Kaydan was pure and innocent.

I knew Luke and Natasha would do the same thing with Piper and her parents. It didn't matter that they were both adults with jobs. And I knew Piper had been talking about getting her own place for a while. It wouldn't surprise me if she and Alexi didn't get a place together now. Yeah, they were cute and deserved to be happy.

"It'll be okay." I said. "Luke and Natasha like you."

"Yeah, but that was before they found out I was bonking their son."

Sabine laughed. "Yeah, that does change a few things." She turned to her little sister. "Don't ever grow up. Stay young and virginal forever. Dating and sex are just complicated."

"You can say that again." I said with a nod, agreeing with her.

"Okay." Kelsey said with as much enthusiasm as any teenager would have when someone older tells them not to do something.

"Well, I gotta go." Sabine said.

"Us too." said Kelsey. "We need to get back to my house and get ready for the party."

"Okay." I said. "Who's driving?"

"Jayce. She just got her license."

I nodded. I walked over to the counter and opened one of the drawers and pulled out a notepad and pen. I wrote my number down on two separate pieces of paper and tore them out, then went back to the island and handed each, one of the papers. "Okay. You girls be safe. No drinking and driving. If you drink, call me and I'll come and get you. Understood?" Yeah, I was sounding like Stefan when I'd been a teenager and had gone out to parties.

"Understood." They said as they took them. And they left.

It was just me, Piper, Bronson, and Carlos now. We spent some time talking about things that didn't involve the case and some things that did. I told Piper about my talk with Ila—Bronson and Carlos already knew. I'd told them this morning. Piper had been horrified, but had listened. She hadn't heard anything about other girls being raped. So we'd all concluded that it was being hush, hush right now. If it was happening to angel girls, the angels would have said something—spread the word around.

Around nine o'clock, Alexi came in followed by Kaydan. Piper's eyes lit up and so did Alexi's. I could see that they were in love and I didn't have Sabine's ability. But I didn't need it. It was right there, written on their faces.

Alexi crossed the room to Piper and kissed her. "Hey, been here long?"

She smiled. "Yeah, but it's okay. It gave me and Morgan time to catch up."

"That sounds nice. You ready?"

"Yep." She looked at me and smiled. "I'm glad we had this talk. I've missed you."

"I've missed you too." I said. "And Sabine. Now go out with your boyfriend and get busy."

That made her blush, but she nodded. I watched her and Alexi leave with a bit of envy. I wanted someone to come home to. But one look at Kaydan took care of any thoughts of that. I knew he was thinking the very same thing, and he was thinking it with me. He'd said the other night that if we'd stayed together, we would have gotten married and had a child. And the look he was giving me said he was trying to picture me pregnant.

Kaydan crossed the room, bent down and kissed me, like he did it every day. "Hey, how's your day been?" he asked.

"Okay." I said and winced when I saw the grins on Bronson and Carlos's faces. "Haven't found any dead bodies yet. So I guess that's a plus. But we're having trouble trying to link our suspect to the crime."

He kissed my shoulder and up to my ear. "I'm sorry. But I know you'll get him."

Oh boy, this was getting dangerously familiar. Kaydan was making his move. Again.

"So Kaydan, have you met agent Bronson and agent Carlos?" I said trying to get us somewhere, anywhere that didn't involve us talking about getting naked.

Kaydan sighed and pulled back. "No." He looked at the two men in the room. "Hi, I'm Kaydan. I'm Morgan's . . . friend. It's nice to meet you."

"Likewise." said Bronson with a big smile. "We've heard so much about you."

"Really?"

"Yep." Carlos said. "Really."

That seemed to brighten him up. He put an arm around my shoulders. "Well, I am an importance in Morgan's life. So that does make sense."

What the hell?

I started to open my mouth to say . . . I don't know, anything when my cell rang. "Montgomery."

The voice on the other end was small and sounded frightened. "Morgan? It's me, Jayce. I need your help. I don't know what to do."

My alarm level went up. "Jayce? What's wrong? What's happened?"

She started crying. "The p-p-party wasn't what we th-thought. There's some things . . . I don't know, I think it's some kind of orgy or something."

"Where's Kelsey? Put Kelsey on the phone."

"I can't." she cried.

"Why not?'

"Because he locked her inside the other room and I can't get in." She was sobbing now.

Oh God! Oh dear God, let me be wrong. "Who locked her into a room?"

I was trying to keep my voice calm, but it was hard. Kelsey was like a baby sister to me.

"Greg. He showed up and he and Kelsey started talking. Then he asked her if she wanted to go somewhere private, and when she said no, he got mad. So we were going to leave, but he . . . he got madder and then he hit her and locked her in a bedroom with him inside. I think I heard her scream."

I felt my body start to vibrate with so much anger, I was pretty sure I was going to combust. "Whose party was it?"

"I don't know. I think Greg said his name was Ivan. I think it's his house." Got him.

"Okay, you need to try to get out of the house if you can. If not, lock yourself in the bathroom. Okay?"

"Okay." she sniffed.

"Now I need an address." She gave me the address and I told her to hold tight. I hung up. "Call for back up." I told Bronson.

"Where are we going?" he asked.

I told him.

"Shit." Carlos spat as we made a run for the SUV and I ignored Kaydan and his questions.

We got in and took off. I prayed we'd make it in time. God help Ivan and Greg if we didn't. Not heaven nor hell would protect them. The hell with my badge and the code. If Kelsey was hurt or if raped or dead? Well, they were going to learn what pain and a slow death was.

Because I was going to kill them. And there would be pain involved.

CHAPTER EIGHTEEN

Bronson drove fast as we raced against time. He'd turned on his siren and flashing lights, and cars moved out of our way. I prayed the whole car ride there that we'd get there in time. Kelsey was only fifteen, too young to have to deal with this. I prayed that God would give me strength to not do something stupid and reckless if we were too late.

If we were, I knew myself well enough to know I'd lose it.

I did not want to find her body. I did not want to add her to the victim list. And most of all, I did not want to have to tell Cam and Sofia that their youngest had been murdered because I was too late to get there. I didn't think the Kincaid family could handle that. These people were kind and full of life. Always laughing and making jokes.

But unfortunately I knew bad things happened to good people.

Twenty minutes later we arrived at the house. It was a two story house that looked like every other house on the block. White with blue shutters.

There were so many cars parked that there weren't any spaces left for us and the now police cars. But it didn't matter. We all parked in the street. I jumped out and the head cop there stopped me. He was twenty pounds overweight with brown hair and eyes.

"So what are we doing here again?" he asked in a snippy tone.

"I got a call from a girl at this party. She and her friend are in trouble. So we're here to get them out." I said just as snippy.

He looked at me and then at the house. "There's demons in there."

"Yeah, so?"

"Well, agent whoever, I'm not taking my men in there until I know what we're up against."

Whatever control I'd had before was now gone. I lit into him. "There is a fifteen-year-old girl in there who might me getting raped at this very minute, maybe even killed. I'm not going to stand out here while you try to grow some balls."

He puffed up like a blowfish. He was mad because I'd brought his manhood into this. Men seemed to have a thing about their dicks that I never got. You didn't hear women walking around talking about the size of their vaginas. So I never understood men's fascination with their size.

He narrowed his eyes at me. "I understand you're harder to kill, but my men and I aren't bullet prove. What if they attack? Or resist arrest?"

"Then I'll make an example out of them for the others."

"You would do that?"

"Yeah, I will do that." And then I turned and headed for the house. He and his men could come along or stay behind. I didn't care. I was going to get Kelsey out of there even if I had to do it by myself.

The music coming from the house was so loud that I didn't even bother knocking or ringing the doorbell. They wouldn't have heard it anyway. I stepped inside with Bronson and Carlos on my heels. I looked around the room and my stomach rolled. Orgy was a soft word to say what was going on here.

There were couples going at it on sofas and in chairs and some up against the walls. There was a young girl who looked no older than Kelsey tied to a table naked. One man was shoving himself inside of her, while another shoved himself into her mouth. Two more men walked up and sank their fangs into her flesh.

"Dear Lord." Carlos breathed.

I looked around until I found the source of the music. I walked over and pulled the cord out of the plug. The music stopped, and we were now left with the sounds of moaning and a few cries of girl's saying stop.

I pulled out my gun, aimed it toward the ceiling and fired. BANG!

The whole room became silent after that. Everyone stopped and turned to look at me.

"Okay." I said, putting my gun away. "Now that I have your attention. I'm Special Agent Montgomery. I'm with the PCU. You're all under arrest."

One of the male demons stomped up to me, his body bare of clothes, his dark brown eyes narrowed. "You cannot touch us." he spat. "We are under the protection of Ivan and his master Samael."

I leveled my gaze with his. "If you resist arrest, that charge will be added to the one you are being accused of."

"And what are we being accused of?"

"Rape for one."

He gave a bark of laughter. "Look around cop. Does it look like any of these whores are being forced?"

I did look around and what I saw were not willing whores, but young girls who could barely stand or keep their eyes open. Pixie Dust. They were all drugged.

"Everyone put your hands up. You're under arrest for the rape of these young girls." It was the only charge I had at the moment. But I was sure once we took a better look, we'd find something nastier.

The sound of footsteps running down the stairs made me look up. Kyriss came down the stairs in a rush and stopped so fast he almost fell. "What the hell?"

My eyes widened for a second before I regained my surprise. I had not expected him to be here, but I should have. His name was on the list. I looked at Carlos and pointed toward Kyriss. "I want him in cuffs and in the SUV now."

Carlos nodded and made his way to Kyriss. Cops filed in and it didn't take them long before they were cuffing the demons and checking the girls for pulses. I made a run up the stairs. Jayce had said that Kelsey was in one of the rooms. I went to every room and checked them, my heart pounding.

I came to one that was locked and I beat on the door. "Open the door! It's the police."

The door opened and Jayce came running out into my arms. "Morgan! I'm so happy you're here." she cried.

"Where's Kelsey?" I asked.

She pointed to a door down the hall I hadn't checked yet. "In there."

"Okay. Go down and find Bronson or Carlos. I'll be right behind you."

She nodded and did as she was told.

I waited until she was gone, and then I walked to the locked door. I didn't bother with knocking on it. I could hear crying protests coming from the other side of the door. I planted my foot and kicked the door down. After that, I blacked out for about a minute.

When I came back to reality, I was on top of the boy I assume was Greg. I was beating my fist into his face over and over again. Hands were pulling at me and someone was yelling for me to stop.

"Morgan!" Bronson yelled. "Stop. You're going to kill him. Now stop. You've saved her. Think of Kelsey."

I was thinking of Kelsey. I was thinking I was going to kill this bastard for what he'd done to her and I didn't care if he was human or not.

"Morgan stop!" Bronson's arms were around me now and I was fighting him. "Just stop. Go check on Kelsey."

That snapped me out of my rage. I was breathing hard and my fist was throbbing, but I ignored it and made my way to the bed where Kelsey was laying. Her shirt was ripped, her skirt pushed up, and her underwear pulled down. There was some blood between her thighs, but I ignored that too. If I thought too much about it I was going to be beating the shit out of Greg again.

"Kelsey." I said. "It's me. Morgan."

She looked up and relief filled her tear streaked face. "Morgan?" Then she burst into tears. "Oh, Morgan. Oh God."

I wrapped my arms around her and held her tight. "It's okay. You're safe now." She clung to me and my heart broke.

Carlos walked in and I could see sadness behind his eyes. "The girl on the table is barely breathing, but she's fighting. The EMTs are working on her. The other girls are on their way to the hospital. And everyone has been cuffed." He dropped his eyes to the floor. "Ivan is nowhere to be seen. We can't find him anywhere."

Why didn't that surprise me? He'd probably took off the second he saw the police.

I nodded and pulled back to look at Kelsey. "We need to get you to the hospital. Would it be okay if Carlos carried you out to the SUV?"

She nodded and I helped her pull up her underwear. Carlos walked over and she clung to him. "It's okay." he said picking her up. "I got you." And then they were out of sight.

I looked over at Bronson and he looked up. "He's breathing."

"I don't care." I said and I walked out.

I made my way to the SUV as Carlos was putting Kelsey in the back. I got in after her and was relieved when I saw that Carlos had put Kyriss in front. I got in and Kelsey was once again in my arms hanging on for dear life. Carlos got in on the other side by Jayce. He wrapped her in his arms to make room for him. She didn't seem to mind the comfort. She clung to him.

Kyriss turned his head and looked at Kelsey, who was crying softly. "Is she okay?"

"Shut up." I snapped. "Shut the fuck up. You don't get to talk."

He turned his head back around. "I at least get my one phone call, right?"

"Yes." Carlos said. "Now shut up."

Kyriss smiled as Bronson got in and turned the key. "Where to?"

"Hospital." I said. "You can drop us off and then take him to the station so he can make his one phone call, then come back for me."

"Good." Kyriss said with a big smile. "I know exactly who I want to call."

CHAPTER NINETEEN

The hospital was buzzing with doctors and nurse's running from one new patient to another. Most of the young girls from the party were here and being looked at. Carlos helped me carry Kelsey into the ER. We had just walked through the doors when one of the doctors stopped in his tracks and just stared at us, his face turning ghostly white.

Cam stood there as realization crossed his face. His eyes looked his daughter over from head to toe and anger filled his eyes as they fell on the blood that was on her legs. "Kelsey?"

At the sound of her father's voice, Kelsey turned her head to look at him. There was a bruise starting to form on her face and tears filled her eyes all over again. "Daddy." she cried.

That was all it took to get him moving. Cam crossed the room and took his daughter from Carlos. She clung to him and started crying harder. My heart broke and it made me want to go beat the shit out of the bastard who'd done this all over again. God help Ivan when he was found and apprehended. I'm not sure it was going to be safe for me to be alone with him.

Cam looked at me and that expression on his face said it all. He knew her being alive was my doing. His gaze left mine and landed on Jayce who was standing next to me. "Are you okay, Jayce?"

She nodded and sniffed. "Yeah."

"Come with me and I'll have someone check you out." he said. She didn't argue, she just followed him as she was told.

I turned to Carlos. "You should get back to the SUV. Bronson's waiting."

"Okay. I don't think this'll take too long." Carlos said, then he turned and left.

I pulled out my cell phone and made a few calls. When I was done, I put my phone back, leaned against the wall, then slid down it as my legs gave out. Tears slid down my face and my chest shook as I began to sob. I pulled my knees up and wrapped my arms around my legs as I laid my forehead down on my knees. I'd been so good on the way here. I'd been so strong. But now I was alone and I didn't have to be so strong anymore.

So much stuff had happened in the past few weeks. Hell, make that months. Some stuff had happened back in December, stuff I wasn't ready to talk about yet. It had been one of those situations where one minute I was so happy and planning for a life with the man I loved, and then the next, everything shattered. A part of me was gone and I suddenly felt empty.

Now I was homeless and in less than a week, I'd probably be jobless too. Okay, I wasn't exactly homeless, I had a home here with Stefan and Nate. But even at that, there were a lot of things to consider. Like for instance, my cat. I'd gotten her a year ago. She was still at my old house with Daniel. The hotel I'd been staying in hadn't allowed pets. So she'd stayed behind. I also needed to get my ass on the ball and send some movers to go get my stuff. But until I knew where I was staying, I didn't think I needed to go move everything out of the house just yet.

Daniel could just deal with it. After all, he was the one with the problem.

I'm not sure how much time passed, but it must have been a while. I heard the sound of running feet. One pair of boots. One pair of heels. The voice that boomed through the hallway was unmistakable. "Where is she?" Julian said.

I raised my head up to see him and his mother running toward me. "Cam took her that way." I nodded in the direction Cam had gone. Julian and Sofia didn't stop. They just kept running down the hall past me. I didn't hold that against them. They were just worried about Kelsey.

I leaned my forehead back down on my knees. I continued to cry softly. This was my fault. I should have gotten there sooner, then maybe I could have stopped it faster. Then the Kincaid's wouldn't have had to go through this.

"Morgan?"

I looked up to see Sabine standing in front of me, her face pale, eyes bloodshot. "How is she?" I asked.

"She's okay. He didn't rape her. He just bit her." Sabine looked like she wanted to cry again, but instead took a deep breath and sat down next to me on the hard floor. "You saved her."

I shook my head. "I wasn't fast enough. I didn't get there in time."

"Hey, did you hear what I said? He did not rape her. So that counts for something."

Did it? He'd still beat her and fed from her. So did it really count? Part of me didn't think so. But the other half knew it could have been a hell of a lot worse. She could have been murdered tonight. Instead of bringing Cam's battered daughter to him, I could have been sitting down with him and his family and telling them that their daughter/sister had been murdered.

How could I have faced Julian and Sabine then? Hell, how could I have faced my own father, biological or not? I would have killed Greg tonight, then I'd have turned in my badge. Made it easier on the PCU. I'd have just quit. I wouldn't have been stable enough to be a cop after that. Hell, I would have been sitting in a jail cell right now if that had happened.

Sabine laid her hand on mine and I winced at the pain. "Your hand. It's bleeding."

"I don't think it's my blood." I said.

She ignored me and stopped a passing nurse and asked her to bring back some stuff to clean my hand. A few minutes later she was back and handed Sabine some gauze, alcohol, and bandages. She cleaned my hand and curse. "Shit, Morgan, I think you need a few stitches."

"No, I'll be fine. It can heal on its own."

"No, it can't. Stop punishing yourself. And yes, I know damned well what you are doing." She glared at me. "I'm your best friend remember? So stop. You did everything you could. So stop being so damned stubborn." She got up off the floor. "Come on, let's get that taken care of."

I got up and followed Sabine into a hospital room and sat down on the bed. She washed her hands and put on gloves. It only took three stitches to fix my right hand.

Sabine was in the middle of wrapping gauze around it when Bronson and Carlos popped their heads in. Bronson looked down at my hand and raised an eyebrow. "Stitches?"

I nodded. "Yeah. Three."

"Ow." said Carlos.

"We have Kyriss in an interrogation room with men at the door." Bronson said. "He made his phone call and seemed pleased after whoever promised to come and get him out."

It was probably Constantine. I cringed at the thought of having to deal with him again. God only knew what story he'd cook up with Kyriss this time. "Okay." I said. "We'll go in a few. I still have a few things to do here first." I looked at Sabine. "I know you're not going to like this. But I need to talk to Kelsey. Cam and Sofia can stay. But I really need to get a statement from her if I can."

Sabine nodded. "I understand. Let me go ask dad." She left the room and was back in a matter of seconds. "He said it was okay, as long as it was only you."

"Okay." I said. I looked at Bronson and Carlos. "I'll meet you in the hall." They nodded and Carlos handed me his note pad and pen. I followed Sabine into a room that was two rooms down from the one I'd been in.

Kelsey lay in the hospital bed under a white blanket and was wearing one of those hospital gowns with little blue flowers. Julian sat on one side of her and was holding her hand. Sofia sat on the other side and seemed to be doing her best to keep control of her emotions. Later when she was alone, she'd break down and cry. Cam stood at the end of the bed in his doctor coat and wore his doctor face. But I knew all too well that underneath he was being a father who was trying to do what was best for his daughter. If Kelsey got upset, he'd stop the interview.

I walked in and every head turned my way. Julian was not all smiles. Tonight he looked like he wanted to commit murder. Tonight these people were not my friends, but the family of . . . an almost raped victim. And tonight I wasn't their friend either. I was a cop doing my job even if that meant making everyone unhappy.

I guess we'd see how much Julian thought I was sexy after I was done here tonight.

"Hey," I said. "How are you feeling?"

"Okay." Kelsey said.

I looked around the room. "Where's Jayce?"

"Her parents came and got her and took her home."

"Oh." I looked down at the floor. I didn't want to do this. Hell, I wasn't even sure I was the right one to do this. I was too close to this family. How was I going to do this? I mentally slapped myself and took a deep breath. "Kelsey, would it be okay if I asked you a few questions about what happen?"

Kelsey bit her lower lip and looked to her father. He nodded once. "Yeah, that would be okay."

I flipped the note pad over to a clean sheet. "Okay, let's start with when you arrived at the party. Did anything seem strange to you?"

"No, it seemed like a normal party. There was music and drinks and people dancing."

"Were these drinks alcoholic or none alcoholic?"

"Both I guess."

This was going to be one of the hard questions. "Did you drink any of the alcohol?"

Kelsey looked down and didn't meet anyone's eyes. "Yes. I had a drink. Maybe two."

"Okay. Did it taste weird to you or look funny?" I asked.

She shook her head. "No."

I flicked my eyes around to see the reactions of everyone in the room. It was as I'd expected. They were staying calm. It was a sure sign they were all trying to control themselves. "Okay, let's move on to when Greg got mad. Can you tell me what happened?"

"Jayce and I were talking and having a drink when Greg walked over. I was really happy to see him and he seemed happy that I came. We started talking about school and what we had planned for the summer and stuff like that. Then after a while, he changed. I can't explain it, but he was acting really weird. And then he asked me if I wanted to go somewhere private with just the two of us. I wanted to, but I just . . . I don't know."

"It's okay. You can take your time." I said.

She swallowed hard as tears came to her eyes. "I told him that I just wanted to stay by the drink table for a while, then . . . everything changed."

"How?"

"The music became louder and . . . people started taking their clothes off. There was this one girl who laid down on a table and . . . guys started doing things to her." There was no way I was asking her what things. I already knew what girl and what things had been done to her.

"Did any of these girls fight back or act like they wanted to?"

She shrugged. "I guess. Most of them couldn't even stand. They seemed sort of . . . drugged."

"Okay, so what happened after the girl on the table?"

"Greg leaned in and whispered in my ear. He said we could go upstairs and he could teach me some things. And if I wanted, we could bring Jayce along. But he mainly wanted me." She looked down and I knew whatever she was about to say next, no one was going to like it. "He said he wanted me on my knees and he wanted me . . . to suck him off."

I saw Julian's hand tighten into a fist and his jaw lock. The storm in his eyes changed from murder to downright homicidal. Sabine made a sound that sounded like a sob, but when I turned to look at her, she wasn't crying. My gaze moved to Sofia and her composer was starting to slip and so was Cam's. I wasn't far behind. My hand gripped the pen so hard that it broke in half.

Shit. I cleared my throat and continued forward. "What happened after that?" Yeah, I was so going to hell after this.

"I told him I was leaving. After that, everything happened fast. I walked away, but he grabbed me by the arm. Then he hit me and dragged me upstairs into a room and locked the door. He threw me onto the bed and then he . . ." She trailed off as a sob escaped her. "I tried to fight him, but he was stronger. He overpowered me and pulled down my . . . you know, and he sank his fangs into my inner thigh and then . . . he started doing other things. I kicked him and that made him madder. Then he was on top of me trying to push himself inside me, but I did my best to not let him." She leveled her eyes with mine. "And then you were there and he was no longer on top of me and you were . . . trying to kill him." A small smile filled her eyes then.

I smiled a little at that. "Yeah, I was trying to kill him."

"But you didn't because Elliott made you stop."

"Pity." Julian muttered.

"Is that all?" asked Cam.

I nodded. "Yeah. I need to go and interrogate an annoying little parasite."

I placed a hand on Kelsey's leg. "You feel better." And I turned and walked out before my expression gave me away.

I was halfway down the hall when I heard my name. "Morgan!"

I turned to see Julian jogging toward me. "Yeah?"

The next thing I knew he had me in his arms in a tight hug. "Thank you." he said, his lips in my hair. "Thank you so much for saving her. I love you."

I hugged him back. "You're welcome. And I love you too."

He pulled back and wiped a hand over his eyes. "I don't know what we'd done if . . . you know happen. Or worse."

"But it didn't. So there's no need to assume what you would have and wouldn't have done."

"I know." He gave me another hug. "I owe you cupcake." And then he turned and went back into the other room.

I found Bronson and Carlos and we headed for the SUV. I needed to talk to Kyriss before his hotshot Lawyer showed up and ruined everything. I needed to know why he'd been there and if he had any idea where Ivan was. I'd been soft on Ivan, but tonight I wouldn't be so soft with Kyriss. If he knew something he was going to tell me one way or another.

Even if I had to inflect pain.

CHAPTER TWENTY

I walked toward the interrogation room with purpose and determination. Bronson and Carlos were letting me run the show, so they were going to wait out in the hallway. The police officer standing outside the door gave a nod as I walked up. I opened the door and went in as he stepped away. I needed privacy with Kyriss. I wasn't going to hurt him, but I wasn't going to be kind either.

I shut the door and walked over and took the seat on the other side of the table. I laid the file in my hand down flat and I sat up straight. Kyriss was slouching in his seat, like he was relaxing in his favorite chair. There was a smile on his face that seemed smug.

"Find something funny?" I asked.

"Nope. I'm just buying my time." he replied.

"On what?"

"On when I can get out of here. When my phone call gets here—"

"Yes, I'm looking forward to seeing Mr. Gonzales again." I said cutting him off. "Tell me, how's his face and ribs?"

He laughed. "Yeah, he was pissed about that too. But I guess he kind of had that coming."

He had, but I wasn't here to talk about Constantine and his broken bones. "Can you tell me about the party tonight?"

"It was a party. What about it?"

"Were you aware of the illegal activity going on there tonight?"

"What illegal activity? It was an orgy. I'm pretty sure those aren't illegal."

"Why were you there?"

He shrugged. "I like sex." He gave a half grin.

I rolled my eyes. "Are you aware of the seriousness of your charges?" He gave me a blank expression. "You are being charged with supplying alcohol and date rape drugs to minors."

He raised up his hands. "Whoa, wait a minute. I didn't rape anyone. I was just there for the sex. And the woman I had sex with was legal and then some. And I can assure you, she was very willing. You can ask her. Her name's Tabitha Rossi. We went together."

"Oh, I can assure you, I will be having a talk with her. And if I find out that she was even a hair under eighteen or had even a drop of Pixie Dust in her blood stream, you will be going to jail for a very long time."

He looked nervous after that and kept eyeing the door. He whispered, "Shit man, where the hell are you?" under his breath.

"Now moving on. Can you tell me where Ivan is?"

He shook his head. "No. Why would I know where he is?"

"I don't know you tell me?" I pulled out a sheet of paper from the file and slid it over to him. "Ivan gave me a list of names of people who attend special parties thrown by Samael. And guess what, your name's on the list."

He looked at it. "Yeah, so? My name's on a list of people who are into group sex, so what? That doesn't mean Ivan and I are buddy-buddy. I'm not into men. Only women. And when I go to these things, I always find a private room. I mean, forgive me, but, I don't exactly want my junk revealed to a room full of other men. I don't get off on other people watching me have sex."

"Then why go to these parties?"

"I told you, I like sex. A lot." He gave another half-grin. "I'm good at it."

I didn't smile. "Were you aware that Ivan was having young girls raped?"

"No." But something about the way he said it made me think he was lying.

"Did you know that he had Ila Shaylee raped?"

"That's Delisa's baby sister. Why would he have her raped?"

"Because he's a sick twisted son of a bitch that needs stopped."

Kyriss stared at me for a long moment. Something formed behind his eyes and I could see the wheels turning in his head. He was trying to find a lie. After a moment he sat back and crossed his arms over his chest. "I don't believe you. I think you're lying. You're just fishing—trying to get me to give you something that will incriminate Ivan. But I'm not. He hasn't done anything wrong."

That did it. I pulled out three pictures and laid them down face up one at a time in front of him. The first was of Delisa, she was laying on her back in a dark alley, her neck broken. The second was of Kendra, she was laying naked in a bed—blood was all over her chest. And the last picture was of Flynn. His hands were tied behind his back and his back was a bloody mess.

Kyriss stared at the pictures looking horrified. Good. I needed him horrified and disgusted.

"Ivan did this?" he asked in disbelief.

"Yeah." I said. "Turns out the man everyone keeps saying is a good guy and would never hurt anyone, has another hobby besides polygamous sex. It's called torture, rape, and murder."

He shook his head. "I don't understand. Why would he do this? He loved Delisa. He wouldn't kill her."

"Sometimes love makes us do unthinkable things."

He looked up at me then. "I'm sorry, I just can't believe he'd do this."

"Well, I can. I know he lied about where he was the night of Delisa Shaylee's murder. I know that night he and her had an argument about someone she was sleeping with. I know Kendra Farris and Flynn Garwood's names were on the list of his lovers. I know he had Ila Shaylee raped and that he watched while it was being done. And I know he likes raping young girls. So this," I tapped a finger on one of the pictures. "This right here can't be much of a stretch for him. Murder. Rape. Torture."

"No. No, he wouldn't do this."

"Well, he did. And now I need to find him and put him away before he does this to someone else. Who knows, maybe you're next." Maybe if I scared him, he'd start talking. "Help me stop this, Kyriss." I could see the confliction in his eyes. He was close to breaking, to telling me everything I needed to know. So I went for it. If he wouldn't break after this, then nothing would. "There was a young girl at the party. Her name was Kelsey Kincaid. She's fifteen. She went to the party with a boy named Greg. He tried to rape her." I forced my voice to stay normal, but it was hard. All I could see was her in that bed bloodied and scared.

Kyriss's head jerked up so fast it was amazing it didn't snap off. "What did you say? What about Greg?"

"You know him?"

"Um . . . yeah. He's my nephew. I mean, you are talking about Greg Martindale, right?"

My mouth fell open and I suddenly wanted to beat the shit out of Kyriss just like I had Greg. Nephew? Greg was Kyriss's nephew?

"Nephew?" I choked out. "That piece of shit is your nephew?"

"Yeah, I have a sister. Or well, I had a sister. She died five years ago. Since then, I've been trying to keep an eye on him, but it's hard. Greg has a mind of his own. And I don't understand, did you just say that he tried to rape someone?"

I nodded, still unsure I had heard him right. "He tried to rape a friend of mine's sister, Kelsey Kincaid. But he didn't succeed because I beat the shit out of him. He's in the hospital."

"Kelsey? That's Bini's sister."

Bini? What the hell?

"You know Sabine?"

I'm not sure what would have happened or what he might have said, because there was a sound of a commotion coming from outside in the hall. I heard someone say, "You can't go in there." just before the door to the interrogation room opened and Balian stormed in. He looked pissed and ready for a fight.

He stepped in. "This interrogation is over." His voice was stern.

"Finally." Kyriss said. "I was beginning to think maybe you were going to just leave me to my fate." He stood up.

"Sit down." I said.

Bronson and Carlos ran into the room. Balian looked at Kyriss and said. "Come on, let's go."

I pointed at finger at Kyriss as I felt something deep down in my core wake up. "You sit your ass back down." I turned to Balian. "You need to leave. You have no business being back here. Now get out!" I stood then and dared him to do something about it.

He stepped further into the room and leveled his fiery gaze on me. "You! I have had about enough of you and your shit! You want to find a killer, then fine. But leave my people the hell out of it!" He moved toward me like a raging bull and I moved back until I was up against the wall.

"I am doing my job, Mr. Ivanski, I can't help it if your people are involved." It was the truth and he knew it. "Now step back and let me do my job."

"I do not give a fuck about your job!" he yelled. "I want you to back the hell off!"

I got right up into his face. "Make me."

It was meant as a bluff. Balian was a demon and they were dangerous. Unpredictable. You never knew what to expect from them. But I guess what happened next I did sort of have it coming. Balian struck out with his hand, wrapped it around my neck, and shoved me hard against the wall. My brain rattled and I saw stars for a split second.

Balian leveled his dark blue eyes into my dark teal ones, and I saw him then for what he truly was. A demon. But not just any demon. A very old and very powerful demon. There was a strength about him that made my body tighten in places it hadn't in months. The mixed signals he was radiating was making me rethink everything I'd thought about him.

The hand pressing tightly on my throat and cutting off my air supply, said he wanted to kill me and that he was strong enough to do it with just his hand. But the raging heat in his eyes said he wanted to . . . well, fuck me. My heart skipped a beat as I felt something inside of me begin to bloom. I didn't understand it, but something deep inside of me recognized his strength. Recognized him.

My soul cried out as an electric spark began to spread throughout my body and into his like a kiss. Like an electric kiss. And that's what I wanted I suddenly realized. I wanted Balian to kiss me, to take over my body in every way imaginable as long as he was using his lips to do it.

There was the sound of guns being drawn, safety's clicking off. "Remove your hand from around agent Montgomery's neck!" Bronson shouted.

Kyriss flew across the table and stopped, standing in front of Balian as if he were protecting him from the bullets that were about to start flying.

I went for my own gun and somehow managed to push it up under his chin. Balian's body became still as anger filled my eyes along with a look that said, "If you don't let me go and step back, I'm going to blow your fucking head off."

He might have been sexy and made parts of my body tighten, but that didn't mean I was going to let him bully me either. I didn't take shit from people, especially from men. No matter how sexy there were.

"Um . . . do you want us to step outside? I could guard the door." Kyriss said.

Balian blinked and slowly, he removed his hand. The heat left his eyes and he stepped back. I took a breath. I hadn't realized that I'd stopped breathing. "Are you done with him?"

I nodded and swallowed hard. "Yes." My voice was shaky. "Yes, he can leave."

He turned to Kyriss and nodded toward the door. "Go." One word, but yet it held so much power. He started walking for the door, but stopped when I called his name.

"Balian." He turned and faced me. "This isn't over. You're not getting rid of me that easily."

He smiled at that. It was one of those smiles that held so much promise. "Oh, I have a feeling nothing is ever easy with you." And with that, he turned and walked out.

I stood there unable to move and unable to speak. My heart was pounding so loud I could hear it in my ears. My breathing was now labored and I was telling myself to breathe. What was it about that man that made me act like that? Like he was the reason for my existence.

"What the hell was that?" Carlos asked. "I wasn't sure if I should shoot him or give you some privacy."

"Are you okay?" asked Bronson. "Are you hurt?"

I shook my head and found my voice. "No, I'm fine." It was a lie of course. I wasn't fine. Not even close. But I wasn't going to tell them that.

"Okay, well, I think we should call it a night. Ivan's nowhere to be seen. So I say we all go home and get some sleep."

"Sounds good." Carlos said. "I'm beat. See you guys tomorrow." Then he left.

I put my gun back in my holster and started to turn to leave, but stopped when Bronson called my name. "Morgan."

"What?" I asked stopping.

"We need to talk about what happened back at that house."

"What about it?"

"Don't give me that tone. You're lucky that that kid was supernatural. If he'd been human, you would have killed him."

I stood there and just looked down at the floor. "I know that."

"Do you?" he asked sounding frustrated.

I shrugged. "What do you want me to say Elliott? I'm not going to apologize for what I did. I remember the day Sofia and Cam brought her home from the hospital. She was so small. Six and a half pounds. I remember the day she said her first word and started walking. I was there." Tears filled my eyes. "I remember because I was spending the night with Sabine, because my mom and Stefan were on one of their romantic weekends. I've known her since I was eight years old and I've always thought of her as a baby sister. So no, I'm not going to apologize for putting that piece of shit in the hospital. I'm just not."

"I'm sorry." Bronson said. "I'm sorry you had to see that. But you know just as I do, that sometimes the people we love get hurt. And doing what you did . . . well, it was wrong. You allowed your personal feelings to cloud your judgement. You can't do that and do this job. You have to learn to separate your personal feelings from the job and you know that. If you can't, then maybe you need to find a new line of work."

I knew he was right and that pissed me off. "Maybe so. But I know one thing, if I'd walked into that room and she'd been dead? There wouldn't have been any pulling me off him. Supernatural or not? I would have killed him." Then I turned and walked away.

Bronson took me home after that. There had been no more talking. But it was fine, I wasn't in the talking mood. I was looking forward to my bed. I could hear it calling my name. But sleep wasn't going to come for me right now, because as soon as I'd walked into the sitting room, I was bombarded with a hundred and one questions.

"Oh my God." Kaydan said jumping up from the sofa. "You're home. I was so worried. You just stormed out of here and I wasn't sure what was going on." He wrapped his arms around me and I fought the urge to snap at him.

"Everything's fine." I said. "We got there in time. Kelsey's okay. Physically. Mentally, I'm not sure. She was almost raped tonight."

"Dear God." Stefan said. "Poor Cam. He must have been frantic. And Sofia . . ."

Kaydan let me go so I could see Stefan and Nate sitting on the sofa.

"Yeah, everyone was shaken up. But it's fine now. She's safe and her attacker is in the ICU with a broken face." I looked down at my hand. It didn't hurt anymore.

"What happened to your hand?" Nate asked.

"I tried to beat someone to death tonight."

"Oh."

I yawned. "I'm tired. I'm going to bed. I've dealt with a lot of shit today." And his name was Balian.

"Okay, I'll go up with you." Kaydan said.

I sighed. "Not tonight."

"I know. Just sleep."

It wasn't just about the sex or the sleeping next to him I was worried about. I knew this man well enough to know, if I allowed him to stay with me tonight, then he'd be one step closer to thinking we were together. And we weren't.

And that was the problem.

"Not tonight Kaydan. I'm too tired and I'm not in the mood to deal with your puppy love shit." It was harsh and I regretted saying it the moment it came out of my mouth. But it was the truth nonetheless.

His face fell and I could see pain in his eyes. "Is that what you think this is? Puppy love?"

That dark beast that was inside of me earlier at the jail woke up again and took over. "Honestly, I don't care. I've dealt with under age raped victims tonight. One of which was my best friend's sister. My only suspect has gone AWOL. And to top it off, I got into a fight tonight with a demon that confuses me to no end. I think with that and every other fucked up thing in my life, takes precedence over your old feelings for me. There is just too much going on right now for me to give a shit." Yep, I was a horrible person. I deserved everything that was coming to me.

Kaydan nodded. "Right. Well, I guess I should go then. I wouldn't want to inconvenience you anymore with my old feelings." And then he stormed out of the house, slamming the door as he left.

"Wow." Stefan said. "That was cold. Don't you think you were being a tad bit harsh?"

"Yes." I said. "But it was the truth."

"Maybe you should tone down on the truth a bit." Nate said with a half-smile. "I think you just broke lover boy's heart."

"I know, but I'm going to bed. I'll fix it later."

"Okay. Night." said Stefan.

"Night." I said. "Night Nate."

"Night."

I went upstairs, stripped out of my close and into my PJ's. I fell onto my bed and was out like a light being turned off. I'm not sure how long I laid there when I heard my cell phone ringing. I popped an eye open and looked at my clock. It read 2:35 am.

I groaned as I grabbed for my phone and answered. "Montgomery?"

"Morgan, it's Elliott." Bronson said on the other end. "They found Ivan."

I sat up. "When? Where did they find him?" This was good news. Now we had our suspect back and he had a lot to explain.

There was a hushed pause and then Bronson said. "Morgan . . . Ivan's dead. They found his body."

CHAPTER TWENTY-ONE

"*Well, there goes our only suspect.*" Carlos said as we stood over Ivan's dead body.

I had been in shock and unable to speak for a long minute when Bronson had said that Ivan's body had been found. He had been our only suspect, the only one with a motive for the killings. Now we were back to square one.

I stood there and stared down at the body. If Kendra and Flynn's murders had been horrible, then Ivan's was just downright gory, and I was surprised that Carlos hadn't lost his cookies. Ivan's body lay on the concrete of a driveway in front of the same house that had been used for an orgy only hours earlier. There was so much blood I wasn't even sure there was any left in his body. There were small slashes on his torso and a small double edged dagger pushed up through his throat and exited through the back of his skull.

"I need a pair of gloves." I said as something caught me eyes.

Bronson handed me a pair. "See something?"

I took them and put them on. I bent down and examined the wound around where the dagger was. There was torn skin that only meant one thing. "Shit." I said.

"What is it?"

"Whoever did this turned the blade."

"Why?" asked Carlos. "Why would they do that?"

"Because they wanted to make sure he was dead." I said.

"Explain." Bronson said. "How do you know that?"

"Because I've had sword training. When I was ten, one of the first things Stefan taught me was to turn the blade. When you are fighting with a dagger or a sword and you have stabbed your opponent? Well, you turn the blade. It's to make sure the wound won't heal. And . . . that they die. And this was what our guy wanted. He wanted to make sure Ivan didn't heal." I bet twenty bucks that when Ming checked the body that he'd come to the same conclusion.

"Wouldn't the dagger through the throat be enough to kill him?" asked Carlos.

I nodded. "Yeah, but our guy wanted to make sure. Maybe he was scared that Ivan wouldn't die. Or perhaps he was that . . . pissed off. Killing someone like this only means one thing."

"Our victim knew his killer and the killer was punishing him for something. Dagger through the throat is sort of personal." Carlos said and I nodded.

"Okay, so what about the slashes on his chest?" Bronson asked.

I looked at them. "They look the same as the others. Some are deep and some aren't. But the intent was the same. He bled out slow until our killer was ready for him to die." I stood up and took off the gloves and stuck them into my jeans pocket. "By the looks of all the blood, he was killed here."

"I spoke to the neighbors, no one saw or heard anything." Carlos said.

I frowned. "They had too. This much torture before death is going to make you scream. So they had to have seen something." Unless someone had used some kind of spell to inflect silence.

"What I want to know is how did they get him out of the party without being seen and why bring him back here to be tortured?" Bronson said. "And another thing, why wait? Why not grab him, bring him out here and kill him for one of the party goers to find?"

It was a good question. Why had the killer waited to torture and kill Ivan? Was it some kind of message? And if so, what were they saying?

Bronson motioned for the medical team to do their thing. We stood there and watched as they put Ivan's body on a gurney and put him in the back of a morgue van and drive away. "Well, I guess we should go home and get some shut eye, then meet back at the morgue." Bronson had no sooner said it when there was a shrieking sound so shrill, that it made my skin crawl and want to run away. "What the fuck was that?"

The remaining police officers stopped in their tracks and looked around. I pulled out my gun because I knew exactly what it was.

"Morgan, talk to me." Bronson said, pulling out his own gun. "What the fuck was that?"

"The shadows." I replied. I darted my eyes around as the shrieking persisted. Got closer.

"The what?"

"They're known by three names. One is the shadows, the second is the forgotten. And the third is a little more known to humans."

"And that is?" Carlos asked.

"Banshee's."

"As in old fork-lore?" Bronson asked.

I shook my head. "No, as in your worst nightmare. They're fairy souls called up from hell."

"Well, shit. How do we kill them?"

"Aim for the head and the heart. And don't let them get a hold of you. They'll tear you to pieces."

Bronson and Carlos yelled it down the line and everyone went for their guns. It didn't take long for the first banshee to show her ugly face and in less than thirty seconds there was a whole swarm of them. Banshees weren't known for their attractiveness. They had pale, ghostly white skin, long jet black hair, and eyes made of red-orange flames. They wore a long white dress, their feet were bare. Sharp claw like fingernails extended from their fingertips and sharp pointy teeth showed in their mouths, sort of like that of a piranha.

They hovered in the air like a graceful death angel, preparing to rip apart everything in its path. And it just so happened, we were its prey of choice tonight.

"Oh heaven on earth." Carlos murmured.

It was going to be more like hell, but I didn't have the heart to tell him that. "Oh, and by the way." I said. "You might want to watch out. They can spit fire."

"Oh, joy." Bronson breathed. "Just when I thought this was going to be boring."

The first of the banshee's attacked so fast there was barely anytime to react. Gunshots rang out and the shrieking continued. I shot one in the head and another in the chest. They both disappeared like smoke. I turned to see one of the banshees hover in front of us. She opened her mouth and I knew what was coming next. I lunged for Carlos and Bronson and we went down as flames shot out of her mouth like a torch. I rolled over and took aim of her chest and fired. The bullet hit her and she disappeared. I quickly turned my gaze toward Bronson and Carlos. Carlos was rolling around on the ground and Bronson was patting out the few remaining flames on his pants.

There was so much chaos around me that it was starting to get hard to decipher the screams from the banshee's and those of police whose bodies were being ripped apart like they were nothing but a pillow made of stuffing.

I got up and made a run for my car and Bronson and Carlos followed. We continued to shoot as we ran. My eyes darted around and I saw that the cops who were still standing were doing the same. One was yelling into his radio that we needed backup. That was a good idea, but the only problem with that was it gave the banshee's more victims. These people weren't trained for this. They were humans and because of that, they were all going to die.

The only way we were going to kill these things and win, was to get up close and personal. And these humans weren't cut out for that.

We made it to the car and ducked behind it just as another banshee spit fire at us. "Fuck!" Carlos yelled.

I went for my keys and prayed that Stefan was still the paranoid freak he'd been before I'd left. I went for the trunk, slid the key in, turned, and opened it. To my great relief Stefan had done exactly what I had been praying for. He'd stocked the back of the trunk with every weapon you could ever want. Swords, daggers, throwing stars, bow and arrows, guns and ammo, a whip, and a whole bunch of other toys that would make any Rambo or James Bond fan salivate at the mouth. I suddenly loved Stefan more for his outgoing paranoia. It had driven me crazy as a teenager, but right now I was grateful.

"Holy shit!" Carlos exclaimed. "What are you preparing for, a war or something?"

"Yeah." I said. "We are. Remember?" I grabbed one of the weapons belts and put it on and slid a few daggers in the sheaths. "Pass some of this stuff around. Remember, head, heart, turn blade and pull out."

"Okay." Bronson said. "What are you going to do?"

I grabbed two of the swords and held them tightly in my hands. "What I was created to do. Fight." And then I took off toward the chaos.

I could hear him screaming out my name, but I didn't stop to see what he wanted. I already knew. He thought I was running to my death. And maybe I was. But I was harder to kill than the human men here tonight. And I had something they didn't. Power. And lots of it.

Bullets weren't really doing anything but making the banshee's angry and maybe slowing them down. But with my power and the two swords in my hands, it was bound to be enough. Or so I was hoping. I'd never really used it like this before. At least not for real anyway. I had practice sessions where I learned how to summon it, but actually using it to kill . . . well, that would be a no.

"Okay." I told myself. "I can do this."

Over the shrieking I could hear a whooshing sound. I looked up to see a news helicopter flying over the crime scene. Great, just great. Now this was going to be all over the news. And I knew by tomorrow morning Daniel and everyone else in Boston would see it and me, and know that I was doing the one thing I had been told not to do. But that wasn't my problem at the moment. Not getting ripped to shreds was. So I wasn't going to worry about them seeing me.

I cleared my mind and searched deep down. There, in the core of me, was my power. It sat there in waiting, ready to be used. I grabbed onto it and forced it up through me. It started as a small spark at first on my hands, then without asking it, my body ignited in power. I was now in flame.

And as I had hoped, the banshee's came for me. For my power.

They came for me, shrieking and slashing out with their claws. I swung the swords in my hands and caught one in the chest. I pushed the blade in deep and turned the blade. When I pulled it out, she vanished into thin air. Another one came at me, but this time she caught me with her claws. But she didn't hang on long, because the red-fire that consumed my body started burning hers. She let out a hissing shriek and let me go.

I bit down on a scream of my own as her claws sliced my skin. Red blood began to pour from the wounds down my arm.

I swung the swords and took them down one by one. It was a slow process, but it seemed to be doing the job. Over my shoulder I saw Bronson and the others doing as I'd instructed. They were killing the banshee's up close and personal too.

I turned my attention back to the fight. There were still so many banshee's, flying and slashing and shrieking. I moved with a grace that was almost a dance. I was good with a sword. Always had been. I swung the swords and cut down most of what was in my path. But by this point the banshee's had gotten smart and didn't get too close to me. But that didn't matter, I switched the sword in my right hand to my left. I pulled out one of the daggers and threw it. It lodged itself into the chest of one of the banshee's and she vanished.

I repeated this three times until there weren't more than five Banshee's left. The last five came at me with a vengeance and I cut them down like melting butter.

When all of the banshee's were dead and the chaos stopped, I pushed my power back down along with the red-fire. I turned to see every cop stare at me as if I'd grown a second head. Bronson and Carlos smiled when I got back to the car.

"Wow." Carlos said. "You were like a flaming angel."

I smiled back. "Thanks." We were all covered in blood, and I for one could use a shower.

I turned toward the open trunk to return the swords when Bronson yelled, "Morgan, behind you!" But it was too late. A sharp pain went through me as claws sliced through my back. I went down to the ground in a heap of pain, but ignored it. I took one of the swords and swung it behind me and shoved it into the banshee. She shrieked, but held on. I turned the blade, then pulled out. It was over. The banshee was dead.

Bronson and Carlos ran over as I tried to sit up. "Don't get up." Bronson said. "The EMT is on its way."

"I don't need to go to the hospital." I said. "I'm fine."

"No, you're not." Bronson said. "You're bleeding and your back looks torn to shreds."

"Honestly, I'm fine. I'm already healing. It wasn't that deep."

Neither of them looked like they believed me. But that wasn't my problem. I wasn't human. I healed a hell of a lot faster.

"Are you sure?" Carlos asked.

I stood and winced at the pain. "Yeah, I'm sure. And I already know a doctor. So I'm good. I just need to go home and clean up."

"Okay." Bronson said. "As long as you promise you'll have your doctor friend check you out."

"I promise." I said. "Do you two want to come over for breakfast and brainstorm?"

"Are you making pancakes?" Carlos asked with a smile.

"Yeah." I said with my own smile, then winced at the pain. I was hurting more than I let on. I needed to get home and call Cam. Hopefully he'd come over and fix me up.

"Then I'm in." he said.

"Me too." said Bronson.

Great, it could be a party. Or well, not a party so much as a moping fest. Yeah, when I got home I was going to need a stiff drink.

CHAPTER TWENTY-TWO

Bronson, Carlos, and I sat on the sofa with a bottle of beer in our hands. It might have been six in the morning, but we all needed a drink. And coffee wasn't going to cut it. I had called Cam and he was on his way over with his doctor bag.

We all sat there and just stared off into space. Ivan was dead and we'd been attacked by banshees. We all looked like hell and felt like it too.

Cam walked in and stopped in his tracks. He took one look at us and just shook his head. But we weren't the only ones who looked like hell. Cam looked tired and somber and I suddenly regretted calling him to come fix me up. He'd had a long night.

"How's Kelsey?" I asked as he made his way over.

"She's okay." he said setting the bag down. "She's at home asleep."

If I knew Julian—and I did, he was most likely in bed beside his baby sister with her in his arms.

Cam looked me over. "What do you want me to look at first?"

"My back."

He nodded. "Okay. Remove your shirt."

I did what I was told, first removing my shoulder holster and setting it on the coffee table, then pulling off my T-shirt and dropping it to the floor. Bronson and Carlos stared at me with open mouths. I smiled inside. I had always been comfortable with nudity. With mine and others. So when I took off my shirt and revealed my black lace bra, it didn't faze me at all. But it had the two men sitting next to me.

Carlos seemed to be foaming at the mouth as he said. "Shit."

"Nice bra." Bronson said, face a hint of red as he tried to not look.

"Thanks." I said as I leaned forward so Cam could see my back.

Cam gave a little chuckle, but kept what he was thinking to himself. He ran his fingers along my back checking the wounds. "Hmm."

"What?" I asked.

"It seems that you have healed most of the damage." he said. "There's nothing here that a shower and a few hours sleep won't fix." I leaned back. "Let me see your hand." I gave him my hand and he removed the bandage and sure enough, it was healed. "I need to remove the stitches so they won't heal into your skin."

At that moment Stefan and Nate came down the stairs. Sleep was still in their eyes and they were still in their PJ's.

"What the hell got ahold of you?" Nate asked.

"Banshee's." I said as my cell phone rang. I answered it. "Montgomery?"

"You're on TV." Avery said on the other end.

I picked up the remote and turned on the TV and sure enough, there I was. It was in big lettering too. PCU TAKES DOWN UNKNOWN CREATURES. The news lady was talking and explaining what was being seen. "As you can see," she said. "the news chopper got to the crime scene as some kind of creatures attacked the local PCU team. And for those of you who are unfamiliar with the term, that is short for Paranormal Crime Unit." she said in a voice that was supposed to be exciting. "We are told that they got a call that a body had been found by a local cop doing his rounds of the neighborhood, after a raid had been done on one of the houses. The details of that are still being kept unknown. But we have been told that the body found was of a demon named Ivan. He had been a suspect in the murders from the last few days."

Her voice continued to be upbeat as she delivered the next exciting news. "In the video you are seeing shows the PCU and the local police fighting the unknown creatures. And we want to warn you, this next part may be disturbing to some of you. As you can see, one of the agents has grabbed some kind of sword and is now in flames. We have been told that the agent's name is Special Agent Morgan Montgomery. We have also been told that she is not human and is an angel and that she's been suspended for causes that the head of the PCU will not comment on."

She continued talking and we all continued watching. We watched as I fought the banshee's all the way to the end when the last banshee sank her claws into my back. Stefan and Nate had hissed at that part.

"Morgan, are you still there?" Avery asked.

"Yeah, I'm here." I said. "How bad is it?"

"Well, grandmother is about to explode."

That was all she got out before Camille came onto the phone. "Morgan! What the hell were you thinking? You could have been killed!"

"Camille, I'm fine. And it's my job."

She started yelling and I had to pull the phone to keep my eardrums from busting. I flashed a look toward Stefan and he was shaking his head. Camille went on and on with her rant until I heard Asher take the phone away from her. "Morgan, are you okay?" he asked.

"Yeah, I'm fine." I sighed. "I didn't mean to cause trouble."

"No, it's fine. It's your job. You can't predict the future. You had no idea those things were going to show up."

I smiled. "Actually, I can predict the future, but you're right. I didn't know those things were going to be there."

After a few more minutes we said our 'I love you's' and hung up. I tossed my cell on the table and sighed. Leave it to Camille to go off the deep end.

"How bad is it?" Stefan asked.

"Depends on what you're talking about." I said.

"Your case." I laid back and took a deep pull from the beer in my hand. "That bad, huh?"

"You have no fucking idea. We only had one suspect and now he's dead."

"Then I guess he wasn't your man." Cam said as he finished working on my hand and moved over and checked out Bronson and Carlos.

He had a point. "Okay, let's look at what we have." I said. "Delisa and Ivan were having kinky group sex, and one of the men in their bed was causing problems. The night she was killed, she and Ivan has a fight about whoever this man is. She's killed and Ivan moves on overnight. Then Kendra Farris and Flynn Garwood are killed. And their names are on a list that Ivan has given us of all of his lovers. And they've been kill the same way as Delisa, except for the cuts. But we know that whoever is doing this is targeting the names on the list."

"Makes sense." Bronson said.

I nodded and continued. "So this guy is killing people on a list of lovers, so we go after Ivan, but everyone says he's not capable of doing these horrible things. But we know that's not true, because Constantine said that Ivan liked to have young girls raped and liked watching it." I saw Cam flinch. "So we know that's a lie. But now Ivan's dead and we're back at square one. But the killer murdered him differently. Why?"

"Maybe it was meant as a message." Carlos said.

"Explain." Bronson said.

"Well, everyone says that Samael is a hard man. So if that's true, wouldn't he take matters into his own hands? I mean, yeah, sure, he's a demon and he likes destruction, but Ivan was causing too much attention. So maybe he did him in."

"I guess so. But I don't see it." I said taking another sip of beer. "Constantine said that Lilith had a thing for Ivan. So I can't see him killing him. But on the other hand, Ivan's murder was different. So if Ivan wasn't the killer all along and it was someone else, then why kill Ivan differently?" I sighed and rubbed a hand over my face. "I feel like I'm missing something. Like the answer to this is right in front of me. But I can't see it, because none of this is making any sense."

"Sure it makes sense." Stefan said.

I raised an eyebrow. "How?"

Stefan smiled. "To the killer." He chuckled when I frowned at him. "It doesn't matter if you understand the motive or not because the killer does. Think like him. He knows why he did it. Look at your facts. There is a connection to these bodies and I'm going to guess it has everything to do with that list you have."

Leave it to Stefan to find the missing piece but still manage to make it complicating.

"So it goes back to what I've said all along, it's someone in his bed." I said.

"Probably."

"Great. Just fucking great." I got up from the sofa. "I'm going to go take a shower and then I'll be down to make those pancakes."

"Need some help washing?" asked Carlos with a devilish grin.

"No." And then I headed upstairs.

I got to my room and stripped out of my clothes and went into the bathroom. I turned on the water and stepped inside. The water was warm and felt nice on my body. I could feel a few aches around my shoulders so I bent my arm back and rubbed the sore spot.

I stood under the water for a long time as it washed away all of the blood. My mind switched from one thing to the next until it stopped on Balian. Last night had been a different side of him. A side I wasn't so sure I liked, but found myself attracted to. Maybe it was his power or the way he held himself. I didn't know, but whatever it was it had seemed damned sexy and exciting.

And maybe a little scary.

Last night something had happened between us, something electric. And if I was being honest with myself right now, I was imagining him naked and pressed up against me.

As if my mind had conjured him up, I felt hands on my shoulders and my body relaxed into him. I didn't have to turn around to know who it was, because I already knew. "Are you real or a hallucination?"

His lips brushed my skin as he whispered in my ear. "I am whatever you want me to be, little orchid." Balian said, and then he pressed his lips to my neck.

I closed my eyes and moaned. I turned and sought out his mouth and when I found it, I kissed him hard and deep. He was a hallucination, so I could do whatever I wanted, right? And what I wanted was to kiss him and have his hands all over my body. And that was exactly what happened. I kissed him and he kissed me back, his tongue moving with mine, exploring. His hands went around my waist and he backed me up against the shower wall.

My hands explored his body, even though I couldn't see it. But I didn't need to, I could feel it and that was enough. It was tone and warm and wet from the shower. And his body felt so damned real it was almost crazy. And when he lifted one of my legs and wrapped it around him and pressed his erection against me, I thought I was going to go right then.

His lips broke from mine and he stared into my eyes with so much heat, so much wanting, so much lust. And I knew right then that I was in trouble. I was in danger of dreaming him up every time I was in the shower.

Yeah, what a hell of a hallucination to have while naked and wet.

Perhaps I was unconscious in the shower and dreaming him up. Or if I was unconscious perhaps I was drowning. Or maybe I was having a really hot vision of the future. Either way I was in trouble. And there was no way of stopping it. Or saving me from a fate of becoming addicted to a man who was undoubtedly unhealthy for me.

Balian stared into my eyes and my heart melted. "I believe it is about time I stake my claim on you." And then he kissed me.

Stake his claim on me? What did that mean? It didn't matter, because he started rocking his hips back and forth against me. My breathing picked up and my heart raced as I felt myself come closer and closer to the release I'd been wanting for months now. Moans escaped me as he took my lower lip between his teeth and bit down slightly. He wasn't even inside me yet—

"Morgan?" A voice called from outside the bathroom door.

The next thing I knew I was falling and had landed hard on the shower floor. "Shit!" I said as there was a thump.

The bathroom door open. "Morgan, are you okay?" Nate asked walking in. "It sounded like you fell. Are you hurt?"

I righted myself into a sitting position and thanked God that I had a shower curtain and that it was closed. Nate seeing me naked would not be a good thing. "Yeah, I'm fine. I just slipped. That's all." Okay, yes, even I was aware that my voice was breathy and sounded like I'd just ran a marathon.

"Okay." he said. "I just came up here to make sure you were okay. You've been up here for over a half hour." He paused and then when he spoke there was no doubt that he was blushing. "I knocked on your door, but you didn't answer, and when I came in . . . I heard you . . . moaning and . . . I didn't mean to interrupt you."

I frowned even though I knew he couldn't see me. "Nate, what are you talking about?"

"You know . . . it. I mean, I understand, it's been a while for you and—"

What the hell was he talking—oh my God! "Oh God, no. I wasn't doing that. I swear."

No, I was imagining a demon taking over my body with his. Taking me over to the point of no return. To the point of self-destruction.

"Oh, okay. Well, I guess I'll leave you to get back . . . to your shower then." he said.

"Okay. I was done anyway. I'll be down in a few minutes."

"Okay." And then he left shutting the door behind him.

I sat there horrified. I had a feeling that he didn't believe me and thought I had been doing . . . something I hadn't. God, why did my mind have to choose that moment to daydream about Balian and his body? Why did I have to allow myself to get carried away with a hallucination?

"Shit." I said.

I got up and turned off the water. I got out, dried myself off, and slipped on some clean clothes. I had just pulled my shirt over my head when I heard the sound of flapping. I looked around, but saw nothing. So I ignored it. I was just about to walk out the door when I heard it again. I stopped and turned, that's when I saw it. On my bedroom wall hanging upside down, was a bat.

I swallowed the scream that was in my throat. "How . . . how did you get in here?" Maybe I should have asked how it got here. It was daylight and bats didn't go out in the day. Or at least I didn't think they did. So I wouldn't bet money on it.

The little brown bat stared at me with its little blue eyes and seemed to be asking me something. I swallowed hard and looked at my window. Was it asking to be set free? Maybe. I slowly walked to the window and opened it, all the while watching the bat.

When I had the window open, it came off the wall and flew out the window. My heart fell in my stomach for about a second as I watched it fly away.

I wasted no time. I shut my window, ran for the door and down the stairs. When I got to the landing I went for my gun. With my gun in my hand I ran out of the room with everyone asking me what the hell was going on. I ran out the front door and didn't stop until I was in the driveway. I aimed as I turned in a circle, trying to find what I was looking for.

"What the hell is going on?" Bronson asked as he and Carlos stopped next to me, their guns drawn.

Stefan, Nate, and Cam were outside the door with confusion on their faces.

"Morgan?" Bronson repeated. I didn't answer him. I was too busy trying to find it. Where the hell was it? "Morgan, what are you looking for?"

When I answered him, my voice was shaky with a hint of fear. "Vampire." I said. "There was a fucking vampire in the house."

CHAPTER TWENTY-THREE

"How do you know it was a vampire?" Bronson asked as he looked around.

"Because I saw it." I said. "Whoever it was, was in bat form."

Or it could have been just a plain old bat. But if that was the case, then how did it get into the house? My mind flashed back to the day in the grocery store parking lot.

The demon I had talked to that day had been cocky and a hard ass. But I'd gotten the feeling that something wasn't right with the whole situation. Especially when I'd asked him what he wanted.

"To warn you." he'd said.

"To warn me about what?"

"That he is coming."

"Who's coming for me?" I'd asked.

"Oh, no. If I told you it would ruin the surprise."

Those words repeated in my head over and over again as I scanned the driveway for anything that didn't belong there. But I found nothing. Everything was as it should be, but still I had an uneasy feeling. Something with this wasn't right. Was it connected to the murders? Maybe. I mean, it seemed off that all this had started happening the night I got back into town. So maybe there was some kind of connection. But what? And why?

Those were the million dollar questions.

But then something else popped into my head, something the demon had said before he'd walked away that day. *"You are going to be fun. I look forward to playing with you."* He'd said those words with a tone that was mocking and filled with promise of things to come in the future. So was this a game? Was someone playing a sick and twisted game? A game where bodies start piling up and they watched and waited to see if I was going to solve this or catch them before the next body was found?

Yeah, if demons were behind this then I'd say yes. It sounded like something they'd do.

Then a horrible thought formed in my head. When I was nine, the night my mother disappeared, there had been a demon looking through my bedroom window. It had been the hideous kind, with horns and claws. I'd never gave it much thought until now. I've always thought I'd seen things that night. But maybe I hadn't. Maybe there really had been someone looking through my window.

"I don't see anyone." Carlos said.

"He's—it's gone." I said and lowered my gun.

"Are you sure you saw someone?" Stefan asked.

I nodded, but didn't say anything. I just walked past him and went into the house. I felt tired suddenly, both mental and physical. Things were starting to take shape in my mind, things I wasn't liking. A picture really and it wasn't of rainbows and blue skies. It was something that was much worse.

I sat down on the sofa, set my gun down on the table, and then put my head in my hands as I set my elbows on my knees. I told myself to breathe.

"Morgan, what's wrong?" Stefan asked with a hint of concern.

I looked up at him. "The night when mom left, there was a demon outside my window watching me. Then when I come back, all this shit starts happening. And the day after I come home, I'm confronted by a demon who tells me that someone is coming for me." I saw something form behind his eyes. "You know something, don't you?"

"Morgan, now is not the time for this."

"When is?"

"When I have no other options and my hand has been forced." Stefan's voice was stern, which meant this wasn't up for discussion. "You look tired. Why don't you stay here and relax and Nate and I will make breakfast."

"We will?" Nate said sounding horrified.

"Yes we will."

"But we don't even know how to cook."

"It's only pancakes and bacon. How hard can it be?" Stefan said matter of fact.

He walked past me with Nate on his heels. "This isn't over." I said.

"I know." And he sounded sad about it.

I sat there and no one said anything. Whether that was because they were just as exhausted as I was and confused about this case, or the fact that there was a sudden tension between me and Stefan, I didn't know. But one thing was clear, Stefan's happiness that I was home was now gone, replaced with an uneasiness. Something was going on and he was hiding something from me and we both knew if I had it my way I'd get the truth out of him. Granted, we would probably fight, but whatever was going on would be out in the open.

A half hour later breakfast was done and we all ate in silence. Although I wouldn't really say we ate. It was more like we picked at it and held back a wince every time we swallowed. Somehow Stefan and Nate managed to burn the pancakes and bacon. I think Bronson and Carlos only ate it because they were trying to be nice.

Another hour after that Bronson and Carlos left and we agreed to meet up at the morgue later when Ming was done examining the body. Nate and Stefan went to work, which left me home alone. But I didn't mind it. After the night I'd had I needed some time to myself.

I went out to the car and got all the weapons used out and carried them to the kitchen and set them on the counter top. I got out the special cleaner and went to work cleaning and polishing the swords and daggers. I cleaned my gun and put in a new clip. After that I went upstairs and grabbed all of the dirty clothes from my room, Stefan's, and Nate's. I put them in the washer and went for a much needed run.

My mind was running almost as fast as I was. It switched from one thing to another quickly, never staying on one thing too long. But in the end I forced my mind to focus on the case. I still felt like I was missing something. Everything had led to Ivan, but now he was dead. Probably killed by the same killer as Delisa, Kendra, and Flynn. But what had we missed? We'd talked to almost everyone but three on the lists and they hadn't screamed jealous lover or killer.

So if our guy was a lover, then what was the motive, because so far, killing in a jealous rage was sort of out of the question. None of these people had seemed jealous. In fact, they'd seemed the total opposite. They'd all said that it was just sex. Nothing more. Most of them were already in a committed relationship with someone else and had been sleeping with Ivan and Delisa to spice things up.

I would have liked to say that one of those people were our suspect, but it didn't feel right. And I had no idea why.

But then something unexpected popped into my head. *What about Constantine?* A voice in the back of my head asked. It was a good question and I had forgotten about him. He could be our guy. He could have helped Ivan kill the others and then turned around and killed Ivan. A partnership gone bad. Yeah, sounded like a good angle. But how was I going to prove it? I hadn't a clue.

But it was a good theory.

When my run was over, I hit the shower and changed into jeans and a red T-shirt. I went back downstairs and put the clothes from the washer into the dryer. As I waited for the clothes to get done I called Sabine to find out how Kelsey was doing. Her phone went straight to voice mail. So I left a short message.

After that I called Avery. She answered on the second ring. "Hey." she said. "How's it going?"

"Depends." I said. "How's things there? Camille still fuming?"

"You could say that. How long are you working tonight? Dad wanted me to ask you to come over to dinner."

"Not too late. I have to go to the morgue to see a body, then I have to talk to a possible suspect. But after that I should be free."

"Good, then it's settled. You're coming for dinner." Avery said. "Then we can hang out a bit and catch up."

I smiled. "I'd like that." After everything that'd happened in the past few weeks a nice meal with my family sounded good. Okay, that wasn't true. If I went over for dinner Camille was going to start on me and on my job. But listening to my grandmother bitch for a half hour was better than coming home to a dark and empty house.

"So, meet any cute guys while I was gone?" I asked.

"No, not really." she said. "I met one guy, but he turned out not to be the one. Have you met anyone since coming home?"

I was silent for a moment. "I wouldn't really call it meeting someone."

"Who is it?"

I took a deep breath. "His name's Balian Ivanski."

She giggled. "I've heard of him. He's only been in town a year or so. I think. I'm not entirely sure because I don't really keep up with that scene. But I have a friend who does and she said he was like the royalty of demon bachelors."

Avery and I talked a bit more, then hung up after I promised to show for dinner. By that time the clothes in the dryer were done and I folded and put everything back in their rightful places. And since I had been doing Stefan and Nate's laundry since I was nine, I knew where everything went. Even their undies.

After that it was time to meet up with Bronson and Carlos at the morgue. So I put on my shoulder holster and grabbed my keys and headed out the door to see what else was going to find me.

CHAPTER TWENTY-FOUR

"You know," Ming said as we entered the morgue. "I'm starting to get the feeling that you guys like coming here."

Carlos laughed. "Not really. But our company has to be better than the dead bodies. At least you can have a conversation."

Ming shrugged. "Actually, you'd be surprised how much the dead actually talk."

"Man, you need a life"

"I have a life."

"Then you need to get laid."

I just shook my head. "If you two are done, I'd like to find out how our victim died."

Carlos stuck his lower lip out. "You're no fun."

"I'm lots of fun. But I'm on a time limit. I have to go to my grandmother's for dinner."

"Yes, and I would like to have a few extra hours of sleep." Bronson said. "And an actual meal."

Ming laughed. "Yes, that would be nice." He walked over to Ivan's body. "But unfortunately I don't think I know any more than you already know."

"Cause of death?" I asked.

"A wound to his throat. The dagger used to sever his trachea was also used to make the slashes on his body, and those on Kendra and Flynn's. So you're looking for the same guy."

"Shit." Bronson said. "I was afraid you were going to say that."

Yeah, that made two of us. But I'd already figured we were looking for the same killer. "Anything else?" I asked already knowing the answer.

"Nope." Ming said. "Everything's pretty much the same. Cuts on his body, both deep and not. He bled out slow. The only difference is how he died. But other than that, it was all the same. I wish I could give you more, but I can't. I'm sorry."

"It's okay." I said. "We'll figure something out." It was a lie of course. We were running out of suspects and no one was really talking. I turned to Bronson. "Did you find addresses for the last few names on the lists?"

He shook his head. "No. Which is weird. They have to sleep somewhere. But I have a source that said they'd be at Illusions tonight."

"What's with that club?" Carlos asked. "Why is it when we need to talk to someone they're at Illusions?"

"Because it's an underworld club." I said. "Most of them are safe havens. Humans aren't normally allowed in them. It's rumored that most underworld clubs have underground housing for the supernatural. And if it's true and Illusions has one, then it makes sense why all the demons are always there."

"Because they live there." Bronson said. "Which is why we can't find any addresses."

"Exactly." I said. "Let's go to Illusions and talk to the last three on the list."

Bronson and Carlos nodded and we turned to leave but stopped when a man wearing a grey suit walked into the morgue. "Excuse me, you three wouldn't happen to be from the PCU by any chance?" The man asked.

"Yes." Bronson said. "How can we help you?"

"Oh good. I'm Detective Mark Sanders. I was sent to warn you that there are a dozen news reporters waiting outside to talk to you." Sanders said. "My boss didn't want you to be ambushed."

Sure he didn't. Local police didn't care about the PCU. They didn't even like working with us. And given the fact that a bunch of cops got killed this morning I doubted the Seattle police department liked us even more.

Bronson smiled. "Thanks for the heads up." He looked at me. "I knew this was coming. And honestly, I should have called a press conference sooner."

"What do you want to do?" I asked.

"I'll start the press conference and then I'll introduce you as our expert."

"I'm no expert, Elliott."

He shrugged. "Yeah, well, you know a hell of a lot more about this supernatural politics shit than anyone else. So that makes you the expert." He turned to Carlos. "Is that okay with you?"

Carlos nodded and smiled. "Yep. I'm okay with just standing there and looking pretty."

Bronson rolled his eyes but he was smiling. "Okay, Sanders, go out and let them know there's going to be a press conference."

"On it." Sanders said and then he smiled as he looked me up and down. "You're prettier in person." And then he was off doing as he was told.

Carlos laughed. "I think he likes you." I didn't even say anything to that. I just shook my head and walked out. Carlos caught up to me and draped an arm over my shoulders as we walked. "You know, he was right. You are prettier in person."

"You know Rafe," I said. "I'm not human. Which means I'm fast and could have you on your back before you even had time to react."

"That sounds like fun. I'd let you ride me for an hour."

This time I elbowed him in the side. "Ever heard of sexual harassment?"

He just laughed. "Hey, I'm a guy. Inappropriate thoughts are hard wired in at moment of conception."

I couldn't help it, I giggled. "You are such a pervert. You and Julian would get along great, because he's a pervert too."

"Enough you two." Bronson said catching up with us. "Head in the case. You can focus on your hormones after."

Carlos only laughed, but nothing else was said.

When we walked outside there was a frenzy of reporters everywhere. Yelling questions at Sanders that he couldn't answer. But he seemed to be handling it like a pro. "I cannot answer that. You have to wait for the PCU agents." He turned his head toward us as we walked out and relief filled his eyes. He turned back to the crowd of reporters. "One moment please." Sanders made his way to us. "Thank God. I wasn't sure I could hold them off much longer."

Bronson patted him on the back. "Thanks. We'll take it from here." Bronson walked up to the crowd and began to speak. "Thank you all for coming. I'm Special Agent Elliott Bronson, from the PCU. As you all know, there have been a string of murders in the area. We would like to clear up any confusion and answer all your questions. But please keep in mind that this is still an ongoing investigation and there are some details that will be kept confidential." Bronson gave his best smile. "Now to answer any questions you might have I would like to introduce you to our supernatural expert, Special Agent Morgan Montgomery."

Now it was my turn to step up and address the reporters. This wasn't my first press conference, but this was the first time I actually spoke. Back in Boston, I had been pushed back into the background and Daniel or one of the others had done the talking at these things. But I hadn't minded. I didn't like the idea of explaining to a bunch of humans about something they just didn't understand.

But here I was, about to do exactly that.

I stepped up next to Bronson and didn't even have to open my mouth before the first question was asked. "Agent Montgomery, is it true that the first victim was Princess Delisa Shaylee?"

"Yes." I said. "It is true."

"How is the king of the fairies dealing with his daughter's death?"

How to answer that? "King Androcles and his family are in mourning at this time. Next question."

"Agent Montgomery, is it true that all these murders are connected to the Shaylee case?" A reporter asked.

"Yes. We believe so."

"Can you clarify on that?"

"Not at this time. That information is confidential."

"Can you tell us anything about the raid that happened last night?" Another reporter asked.

I nodded. "Yes. We received a call from one of the guest attending a party, from there I can't go into much detail. All I will say is that there were some arrests made."

"Agent Montgomery, is it true that you are from the angel community?"

"Yes . . ." Where was this going?

"Is it true that you were suspended for your inhuman nature and because you were believed to be a danger to your team?"

I stopped breathing. Seriously. That had caught me by so much surprise I had no idea how to react. I stood there stoned faced and tried to remember how to breathe and speak. And when I found my voice, I was very careful how I phrased my words. "I'm sorry." I said. "I don't see how that is relevant to this case. Please keep your questions to the case at hand."

"But is it true?" The reporter asked.

"What's your name?"

"Oliver."

"Well, Oliver, that is a very personal question. And I'm not going to answer it for so many reasons. What I am or am not, has nothing to do with this case. It does not affect my job. Never has and never will. I do not see how the reasoning behind my suspension is any of your business."

"But with you being suspended doesn't that mean you're going against protocol working this case? Wouldn't you be going against orders?"

"Agent Bronson and agent Carlos needed my assistance and I am assisting them. So no, I'm not going against my orders." Okay, I was, but this prick didn't need to know that. I could get in a lot of trouble and I probably was. But that didn't mean I left two fellow cops to deal with this alone. And yes, I was aware I was being a bitch about it, but he'd gone too far.

"Okay." Bronson said. "I think that's enough questions for tonight." And with that, he put his hand to my back and led me away.

I breathed a sigh of relief. "Thanks."

"No problem. Are you okay?"

"Yeah, I'm fine." It was a lie.

"Okay, let's go talk to the last names on the lists. You talk to Tabitha Rossi and . . . Balian Ivanski. Carlos and I will take the other one."

I nodded. "Okay. Sounds like a plan." I only hoped it was as easy as it sounded.

CHAPTER TWENTY-FIVE

Tabitha Rossi was exactly how I'd pictured her. She was tall, beautiful, and her C cup made my A cup seem like a joke. She had short spiky red hair and dark green eyes. She wore a black dress that was so short and low cut that it left nothing to the imagination. Tabitha was one of those women Sabine would call a ho in stilettos. And that was exactly what she was.

She was also the woman Ivan had been tongue wrestling the night we'd come to talk to him.

I sat across from Tabitha at one of the tables in the club. Her legs were crossed and she seemed board as she examined one of her red painted fingernails. I could tell just by the way she was acting, she didn't want to be sitting here and talking to me. But she didn't have a choice. I'd kindly explained to her that if she didn't answer my questions here, then I'd take her to the police station and she could answer them there.

She chose Illusions.

"So, Miss Rossi, where were you the night Delisa Shaylee was killed?" I asked.

She rolled her eyes. "I was here with a friend."

"His name?" She gave me a look. "Don't play coy Miss Rossi."

"His name's Grady." she said with a huff.

"Do you know of anyone who would want Delisa and Ivan dead? Was there ever anyone who acted uneasy around them or jealous?"

"No. Not really. I mean, Ivan and Delisa were nice to everyone."

I doubted that. "Even you? I see that your name is on a list of lovers who were in their bed."

"Yes, so? That list means nothing. Was I sleeping with them? Yes and No. I'm not into women agent Montgomery."

"Then why were you in their bed?" I asked her.

"Because Delisa had a fancy for me and she knew the only way I would get naked with her was if Ivan joined us. I only allowed some kissing and touching, but everything else I drawled a line to. Ivan was the only one allowed to do that."

"So they never drugged you or forced you in any way?"

"No. They only did that when someone wasn't willing. And I was willing."

"But not completely. You just said there were things you didn't allow Delisa to do."

"If you mean not allowing her to go down on me or rub herself against me, then yes, I guess you're right. But they never drugged me or anything like that. And besides, I wouldn't really call Ivan my lover. We weren't together all that much for that. I mainly split my time between two men. And trust me, they're a hell of a lot better in bed than Ivan ever was."

I wanted to laugh. Tabitha's voice had turned from board to disgust to finally settling on a purr as she mentioned the two men.

"Do these men have names?"

"Yes, one is Grady. He's the one I go to when the other isn't available or well, not allowing me in his bed."

"And this man is?"

"Balian Ivanski."

I had been taking notes, so when she said Balian's name I'd stopped mid-stream of making a note. I looked up at her and did my best to hide my shock and my sudden need to rip her hair out. "Balian Ivanski?"

She nodded. "Yes. He's the one I prefer."

"Okay, well, last night you were at a party with Kyriss."

"I was. But Kyriss and Grady aren't the men or man I want to be with. I have plans for Balian. Permanent plans. It's only a matter of time before he decides he's ready for a mate and wants to settle down. And I plan on it being me."

Okay, it didn't really bother me that Balian had slept with her. The problem was, I was having a hard time seeing him with her . . . forever. Balian struck me as the kind of man who always went for the best in everything. And settling down with a woman who was known to be loose and looked like a whore . . . well, I just couldn't see it. Maybe I was wrong, but I didn't think so.

And besides, I was having a hard time seeing Tabitha being with only one man and having babies. She just didn't seem the mothering type.

I swallowed hard and shook my head. Why did I care if Balian was into red-headed women who were nothing but gold digging bitches. It wasn't any of my business.

"So you admit that you went with Kyriss willingly and he never forced you?" I asked.

"Yes." Her voice changed to one of crying and she put a hand over her mouth as she began to sob. "I didn't want to go, but he threatened to hurt me and when we got there . . . I told him no to the sex, but he got mad and hit me and threw me onto the bed and he . . ." She started laughing as she made eye contact with me. "Was that a little over the top or just about right?"

The bitch was mocking me. And yeah, I was this close to banging her head against the table.

"I don't find that very funning Miss Rossi. There were young innocent girls raped last night."

"Innocent? Whoever is really innocent? Those girls knew what they were getting into. Why else go? Screaming rape is just another way of saying I made a big fucking mistake." She stood then. "Are you done? I would like to go dance now."

"One more question. Did you know Kendra Farris and Flynn Garwood?"

"Yeah, a little. They were the main people in Delisa and Ivan's bed."

"Did any of their other lovers ever seem jealous of them, since Delisa and Ivan preferred them?"

She shook her head. "No. From what I saw, most of them were only doing it because they were having problems . . . doing it. But Kendra and Flynn were into it and never looked back. If you know what I mean. Now can I go dance?"

I waved her away. If she sat here much longer I was going to do the very thing I wanted to do in the last five minutes. Beat her to death.

She walked away and I rubbed my forehead. The ho had given me a headache. That was great. I hadn't even gone to see my grandmother yet.

"Did you find what you were looking for?" I looked up to see Balian sit down in the chair Tabitha had been a few seconds ago.

I looked at him and all I saw was the man who'd been in the shower with me this morning. Granted it had been all in my head, but I could still feel his hands and lips on my skin as if it had really happened. But it hadn't so there was no need to dwell on it.

"Maybe. Mind if I ask you some questions?" I asked him and hoped my voice gave nothing away.

"It would depend."

"On what?"

"On what you asked."

Perhaps now wasn't the right time to do this. But when would I get another chance? So I just went for it. "Where were you the night Delisa Shaylee was murdered?"

"Home." he said and smiled at the expression on my face.

"Can anyone clarify that?"

"No. I was home alone."

"Were you?" Yeah, even I knew my voice sounded strained and came off a tad bit jealous.

Balian smiled wider. "Yes, I was." He tilted his head to the side. "I saw you on TV this morning and again tonight. You were breathtaking as you cut down those banshees."

I rolled my eyes and looked down. "So I've been told."

"I found it intriguing that you were the one chosen to address the reporters."

"Why is that?"

"Because you do not strike me as the kind of woman who likes being front and center. You seem like you are alright with just being in the background."

I shrugged. "You don't know me."

"On the contrary. I know you better than you think."

I doubted that. "Stop straying from the conversation. I'm here to talk about murder victims not me. So stop changing the subject."

Balian sat back. "I am bored with your subject. I want to talk about something else. Perhaps if you are done for the day, we could go somewhere... more private to talk and dine."

I was speechless for a split second and then recovered. Did Balian just ask me out? No, I didn't think so. It didn't sound like it. And even if he had I wasn't interested. I had too much on my plate as it was. I needed to deal with some stuff before I—I mentally slapped myself for going there.

"I can't. I already have dinner plans."

"Oh? What is his name?"

Now it was my turn to smile. "Why do you care?"

"I do not. I was just curious." There was a pitch to his Russian accent that suggested otherwise. Balian did care, a lot.

Liar. I thought. "Hmm, well, I'm going to my grandparents for dinner. And besides, wouldn't you taking me out to dinner cause problems with your girlfriend?"

Balian seemed confused then as he raised an eyebrow. "My girlfriend?"

"Yeah, Tabitha. She is your girlfriend, right?"

He burst out laughing. "No. Why would you think that?"

"Well, she said that you were sleeping together and that . . . when you finally mate—"

"And you believed her?" he said cutting me off. I just gave him a look. "Right. Well, yes, I am sleeping with her. But as for the other no. She does not even know where I sleep."

I raised an eyebrow at that. "Excuse me? You just said that you were having sex."

"Yes. But that is all it is." he said and I just gave him a look. "Okay, listen, there are only four people who know where I live and they are all men. I do not allow women into my home."

"That's sexist."

"No, it is not. The only woman allowed into my home will be my mate. And I can assure you, it is not Tabitha."

For some reason I believed him. And when he stretched out his arm and brushed his fingers across the back of my hand, I didn't pull back. I just sat there very still and watched as his fingers made small circles over my skin. My breathing picked up and I had to grip the side of the chair to keep from falling out of it.

"You know," Balian said. "I came over here to apologize for last night.

I should have never pushed you. I am sorry." A waitress came over and set down a glass with brown liquid and a beer bottle on the table. "Thank you Vika." She said nothing and walked off. Balian pushed the beer towards me. "This is for you. You look like you have had a long day."

I had, but I wasn't taking the beer. "No thank you. I'm still on duty."

"Are you?"

"Yes," I said. "I am." But we both knew I was lying. And despite a need deep down in my soul that wanted him to do more than just hold my hand, I knew I needed to keep a distance from him. I needed to remember that he was dangerous. And at that thought, he started looking even more attractive.

Shit. I needed my head examined.

I pulled my hand away from his and applauded myself for not backing down. "Look, I know what you're doing. And it's not going to work."

He smiled. "And what is it you think I am doing?"

"Seducing me. Making me your next conquest. But you're wasting your time. I can't be seduced."

"Never say never, darling."

"Not gonna happen."

"We will see." And he smiled as heat filled his eyes.

Bronson and Carlos walked up and stopped at the table. I silently thanked them. Who knew what would have happened if I'd been alone with Balian for much longer. "Hey," Bronson said. "Carlos and I are done. We were going to go get a beer and ask you if you wanted to come. But I can see you started without us."

"Yeah." I looked at the clock on my phone. "I have to get going soon. I'm already late. Camille is probably already seething."

Balian stood taking his brandy with him. "You gentlemen can sit here. I will have Vika bring you those beers. They are on the house."

"You don't have to do that." said Bronson. "Carlos and I can go somewhere else and let you and Morgan finish talking."

"Nonsense. I was already leaving. Morgan and I can finish our conversation later when we have more privacy." And with that, he turned and walked away.

Bronson looked at me with raised eyebrows. "Sure we didn't interrupt anything?"

I rolled my eyes and didn't even respond.

Bronson and Carlos sat down as Vika came back with two beers. She gave me a glare and walked off. Okay. What did I do to her? I didn't know, so I didn't worry about it.

"So, did you get anything out of Tabitha?" Bronson asked.

"No. You?" I asked.

"Same. He claimed Ivan was a good person and he didn't know why anyone would want him dead."

"What about Balian?" Carlos asked. "Did you get anything from him?"

I rubbed my forehead. "No. Nothing. The only thing I got from Tabitha was mockery. And Balian, well, he did his best to talk around everything. He was more interested in me than helping to find a killer."

"Yeah, what's the story with you two anyway?" Bronson asked.

"What?"

"Oh come on." Carlos said. "Don't act like you don't know what he's talking about. We've seen the way he looks . . . or well, is looking at you. And forgive my language, but I think he wants to fuck you hard and fast."

"Rafe! Do you have to be so crude about it?" I asked feeling my cheeks warm.

"Hey, I'm just telling it how I see it. And that man is picturing you naked and under him."

"Or on top." added Bronson with a smile.

I glared at both of them. "Men and sex is the last thing I need. Especially with a man like Balian."

"What's wrong with him? You're both single. He likes you. And you've just been dumped. A man like Balian is exactly what you need. Help keep your mind off the shit going on in your life. Off your ex. What better way to get back at the bastard than to have hot rebound sex with a man who's probably a total Sex God in the sack?"

"Then you go have sex with him."

"Sorry, he's not my type. I like women." He smiled. "But you on the other hand . . ."

"You don't understand, Rafe." I said shaking my head. "I can't. I spent the last few years with a man who couldn't deal . . . with some things. He tried, but in the end . . . it just couldn't work."

"Like what?" Bronson asked. "What did he have to deal with?"

I took a sip of the beer. "Sex."

"What? Did he say you weren't good at it?"

I looked down and didn't say anything.

"Shit." Carlos said. "I don't believe it. Maybe he was the one who was bad at it."

I smiled. "Thanks. But that wasn't it. He . . . couldn't keep up with me."

They both gave me confused expressions. "Huh?"

I took another sip of my beer and sighed. "I'm not human. Daniel is human."

"Still not understanding." Carlos said.

"Rafe, what's your idea of a sex marathon?"

"I don't know. All night into the morning. What's yours?"

"All weekend. Friday, Saturday, and Sunday. Most of it without much sleep."

Carlos blinked. "Holy shit."

"Damn." Bronson exclaimed. "How is that possible? Doesn't that like, I don't know, hurt? I mean, I'm all for taking my time and going for seconds or maybe thirds in that department, but three days in a roll without much stopping. I just . . . I can't fathom that."

I sighed. "Yeah, neither could Daniel. Which is why we always ended up fighting every time we had sex. Because once I got started I didn't want to stop."

Yeah, that was one of the many problems in our relationship. To be honest, I think we were headed for a breakup long before this new stuff came up. Not that the new stuff didn't play a major part in it, because it did. In fact, I think it was sort of the final straw of sorts. We'd needed a reason to end it without everyone wondering what had happened. Okay, maybe not for our families, but for the people we worked with. They'd known we were together and if we'd just ended it they would have been confused.

To them, we'd been the perfect couple.

"I'm sorry." Carlos said after a long moment. "I didn't know that. Why do you have trouble stopping? Is it because you're not human?"

I shrugged. "Not sure. I've always been that way since I was sixteen. I'd thought it was that, but Stefan said my appetite for sex is greater than any supernatural he knows. I have an unhealthy appetite for sex even for a supernatural." I sighed. "But I can still go a long time without it just like everyone else. It's the having it that's the problem."

Bronson laughed then. "You sure have problems."

I smiled. "Yep." I took one last drink of my beer. "Well, boys, I got to go. I'm really late and if I don't at least show up to say hi, Camille is going to explode."

"Okay." Bronson said. "I think we should take the rest of the weekend off. No one's talking and we've ran out of suspects. So unless another body shows up or our killer loses his mind and does something stupid, I won't be calling you."

"That's fine." I grabbed my purse. "I'll see you boys later."

I got up to leave when something caught my eye. Standing at the bar was Constantine and he was talking to a cute blond. She was smiling and laughing at everything he was saying. I debated about whether or not I should confront him about Ivan and the murders. In the back of my head he was the only likely suspect we had. He did have access to Ivan and had sounded somewhat disgusted about what turned him on.

But still, I wasn't entirely sure now was the right time for this. What if I pissed him off and he chose another victim? What if he chose Balian? That thought scared me, but I told myself that I might not get another chance to talk to him. So I squared my shoulders and walked over.

Constantine's eyes met mine and he suddenly looked angry and annoyed. "What do you want?"

"Mind if we talk?" I asked giving him a smile.

He glared at me and I knew he wasn't happy. He looked at the blond and smiled at her and said something in Spanish. She nodded and left. I watched her leave wondering if I should fear for her safety. "What do you want to talk about, agent?"

I turned my gaze back to Constantine and saw that he wasn't smiling. "I wanted to ask you some questions about Ivan."

"What about him? He's dead. What more could I possibly shine on his murder?"

"Were you two close?"

He shrugged. "Not really. My mate and I had dinner with him and Delisa from time to time."

"And what occurred at these dinners?"

The vein in his neck began to pulse. "Are you implying that my mate and I had some kind of relationship with them?"

I shrugged. "I don't know, you tell me. Your name wasn't on the list, but since you were his Lawyer and you helped him put the lists together . . . you could have kept your name off for a reason. So tell me, Mr. Gonzales, where were you the night Delisa Shaylee was murdered?"

"I am not answering that?"

"Why? Afraid you might sound guilty?"

"No, because I know my rights and I know you're just fishing." he snarled. He took a threatening step toward me. "I know what you're doing. But it's not going to work. First you accuse Ivan, but now that he's dead—killed by the same killer, you're trying to pen it on me."

I know I was taunting him and I should have just walked away right then, before I made it worse. But I knew he wouldn't hurt me. At least not here. There were too many humans in the club and too many witnesses. No, if he hurt me, he'd do it somewhere else.

"My, you seem to have quite the temper on you. Ever have violent tenancies" I asked deadpanned.

"I'm a werewolf, of course I have violent tenancies."

I smiled wide as I caught something he'd said. "How do you know Ivan was murdered by the same killer as the others?"

Constantine set back on his heels and gave me a look that said, "Oh shit." and gritted his teeth. "Wasn't he? He was killed the same way, yes?"

"Maybe." Now it was my turn to lean into him. "I know you had something to do with it. Or at the very least, are covering for someone. That's what you demons do. It's a reflex. You can't help it. But sooner or later, you or whoever you're protecting are going to slip up. And when you do, I'm going to be there and you're going to jail for a very long time."

"Now look who has a temper. The truth is agent Montgomery, you're no better than the rest of us. You're just a psychotic bitch hiding behind a gun and badge."

He wasn't wrong.

I just smiled at him and left. On my way out my eyes locked with Balian's. He was sitting in an armchair next to a sofa. He smiled and raised his glass to me, but I could see curiosity behind his eyes. He'd been watching me and Constantine. The man with the dark teal eyes was sitting on the sofa and he eyed me with a hint of curiosity. There was something about him that was so familiar it was almost scary. And it had nothing to do with the fact that he was in my vision.

The man with the red eyes sat in the other armchair. He smiled at me and gave a curt nod of acknowledgement. When he spoke his Swedish accent was smooth with a hint of enthusiasm. "Not going to beat anyone up tonight, lilla gnista?"

I didn't even stop as I replied. "The night is still young."

He just chuckled. "Pity. I was so hoping for some entertainment."

I said nothing and continued walking all the way to the car. I got in and took a deep breath. I silently wondered if there was any way I could get out of going to my grandparents. But the thought of Camille showing up at Stefan's and going apeshit took care of that. If I didn't show up she'd blame him for it or my job. She'd accuse me of not caring for her or the family and accuse me of abandoning them. Point fingers and say that I chose Stefan and my job over my blood.

So there really was no choice. I had to go and I had to bear it. Yeah, it seemed like I was doing a lot of that lately. You'd think I was used to it by now.

Spoiler alert. I so wasn't.

CHAPTER TWENTY-SIX

Things at the *Montgomery house were* as bad as I had feared. Avery opened the door before I even got on the porch. "You were on TV again." she said. "And you're really late."

I walked up onto the porch and shrugged. "I know and I'm sorry. I was working." I went inside and suddenly wished I hadn't. As soon as I entered the sitting room, I was greeted by an angry Camille.

"You're late. Dinner was three hours ago." Camille snapped.

"I know. But I'm here now. I was hoping for some leftovers. I'm starving." I set my purse down on the coffee table.

"No. No leftovers. If you wanted dinner, then you should have been here when it was served."

I nodded and sighed. I wasn't going to fight with her. It was just food and I could get that at home. I sat down on the armrest of the sofa and crossed my arms over my chest. "What do you want from me, Camille?"

"I want you to start showing me and this family some respect."

"And how is me being late for dinner being disrespectful?" I asked. This was stupid and a waste of time. We both knew there was more going on here than my being late for dinner. She said nothing and I shook my head. "We both know that there's more going on here. So why don't you just say what's on your mind."

And that's when she exploded into a ball of raging anger. She narrowed her eyes at me and pointed a finger in my direction. "Don't start with that attitude young lady. And you know damn well what the problem is."

I did, but I wanted her to say it out loud. "Say it. Just say what you're thinking so we can get this over with." I knew where she was going to go with this. So I braced myself.

"What do you think?" Camille snapped. "You've chosen them over us again."

"Who? My job?"

"As a start, yes. But mainly him."

"Stefan?" I said. "When have I ever chosen Stefan over you?"

"The day your mother left."

And there it was. Her pointing a finger and blaming Stefan for my mom leaving. But it wasn't his fault and I was getting sick and tired of this. It was getting old.

"You have chosen that man over your family, your blood for years. And now you've chosen a job that is going to get you killed. But you don't care, do you? You just do whatever the hell you want to do and never think about how your choices are going to affect your family. You're just like your mother."

"You mean you, right?" I said feeling my own anger boil to the surface. "You mean I chose him over you. God, Camille, I was nine years old. My mother was gone and he was the only parent I had left. How can you stand there and blame him for something he had no control over? Or blame me for just being a child and choosing the only father I had? The only problem here is you. You just can't handle that you had no authority over my mother, or the fact that you can't control me. It has nothing to do with Stefan or my job. It's you and always been you."

I was so mad by that point that I'd dropped my hands to my sides and balled them into tight fists. I could feel my power wanting out and that dark beast that was deep inside me was awake and wanted out too. But I forced them down. Who knew what would happen if I allowed them loose.

"Okay." Asher said. "Everyone needs to calm down."

"I will not calm down." snapped Camille. "Not until she stops being so damn selfish."

"Selfish? When have I ever been selfish?" I asked.

"When have you not? Tell me Morgan, why did you come back here?"

"Because Stefan got hurt and I had nowhere else to go." A few hot tears ran down my cheeks.

"Enough." My grandfather said. He walked up next to Camille and stopped. "Camille, you've made your point, now it is time to stop."

"I second that." Ember said. "Mother, just stop."

I agreed and figured that was my cue to leave. "I need to go." I turned to leave and I guess Camille wanted the last word.

"See, there she goes. Running off to God knows where just like Lauren." There was a venomous note to her voice. "Always running away when things get hard. I saw you on the news tonight. Do you have any idea what you've done by putting us front and center like that? We don't let humans see our powers. It just isn't done." I'd wondered how long it would take before she went there. It had taken her less than five minutes.

I turned on her. I spun around and leveled my dark teal gaze at her. "It's my job!" I yelled. "If I hadn't acted when I did we wouldn't be having this conversation because I would be dead along with every cop that was there. So stop acting as if everything's a fucking conspiracy."

"Morgan Alexandra Montgomery, watch your language." Camille snapped. "And I don't think everything's a conspiracy. I just don't think it's a good idea to expose ourselves to humans."

"News flash Camille, everyone already knows we exist, so it wasn't like I was revealing myself. And like I said, it's my job. I can't help it if you can't get that through your simple minded head. And about the other stuff? Well, I'm dealing with a lot of shit right now, so forgive me if I act as if I don't give a shit right now."

"Get out!" Camille pointed a finger toward the foyer. "Get out of this house!"

"With pleasure." And I turned and stormed out of the house and didn't stop until I reached the car. I didn't get in right away. I just stood there and tried to calm myself. I took deep breaths and told myself that it was all going to be okay. We all just needed some space. In a few days I'd come back over and try to make everything right.

"Morgan." I turned around to see Grayson. "Are you okay?"

I shook my head. "No. That woman . . . is impossible."

"Yeah, tell me something I don't know." he laughed. "Hey, give her a break. I know she can be over baring sometimes. But she really does love you.

I think she's just scared that you're going to leave and never come back . . . just like your mom."

I scoffed. "Yeah, right. How can I forget? You know, have you ever wondered how they talk about her but yet they don't talk about her?"

Grayson frowned. "I don't understand."

"Think about it. They always talk about how she ran off, not about how she disappeared. I mean, she had a nine-year-old daughter. So why would she willingly leave? Why not fill out a missing person's report?" I looked down. "The night she left, there was a demon looking in my window."

"You think it's connected?"

"I don't know. I'm just trying to figure this out. Maybe she went out to make sure everything was safe and he took her."

"But there wasn't a body found." Grayson said.

"So, humans go missing every day and their bodies never get found." It was a logical enough explanation. But it still didn't explain why everyone claimed she'd ran off.

Grayson stuck his hands into his pant pockets and slumped his shoulders. "You know Morgan, grandmother isn't the only one who's worried you're going to leave and never come back." He raised his eyes to meet mine.

I frowned. "I'm sorry."

He shrugged. "It's not just me and this family. It's Stefan and the others. I've ran into them a few times since you've left, and they all seemed really sad. Sure they talked to you more, but they still seemed sad. I ran into Stefan a few days ago and he seemed really happy that you were home, but I think he's scared that when these two weeks are up, you're going to pack up and he's never going to see you again. I think that's why he went out and found Mariska, so he wouldn't be so lonely."

That took me aback. "You know about Mariska?"

He nodded. "Yeah. And I think it's about time too."

I stood there and realized that maybe Camille had been right. Maybe I was selfish. After all, hadn't I gotten mad when Stefan introduced me to Mariska? Hadn't it been selfish of me to get angry over him wanting to move on? Yeah, it had.

I sighed. "I'm sorry for not calling more and putting my job first."

Grayson smiled. "Don't be. I'm one out of a few people who understand. I know you have a job that's dangerous, but you're also saving people. You used your ability to safe those cops from being killed. Everyone knows that. And in time, so will grandmother. I wish I could do that."

"Why don't you?"

"Because the job I want would only make matters worse. That's why I'm not working and neither is Avery and Cristabel. Grandmother has put her foot down and if we go out and get a dangerous job, well, she'd go beyond apeshit."

I laughed. That sounded like Camille. "If you don't mind me asking, what do you want to do?"

He gave a sad smile. "I want to be a PCU agent like you."

"Then that's what you should do." I said feeling happy that my own cousin wanted to do the same job I did.

Grayson shook his head. "Nah, that's okay. Camille having one grandchild in a dangerous job is enough. She wouldn't recover from having two."

He was probably right.

"Well, I should probably go. I'm starting to get really hungry." I said opening the car door.

"Okay. I'll see you later."

"Okay. Tell Avery I'm sorry we didn't get to hang out."

"I will. Drive safe."

"Okay." And with that I got into the car and drove away.

It was a long quiet drive home. Okay, it wasn't completely quiet. My mind raced all the way to the house. I just kept thinking about Camille and everything she'd said. And about my mom. I hadn't thought about the night she left in years. Well, that wasn't true, but it was close. I thought about her around my birthday and holidays. She'd never sent me anything. I used to think it was because she didn't want me or Stefan to know where she was. But now I wondered if it was because she couldn't. Because she was dead.

But everyone kept saying she'd ran off. But why? What would cause a mother to abandon her only child? There had to be an explanation, because it just didn't make any sense.

When I pulled into the driveway I saw that I wouldn't be walking into an empty house tonight. I got out of the car and made my way inside. Nate was sitting on the sofa and looked up from his beer when I walked in. He gave a slight smile. "Rough night?"

I plopped down beside him. "You have no idea. First, I have to deal with the press, then I have to deal with a smug demon who made a mockery out of those rape victims, then after that, I got into a fight with Camille, where she accused me of choosing everyone over her and being like my mom. But that's not the worst of it. We're now officially out of suspects. Well, except one, but I don't want to talk about it."

"Damn, and I thought I was having a bad night." Nate said. "Want a sip?" He handed me his beer. I took it and took a big gulp before handing it back to him. "Feel better?"

I smiled. "A little. So how was your night?"

"Not as bad as yours. But there was one point of it where I started rethinking my choices and line of work. But other than that low point, it was fine."

"What happened?" I asked as I curled up next to him, wrapping my arms around his bicep and laying my head down on his shoulder.

I felt him stiffen for a second before he answered. "I had a really big fight with dad today at the firm."

"What about?"

"You."

I stiffened this time as I tried to figure out what they could possibly fight over me about. "Why?"

Nate shrugged. "Doesn't matter. Not really. I mean, I got upset this morning when he snapped at you for asking about Lauren. It wasn't right. He should tell you whatever he knows."

I smiled. This was just too weird. Nate taking up for me, who would've thought? "Thanks for taking up for me."

"No problem."

We sat there in silence for a few minutes until I couldn't handle it any longer. "Nate?"

"Hmm?"

"Are you ever going to tell me what's going on? Why have . . . you been so nice to me?" Not that I was complaining. I liked this new Nate.

Nate didn't answer for a very long time. "It's sort of hard to explain."

"Could you at least try?"

He sighed. "I thought I was in love with you."

I raised up as my heart stopped. I hadn't expected that. Nate thinking he was in love with me was a little overwhelming. I swallowed hard as I said. "And now?"

"Well, I love you, but I'm not in love with you. Trust me, I've done a lot of examining over the past few years. And I've realized that maybe what I was feeling wasn't so much as romance or even male hormones—though that was there, but perhaps maybe it was something else."

"Like what?"

"Brotherly love."

I frowned at him. "Nate, you're not making any sense."

He took another pull from his beer. "Every time you were with someone it drove me crazy. Especially Kaydan. I don't know what it is about him, but every time he looks at you or gets this thought in his head that he can be with you. Well, I just want to wrap my hands around his neck and choke him to death." He paused, seemed to be in thought. "And that was why I thought I was in love with you. Because I thought I was jealous. But now I know that's not true. When I found out that Daniel had dumped you, it had taken everything inside of me to not go to Boston and beat the shit out of him. He doesn't deserve you. And honestly, there's no man in this world that does. Including Kaydan. No, especially Kaydan."

His words seemed so sincere and he sighed. "Truth is, when you do start dating again? It's going to take a lot for the bastard to win me over. I'm not going to just sit back and let some guy take advantage of my sister. That would earn him an ass kicking."

There were small tears in my eyes as I said. "Actually, it's the other way around. No one's going to want me. Not now. I'm damaged and no one wants someone who's damaged."

"You're not damaged."

Yeah, but he didn't know the things that had happened to me. What Daniel had done to me. If he had, he wouldn't be sitting here telling me all of this. Instead, he'd be trying to warn men to stay away from me. Not all of it had been physical, most of it had been emotional. But it really didn't matter. There were just some things that just stuck in your head enough to leave an imprint of how someone saw you. So therefore, made you wonder if that was how everyone saw you.

There hadn't been any sex for almost five months, since it'd happened, because he couldn't handle looking or touching me. He'd told me more than once in the past five months that I was disgusting to him and the thought of touching me made him sick. There had been nights after we'd gone to bed where I'd get up and go to the bathroom and cry on the floor.

Although, there had been those cases when we were out of town on a case and he'd opted for his own hotel room.

I laid my head back down on his shoulder. "Yes I am. And you saying otherwise only makes it worse."

Nate sighed, but said nothing else. Not that he had a chance to. Because about that moment, we heard the front door shut and a few seconds later, Stefan and Mariska walked in.

Stefan took one look at me and Nate curled up on the sofa and I saw anger in his eyes. But it wasn't aimed toward me. It was aimed toward Nate. "Now you're curling up with her on the sofa?"

"What do you want dad? Do you want me to be hateful with her or do you want us to get along?" Nate asked in a sharp tone.

"I want to know what the hell is going on."

Nate shook his head. "You wouldn't understand."

"What is your problem?" I asked starting to feel angry.

Stefan narrowed his gaze at me. "You stay out of this."

"The hell I will. You've wanted me and Nate to get along for years, and now that we have, you've got an attitude. And frankly, I'm fucking tired of everyone's attitudes. I've had a long day and all I want to do is come home to a nice and quiet house without having to deal with everyone's drama along with my own." I was sitting up now. "And I'm not going to sit here and let you rip Nate a new one over something stupid."

"Fine." Stefan snapped. "Mariska and I are going to bed." And with those parting words, he took Mariska's hand and led her upstairs.

"Damn." I said. "He's pissed."

"Yep." Nate said. "I was going to watch a movie. Want to join me?"

"Sure. Want something to eat? I'm starving."

"Sounds good. You get the food, I'll set up the movie."

I got up and took off my shoulder holster and set it along with my cell phone on the coffee table. I kicked off my shoes and went to the kitchen to find something to eat. After five minutes of searching I finally settled for Nachos. It took me less than ten minutes to make them. I put two beers under my arms and grabbed the plates and carried them to the sitting room.

Nate had the movie going by the time I got back. The glow from the TV was the only light in the room.

I handed him a plate and he took it with another beer. "This is what I'm talking about." he said taking a bite. "Dad and I can't cook worth shit." I sat down next to him and giggled as I remembered the burnt pancakes from this morning.

We ate as we watched the movie.

About halfway through the movie we were done eating and the moans from upstairs were getting louder and louder. I was sitting on the other end of the sofa, my legs were pulled up underneath me. Stefan and Mariska had been going at it for almost an hour, and I was resisting the urge to scream in frustration. I found myself letting my mind wonder to dangerous places. Places that didn't involve clothing and involved Balian and his hands and his lips and his . . .

"Giving you ideas, huh?" Nate asked with a smile in his voice.

"About five months in the making." I said. "What gave me away?"

Nate chuckled. "Everything. And the fact that you're sitting over there with a look that says that you're three seconds from shooting out the door and jumping the first guy you see. Although, there's another look that suggests that you might be . . . thinking or have the guy already in mind."

I winced at his words, because I did have a guy in mind.

"So, who is he?" Nate asked. When I didn't answer him, he said. "You know, you can talk to me. About . . . whatever. Anything."

I smiled. "I know. And it's . . . complicated. I guess. I just don't know if there's anything to tell. So . . . I'm not sure if it's worth telling."

Nate nodded, and after a moment he said. "So, do you miss it?"

"Miss what?"

"Sex."

I sighed. "Sometimes. But it was the other I missed the most."

"Other?"

"The holding. I miss the holding afterward. And this. Daniel and I never did this. Well, we did the first few months, but after . . . we never just curled up on the sofa like this and watched a movie. He never even held me after the sex either. He'd just roll over and go to sleep."

That little bit was hard to say. I'd been doing my best to keep everything locked up and out of reach of those I loved, and telling Nate this little bit about Daniel was hard. But it did make me feel better somewhat. I wasn't going to tell him everything, but I didn't need to. I think in some ways he already knew.

"I'm sorry." he said. And I believed him. "You know, I could get used to this. The coming home every night to a girl, curling up on the sofa and watching a movie, making out on the sofa, and then maybe taking it upstairs when clothes started feeling too heavy and we wanted them off."

I liked the sound of that. In my head I pictured coming home to a man— my husband, and maybe a baby. My eyes flicked toward the coffee table and landed on mine and Nate's guns that were laying on it. If Nate and I were to have a life where we came home to a family, then he and she were going to have to be okay with our line of work. With the danger that our jobs brought.

"Yeah, might be nice." I said.

"You know, I miss it too."

"What?"

"Sex."

I raised an eyebrow. "Really?"

He nodded." Really. That blond from the other night was the first sex I'd had in weeks. Maybe a few months."

I was shocked. Nate had been almost as bad as me when it came to sleeping around as a teenager. The fact that he was admitting to not being with anyone for a long time was weird. "Why?"

"Because I've grown up and out of casual sex. I mean, come on, I'm twenty-seven Morgan. I think it's time I settled down, you know. Meet a nice girl, get married, have a few babies."

"Do you even want that?"

He seemed to think about it. "Yes, I do. And I know it's only a matter of time before I have to move out and find my own place."

"Why would you have to move?" I asked.

"Because of Mariska. Before long, she's going to be moving in, and she's not going to want dad's older children around as reminders that he's had a family before her. Not while she's trying to convince him to put a ring on her finger and start a new family."

I guess Nate had a point. I didn't know any woman who married a man who was married before her and had children from that marriage, wanting reminders of it. Especially if she was of child baring age. Yeah, nothing pisses off a woman in her twenties or thirties, who marries a man in his forties or fifties, than having to see his grown twenty-something children while she's trying to get him to be her babies daddy.

"And that's what pisses me off." Nate said.

"You don't like her?"

"No. I mean, I like her to a point. I've hung out with her and dad a few times. She's kind of nice. But when someone mentions mom and Elizabeth or even Lauren? She squirms. I guess I get it, but in a way I don't. I mean, are we all supposed to just tip toe and whisper their names when she's around, because it makes her uneasy?"

I didn't have an answer to that.

"I'm sorry." I said. Because what else could I say?

This new reality that was my life, was filled with drama after drama. People I loved were getting hurt by other people I loved. And it was clear that I was the cause of some of it. My friendship with Kaydan was beginning to look nonexistent. I knew he was hurting, but what else was I supposed to do? Sabine was in love with Matt, but was afraid of what would happen if she told him. Piper and Alexi were dating now, and I prayed they'd have a happier ending. As it was looking like Stefan and Nate were now fighting.

"It's okay." Nate said "So, how about we try being brother and sister? Maybe even friends?"

I smiled. "Yeah, I would like that."

We fell back into silence and it wasn't long until everything was lost to sleep. The last thing I thought before I dosed off was that it felt nice to finally have a brother.

CHAPTER
TWENTY-SEVEN

I woke up the next day on the sofa, a small lap blanket had been placed over me. I laid there for a half minute and remembered falling asleep. There was a vague remembrance of Nate turning the TV off and covering me with the blanket before going upstairs to his room.

I smiled a little. Guess he was taking this whole big brother thing seriously.

I got up and went up to my room and changed into a tank and a pair of shorts before padding back downstairs. Stefan, Mariska, and Nate were sitting at the island and looked up when I walked in. There were no warm smiles on their faces. Well, Nate smiled for a heartbeat, but other than that, it seemed pretty doom and gloom.

Stefan eyed me with a hint of anger still visible in his eyes. "So how was your night? Did you make any breakthrough?"

"It was fine and no." And I left it at that as I grabbed a bowl and spoon and sat down at the island. I poured the cereal and milk in the bowl and ate as I tried to ignore that growing tension in the room. The kitchen seemed to close in and whatever had been said before I walked in was hanging in the air like a bad smell. "Okay." I said. "What the hell is going on?"

Stefan looked down as Mariska squirmed in her seat. "Morgan." Stefan began. "Mariska and I have decided to try to get pregnant."

My heart sank and I dropped the spoon in my hand. There was a small splash as milk spilled onto the counter. I felt tears come to my eyes, but they weren't happy tears of joy. They were angry hot tears that burned my throat as I swallowed back the sob that threatened to escape. Nate had been right after all about the whole Mariska wanting a baby. And if he'd been right about that, did that mean he was right about the other?

I took deep breaths and swallowed hard before I spoke. "That's . . . great." It was getting hard to speak. If I wasn't careful, I was going to be screaming.

Stefan studied me. "Why do I get the feeling you're lying? Just say what you're thinking."

Well, if he insists. "Are you out of your damn mind?" I said before I had a chance to stop myself. "You've only been together six months. Don't you think you're moving a little fast?"

"Thank you." Nate said throwing his arms up.

"Nathaniel," Stefan said. "You've already said your peace. Now it's Morgan's turn." He turned to me. "No I don't think we're moving too fast. I love her."

"The way you loved my mom and his?" I pointed a finger at Nate.

"Don't bring them into this."

"Oh, I'm bringing them into this. When you met Charlotte, you dated for two years before you got married. And it was another three years after that before you had Nate. You were with my mom all that time and not once did I ever hear you talk about having children. Now you're with her and all of a sudden after six months, you want a child. Why?"

"Because I love her." he said. "I wouldn't expect you to understand it. And frankly, I think you're being selfish about this."

"Wow, did you come up with that all by yourself or have you and Camille been talking?"

"I am nothing like Camille, so don't compare me to her."

Right, sure. But it sure as hell sounded like what Camille had said last night. "Okay, fine, I'm being selfish. But what are you being?"

"I'm being a grown up. I'm making a decision to move on and live my life. I'm sorry if you don't understand that."

"I understand. But I just met her."

"And whose fault is that?" Stefan asked flatly. "You weren't here, Morgan. What was I supposed to do, wait to move on until you decided to come home? I mean, you sure as hell aren't telling me anything about what's going on in your life. You've shut down and have kept everything bottled up like it's some kind of secret."

"Yeah, well, I'm sure you know all about secrets. Seeing as you're keeping some of your own. I know you know who my father is and where my mom might be. So before you start lecturing me about keeping things from people why don't you look in the fucking mirror." Okay, I might have gone a little too far on that one, but I was mad. And when I got mad I lashed out. And when I lashed out, people got hurt. Usually people I loved.

And that was unacceptable.

Stefan just stood there stone faced and stared at me like he'd seen me for the first time. "Why are you so angry?"

At first I didn't understand what he was talking about, and then I did. He wasn't referring to me being angry about him and Mariska having a child, he was referring to the fact that I'd always been ready for a fight. It had started after my mom had left and like any good parent, Stefan had just assumed that my being angry all the time was because I missed my mom. And I had always thought the same thing. That was why Stefan had never really disciplined me or Nate.

Because he thought it was because of us losing our mother's.

But lately I'd wondered if that was the case from where I was concerned. I'd always blamed my attitude and anger issues on my mom leaving, but was that what it was or was it something else? And what about now? Was I upset because Stefan was trying to have another child with a woman I barely knew or was I upset about something else?

"Just tell me." Stefan said. "Whatever it is, just tell me. I can handle it." I shook my head. "No, I can't."

"Why?" Stefan's voice changed to something that sounded like sadness.

"Because you'll get mad." I said my voice sounding guilty. "Some stuff happened back in December that I didn't tell you about. I know I should have called you when it happened, but I didn't. At first I thought dealing with it alone was what I needed. I didn't want to burden you with my drama and have you come to Boston to take care of me. And besides, you would have probably beat the shit out of Daniel."

Yeah, I had no doubt about that. And I knew Stefan well enough to know that he'd do what I'd just said. He would have gone to Boston and took care of me. And I knew him well enough now to know that if and when I did tell him, he would either get really mad at me for not telling him, or he'd get all sympathetic.

"Please tell me he didn't beat you. Because if that's what you're telling me, I'm taking the first flight to Boston today and when I find him, he's going to need plastic surgery after I'm done." Stefan said, voice full of promise.

I flicked my gaze over to Nate and his face said he'd be joining his father on the plane. I shook my head. "No, he didn't beat me."

"Then what was it? What did he do to you?"

"It doesn't matter."

"Damn it Morgan. Why do you insist on doing this?" Stefan snapped.

I shook my head as I got up and made for the doorway. "I'm not doing this. I didn't come home to fight with you. If I wanted to do that, I'd stayed in Boston and fought with Daniel."

I stormed out of the kitchen and went to my room. I took a quick shower and got dressed. I went back downstairs and put on my shoulder holster, grabbed my keys, phone, and purse, and headed for the car. I had to get out of here. I needed to go somewhere I could be alone. Man, I wished there had been more leads to check up on, then I'd have somewhere to go.

But as it turned out, I did have somewhere to go. I ended up at the grocery store. I grabbed a cart and pushed it through the aisles and grabbed a week's worth of food. When I was done, I went to the checkout and paid.

I was pushing the cart out the door when it hit me. It happened so suddenly that I didn't even have time to brace myself.

I was in the dark room again, still chained up with my arms over my head. The dark haired man with dark blue eyes stared over at me with so much regret it was almost suffocating. My vision-self stared back at him with understanding. She knew she was about to die. And she knew he was going to watch. That Balian was going to watch, because that's who the man was.

Balian stared at my vision-self as anger filled his eyes. It was clear that he didn't agree with this and my vision-self knew if there was any way he could stop it, he would. But she knew it was no use. She was going to die and the man she loved was being forced to watch it.

In the back of her mind she prayed that Nate would find her. She knew if anyone could save her and the man she loved, it would be Nate.

The man with the dark teal eyes walked over and stopped in front of her.

The gleam in his eyes was one of rage and power. There was no sympathy in them and she knew once he killed her, he'd feel no sympathy after.

Then the world shifted and I was back in reality. My hands gripped the handle of the cart tightly as I tried to breathe.

"Morgan?" A voice said beside me. "Morgan, are you alright?"

I turned my head to see Balian. He stood there and looked at me with pure concern all over his face. I swallowed hard and bit back a sob that was trying to rip its way out of my throat. "Y-yes." I stuttered. "Yeah, I'm fine."

I could tell by the way he stared at me that he didn't believe me. I couldn't blame him. I wouldn't have believed me either.

"Are you sure?" he asked.

I nodded. "So, what are you doing here?"

He smiled and raised up a hand holding a white plastic bag. "Even I need to eat."

"Oh." Right, I knew that. It wasn't like he fed off of unexpected women for food. "Well, thanks for making sure I was okay." I started walking away, but Balian called out my name.

"Morgan. Wait."

I stopped and turned back to him. "What?"

"Would you . . . would you mind giving me a lift?"

I stared at him and just blinked. "Um, why?"

Balian smiled and I could tell that he was amused. "It seems that my ride has left without me."

I frowned. I wasn't sure if he was telling the truth or not. I mean, it was hard to believe that he'd carpool, let alone ask for help. He seemed like the kind of man who could get along by himself. He was clean shaven and well dressed. Men like him never asked for anything without asking for something in return.

"Okay, um . . . what's the catch?" I asked.

Balian laughed. "Wow, you really do not miss a beat, do you? Is it really that hard to believe that I need only a simple ride without anything in return?"

"Yeah, well, forgive me for being suspicious. But you don't strike me as the kind of man who asks for help. So I ask again, what's the catch?"

Balian gave me one of those smiles that could make you go weak in the knees. "Why, the joy of your presence of course."

I stood there and debated. I wasn't so sure being alone with him in the car was such a good idea, but he wasn't threatening me either. Yeah, I still felt attracted to him, and that was the whole problem. Being alone with this man was a bad idea for so many reasons.

"Okay, I'll give you a ride." I was so going to regret this.

Balian smiled and followed me to the car. He helped me put the groceries into the backseat, and then got into the passenger side. I started the car and the song I'd been listening to, came on where it had left off. *"Taste on my lips . . . your salty kisses . . ."*

Shoot me now.

Balian looked at me and smiled. "Hmm, interesting."

I raised an eyebrow. "What?"

"Your music."

"Oh. Well, um, sorry if you don't like it. But, uh, my music depends on my mood."

Balian shook his head. "Do not sweat it. I actually like this band. And well, most people do not like my music either."

"What kind of music do you like?" I asked as I ejected the CD and popped in Linkin Park. A few seconds later Chester Bennington started screaming about shoving the keys to the kingdom down someone's throat. And really, that was how I was feeling more at the moment.

"Within Temptation." Balian answered and smiled as he added. "Linkin Park. Bands like that."

Shit.

Okay, we liked the same music. Lots of people liked this band. The fact he was one of them meant nothing.

"Hmm. So, where am I dropping you off?" I asked trying to change the subject.

"Illusions."

I nodded and put the car in gear. We drove in silence for a really long time and I found myself wondering what else we might have in common. I tightened my grip on the steering wheel as I tried not to imagine what it would feel like if he touched me right now. God, he was too close again. I couldn't think with him in the car.

"So, how are you enjoying your vacation?" Balian asked breaking the silence.

I shrugged. "It would have been better if it hadn't been forced or if there hadn't been a murder. But it's fine. It's keeping my mind from dangerous and depressing places . . . most of the time."

"I am sorry."

"Don't worry about it." I said as I pulled in front of Illusions. The car idled and I turned in my seat. "So, can you shine some light on Delisa and Ivan's deaths?"

Balian smiled. "You sure are sneaky. And no, I cannot shine any light on Delisa and Ivan's deaths."

I started to say something but stopped when my cell phone started ringing. I answered it without checking the caller ID. "Montgomery?"

"What the hell are you doing?" Daniel's voice boomed on the other end of the phone.

"I ask myself that all the time." I quipped. Yeah, I was being a smart ass, but I was in a smart ass mood. So sue me.

"Stop being a smart ass and answer the fucking question."

"I'm sorry, but I'm in a smart ass mood. And seeing as you're one of the reasons I'm visiting smart ass land . . ."

"You know, I'm starting to wonder what I ever saw in you." he said.

"Yeah, well, I've been wondering that myself too." I sighed. "What do you want Daniel?"

"What I want? I want to know why I've seen you on the news twice now, and why you're helping out on a case when you've been fired?"

I rolled my eyes. "First of all, I wasn't fired, I was suspended. Second, agent Bronson needed assistance, so I'm assisting. And third, I don't know why you care since it doesn't affect you, not really. You lost the right for an explanation the day you threw me out of the house."

This was all I needed. It wasn't enough that he'd screwed up my life as it was and I was starting to have problems at home, but now he was going to try to put the nail in what was turning out to be a really shitty day.

I quickly looked at Balian and saw that he was listening to every word I was saying. I could tell he was filing it all in to examine at a later date. Probably tonight when he was laying awake in his bed.

There was a chuckle at the other end. "Yes, that was the highlight of our relationship. And another thing, expert, really? What the hell was that about?"

"Not that it's any of your business, but I am a supernatural. Elliott and Rafe aren't and they both agreed that they had no idea what they were talking about."

"Elliott and Rafe? Now you're on first name bases? Haven't you moved up in the world." Daniel taunted. "And to answer your earlier question, I called to see when you were coming for your shit. I sort of need it out of the house."

I sighed. "I don't know. I don't even know where I'm going to be living. I thought I would wait to see where the board sent me."

"Sweetie, the board is going to fire you after what you did. It's a sad reality, but it's the truth. So if I were you, I'd come up with a new career. So I repeat, when are you coming for your shit?"

I laid my head down on the steering wheel. "Daniel, why are you doing this?"

There was no answer, only silence.

"Okay, fine. I'll send someone for my stuff. What do you want to do about Phoebe?"

"Actually, I was planning on keeping her."

I sat up as I felt tears sting my eyes. "You can't do that. You didn't even want her."

"Yeah, but she's grown on me, so I'm keeping her."

"Damn it, Daniel!" I yelled. I was starting to get angry. "You are such a dick. You're only doing this to spite me." Hot tears spilled over my cheeks and I cursed myself for them and allowing myself to do this in front of Balian.

"Probably. But I figured I've deserved it."

The hell he did. He deserved to be eaten by hungry lions while he was still alive and conscious.

I started to open my mouth when I heard the sound of a woman's voice on the other end. "Who's that?" I asked. If I hadn't known any better, it sounded like . . .

"I need to go" Daniel said. "Oh, and you have two days or I'm throwing everything out on the curb." Then he hung up and the line went dead.

I pushed the end button and just stared at my phone. Why me? Why was all of this happening to me? On second thought, I rather not know.

"Are you alright?" Balian asked after a moment.

I sniffed and wiped my eyes with the back of my hand. "Yes." It was a lie.

"Who . . . is Daniel?"

An asshole who screwed me up in more ways than one. I wanted to say, but I didn't. Instead I said. "No one." Yeah, I was still lying, but I wasn't going to tell him about the worse mistake of my life. "And I'm sorry you had to see that."

"Do not be."

"It's just . . . I'm in a really bad place right now and—"

"No, seriously love, I understand. I know what it is like to be broken." Balian smiled at me and I suddenly felt warm inside. "Thank you for the ride. Maybe the next ride you give me will be a little more personal and intimate." My face turned ten shades of red. Balian gave a small chuckle. "You are blushing, little orchid. I think it is cute."

I didn't think my blush could get any warmer, but it did. I wasn't sure I would be able to speak, but somehow I found my voice. "Have a nice day, Balian."

He got out of the car and smiled. "Oh, I will now. Trust me, my dreams will be very sweet." He laughed as he shut the door and made his way to the club and inside.

I sat there for a moment and wondered what would have made Balian broken, he seemed to be very confident about everything. So what would have broken him? I hadn't a clue. But then again, I didn't actually know him. So it was hard to say.

I pulled away from the curb heading home wishing I had somewhere to go, a suspect to interrogate. But wait, I did have a suspect. Okay he wasn't a suspect, but he'd been eluding my questions for a while now.

A dangerous thought popped into my head and I told myself to forget it. To just let it go. It wasn't worth it. But as dangerous as it was, it really was a good idea.

CHAPTER TWENTY-EIGHT

I tried to talk myself out of it, I swear. But in the end my curiosity won out. I'd taken the groceries back to the house and put them away. Then I'd gotten back into the car and drove back to Illusions where I'd been for the past . . . I don't know, how many hours. But it was dark and my ass was getting numb. But that was the cost of an important stake out.

I was going to watch Illusions and see if anything shady happened. And maybe follow Balian if he happened to leave.

My cell phone rang and I answered. "Montgomery."

"Hey, what are you doing?" Avery asked on the other end.

"I'm on an important stake out."

"Who are you watching?"

"Balian Ivanski." I said. She burst out into giggles. "Hey, it's not funny. This really is important."

She laughed. "Yeah, sure it is. So, see anything yet?"

"No. Not yet. And my ass is getting numb."

"Well, I'm sure if you asked him, Balian would massage it. I've heard stories about that man. Heard he was a Sex God."

"Avery, there is no such thing as a Sex God."

"Sure there is. His name's Balian Ivanski." Then she started laughing again.

"And they think I'm the one with the problems." I muttered. "So, what did you want, to invite me over for dinner?'

Her laughter died off. "No. I was going to see if you wanted to hang out somewhere else, since well, you're not welcome here at the moment."

That hurt, but I'd expected it. No way was Camille going to let me go unpunished.

"I'm sorry. But I'm working."

"I know, and it's okay." Avery said sounding a little sad. "Maybe next time. Right now you need to find your bad guy. I understand."

"Thanks." I said as the door to Illusions opened and Balian walked out. I watched as he went to a black BMW and got in. "Avery, I'll call you back. I think I'm on to something."

"Okay. Bye."

"Bye." And I hung up, tossing my phone into my open purse and starting my car.

I followed Balian at a distance, making sure there were always two cars between us. I followed him to a pizza place and watched him get out and go in. Five minutes later he came out carrying a pizza box. He got back into his car and I followed him to Insidious. I thought it was strange that he'd gone there instead of going back to Illusions or maybe a secret loft house somewhere in Seattle. I watched as he got out of the car, grabbed his pizza, turned, and walked—

Oh shit. Balian was walking toward the car. My car.

Shit, shit, shit.

What the hell was I going to do? I looked around for an out, but didn't find one. I had gotten caught. Busted.

Balian tapped a finger on the driver side window. Well, now what? I winced and rolled down the window and waited. For what, I wasn't sure. But whatever it was, it sure wasn't what had happened. "Hello, darling." Balian said with a smile. "Enjoying yourself?"

I swallowed hard. "How did you know I was following you?"

He gave a mischievous smile. "I have my ways." He peered through the open window and tilted his head. "You sure are persistent."

I just shrugged.

He nodded as if he'd decided something. "How about you come in? I have a pizza and there is beer in my fridge. We can play twenty questions. I answer your questions and you answer mine. I think it is a fair trade, yes?"

I shook my head. "I don't think that's a very good idea."

Balian didn't seem all that fazed by my reluctance. He just reached inside the car and pulled out the keys.

"What the hell are you doing?" I asked feeling shocked that he'd just took off with my car keys.

"If you want them back, you will come inside and dine with me." he said as he walked away and disappeared into the dark alley by Insidious.

I sat there for a moment and debated on what I should do. I didn't want to go inside wherever it was he was going. I didn't trust myself and I didn't trust him. Not that he was going to hurt me, because I didn't think he would. But I was worried being alone with him would lead to other things. But I really wanted my car keys back.

With a huff, I grabbed my purse and got out of the car and followed him into the alley. I knew I would regret this, but I didn't really have a choice.

I stepped into the alley and looked around until I saw him at the top of the stairs I'd asked about the night of Delisa Shaylee's murder. I walked up the stairs and he motioned for me to go through the open doorway. I did and stepped into a small hallway. Balian closed the door and unlocked another door and opened it. I went through it without being told and stopped in my tracks.

It was an apartment loft. All the walls were painted a dark gray and all the rooms were one. In the center of the room was the sitting area, with a long dark blue sofa, two matching armchairs, and a glass coffee table in front of the sofa along with a big screen TV. Two smaller tables that matched the coffee table sat between the sofa and chairs. There was a horse lamp on each table. One quick glance, revealed more horses.

Cool, Balian liked horses.

To the left was the kitchen area, complete with a small island and four stainless steel stools. To the right was . . . the bedroom. A big bed sat in the middle of the wall, with what looked like a black satin bedspread. It looked inviting. Too inviting.

"You like?" Balian asked shutting the door.

I nodded as I looked around. "Is this your place?"

"Yes." He turned around as a big husky ran from behind the sofa. Its tail was wagging as it jumped up onto its hind legs, front paws on his chest. Balian patted it on the head. "Hello. Yes, I missed you too." The dog jumped down and walked over to me. I knelt down and offered my hand. The dog wasted no time in demanding that I pet it. "Morgan, this is Mischa. Mischa, this is Morgan."

"She's beautiful." I said as I stroked her fur. She was white with black and gray patches, and big blue eyes. "And she's really friendly."

"Yes, she loves everyone. As long as they pet her and give her food."

I laughed and gave her one last pat before standing and walking over to the island and sitting down. "Sounds like Julian." I said.

Balian smiled and set two plates down. "Help yourself." He walked over to the fridge and I opened the pizza box. I was hungrier than I'd realized. But when I opened the box I froze . . . Was this a joke? I wondered that as I stared down at the green peppers, mushrooms, and light sauce. "I am sorry." Balian said as he set two beers down. "If the pizza is not to your liking. It is just . . . I do not like pepperoni. I never have. Kyriss says that it is not a pizza without pepperoni, but I disagree."

I didn't know if I should start laughing or freak out. In the end I chose laughter. It was just too funny. First the music, now the pizza. "No. This is . . . perfect." I picked up a slice. "You get two points for this."

"I am sorry, I do not understand."

"I know. And I might regret saying this, but that makes you seem adorable."

"You think I am adorable?" Balian asked with a raised eyebrow.

I bit into the pizza. "I think you are a lot of things. Adorable just happens to be one of them."

Balian sat down on the other side of the island. "I have never been told I was adorable before, but I will take it. Are you sure the pizza is alright?"

"Yep." I said around another bite. "I'm sure. This is exactly how I eat my pizza."

Balian stared at me with curiosity. "Hmm, I did not know that."

We ate in silence for about ten minutes. Within those ten minutes I mustered up the courage to ask him about the murders. I needed to ease into it. So I went with the easiest question.

"Are you the owner of Insidious?"

He smiled as he nodded. "Yes and I own Illusions."

"Why were you watching me the night Delisa Shaylee was killed?"

Balian took a sip of his beer. "I was not watching you that night. Well, not at first. I was watching the police do their jobs. I was looking out the window when I saw a red Porsche drive up. I thought it was odd and when I saw you . . . I thought you were possibly the most beautiful creature I had ever seen in the past hundred years or so." He looked down and sighed. "I was curious about you. That is why I watched you and why I showed up at the mansion once I found out your name."

I believed him. I knew deep down he was telling me the truth. Because really, he had no reason to lie to me.

"Who really found Delisa's body?"

"Kyriss. He was on his way up to see me. I told him and Constantine to lie and say that a worker found her taking out the trash. But I suppose that backfired seeing as there are no dumpsters."

I laughed. "Yeah, that kind of gave it away. Do you know who would want her dead?"

Balian shook his head. "No. I thought perhaps you were right. That Ivan had killed her. They had been fighting for the past two weeks over someone she was sleeping with. That was why I sent Kyriss to that party. I wanted to see what Ivan was up to, so I could deal with him. But as you know, Kyriss got distracted." He frowned. "How is Kelsey Kincaid doing?"

I shrugged. "I'm not sure. No one is returning my calls. But if I had to guess, not good."

"I was sorry to hear what had happened. I sort of . . . punished Kyriss for allowing it to happen. And Gregory . . . well, let's just say he will not be around for a while." Balian paused and shook his head. "Anyway Kyriss was supposed to have watched and gathered information, see if anything illegal happened. And if it did, stopped it or called me so I could stop it." There was an angry edge to his voice. I knew right then he wasn't happy with the outcome.

"What were you going to do, Balian? Kill him?" I asked knowing that was exactly what he was telling me.

"You and I both know demons like me have our own set of rules and laws we bide by before the ones handed down by humans. So yes, I would have killed him. I do not condone the drugging and raping of young girls."

I believed him on that too. Balian didn't strike me as the kind of man who allowed those he cared about to get hurt or even those he didn't know. I gazed into his dark blue eyes and knew that if he'd gotten to that party before I had, he'd beaten the shit out of Greg himself, if not killed him. There would have been no stopping him from doing it. That made me wonder what the hell he'd meant by Greg not being around for a while. What the hell did he do to Greg? Was he still breathing?

I knew by the dark gleam in his eyes that whatever it was, hadn't been fun. He hadn't enjoyed whatever it was. Balian didn't like torture.

And I also knew what he was talking about with the rules and laws thing. Supernatural Politics was more complicated and screwed up than human. And messier. In the human world if you messed up, you got jail time. For the really bad stuff, it was either life in prison or the death penalty. But in the supernatural world, it was death without trial. It was sort of like the mafia in some ways. There was no second chances. If you fucked up, you were dead. End of story.

"What about Kendra Farris and Flynn Garwood? Do you know why someone would want them killed?" I asked.

"No, I did not know them that well."

"Their names were on one of the lists Ivan gave me. So are you sure—"

"Yes." Balian said cutting me off. "I know where you are going with this, so just ask the question."

I stared at him and told myself to not be a coward. "Your name was on a list of those who attend a party thrown by Samael. Ivan called it an orgy. Is that true?"

"Yes, he throws them."

"Do you attend them?"

He didn't even hesitate. "Would you think of me any less if I said yes?"

"No. Do you participate?"

"Yes. But not in the way you think. I am not into men. I never have been nor do I ever plan on being. Does that answer your question?"

I nodded and cringed a little.

"Is there a problem?"

I frowned. "No, not really. It's just, I have enough problems trying to tell one man what I want, let alone trying to have two."

Balian gave a devilish smile. "Perhaps the problem is that you have to tell them in the first place. A man should already know what his woman wants without her telling him." I blushed as his gaze became warm. "Are there any more questions?"

"Constantine." I didn't make it a question. I just said his name to see how Balian would react.

He shook his head. "Constantine would not do this. He has too much at stake. And I know him." He tilted his head to the side. "But I am curious, what did you say to him last night? After you left, he was in a really bad mood."

I shrugged. "Nothing that wasn't true." Or so I hoped. If Constantine turned out to be innocent, then I had just pissed off a werewolf for nothing.

"And that was?"

"He's a suspect." I smiled. "But don't worry, he handled it quite well. Called me a psychotic bitch. And that is also true."

A muscle began to flex in Balian's jaw as if he was trying to control himself. "I see. Is there anything else you need to know?"

I shook my head. "No. I think that's everything."

"Good. Now it is my turn to ask the questions. Who is Daniel?"

I snorted. "Wow, you're really going for the punch, aren't you."

"As it would seem. Now answer the question."

I rubbed my hand across my cheek. "He's my recent ex."

"How recent?"

"As of almost two weeks ago." I said. "He was a PCU agent like me. We've been living together for about two years. And when some stuff happened at work and in our personal life, he couldn't deal with it so he dumped me and threw me out of the house."

Balian started to look angry, but I didn't think it was at me. Something told me it wouldn't be good if he ever met Daniel.

"Okay, so who is Phoebe?"

I looked down as a frowned formed on my face. "My cat. I got her a year ago. He's keeping her."

"But she is yours. He cannot do that."

"Yeah, well, he is."

He frowned and shook his head. "I am sorry." I looked up at him then and our eyes locked. There was pain in his eyes. A pain that was so old, yet so fresh stared back at me with regret. "Why were you suspended?"

I opened my mouth and then closed it. I picked up my beer. "I . . . I can't talk about that."

"Why?"

Because I couldn't talk about it with my family and I sure as hell wasn't going to talk about it with him. I didn't know Balian well enough to confide in him. But as I sat there and watched him go to the fridge and pull out a container of chocolate and almond ice cream and set it down on the counter, I started to rethink that thought.

"Ice cream?" he asked seeming to be okay with my silence.

I looked at the ice cream and suddenly wanted to cry. We had three things in common now. Music, pizza, and ice cream. I nodded. "Yes. Thank you."

Balian put the half eaten pizza in the fridge and went to scooping the ice cream into two bowls. He slid one of the bowls to me along with a spoon. I went to work on it as I tried to sort out everything going on in my brain. I could tell him. I mean, he wasn't my family or really my friend. And wasn't that the beauty of it?

He didn't know me like my family did. And in some ways they didn't really know me either. And honestly, I needed to tell someone. And if not my family, then perhaps Balian.

"I'm a supernatural." I said staring into the bowl.

"Beg pardon?"

I looked up and bit my lower lip. "That's why I was suspended. Because I'm a supernatural. I'm being accused of lying about not being human."

Balian looked at me puzzled. "I do not understand. Your eyes are your tell. How can they say you lied about what you are?"

That had been my question too when I'd been relieved of my job until further notice. I'd been so confused it hadn't been funny. I hadn't lied, but yet, they believed I had.

"Because I'd never came out and said I wasn't human. My old team in Boston never asked and neither had the board when I'd gotten my badge. So I never said anything because I thought they already knew. Daniel knew... from the beginning. But he's claiming that he didn't." And that was part of what hurt the most.

"How did they—"

"Find out what I am? We were on a case and I had to use my supernatural strength." I scoffed. "I saved their lives and this is how they repay me. By reporting that their fellow team member was a monster and had fooled them all." That part had been really hard to say, but not as hard as some of the other stuff. "That's why Daniel dumped me."

Balian just blinked. "They are going to fire you for not being human?"

"Probably."

"They cannot do that. It is not against the law for a supernatural to be a cop."

"I know. But they're saying I lied and pretended to be human. Daniel isn't helping. He's doing his best to save his own ass by telling everyone he didn't know he was dating a supernatural." My voice became low and I knew if I wasn't careful, I was going to start crying.

"What did he do to you?" Balian asked.

I frowned at him. "Huh? What are you talking about?"

"There is something you are not saying. Something that is making you sad and I can tell it has something to do with this Daniel. So I ask again, what did he do to you?"

Holy shit, how did he know there was something else? Had I let something slip in my features? I didn't think so. Maybe it was in my voice. Yeah, that was it. My voice had given me away.

"That doesn't matter." I said shaking my head.

"Why not? I think everything about you matters."

"Because . . . the outcome is still the same. Talking about it isn't going to change anything. I'm still going to be broken and damaged and no one is ever going to want me ever again."

"That is not true. I want you. Very much." Balian said. I looked at him dumbfounded. But at the same time I found it sweet and it made me want to cry. "I am sorry. I did not mean to be so forward."

I sat there and just stared at him as I tried to comprehend what he was saying. I didn't understand why he felt the need to apologize for wanting me. I mean, I'd already known that. Anyone with eyes could see the lust and wanting in Balian's eyes. And hell, there was this small piece of me that thought about letting him have me.

I got up and took my empty bowl to the sink and let the warm water wash it clean. I stood there and just tried to talk myself out of giving in to what my body and mind wanted. His hands and mouth on my body. But I wasn't going to give in. Not yet.

I turned off the water and turned around to only run into Balian. My heart jumped into my throat. Not out of fear, but because he was standing too close to me. He stepped forward until my back was pressed against the counter. He put his hands on the counter on either side of me and leaned in, his lips breaths from touching my forehead.

"Balian, you're being too forward again."

I felt him smile against my skin. "My apologies, but can you blame me? You are a very beautiful woman. How could a man gaze upon you and not think you heaven?"

I swallowed hard. How could I answer that?

"Tell me." he whispered. "Tell me what he did to you so I can try to fix it." He pressed his lips to my skin and I found my lips moving.

"I found out that I was pregnant." I said, my voice low. This had been the first time I'd told anyone, and the warmth of Balian hadn't made the confession any easier. There was still emptiness and the feeling that it had been my fault. That I'd been punished for something.

Balian pulled back to look at me. There was confusion all over his face. "If that were true and you are with child, then I do not think you should have had that beer."

I swallowed hard as I shook my head. "It was about five months ago. I was six to seven weeks when I found out. I would have been a little over six months now."

"I do not under—"

"I lost the baby." I said. I spoke fast, because if I didn't, I wasn't going to get through this. "Daniel . . . he was so happy when I told him about the baby. He said he wanted a boy, because he wanted to teach him how to play football and baseball. I was already thinking about names and how I wanted to do the nursery. We'd decided that we'd wait until I was a few months along before we told our families. We only had like two or three weeks." My eyes stung with unshed tears and I felt like I was choking. But I pushed the tears back and took a few deep breaths before I continued. "We were on a case and I fell. There was this crazed werewolf that had been on a killing spree. We had him cornered and when I went to cuff him, he pushed me and I hit a wall. And I . . . lost it. Just like that. I'd only known I was pregnant for a week and then I lost my baby." Another deep breath. "After I lost the baby, everything changed. Daniel stopped touching me. He said I made him sick. And after I was suspended, he dumped me and we got in this big fight. He said that he was relieved that I lost the baby, because he didn't want a child that was a monster."

And that was the end of it. I couldn't talk anymore. If I said anymore, I was going to be sobbing and I couldn't allow myself to do that, to fall apart in front of Balian. And besides, I had shed enough tears over Daniel and his bastard behavior, I was not going to shed more. Balian wrapped his arms around me and held me for what felt like the longest time. And I let him. I felt warm and safe in his arms and that confused me, but I chose not to question it. I could do that later. Right now I was just going to enjoy being in his arms.

And have I mentioned that he smelled fantastic?

Balian pulled back. "I . . . am sorry." he said as he cupped my face in his hands. He leaned down towards my lips and I thought my heart was going to stop as I closed my eyes. His lips brushed mine and I felt butterflies in my stomach start to move and my heart started to pound. His lips found mine and he kissed me deeply as his hands move down and started to work the straps of my shoulder holster.

"This is bad." I said breathlessly as my hands pushed off his suit jacket.

"Extremely." he replied.

"This has to be against the rules."

"Rules are meant to be broken."

Yeah, and I was about to break two of them.

Balian moved me to the island as he finally got my shoulder holster off and he laid it down on the counter, then without pause, he pulled my shirt up and over my head, tossing it to the floor. I pulled at his tie and when I got it loose, I threw it over my head. He picked me up as my hands ripped his shirt open. Buttons went everywhere, but he didn't seem to care as he lifted me up onto the counter top.

Our kisses became frantic, tongues moving together, fingers pressing on skin. My body screamed with the excitement of it, but my brain screamed for a totally different reason.

What the hell was I doing?

I pushed on Balian's chest, breaking the kiss as I pulled back. I had to stop this before I got too carried away. "We have to stop." I said through shaky breaths.

"Why?" Balian asked with his own breathy voice as he leaned in.

I put a hand on his chest stopping him. "Because we don't know each other enough to sleep together. We just met."

"I think we know each other just fine." Of course he did. He wanted sex.

I shook my head. "No we don't. We're practically strangers."

"Are strangers not allowed to make love?" he asked in a low voice. "I want to make you feel better, to take the pain away." He leaned in and pressed a kiss to my shoulder. "I want to make love to you, Morgan."

Hearing my name leave his lips tightened my lower body and I closed my eyes. His kiss wasn't frantic anymore as he moved across my skin, but slow and patient, like he was waiting for me to give him the go ahead.

I swallowed back a moan. "That's not the point." I said, proud of myself for finding some self-control. "I barely know you. And I've just gotten out of a bad relationship. I'm vulnerable right now. And this is not the solution to my problems."

Balian stopped kissing my skin and pulled back to look at me. "I know you are vulnerable. But I can assure you, my attentions are strictly honorable. I would never dream of taking advantage of you. You are ... different. Out of all the women I have been with, you are different." He traced a finger down my temple to my cheek. He pressed a light kiss to my lips. "I can go slow." he said. "And if you want me to stop, I will stop."

I told myself to not give in, to just tell him no. I knew I should have at that moment, pushed him away, grabbed my stuff, and left. This was my out. Balian was giving me an out. But I didn't take it. And I should have.

Instead, I allowed myself to think. To examine this. If I gave in and slept with him, would I feel guilty in the morning? No. Because I was single. There was no one else. But, did I want to put myself through the possibility of guilt? That was also a no. But I didn't think there would be any, so I pushed the whole guilt factor aside.

Balian was a demon. I was an angel. I didn't find anything wrong with sleeping with someone out of my race. I'd been with humans, fairies, and warlocks. But here was the thing, they weren't my enemy. The demons were. And Balian being a demon was the problem.

I'd never heard of angels and demons being together. We didn't like each other enough for that. But as I sat there, I could hear Julian's voice in my head, telling me that it was sex, not a marriage proposal. That I needed to stop thinking and have some fun.

Part of me wondered if I'd accidently transmitted a question about my dilemma to him and he was replying. I hoped if that was the case, that I hadn't given Balian away.

But all the same, it was good advice. It was just sex. Nothing more. No one had to know.

I slowly wrapped my arms around his neck and kissed him. "Okay."

"Okay what?" Balian asked against my lips. "I want to hear you say it. I want the words to leave your mouth."

I took a deep breath as I said. "Make love to me. Take the pain away."

That was all it took. Balian's lips were pressed against mine. It was slow, but with purpose. His arms went around my waist as he lifted me off the counter and began walking.

We landed on the bed in a heap of roaming hands and lips. Hands tearing at clothes and lips seeking out skin. My eyes were closed as Balian trailed his lips down my body slowly and I relished in it. It had been almost five months since I'd had sex. Since I'd felt the touch of someone's hands and lips on my skin. So if Balian wanted to go slow and take his time, it was fine with me. But then again, hadn't that been what he'd promised?

He kissed all the way down and stopped just before the waist band of my jeans. I felt him tug them off and heard the soft thump as they hit the floor. I opened my eyes long enough to see him gaze at my now naked body with so much heat it was almost intoxicating. Then without a word, he buried his face between my thighs.

I closed my eyes as the small moans started to escape my throat. And as his mouth and tongue worked me I screamed in my head, "Oh thank you God!" over and over again.

My hands gripped the comforter as I felt myself getting closer and closer to that point of spilling over. And when the release I'd been craving for five months came, I arched my back as a scream broke from my lips. Balian's hands gripped my hips, pushing them back down. And without seeing him I knew the bastard was smiling.

A few moments later he moved his lips back up my body, but still taking it slow. When his lips found mine he kissed me hard and deep, his tongue moving with mine.

He pulled away, but I kept my eyes closed. There was a sound of a drawer being opened, before more movement followed by foil being torn. He returned his lips to mine for a second, before trailing them down to kiss my earlobe.

"Now I am going to make love to you." he whispered in my ear.

I wanted to say okay, but I couldn't speak. My throat was clogged and talking was going to be impossible at the moment. The only thing coming out of my mouth were moans. Which escaped the moment he pushed himself inside me. I dug my nails into his back and I heard him give a small moan. He gave slow deep thrusts that made my head spin. There was nothing going on in my head but what he was doing. He whispered my name over and over again in my ear. His voice was thick and breathy with his Russian accent. So instead of him saying Morgan, it sounded more like Morgun.

At one point of the love making, he raised himself up so he could stare into my eyes as he continued to move in and out. There was something about it that made it seem so romantic and sexy. It was almost like he was looking into my soul as he made love to me. As he took my body over with his. There was a sparkle in his dark blue eyes that said he'd never grow tired of staring into my eyes and was enjoying the way I was reacting to him.

And when my release came it was with a vengeance. I cried out at the same time Balian gave his own shutter and we rode it together. When it was over he collapsed on top of me and kissed my shoulder. After a minute, he rolled off me and onto his back. We were both panting and slick with sweat. My heart was pounding in my ears and it took me a few minutes to find my voice.

"I can't believe I just did that." I breathed.

Balian put an arm around me pulling me close as he gave one of those guy chuckles and kissed my cheek as he said something in Russian.

"That's really hot. But could you translate?"

He kissed my cheek again. "I said I told you I would find it. And it was hiding here." He moved his hand down and slipped one finger between my thighs.

"Shit!" I gasped.

Balian laughed as he got up from the bed and I watched as he went into the bathroom. I laid there for a few minutes longer, just enjoying the feel of my now sated body. I silently compared every man I'd ever been with, with what had just happened. No one even came close. Balian had been the best sex I'd had in my life. The realization that I'd been having bad sex my whole life made me giggle a bit.

Avery had been right, Balian was a Sex God.

I got up and padded to the island long enough to grab my cell phone.

If Bronson called I needed to be able to get to my phone. I went back to the bed and set my phone on the bedside table as I crawled in under the covers. I had been right. They were satin.

Balian came out of the bathroom and just stood in the doorway as I took in his body. He was toned from one end to the other. His chest was hard and he had a six pack a human man would kill for. He was perfect except for one flaw. And really I wouldn't call it that. On the left side of his chest there was a scar. It started from the curve of his side and made its way down across his chest and stopped just below his belly button. It looked like someone had taken a knife to him. I found it odd because to my knowledge, there wasn't anything that made us scar. That was the beauty of being a supernatural.

"How did I miss that?" I asked.

"You were preoccupied." he said as he made his way to the bed. My cheeks warmed, but the scar wasn't all I'd missed. He set a small waste basket down beside the bed before getting in under the covers beside me.

"How did it happen?"

"It was a very long time ago. I barely remember." He was lying, but I had no room to talk when it came to keeping secrets.

"Well, you're beautiful." I said, admiring his naked body in appreciation. To me, his body was perfect.

Balian shook his head. "No, the scar has ruined my body." I didn't agree with that, but I let it go. There had been a note in his voice that suggested a painful memory. I knew all too well about painful memories. So I didn't press.

I looked down at his left arm. At the skull and sword tattoo that was looking back at me. "You're one of Samael's men?"

Balian studied me and then nodded. "Yes. Is that a problem?"

I thought about it for a moment and realized that in fact, it wasn't. It didn't bother me that tonight I was going to be sleeping with a man who was probably more dangerous than I realized. I straddled him and shook my head. "No. No, it's no problem at all." and then I kissed him.

"Good." Balian said. "Then I can continue with my plan."

"And what plan is that?"

A devilish smile curved his lips as he raised my hips up slightly and then very slowly slid himself inside me. I gave a gasp. "Making love to you the rest of eternity."

CHAPTER
TWENTY-NINE

I *woke to the feel of lips* brushing the curve of my neck and fingertips slowly sliding across the length of my side. I gave a happy sigh as I snuggled closer into the warm naked body beside me.

"Good morning, little orchid." Balian whispered in my ear. "Or should I say, good afternoon, seeing as it is two in the afternoon."

I smiled as he kissed my shoulder. "Good . . . afternoon." I said not surprised about the time. Balian and I had made love well into the early morning. Like the first few signs of daylight morning. Last night had been the best night of my life and it had gotten better when Balian had proven that he could keep up with me.

But as good as the sex had been, it was after the love making that had sealed the deal. Balian had held me. I had fallen asleep in his arms with my head laying on his chest. That had meant almost more to me than the sex.

I rolled over onto my back and gazed up at Balian. He was giving me a curious look. "What?"

He smiled as he propped himself up onto one elbow and trailed his other hand across my now bare skin. The sheet was down around my waist and my girls were out in the open. "You are revealing yourself."

I raised an eyebrow. "Revealing myself?"

"All of the women I have been with would not have . . . been so brazen about their body. They would have pulled the sheet up to cover their breasts."

"Is my being brazen a problem?" I asked.

He smiled. "No. It is just that with most women, me seeing their body during the love making is one thing, me seeing it after is another."

"Well, I'm not like most women."

Balian leaned down and kissed the top of one breast. "Yes, I am finding that out. And it is refreshing."

He positioned himself on top of me as his lips found mine and he kissed me hard and deep. My world spun. He pulled back and pushed himself up by his hands that were on the pillow on either side of me. Which gave me a great view of his body all the way down to what was under the sheet. His Mr. Happy was very happy. So happy in fact that it was standing at attention.

"When do you have to go back to work?" he asked, his voice starting to get husky.

I sighed as I smiled. "Well, unless I get a call saying that another body's been found, not until tomorrow. Why?"

"Good. Because I am going to hold you hostage in this bed until I have to get ready for work."

I giggled as he leaned in and kissed me. A soft moan escaped my lips as he pushed his erection between my thighs and moved against me. Everything was starting to get so hot and heavy that I forgot to remind him about one small detail.

But gratefully he remembered before disaster struck. "Wait." he said pulling back and reaching for a drawer. He opened it and pulled out a silver square wrapper. A condom. Great, I'd almost messed up and had unprotected sex with a demon/vampire. And with the way my luck was going as of late, I'd turn up pregnant. I watched as he tore open the wrapper and slipped on the condom. "So, where were we?" he said leaning back over me.

His erection found me again, but this time it entered me. At that same moment my cell phone began ringing. "Shit." I muttered.

"Ignore it." he said as he began pumping.

That wasn't exactly hard at the moment. I was too busy focusing on what he was doing to even care. Bronson or whoever could just wait until Balian was done ravishing my body. And if last night was any indication, they were going to be waiting for a while.

Thirty minutes and two screaming orgasms later, Balian collapsed on top of me. We were both panting and my cell phone had stopped ringing, but Balian's had started.

"You . . . should get it." I panted.

"Ignore it." Balian said as he started kissing his way down and stopping to show one of my breast's attention.

"It could be important. It could be . . . I don't know, something could be wrong. Maybe someone got locked out or can't find the vodka. Or maybe a shipment didn't show up . . ." Balian's lips had moved farther down my body to a spot that had become very sensitive.

The ringing had become persistent and I was finding it distracting. I wanted nothing more than to concentrate on what Balian and his lips and tongue were doing, but I couldn't.

"Balian." I breathed. "Please, answer it. I can't concentrate." His eyes flicked up and I saw a hint of anger as he stopped.

Balian growled as he got up out of bed and went in search of his cell phone. He dug around in his pants that were on the floor until he found it. It was still ringing.

"What?" Balian growled as he answered. There was some mumbling on the other end. "I am in the middle of something. Can this not wait?"

I sat up in bed and had a feeling that my adult play time was over.

"Kyriss, if you do not stop and tell me why you have interrupted me, I am hanging this phone up." There was more mumbling. "Kyriss!" Balian's voice sounded impatient. I had a feeling that if Kyriss didn't have a good enough reason to be calling, Balian was going to wring his neck.

I'm not sure what Kyriss said, but something changed in his face. He went from impatient to downright pissed.

"Why?" Balian asked. "Why must he speak with me now? He will see me tonight." More mumbling. Balian sighed. "Yes, you are right. Give me an hour and I will be there." Then he hung up. He tossed his cell onto the bed and frowned. "Something has come up. I am afraid I am needed elsewhere." He sat down on the side of the bed. "I am sorry."

"It's okay." I said.

I started to get up, but Balian grabbed me and wrapped his arms around me, pulling me onto his lap. Now I was straddling him. "It is not alright" he said kissing me. "But there is no way I can get out of it and stay with you." Then he kissed me hard and deep, one arm around my waist, and his other hand in my hair.

Damn, this man was just too cute. I wrapped my arms around his neck and moved even closer to him, fully knowing how easy it would be to convince him to ditch whoever and let me ride him instead. We were both naked and I could feel that he was ready despite the fact he'd just gone two minutes ago. I kissed him back as butterflies began to fly in my chest.

"Mind if I use your shower?" I asked as I pulled back.

"Of course. Anything you need is yours. There are extra tooth brushes in the second drawer on the right."

"Thanks." And I kissed him as I realized something. I realized that it could be easy to allow myself to love him. To say those three little words every day. It would be easy to come home to him every night and wake up next to him every morning. It seemed so easy that in a way it kind of scared me.

I pulled back and smiled as I got off the bed. I made my way into the bathroom. It was almost as big as the one I had back at home. The walls were painted a light gray, the tile was white with swirls of gray and black, the counter top was black with a white sink and stainless steel faucet, and the shower curtain matched the walls.

I opened the second drawer and picked out a purple toothbrush and after some searching found the toothpaste. I scrubbed my teeth and when I was done, came to a standstill. I didn't know what I was supposed to do with the toothbrush. Putting it in the holder with Balian's seemed weird, but throwing it away seemed wrong. So I made a compromise. I set it on the counter. I'd let him decide what to do with it.

I turned on the shower and climbed inside. The water was warm on my skin. I was halfway through washing when I felt arms wrap around my waist and lips press down on my shoulder. "What are you doing?" I asked turning around.

"Conserving water." Balian replied.

I laughed. "Liar."

He smiled. "I have decided that I need you one more time before you leave."

Memories of my hallucination . . . vision flashed through my mind. It was sort of like déjà vu. "I thought you didn't have the time?"

He pushed me against the wall and pressed himself against me. "Well, I guess it is time you show me how this quickie works."

An hour later, I was clean and satisfied. Balian's quickie turned out not to be so quick. And his one more time turned out to be twice. I walked out of the bathroom and picked up Balian's shirt from the floor and slipped it on. There weren't very many buttons left, but I buttoned the ones that were there.

I looked around the apartment and sighed. Despite my happy feeling I knew it wasn't going to last. I was going to have to go home soon and face a million questions. Suddenly I realized that I didn't want to go home. I wanted to stay here. I didn't feel like facing Stefan and his new attitude. Last night I told myself that no one had to know. But Stefan wasn't stupid. He might not know who I'd been with, but he'd know I'd been with someone.

I blew out a breath as I walked around the room. I stopped in front of a shelf on the wall. On it was a black picture frame with a black and white photograph of a girl inside. I'd never seen her before, but she was really pretty. She had curly black hair, flawless white skin, eyes that sparkled, and a smile that was breathtaking. I wasn't sure what decade it had been taken in, but she wore one of those dresses that came with a corset and she was riding a horse.

I frowned as I continued walking. I picked up my clothes as I made my way to the bed. I laid them down as something caught my eye. On one of the night stands by the bed, there was another picture frame and in it was another picture of the same girl who was riding a horse. But only this one was different.

She still had the same flawless skin, but her eyes seemed to be shining and sparkling with love for the man staring back at her. The man was Balian. His arm was around her waist and he was smiling and gazing at her with the same look of love as she did him. There was so much love in their eyes it was almost pouring out of the picture.

I don't know why, but I suddenly felt jealous. It was silly. I had no claim on Balian. We'd just had sex. Granted it was amazing sex at that, but just sex all the same. My jealousy over a man that wasn't even mine was just stupid. A waste of time and breath.

Balian came out of the bathroom, a towel wrapped around his waist and his chest looking very yummy. "Leaving so soon?"

"Yeah. I um . . . probably should go." I said. I didn't want to go, but I couldn't bring myself to say that. He nodded and looked kind of sad. Like he didn't want me to go either.

He crossed the room to me and my heart went thump, thump, thump. He stopped in front of me and pushed a strand of my wet black hair out of my face. "Can I see you again?"

I smiled and bit my lower lip. "Maybe. When?"

"Tonight. You could come by Illusions later and I could leave early and we could come back here, if you want."

It was a bad idea. "Okay. I'd like that."

Balian smiled and kissed me. "Then I will inform Chiron that you will be coming. It is a private party tonight. Invitation only."

"Okay. Then I'll see you tonight."

"Tonight."

He stepped back and I sat down on the bed and pulled my knees up. "So, who's the girl in all the pictures?" I asked allowing my curiosity to get the better of me.

The smile that had been on his face faltered. When he spoke, there was a hint of pain in his voice. "Would you get mad if I said I did not want to talk about her?"

I frowned, but shook my head no. It was clear from the sound of his voice that she was a sore spot.

I sat on the bed and watched Balian get dressed; black boxer briefs, black suit with a white dress shirt, black and blue tie, and black vest, belt, and shoes. I watched how his muscles moved as he put on his shirt. There was a sparkle in his eyes every time he caught me watching. When he was fully dressed, he put his cell phone and wallet in his pocket. He walked over to me and bent down, placing a kiss to my lips.

"I shall see you tonight." he said. "Feel free to stay as long as you like. Or if you want, you could stay here in this bed and wait for me. When I am done, I could come back and we could finish what we started."

I just smiled at him. It sounded so good, but I knew if I didn't at least show my face at the house, Stefan would go in a panic and come looking for me. I didn't have to check my phone to know he'd probably been the one calling.

I kissed him again and this time there was a little more heat behind it. I raised up on my knees as Balian's arms went around my waist, pulling me in closer and tighter to his body. There was a strength to it that suggested . . . I don't know, possession. Claiming.

I pulled back. "You should go." I said breathlessly. "If you don't, we're going to end up in this bed naked again. Then you're really going to be late."

"Yes, that would undoubtedly be unheard of." Balian said. There was a sarcastic and bitter note to his voice. "Tonight." He gave me one last kiss, then left.

I sat back down on the bed and sighed. I wasn't ready to go home and face the music of questions of where I'd been last night. But as I looked over at the night stand by the bed, the picture of Balian and the mysterious girl smiling at each other, I began having second thoughts.

Who was she? And why wouldn't Balian talk about her?

I rubbed my forehead and decided that it didn't matter. After tonight Balian would be a distant memory and nothing more.

I got dressed and put on my holster and was just about to walk out the door when Mischa padded up and gave a small whine. I bent down and petted her. "I'll be back tonight." I got up and she whined again as she scraped a paw on the door. At first I wasn't sure what she was doing, then I understood. "Oh." I said. I hooked her to her leash and grabbed the doggie bags and scooper that was by the door.

I took her for a little walk so she could do her business, when she was done I took her back to the apartment. I tossed the used bag in the trash, gave her a pat, then left. I got into the car and just sat there, not even bothering to put the key in and start it. I just sat there and tried to figure out where I was going. I didn't want to go home, but there really wasn't anywhere else I could go.

I looked down at my phone, it was flashing with unread texts and voice mails yet to be listened to. I sighed as I tapped the screen and brought my phone up to my ear. There were seven voice mails. Most from Stefan. "Hey babe, just wanted to see where you were. Saw that you didn't come home last night. Just wanted to make sure you were okay. Love you."

The last one was from Nate. "Hey sis." There was a chuckle. "Never thought I'd say that. Kind of weird. But anyway, dad's driving me nuts and I promised I'd call you. Hope you're okay. Talk to you later. Love you, bye."

I smiled a bit at that one. Yeah, it was weird hearing Nate call me sis. But it was nice. None of the voice mails were from Bronson, and I was kind of disappointed. Not that I wanted anyone else to die, I just wanted somewhere to go and something to do other than sitting here.

The texts were pretty much the same. Stefan was worried and wanted to make sure I was okay. Nate trying to make Stefan happy by texting me, but not really expecting a reply.

I sighed as I started feeling guilty about last night. Was this going to be my life? Moving back to Seattle and back into the house and having Stefan hovering and calculating my every move? I groaned as I realized that was exactly what was going to happen.

Yeah, there was no way in hell I could go back to that house right now. I needed time to get my head together and think. But where was I going to go?

My stomach growled giving me the answer I needed. Food. I needed food. Okay, I'd go find some food and eat and then figure out my next move.

I just hoped I'd like what my brain decided. If not, then I was screwed.

CHAPTER THIRTY

I ended up at the food court in the mall. While I was there, I did some retail therapy. And I knew I should have called Avery and invited her and Cristabel out to shop. Hell, I should have invited them and Sabine and Piper. But I didn't. I could feel one of my moods coming on. It wasn't anger, just a little remorse that would make me grumpy if forced to explain where I'd been all night. Which was why I hadn't invited my friends out to go shopping. Because I was sure word of my all night disappearance had been spread.

And until I could calm down a little, I wouldn't be going home.

I told myself as I walked through the stores that it was stupid for me to feel guilty for being happy about indulging last night . . . and this morning all the way into this afternoon. It had been my right to allow myself some reckless behavior. And it wasn't like this was going to lead to anything. Balian and I were just having fun. Soon I'd be back in Boston and finding out my fate.

And by some small chance I did get fired and moved back home? Well, there wasn't going to be any Balian and me. This was only a two night thing. After tonight, I was done. I would move on and so would he. There was no future for an angel and a demon. We were on opposite sides. And when the war started, we'd be enemies and have to kill each other. So no, no future there. It was just sex and a good time. Just me needing to get over Daniel.

I took pause at a shirt rack when I realized something. I didn't want to kill Balian. I didn't want to kill anyone. But I knew there would come a day soon, when I wouldn't have a choice. I could feel it in my bones. The war was coming. One day in the near future Samael was going to attack and I'd have to turn in my badge anyway. Because I'd have to start killing instead of protecting.

I shivered at the thought.

I continued to shop. I didn't really buy anything, just a few shirts and some lingerie from Victoria Secrets that had me imagining Balian taking it off of me.

After I was done with the mall, I took my bags to the car and put them in the back seat. I still didn't feel like going home so instead I decided to go for a walk. It was a nice spring day, the sun was out and it wasn't raining for a change. So I walked so that I could clear my head. I passed coffee shops and boutiques, the Space Needle was off in the distance.

I walked enjoying the nice warm day, my mind still going over everything that had happened last night with Balian. I could still feel his hands on my body. Last night had been the best night of my life and it made me kind of sad that after tonight, we wouldn't be seeing each other anymore. Although, that wasn't entirely true. I was sure that if I moved back to Seattle, I would be seeing him a lot in passing. And there was also my vision. I still didn't understand that. Why he was there and why my vision-self was in love with him.

That made no sense to me at all. But nothing of the vision did. And me being in love with Balian was one of a million things about the vision that confused me.

I was walking passed a cafe when I felt the sense of someone following me. A demon by the feel of it. I glanced over my shoulder, but saw no one I recognized, so I picked up my pace and ducked into an alley way. I peered around the corner and scanned the crowd of people. Everyone who came close felt human except one.

He was tall with dark hair and a demeanor that screamed demon. I waited until he was just about to walk pass the alley and I pounced. I grabbed him and pulled him into the alley and slammed him against one of the brick buildings. The surprise on his face was almost comical. He had not expected me to realize that he was following me. Stupid on his part.

I drew my gun from its holster and aimed in nice and steady at the demon. "Who are you and why were you following me?" I asked him, my voice gaining an edge.

The demon stared at me wide-eyed and swallowed hard. Yeah, he knew he was in deep ship. "I . . . ah . . ." He was stuttering.

"Spit it out."

"I think you're really hot." He spoke fast. "I saw you in Illusions and thought you were hot and wanted to ask you out."

I raised an eyebrow. "Do you usually stalk women you find hot and want to date? Am I going to have to watch you?" I didn't believe his story. Not even a little. Something else was going on here.

The demon shrugged. "What can I say, I like to get to know a girl before I ask her out." He gave a smile, but the look I gave him made it disappear.

"Give me your name."

"Jacob."

"Well, Jacob, here's the thing. I don't believe a damned thing coming out of your mouth. So, here is what you are going to do. You are either going to tell me the truth, or I'm going to shoot you." I was done playing games.

Jacob swallowed hard again and I could see his mind run through his options. This demon did not want to tell me, that was obvious. It was obvious in how wide his eyes were and the sudden fear that filled his body. "See, here is the thing. I can't tell you."

I frowned at his words. A thought crossed my mind and I grabbed his left arm and turned it over. His white skin was clean of any tattoos. He did not bare the mark.

"No mark, Jacob, which means you're low on the food chain. Expendable."

"Yeah, I'm expendable. So shoot me, because he won't care." Jacob said, his body relaxing into the brick wall, like he had decided that I was going to kill him and had come to terms with it.

"He who?" I asked him. He just gave me a look and didn't answer. And then I realized why and I felt confused. "Samael? Why would he want you to follow me?"

Jacob shrugged. "Don't know. He never said, I never asked, I just do what I am told. Samael tells me to follow someone I follow them."

Okay, hadn't seen that coming. It made me wonder if perhaps I hadn't been right to a point. If perhaps this case I was working on involved demons playing a game with me. But where did Samael fit into it? Was he behind this somehow? And if he was, then why? Maybe some of his demons had done something he didn't like and he was making an example out of them. After all, Ivan's death was very public and so were Kendra and Flynn's. But where did Delisa's death fit into it?

I had no idea how this all fit together, but I did know one thing. I didn't like Samael wanting me watched. "Okay, so this is what I want you to do." I said as I holstered my gun. "I'm letting you go, and I want you to tell Samael that I want him to back the fuck off. If I catch anymore of his men following me or watching me, I will kill them. Now repeat what I just said so that I know you heard me." He did word for word. "Good, now go before I change my mind and kill you instead."

Jacob ran out of there so fast it was almost funny. It was clear that he believed me.

Smart demon.

After that I went home and prepared myself for all of the fallout. I prayed that Stefan would just leave everything alone and not ask where I'd been all night. I had decided on my way home that I would keep the demon following me and why to myself. Stefan didn't need to know that. It would just cause him to worry and I didn't need him to worry. If this thing with Samael became of something, I would take care of it. So, I searched all of my memories of last night and this morning with Balian and found my happy bubbly mood.

I walked into the sitting room to find Stefan, Nate, and Matt all sitting on the sofa watching TV. They were laughing and drinking some beers. There was a half-eaten pizza on the coffee table.

"Hey babe." Stefan said. "Have a good day?"

"It was okay." I said. I set my bags down on the floor and sat down in one of the chairs. "Actually, my whole night was great. All the way through the morning and late afternoon."

"So," Stefan began. "where were you last night?"

Okay, so I guess I couldn't get out of this without explaining myself. Or could I? "I was out." There, that was a nice simple answer that gave nothing away.

"Yeah, kind of figured that out. But where did you go? I called this morning, but you never answered or returned my calls."

I sighed. "Stefan, I'm twenty-three and I'm a big girl. I can take care of myself. And trust me when I say, you really don't want to know where or who I was with last night. Because you're not going to like the answer."

Yeah, telling him I was with a demon last night . . . well, I had a feeling it wouldn't go over very well. Stefan might have an open mind about races mixing, but I didn't think he'd be okay knowing that I'd been with a demon.

"So, you were with someone?"

"Yes." I wasn't going to lie to him, just wasn't going to tell him with who.

"Are you going to see him again?" Stefan asked. When I didn't answer he just nodded. "Right. Well, just be careful. I don't want you getting hurt."

"I'm always careful." I said, my voice almost a whisper.

Damn, why was I feeling like I was a child being scolded by her father for doing something wrong? Probably because I was.

"Morgan." Stefan said. "Look at me."

I turned my eyes up to meet his, not realizing that I'd been looking down at the floor.

"I'm not mad at you. I'm just worried. You've just gotten out of a bad relationship. I don't want you getting hurt, that's all. You have no reason to feel guilty for what you did last night . . . with whoever it was with."

"I know. But why do I feel guilty?"

"Maybe because you've just gotten out of a relationship. Rebound sex has a way of making you feel like shit the next morning." Nate said, speaking for the first time.

I raised an eyebrow. "What would you know about rebound sex? You've had less long-term relationships than I have."

Nate smiled. "Remember that girl I dated after you moved to Boston?"

I nodded. "Yeah, her name was Addison. You dated for what, eight months?"

"Close, it was ten months. And I really liked her—everyone did. When she dumped me, I went on a little bender."

Matt laughed. "Little bender? Man, you drank more liquor and fucked more women in two weeks than a rock star does in a month."

Nate's smile widened. "Yeah, but the point is, I regretted it in the end. I still do."

"Does this mean I'm going to regret being with . . . him for the rest of my life?"

"Well, as I see it, it would depend" Matt said. "How do you feel about this guy? Is it just sex or is there something else?"

"I don't know. I guess it's just sex." I couldn't believe I was talking about this with them. Okay, Nate and Matt were one thing, but with Stefan? It was just weird.

"Good." Nate said. "If you were having feelings for him it would be worse. But since it's just sex that means no one's going to get hurt."

"Hey." Julian said walking into the room. "What's going on? Why does Morgan look like she wants to bolt from the room?"

If he only knew.

"We're talking about sex." Matt said.

Julian smiled. "Oh goodie. My favorite topic. So glad I stopped by."

I needed to change the subject. "How's Kelsey doing?" I asked.

Julian frowned and slumped his shoulders. "Not good. She's starting to have nightmares."

"I'm sorry. How are your parents handling it?"

"The best they can. Mom won't let her out of her sight. Dad . . . he's considering sneaking into the guy's hospital room and castrating him." Julian looked sad but seemed to brighten as his eyes fell on the pink bag by the chair. He took a few steps and picked it up. "What's this?"

"Nothing." I said, but it was too late. He was already reaching inside.

Julian smiled as he held up the white and black bra and panty set. He raised an eyebrow. "Who's the lucky bastard that gets to see you in this?"

"None of your damn business."

"Ah, so there is a lucky bastard after all. Anyone I know?"

I stood and took the undies away from him and put them back into the bag. "Doubt it. He's staying anonymous for his and your protection."

Julian smiled wide then. "Oh? Is he dangerous?"

I grabbed the other bag and my purse from the floor. "Maybe."

"Hot." Julian said as he wiggled his eyebrows.

I laughed. "Yeah, I guess. Hey, could you do me a favor? Could you and some of the others make a trip to Boston and get my stuff?"

"Sure. Is it in boxes?"

I shrugged. "Probably not. Most likely it's outside in the yard." I grabbed my keys and took off the house key and handed it to him. "Here, just in case.

I'll text you the address and Daniel's cell number. You might want to call first."

"Okay. I can do that."

"Thanks." I turned to go upstairs. "Now, if you'll excuse me, I need to go upstairs and get ready for a date with the dark side."

"Is this serious?" Stefan asked as I headed for the staircase.

I shook my head. "No. It's more like a . . . two nightstand."

"Oh, Morgan?" Julian said. "Just so you know, your secret is safe with me. And you're right, he should stay anonymous."

I stopped in my tracks and turned to look at him. I'm pretty sure the look on my face was priceless. "How do you kn . . . oh my God. I wasn't imagining it last night, was I?"

"No. I don't know how or why, but you were transmitting pretty loud last night. But all I have to say is, good choice."

Holy shit.

I stood there and bit my lower lip. "You didn't happen to hear . . . anything else, did you?" I was starting to feel mortified. If he told me he heard all of it, I was going to scream.

Julian smiled. "No, just heard your panicked indecision and his name. I put up a block after that. I was afraid I'd hear more than I really wanted."

"Oh, thank God."

"Yeah." he laughed. "But I was happy you listened to me. And now I'm going to give you another piece of advice. Go and get busy."

I laughed and went up to my room as I heard Matt ask Julian about details. I text Julian the address and Daniel's number, then I took a shower and did all of those girly things. I put on the lingerie and took my time finding the perfect outfit. I didn't want anything real dressy just in case I got a call about a body. It needed to look professional and sexy all at the same time. Something I could use for work and something that I could use to make Balian drool. So, I settled for a pair of black leather pants and a red silk top I'd bought at the mall today. I finished the look with a pair of black leather ankle boots and my shoulder holster. I left my hair down.

I threw some clean clothes into a duffle bag, grabbed my purse and keys, and headed back downstairs. Julian was sitting in a chair. He smiled when he saw the duffle bag. "Is this your way of saying don't wait up?"

I just smiled and made my way out the door. I put everything in the passenger's seat and got in. I drove to Illusions and parked in front of the building. Balian had said it was a private party, so I didn't have to worry about a line. I grabbed my purse and got out of the car and headed for the door and smiled at Chiron as I approached.

"Hey." I said. "My name should be on the list."

He nodded. "It is. Balian told me to expect you. Go on in."

I smiled at him and went inside. The club was the same as it had been the night I'd arrested Ivan. The music wasn't as loud, and the room was full of demons. Some were sitting and talking, others were on the dance floor. There was a sofa and two armchairs to one side of the room with a small coffee table.

Sitting on the sofa was the man with eyes like mine and a woman with long white blond hair. Sitting in one of the chairs was the man with red eyes. He smiled at me as I walked in that direction. He wasn't who I was looking at. Constantine was sitting in the other chair glaring at me. There was a tall woman standing next to him with long dark hair and eyes and mocha skin like his.

I was four feet away when he stood. "What the hell are you doing here? Who have you come to arrest now?"

I wanted to be mean and say you, but I didn't. Instead I smiled sweetly at him. "No one. I came to see Balian. Could you let him know I'm here?"

"And why would I do that . . ." His face began to turn pale. "Oh, don't tell me he's . . . of course he is." Constantine shook his head.

The woman who had been standing by the chair put her hand on his arm. She was really pretty. And very pregnant. "Con, who's this?"

I offered her my hand. "Special Agent Morgan Montgomery." I said.

Her face became cold as she said. "So, you're the one who broke my mate's ribs."

I smiled. "Well, he deserved it." I looked at Constantine. "Aren't you going to introduce me to your mate?"

He rolled his eyes. "Morgan, this is Valentina. My mate."

"It's nice to meet you. When are you due?"

"Three weeks. Thought I'd get out one last time before the baby comes."

I nodded. "Yeah, makes sense. Although, I could think of other places to go than a night club."

Constantine narrowed his eyes. "Go away. Whatever business you have with Balian, just stop it now and go away. He doesn't need someone like you."

"Like me? Is that an insult?" Yeah, I was baiting him, but it was fun.

I knew Constantine didn't like me, but I really didn't care. I hadn't come here to see him. I'd come to see Balian.

Constantine smiled. "Yes. I know your kind and you only want one thing. And once you have it, you'll be gone."

"I think you have me confused with a man. I'm not a love them and leave them kind of girl. Now, would you go and tell Balian I'm here before I have to re-break your ribs in front of your mate?"

He growled. "Fine."

"Good little wolf." I said as he walked away.

"That is very brave of you." The man with the red eyes said. "Standing up to a werewolf is usually not done."

I looked at the man and smiled. "Well, I'm not your usual kind of girl." And I walked away toward the half open door I assumed was Balian's office.

I leaned against the wall by the door and listened as the voices from inside drifted out. ". . . out of your damned mind?" Constantine had been saying. "She's a cop."

"Yes, I am aware of that. And your concern is?" Balian said.

"Don't do this. She's going to get you killed. I am begging you as your Lawyer and your friend, Balian, do not take her home with you tonight. Stop this before it even starts. Let me try to get you out of this stupid arrangement."

"You and I both know that it is not possible."

Arrangement? What the hell?

"Let me try. This girl—this whore is going to get you killed."

"I would be very careful what you say next." Balian said, his voice cold with a dangerous edge. "You are walking on a very thin sheet of ice and you have just crossed a line."

"I'm sorry." Constantine said. "But you don't know anything about her."

"And you do?"

"As a matter of fact, yeah. I've been checking her out. She doesn't have that great of a track record with men. And her mother—"

"Yes, I know about her mother. I know more about her than you think. I know what I am doing, Constantine. I know this woman and I—"

"Don't. Don't you dare say it."

"Why not if it is the truth?"

"Because it's not the truth."

I heard Balian sigh. "But it is. You know who she is. How could you believe she is not?" There was no answer. "See. Now leave. You and I will continue this conversation at another date."

"Balian . . ."

"Must I repeat myself?"

"No. I'm going. But I'm letting you know that I don't trust the fucking bitch." Constantine walked out and when he saw me, he said something in Spanish I was sure meant whore. Or maybe bitch.

I only smiled at him and watched as he went back to his mate who was now standing by Kyriss. Kyriss looked in my direction and smiled. He said something to Constantine and laughed at whatever was replied. A tall woman with milk chocolate skin walked up and wrapped her arms around Kyriss. She had long black hair and dark eyes. She was cute. Like Rihanna cute.

Kyriss kissed her and she smiled at something he said. She removed one arm from around his neck and placed the hand on Valentina's belly. The baby must have kicked because she smiled and gave a small giggle. Valentina's eyes flicked up and she caught me watching. She said something and the other girl looked up and planted her dark gaze on me and glared.

Wow, these women didn't even know me, and they had already decided that they hated me. But they weren't alone on that one. Tabitha and Vika stood by the bar and glared daggers into me.

"Morgan?" I turned to see Balian standing in the doorway. "You came. I was afraid you had changed your mind."

I shook my head. "Nope." I said with a smile as my soul began to sing a happy song.

Balian stepped out and wrapped his arms around me and kissed me. "I am glad. I will be with you in five minutes. I still have a few things I need to take care of."

"Okay. But I think I'll wait outside. I don't think I'm welcome here."

He frowned. "It will just take some time. They will come around."

He made it sound as if I was going to be staying in his life. Which wasn't going to happen.

"Maybe. But I'm still going to wait outside."

"Alright." Then he kissed me hard and deep. It almost made me weak in the knees, but I managed to pull away and walk toward the door without falling.

I passed opened mouths and wide eyes on my way out. I only smiled which only added to some of the glares. There were some people coming in as I was going out and I bumped into one of them. "Sorry." I said looking up at him.

He smiled all the way up to his glowing green eyes. "No problem." he said.

I smiled back as something chilling went through me. But I brushed it off and went outside. I had just stepped out the door when I saw him. Chiron was laying on the ground and he wasn't moving. I went over to him and bent down to check for a pulse. There wasn't any.

I cursed as I fished out my cell phone and called it in. Then I called Bronson.

"Bronson?" he said answering.

"Hey, remember when you said we could have the weekend off if the bad guy didn't kill anyone else?" I said.

There was a pause followed by a curse. "Who?"

"Chiron. The bouncer from Illusions. I was here to . . . see Balian and I was just leaving—"

"Wait. You went to see Balian? Why?"

"Personal reasons."

"Shit." he muttered. "Okay I've got to call Rafe and then we'll be there…"

I had stopped listening because something had caught my eye. I leaned in and studied Chiron's neck. I cursed as I realized his neck was broken and—oh my God.

"Bronson." I said trying not to panic and pulling out my gun. "I think the killer is here."

"What? Outside?"

"No. I think he's in Illusions." My heart began to pound as I suddenly realized why the man had given me chills. He was tall with dark hair and glowing green eyes. That fit the description the old lady had given at Kendra and Flynn's house.

"Are you sure?" he asked.

"Yes. I think I just ran into him on my way out. And Chiron's neck looks broken."

"Okay. Wait for backup. I'm on my way." And he hung up.

Okay, there was no way I was going to stand there and wait for backup. The bastard could have everyone dead before they got here. So, I made a decision. I put my purse back in the car and switched off the safety on my gun. I was going in there. Because there were innocent people in there and . . . Balian. Oh God, Balian was in there. My heart began to beat faster as panic washed over me. The realization that he was in there sealed it.

I walked to the door and asked for forgiveness for going against protocol. I went inside, my gun aimed and ready to shoot anyone and anything. When I made it inside I saw my bad guy. His back was to me, so he never saw me walk up behind him. I put the barrel of my gun to his head and said. "PCU, put your gun down and put your hands where I can see—"

I was hit from behind and fell to the floor, my gun skidded across the floor and I started to go for it when I heard the sound of a shotgun being cocked and someone say. "Go for that gun and I'll blow your fucking head off!"

I froze. A cold sweat washed over me as a face to the voice began to fill my head. No, this couldn't be. But when I turned around to face the man with the shotgun, I soon realized it was exactly who I didn't want it to be.

And who I least expected to be holding me at gun point.

CHAPTER THIRTY-ONE

didn't really panic; I was more confused than anything. I took in everything that was going on around me with such detail, that later when I looked back on it, I realized there had been no way for any other outcome. The things that had transpired that night had awaken something that should have never been awaken in the first place.

There were ten of them, dressed in black and each had a shotgun in their hands. They were spread throughout the room. Constantine and Kyriss were standing in front of Valentina and the dark-skinned woman, both of which looked scared as hell, but at the same time, looked ready for a fight. Tabitha and Vika were still standing by the bar, their fangs extended. On the floor by the chair he'd been sitting in, lay the man with the red eyes. He was bleeding on the forehead.

Shock ran through me as I tried to figure out how they'd been able to knock him out without being killed. He was one of Samael's men and he'd bared the mark. My eyes moved to the sofa and the man and woman were now standing in front of it. They looked neither worried nor scared. But the man did however looked pissed. There was an anger in his eyes that said these men were going to pay greatly for this. I recognized the look. I'd seen it a few times in the mirror. The familiarity of who he was washed over me, and I prayed I was wrong.

I darted my eyes around until I saw Balian. He was standing a few feet away from Kyriss. Our eyes locked and I saw fear. But it wasn't fear for himself, but for me. He asked me with his eyes if I was okay and I gave a small nod.

I turned back to the man with the shotgun and realized I had been way off. Theophilus held the shotgun in his hands like a pro. His blue green eyes swirled with unchecked anger. "Get up nice and slow." he said.

I slowly stood and raised my hands up without being told. I knew the drill and I knew what came next. "Is he alive?" I asked nodding toward the man on the floor.

"Yes."

"Mind if I check for myself?"

"Don't trust me?" he snapped.

"Well, you're the one with the shotgun holding everyone hostage. So, forgive me if my trust level is a little low."

Theophilius glared at me. "Fine, but no funny business. One wrong move—"

"I know, you'll blow my fucking head off." I said walking over and bending down to check red eyes pulse. I breathed a sigh of relief when I found one. "He's breathing."

"Told you."

I looked up at him. "How? How are you not dead? He bares the mark."

Theophilius smiled smugly as he rolled up his sleeve. On his left forearm there was a tattoo of gold angel wings with a sword through the middle of them. "Like it? It's new."

I didn't understand. "That doesn't tell me anything. It could just be a tattoo."

"But it is not." he said proudly. "I met this group of rogue angels a few months ago. They figured out a way to make the mark work in their favor. And as you can see, it worked."

Rogue angel group? That was the first time I'd ever heard of them. So, they must have been something new. If I ever made it out of here alive, I'd have to ask around.

"Why are you doing this?" I asked standing up. "Why did you do it?"

"You know why."

I shook my head. "No, I don't. I don't understand how you could brutally murder five people."

Theophilius gave another smug smile. "Don't you mean six?"

It took me a second before I understood what he was saying. "You knew she was pregnant."

"I knew."

"And you still killed her knowing she was going to have a baby?"

"Not just a baby, but his child!" he snarled, aiming the shotgun at me again. "I went to her that night and begged her to come home . . . with me. So, we could be together."

"But she said no because she was pregnant." I said, guessing what had happened.

He nodded. "Yes, but not at first. We had a little reunion against one of the buildings walls. After, she said we couldn't be together anymore because she loved him—a fucking vampire and she was having his child. So, I snapped. I didn't mean to do it, it just happened. But now . . . I know it was for the best. She was dishonoring her father and her family. And if she'd had that child . . . half-breeds are not done. We do not mix outside our species." His voice became angrier with every word he spoke, and I knew nothing good was going to come of this.

He'd killed Delisa as an honor killing/crime of passion. But what about the others? Theirs still made no sense. "What about Kendra Farris and Flynn Garwood? They did nothing to you, so why kill them?"

"Do you not know? Surely you did not forget that quickly?"

"I have no idea what you're talking about."

"Ila. I know she told you what happened to her."

I thought back to a few nights ago when I'd gotten a call from Ila Shaylee. I'd met her outside the gates of the fairy world, and she'd told me about a party she'd gone to where Ivan had had her drugged and raped.

"Okay, but what did they have to do with what happened to Ila?"

"Don't you see? Flynn is the one who'd raped her. So, my men and I raped his mate and made him watch so he'd know what it was like to feel helpless. To hear the one, he loved cry out his name and beg him to make it stop. To know if she was allowed to live, she'd be ruined, and no one would ever want her." His voice got a psychotic edge.

Oh my God. Everything started making so much sense to me. Kendra, Flynn, and Ivan's murders had nothing to do with Delisa's. Hers had been by chance—out of anger. But the other three . . . this had been about Ila all along. Ivan had had her drugged and raped and Flynn had been the one who'd done it. And since Kendra had been Flynn's mate, she'd shared the punishment.

And the punishment had been death. See, like I said, supernatural laws were messier than human.

"I see where you might think killing them was poetic justice, I really do. But killing them doesn't change anything. It won't fix it. It's only made you just as bad as them." I said, my voice calm. "You say you killed Flynn because he raped Ila, but how does raping Kendra fix it? Rape is rape. It doesn't matter how much you try to justify it."

"Maybe not, but Ivan and the rest deserved everything I did to them."

Something else started to click just then. "You were the one who sent those banshees." Now it was so obvious I cursed myself for not figuring it out sooner. Banshees were fairies and the only one who could call them up and control them, was another fairy.

He smiled. "Cool wasn't it? Not as easy as one would think, though."

I shook my head. "Actually, it wasn't. Banshees, really? Is that the best you could do?"

Theophilius walked up to me and pushed the shotgun into my chest as he snarled. "You haven't seen my finale yet." I had a bad feeling about this. "Take off your shirt."

I raised my eyebrows. "Excuse me?"

"It's for my finale. It's really going to be explosive. I have decided to rape every female here. And I think I'm going to start with you. Now remove your shirt."

"Go to hell." I said.

"One day." he said putting his shotgun in a holder behind his back. Then he pulled out an ugly looking double-edged dagger. "Now, remove your shirt or I'll do it for you."

"No!" Balian yelled taking a step forward. "Keep your hands off her. Or I swear, I will kill you. All of you."

The fairy beside him pushed his gun into his side. "Not another step." he said and Balian hissed.

Theophilius turned his head to look at Balian and smiled. "Aw, isn't that sweet, he's trying to save you." He turned back to me. "Don't you think that's sweet agent? He's willing to die for you. Why do you think that is? Have you been a naughty little girl, agent Montgomery? Have you been fucking the vampire?"

I said nothing as I locked eyes with Balian. I shook my head slightly no. I knew what he was thinking, and it was only going to get him killed.

"No?" Theophilius asked. He leaned in and nipped my earlobe. "I know what you are and who you are. I can smell him all over you. Can sense hell inside you. You are nothing but a fucking half-breed whore. I am going to take you in front of your little lover friend and make him watch. I will make him feel your pain along with his own. And when you start begging him to make it stop—to help you, that is when I will kill you."

This guy was crazy. He'd lost his damned mind. If he'd ever had one that is. I was betting on the latter.

I started walking backwards, away from him. There was no way in hell I was letting him or anyone else rape me without a fight.

Theophilius sighed as he handed the dagger to one of the fairies. "Go get her."

The fairy smiled as he put his shotgun in a sheath behind his back and took the blade. I continued to move backwards, trying to come up with a way out of this that wouldn't get me hurt or anyone killed who wasn't the bad guy. I came up blank.

The fairy came at me with a stalking stride, the purpose of pain in his eyes. He gripped the dagger tightly in his hand. He was about two steps away from me when it happened. First, there was a hiss, then a blur of movement. I was knocked down by the edge of impact of another body. I landed on the floor hard. I rolled over in time to see something so horrifying, that I was sure I'd have nightmares for the next six months.

Balian had the fairy by the hair, his fangs were extended, and he was hissing. The fairy had dropped the dagger and there was fear in his eyes. It happened fast, one second Balian was just holding the fairy by his hair, the next he was sinking his fangs into his throat, ripping it out. Blood ran down his face as he tossed him to the floor. In a matter of moments there were fairies on him, their fists and guns beating into him until he went down to his hands and knees.

Before I knew what was happening, Theophilius was on me, the dagger now in his hand. "Demissi!" he yelled. "Hold her down."

Demissi was there in a flash, his hands gripping my arms, holding them down. I fought against his hold and did my best to turn my body away from Theophilius. He might rape me, but I wasn't going to make it easy for him. I was going to fight even if it killed me.

Theophilius grabbed the hem of my shirt and began cutting it away with the dagger. But that wasn't the only thing it cut. I was still fighting, still trying to turn my body away from him. The dagger sliced my skin and I hissed at the pain. And that had been the wrong thing to do, because Balian had heard me cry out. There was more hissing, but not from me. I risked a glance in the direction of the hissing and saw Balian. And he looked murderous.

But there wasn't anything he could do. There were just too many fairies on him. And that, I think, is why he looked so angry. Balian was helpless to help me, to stop this from happening. The fairies were still beating him and my heart broke as I began to get my own anger.

A few feet away from him lay a demon. He was bleeding from somewhere on his body and I couldn't tell if he was breathing. I didn't know his name, but I still felt angry that he was hurt. I knew deep down that it was because he'd been trying to help Balian. And as I looked around the room for the second time that night, my anger grew to a new height. A group of demons stood in the back of the room pretty much the same way the men in the front were standing. The women behind them, as if they were protecting them.

None of the women looked scared. Actually, they looked pretty pissed off. There were hisses and growls coming from that side of the room.

I wondered silently if there was a way out of this. If there was a way, I could get these women out of here. Could I bluff Theophilius? I wasn't sure, but I had to try.

"Stop!" I yelled kicking out with my legs. "Just stop!"

The toe of my boot connected with Theophilius and he fell backwards onto the floor. When he righted himself, his eyes were blazing with anger. "You little—"

"No, stop." I said trying to turn over. "Just stop. Let . . . just let them go."

Theophilius tilted his head to the side. "What was that?" he asked in a clipped tone.

"You win. You can have me. I'll do whatever you want. I'll strip down right now and do you and your friends like any good whore would do. Just let them go."

"Who?"

"The women."

"No!" Balian said in a raspy voice. "No, Morgan. Please do not give in."

I ignored him as I slowly sat up and finished tearing what was left of my shirt and bra. My small breasts were revealed to the whole room. It was a good thing nudity didn't bother me, because if it had, I wouldn't have had the guts to sit there and let every man in the room stare at my breasts like they were some amazing find. I just hoped that Theophilius would take the bait. And by the way he was drooling I was pretty sure he was trying to picture his mouth on them.

"These are yours." I said. "All you have to do is let them go. And I'll do things to you and your men I haven't done to anyone in years."

Please oh please take the bait. I thought. All I needed was him preoccupied for a few minutes. And what better way than him trying to see if he could fit all of my breast into his mouth.

He seemed to think about it for a second and then said. "No."

"Then at least let Valentina go. She's pregnant and no use to you."

That seemed to perk him up. "Pregnant, huh?" And laughed. "Keenan, would you mind?"

A blond-haired fairy with grey eyes walked up to Valentina and half pulled half dragged her out from behind Constantine. She screamed and he yelled "NO!" When he started to move forward another fairy hit him with the back of his shotgun. He went down and Kyriss grabbed him by the arms trying to hold him back.

Theophilius smiled as he stood and turned toward Valentina, the dagger was still in his hand. "Let's see what's inside you." he said. I suddenly felt sick as I realized what he was about to do. When he put the tip of the blade to the top of her stomach and pushed down, I knew I had to do something. Anything to make this stop.

Demissi pulled me up from the floor and pinned my arms behind my back. Pain shot through me at the odd angle.

Valentina began to scream as blood started to run down her stomach. Constantine started to fight Kyriss's hold on him. Balian moved forward, still on his hands and knees, but stopped when a fairy with yellow eyes stepped in front of him. One of the fairy's grabbed a handful of his hair and jerked his head up. The fairy standing in front of him pushed his shotgun into Balian's throat.

Panic went through me as I locked eyes with the man with eyes like mine. His hands were in tight fists at his sides and the look of murder was written on his face. And that was when I made my decision. I couldn't let this go on any longer. I wasn't going to just stand by and watch as Theophilius cut Valentina's baby out of her. And I sure as hell wasn't going to watch them blow Balian's brains out either.

My eyes darted around the floor until they found my gun. It was maybe ten feet away. If I could get to it, then I could stop this. All I needed was a distraction.

And I got one.

Kyriss was still trying to hold Constantine back and Constantine was still fighting. A growl escaped his throat and I knew what he was going to do. And so, did Kyriss.

"Constantine no!" he yelled. "Please don't shift." But it was too late.

The growls became more ominous as his body began to change. I'd never seen a werewolf shift before and I prayed I never saw it again. It looked painful. Bones snapped and cracked as skin melted away to reveal fur.

Kyriss let Constantine go and stepped back in front of the dark-skinned girl protectively. "Whatever happens next, stay behind me." He said to the girl. "If I go down, fight like hell."

"I will." she replied.

I've seen pictures of black wolves in the wild. They weren't that pretty. But Constantine? He was . . . beautiful. He was solid black with glowing green eyes. And he was huge. I'm talking like the size of a horse huge. He stood on four legs, had a long fluffy tail, and sharp canine teeth. He trained his glowing green eyes at Theophilius and Keenan. The look in his eyes were neither human nor demon. Just animal. Like he'd been hunting all night and he'd found his prey.

And Theophilius and Keenan were definitely his prey.

Here's a lesson for anyone out there thinking about coming between a male and his mate. Don't. Because if you do, then you are either going to end up hurt or killed. And in this case, possibly eaten.

And by the looks of all these men, Kyriss, Constantine, Balian, and the man with eyes like mine, they weren't just protecting the women. But their women.

Constantine growled then lunged. A shot rang out and he fell to the floor as bullets from a shotgun hit him in the upper thigh. There was a barking whine and he landed hard. Blood poured out of the wound and I took my chance as everything became chaotic.

I moved my head forward, then pulled it back as fast and with as much strength as I could. Demissi yelped and let me go. I spun around and punched him, and he stumbled backward. He regained his balance and grabbed me by my hair and pulled. A split second later he threw me across the room and my head smacked the wall. I saw stars as I tried to regain my baring's. Demissi came at me and I ducked his blow and planted my fist in his stomach, and he bent over.

I made a run for it and dove for my gun, but it was no use. It was kicked out of my hands and slid to the other side of the room. I was kicked in the chest with a boot. Pain shot through me and I gasped for air as the wind was knocked out of me.

"You know," Theophilius snarled. "You're really starting to piss me off. Maybe I'll kill you first, then I'll rape you."

Ew! This man had just gone past crazy and went straight to insane. But after all, he was a psychopath so I really shouldn't have been surprised.

I took deep breaths as I got on my knees. "You're insane. Ever thought about medication?" That statement earned the end of his shotgun being smashed into my face. That hurt. I spit out blood. "Scratch the medication. Perhaps anger management."

He hit me again with the end of the gun. He hit and kicked me over and over again and didn't stop until there was the slightest sound of police sirens. Theophilius stepped back and looked around dumbfounded.

"Hear that." I wheezed. "It's over. You're not going to get away with this."

"Watch me." he said. "Haldar." One word was all he said and the fairy with yellow eyes made for the door.

I got back onto my knees and after several try's, managed to get to my feet. "It's over." I repeated with a wince. "Even if you manage to escape, there is no way in hell Samael is going to let you live. He will find you and your men and kill you and anyone else who might be involved. So, it's over one way or another." I breathed in deep and cursed. Something was broken.

I could hear yelling coming from the doorway followed by the sound of gun fire. Apparently Haldar was telling the police to stay back or they were going to kill everyone.

Yeah, that was original. I wonder if he thought of that on his own or saw it in a movie?

I risked a glance over at Valentina and my heart broke. Constantine was in his human form now and had somehow crawled over to Valentina despite his damaged leg and now he was holding his mate in his arms. Blood pulled under her as it poured from the wound in her stomach. Her eyes were open and glassy, and she was breathing. But not for long if she didn't get out of here and to a hospital soon.

A fairy walked over and handed Theophilius my gun and he put his shotgun back into the sheath behind his back. "Want to know what I think about Samael?" Theophilius asked. Before I had time to ask what, he hit me again, but this time it was with the end of my gun. I started to fall but caught myself on one of the bar stools. "Demissi!" he yelled. "You can have this one first." His voice was cold and so were his eyes as he trained the gun at me.

Demissi walked over and grabbed me by the hair and shoved me down onto the floor. He knelt down in front of me on his knees. I saw pure evil in his eyes. He was going to enjoy this. Enjoy hurting me. He undid his pants and pulled himself out. He was already hard.

"No!" Balian yelled. There was a crack like sound followed by a grunt. I turned my head to see Balian doubled over again. Blood was running down the side of his face.

I turned my head back around as I felt Demissi start tugging at my pants. I stared at him for what seemed like a long time but was really only a few seconds. If I'd been the only victim here, I might have not fought as hard. I was starting to feel weak. But the truth of it was, I wasn't going to be the only victim. Once they were done with me, they'd kill me and move on to someone else. So, I had to keep fighting no matter what.

I stared at Demissi and felt calm. I raised up one of my legs and took a painful deep breath as I shoved the spiky heel of my boot right through his groin. Demissi screamed. "Fucking bitch!" He crumpled to the floor in the fetal position. Blood poured from the wound I'd made in his manhood. "Bitch just cut my dick off!" Actually, I hadn't. He would heal, but right now it probably felt like I'd just cut it off. Theophilius kicked me and I felt something snap. If he kept this up, I wouldn't have any more ribs left to break.

"Enough!" yelled a man with a strong voice that sounded Italian. I looked up to see the dark teal eyed man. His hands were still in tight fists at his sides and murder was still written on his face. "Hit her one more time and I will call up the power of hell and Lucifer and I will destroy you in the very place you stand." There was so much power and authority in his voice, I was surprised Theophilius didn't drop his gun and fall to his knees. I would have if I hadn't already been laying on the floor.

The sound of his Italian accent sparked something inside me that I hadn't expected. It was familiarity and more. Much more. It came with a name and a knowledge that scared me more than the possibility of death.

I took a few shaky breaths and forced myself up onto my feet. It was slow going and very painful, but I did manage to stand. For how long, I didn't know.

"Shut up!" Theophilius yelled at Samael. "Don't you fucking move."

"Do not use that tone with me." Samael snapped.

Samael stood there and stared Theophilius down, almost daring him to do something stupid. And I'm pretty sure he would have if he hadn't turned his attention to a movement to his right. I turned to see Balian start to run towards Theophilius. I was surprised that he'd been able to get up from the floor, let alone run. But Balian was up, but he wasn't going to be fast enough. He'd taken just as much damage as I had.

It all happened in slow motion. Theophilius raised my gun and took aim at Balian. I yelled, "No!" my voice sounding so far away. I moved my feet and told them to move faster. The gun went off just as I threw myself at Balian. Bang, bang, bang. We fell to the floor. We landed with a thump. There was the slightest twinge of pain in my chest, but I ignored it. I didn't care about me at the moment. I only cared about Balian and his safety.

"Are you okay?" I asked, my breathing becoming shallow, harder to do.

"Yes. I am fine." he replied. "You?" His question made the twinge of pain in my chest worse. I gasped as I rolled off him. There was so much blood coming from my chest that I wasn't sure where it was all coming from. Balian sat up on his knees and pressed his hands on my chest. "No, no, no! Not again." he screamed. "I will not lose you. Not like this."

I felt confused and didn't understand what he was talking about. But it was obvious that he'd lost someone in one of his previous lives and it had left scars. And my being shot was bringing back a bad memory I could only suspect he'd been trying to forget. My heart broke as I realized I was probably going to die here in his arms and become another bad memory.

I stared up at him and tried to smile but failed. I was just in too much pain for assuring him I was alright. But it didn't matter, because we both knew I wasn't alright. I'd just been shot in the chest and if the bullet hit my heart . . . well, I wouldn't have to worry about losing my badge.

There was the sound of more gun fire. I turned my head in time to see a chunk of the ceiling fall to the floor. Glass broke and I heard more guns going off.

"What . . . what's happening?" I asked in a shaky breath.

"Shoot out." Balian replied pulling me behind a knocked over table.

I closed my eyes as I heard the sounds of guns being fired, werewolves growling, and vampires hissing. The demons were starting to fight back.

I felt light as a feather and was just about to pass out when I heard someone scream my name. "Morgan!" I opened my eyes to see Balian. "Morgan, darling, do not go to sleep. Open your eyes." he said. I didn't want to open my eyes. I wanted to feel light again.

I raised a hand up to his cheek and he covered it with his own hand. He turned his head slightly and placed a soft kiss to my palm. One silver tear ran down his face. I was dying and we both knew it. He shook his head. "No, no, no." His voice cracked, began to sound a bit unstable. "No, please no. Morgan, no. You have to stay . . . here . . . with me." But we both knew his plea was useless.

I closed my eyes again.

"Morgan!" It was Bronson this time. "Morgan look at me." he said as he removed Balian's suit jacket back to look at the wound. When had he taken it off? "We need an ambulance now!"

"Val . . . Valentina . . . s-she needs . . . it w-worse." I stammered. "Her . . . b-baby . . ." I was gasping for air at this point. Whether it was from the broken ribs or the gun shot, I wasn't sure.

Carlos was there and pushed Balian back. I would have yelled at him for it, but I couldn't speak anymore. I turned my head and found Balian staring at me ghost faced. I stretched out my arm and he grabbed my hand and held onto it as if letting go would mean death. His death. Mine.

The last thing I remember was staring into those dark blue eyes that reminded me of the sky at night and seeing a piece of my soul reflecting back at me.

CHAPTER THIRTY-TWO

I could hear faint voices of people around me. I could only make out bits and pieces of what they were saying. Some told me that they loved me, others begged me to wake up. I didn't understand why they were saying these things and when my eyes fluttered open, I became even more confused.

I was laying on my back and the room was all white. Well, I guess it was, I could only see the ceiling. I heard something beeping and the sound of arguing. Angry voices carried into the room. Although with as loud as they were, they could have been inside the room or down the hall. They were that loud.

"This is your fault." A woman said harshly. It took me about a second to place the voice. Camille.

"How is this my fault?" Stefan returned with his own harsh sounding voice. "I didn't tell her to go to Illusions and get shot."

"No, but you encouraged her to go after a career that is dangerous and unladylike." Her voice was full of scorn as she continued to blame Stefan for what had happened to me. Typical. This was so typical of Camille.

Stefan gave a laugh that was both mocking and harsh. "I'm sorry, but I thought it was a parent's job to encourage their children to want to be all they can be and have a mind of their own. Oh, I forgot, you like to encourage your children to never leave and do as you want and think."

"You little piece of shit. You have no right to accuse me of such a thing.

And Morgan isn't your child. She never has been. Your blood does not run in her veins."

"I know that. But we both know whose blood does run in her veins. So, tell me this, Camille. Would you have liked him to step up all those years ago and raised her instead of me? Would you have wanted to have fought with him over Morgan?"

There was nothing but silence. Who was he talking about? My father? I got a sudden memory of something that had happen or something I had realized. I remembered going to Illusions to see Balian for an all-night . . . booty call. I remember everything going to hell after that. I'd been held hostage and I'd been shot. But it was before that. The part when I realized that the man with eyes like mine was Samael. But not just Samael the most powerful and feared demon, but someone else.

"That's what I thought." Stefan said. "So, before you start blaming me for how she turned out, remember, it could have been worse. I did my best with her. And frankly, I think I did a damned good job given the circumstances."

There was more talking but lower, so I couldn't hear what was being said. But when a warm soft hand gripped mine, I forgot all about the voices. As a reflex, I squeezed the hand holding mine. There was a jerk and the sound of a chair being scooted back. Two seconds later Nate's face appeared, and I could see the worry on it start to disappear. His bright blue eyes were bloodshot, like he'd been crying. His wavy blond hair was disheveled.

"Morgan?" he said as he brushed a hand over my hair.

"Nate." I croaked. My voice was barely a whisper. My throat felt so dry it was almost sore.

"Dad!" Nate yelled. "Morgan's awake."

There were footsteps and then Stefan was in the room. He didn't look any better than Nate did. He took one look at me and I swear I saw tears glisten in his eyes. "I'll get the doctor." Then he ran out of the room.

Camille stormed in followed by Asher. I found it odd that I hadn't heard him speak. What was up with that? All the times I'd remembered Camille and her ranting, he'd always been there to tell her to let it go. So why not this time? What had changed?

Camille came in with the look of seniority all over her face with a hint of worried grandmother. The last was fake and the first was just wishful thinking and her being conceded. She had always had a stick up her ass for as long as I could remember. Had always accused people of acting the same way she did. But with Camille, it was okay when she did it, justifiable. But when someone else acted that way, they were being disrespectful and selfish.

My grandmother was one of those people who acted as if nothing ever bothered them. But you knew they were thinking really hard on the situation and bitching in their head about it.

Yeah, that was Camille alright.

Asher stepped around Camille and walked over to the bed. "Hey, you're awake. How do you feel?"

I thought about it. "Sore. Like I've been shot in the chest."

He smiled. "You were shot in the chest."

"This is no time for jokes." Camille snapped. "This is serious. Morgan could have died."

"Yeah, that would have been terrible." I said with a mocking whisper.

Stefan walked in with a man at that moment. He had dark greying hair and pale green eyes. "Miss Montgomery. I see you've come back to the land of the living. I'm Dr. Stevens." he said with a smile. "How do you feel?"

"Sore." I said. "My chest is sore and my throats dry."

He nodded as a nurse came in. "Okay. I need to check your chest, so I need everyone out."

Everyone stepped out and Dr. Stevens started checking the wound on my chest. To no surprise from me, I was completely healed with no scarring. But the doctor took in a breath and just shook his head as if he didn't believe his eyes.

"No matter how long I treat supernaturals, I will never get use to this." he muttered.

"Which part?" I asked.

"All of it. The healing process, the sleep required. All of it. I treated a werewolf a year ago with a serious head injury. He slept for over a week. If he'd been human, I would have said he was in a coma. And you, well, you were very lucky agent Montgomery. If you'd been human, you might have died. Hell, I've lost patients with less serious injuries than yours. Do you know how lucky you are?"

I shrugged. "No. And I could have died just like any human, doctor. The bullet hit my chest and I'm guessing it was damned close to my heart."

He nodded. "Yes. In fact, it did hit your heart. You had to be revived twice. Once on the way here and the second on the operating table." he paused. "I was certain I was going to have to go out and tell your family I was sorry for their loss."

"But you didn't."

"No, I didn't. You pulled out."

See, this was the whole problem with humans treating supernaturals. They didn't understand the healing process. Couldn't comprehend it. They were used to humans bleeding and dying of serious injuries. The chance of a supernatural dying in a human hospital over their injuries was one out of a thousand. Maybe more. We were harder to kill. It took more for us to die and it frustrated the humans. It didn't take much for them to die and they grew old. We didn't.

I would never see wrinkles or have greying hair. I would never grow old and die. If I ever got married and had children and they had children, well, I would still look the same. Never a day over twenty-five or thirty.

"So, what is the verdict?" I asked. "When can I go home?"

Dr. Stevens stood there, his face a mask of uneasiness. He didn't want to be here, and he didn't like what he was about to say. "Well, if you'd been human, I'd say in a week. Maybe two."

"But I'm not human. So, stop comparing me to them." My voice was hard and cold. Colder than it had ever been. A part of me didn't like being compared to a weak human. It was a dark part, that I'd only felt a few times since coming home.

He didn't flinch once. "Do you not realize that you've been asleep for a week straight?"

A week, huh? Well, it could have been worse. "And your point is, doctor?"

"I'm not sure. It's just . . . I'm fascinated and scared."

"Of me?" I phrased it as a question, because I didn't want it to sound as if I was accusing him of anything.

"Yes." he said honestly. "Yes, I'm scared of you. All of you. You're faster and stronger and harder to kill than me. And I mean no offence."

"None taken." I said. "I understand. Trust me. So, when can I go home?"

"Well, I guess since you have no wound . . . tomorrow."

I breathed a sigh of relief. I got to sleep in my bed tomorrow night.

The nurse that was in the room opened the door and I heard her say that everyone could come in. A few seconds later Nate came in followed by the gang. Julian walked in with a big smile on his face. But his eyes showed how he really felt; they were blood shot just like Nate's. "Hey there beautiful." he said walking in.

"Hey." I said.

My eyes moved around the room from one face to the other. Camille still seemed angry and Asher seemed off somehow. I couldn't put my finger on what was wrong, but something told me I was better off not knowing. A small part of me felt that that was unacceptable. This wasn't the Asher I knew and loved. Not the uncle who on more than one occasion took up for me. No, this Asher was distant, and I knew whatever was going on, it had something to do with Camille. And he was taking her side.

Stefan stood to the far side of the room with Mariska standing next to him. She regarded me with caution. But who could really blame her? The last time I saw her I was yelling and mad about her and Stefan wanting a baby. I needed to apologize to both of them about that. But I'd do that later. Right now, I just wanted to enjoy my family.

I continued to scan the faces. Most of them were the same, worried and relieved. When my gaze fell on Piper my heart almost stopped. There was a hint of pain in her expression. "Piper, are you okay?" I asked her.

She nodded. "I'm fine." she was lying. I knew she was in pain just being here. I knew she was feeling the emotions of every patient in the building.

I moved my eyes to Sabine. She looked worn out. My eyes moved to Matt and I frowned. I knew Sabine had a thing for him, but did he? I hoped if he did, he'd make a move. God knew at least one of us needed to have a happy ending with love. And why not Sabine? She was a good person. She was beautiful and smart and funny. And she deserved to be with a good man like Matt.

"What are you thinking about so hard?" Alec asked.

My eyes found him, and I smiled. "Nothing. So, where's Kaydan and Alexi?"

No one said anything for a long moment, and in the end, it was Matt who answered. "Kaydan was here earlier. He and Alexi left. He . . . he just needs some time."

"Time for what?"

"Do I really have to answer that?"

Well . . . I guess he didn't. I already knew that answer anyway. Kaydan was trying to deal with my rejection.

"Guess not." I whispered.

There was a small knock on the door, and we all turned to see Kyriss standing in the doorway. He wore faded jeans low on his hips, a white T-shirt, and an uneasy expression on his face. In his hands he held a clear vase full of white lilies.

"What the hell are you doing here?" Nate snapped.

Kyriss raised up a hand, palm up. "Hey, this wasn't my idea. The only way I could get him to stay in that hospital bed, was to agree to come check on her."

There were a few groans throughout the room. What was I missing? Who was Kyriss talking about?

"What's going on?" I asked.

Kyriss raised an eyebrow. "You didn't tell her?"

Stefan sighed. "No, we didn't tell her. She's been through too much already and she just woke up. I didn't want her getting upset."

Okay, what the hell . . . "Tell me what? Would someone please tell me what the hell is going on?"

Stefan glared at Kyriss. "Thank you. Thank you very fucking much. It isn't enough that your kind have already wrecked one family's life, but you must continue to wreck mine. Seriously, why don't you and the rest of them leave us alone? We don't bother anyone."

There was a deafening silence. I'd never seen this side of Stefan before. He'd always had an openness to everything and everyone. I'd never heard him say a cruel word about anyone in all the years he raised me.

Then as if he'd realized what he'd said, Stefan dropped his head. "I'm sorry." he said. "I shouldn't have said that. I . . . I haven't been sleeping. It's been a long week and honestly, I'm not mad at you—with any of you."

Kyriss smiled not seeming bothered or even offended by what Stefan had said. "I get it. Don't worry, I've spent most of my time going from one hospital room to another this week. You were lucky you only had one. And I understand you wanting to protect her, but she needs to know."

Stefan nodded. "You're right." He turned to me and I saw guilt in his eyes. "Morgan . . ."

"I'll tell her." Nate said. He sat on the end of the bed and took my hand in his. I suddenly felt cold. "Morgan, when you came to the hospital you were hurt really bad." he paused. "What do you remember about being shot?"

I shrugged. "Not much. I remember the gun going off three times."

Nate nodded. "Well, all three bullets found a place to go. Two hit you. The other bullet . . . it hit Balian."

I stared at him and just shook my head. "No, no that's not possible. He was fine. I saw him. He was hurt, but not like that." I was beginning to ramble. "I . . . I have to see him." I started to throw off the blanket, but Nate put a hand to my shoulder and pushed me back down.

"No. You're not going anywhere."

"But I have to. I have to make sure he's okay. That he's not dead."

"He's not dead." Kyriss said. "He's fine. The doctor thinks there was too much adrenaline running through his body. That's why no one noticed. He passed out after you did. Guess he didn't have to be such a tough bastard anymore." He smiled. "But anyway, I promised Balian I would check on you and give you these." He held up the lilies. Stefan walked over and took them.

"They're beautiful." I said with a smile. "Tell Balian I said thank you."

"I will." he said. Just then there was the sound of a crash. Kyriss sighed deeply. "If you'll excuse me, I need to go kick a hardheaded demon's ass." Then he turned and left. A few beats later I heard him say. "What the fuck do you think you're doing? Get your ass back in that bed before I call Grady to come give you a hard sedative." There was a mumbled reply I couldn't hear. Then I heard Kyriss say, "Hard, heavy, doesn't really matter. As long as it knocks you the hell out."

I smiled to myself. It was kind of funny that someone like Kyriss was able to kick Balian's ass. I would have liked to have been a fly on the wall. But Stefan was right. I had been through too much. I needed to stay here and rest up. Although, everything inside of me wanted to get out of this bed and go to Balian. There was a part of me that needed to see that he was okay for myself.

Stefan set the lilies on the small window seal, then grabbed the small white card and handed it to me. I took it. The handwriting was neat and perfect. But then again, everything about him was perfect.

A kiss so bittersweet, that only it shall wake thy sleeping beauty. Get well soon, darling. With love, Balian

His words were sweet, and I had to stop myself from smiling. I couldn't let anyone know what I'd done with Balian. Not because I was ashamed of it, but because I didn't need a lecture. Balian was a demon/vampire and I was an angel. I knew what would happen if these people found out I'd slept with him. I'd never hear the end of it. Fairies weren't the only ones who didn't mix their bloodlines.

"That was nice of Balian. To make sure I was okay." I said, hoping my voice wouldn't give me away. "And to send flowers. That was sweet."

"I think it's inappropriate." Camille snapped. "That thing had no right to send you flowers. Or to even send one of his minions to deliver them."

I suddenly felt angry. Although, I was surprised that Camille had been able to keep her mouth shut this long. "He's not a thing. He's a man and he has a name."

"Morgan, he's a demon and a vampire." Camille said with venom in her voice.

"He's my friend."

"They are no one's friend. They only think about themselves. He is dangerous and I forbid you from seeing him."

My mouth fell open. "Forbid me? I'm not an adolescent teenager, Camille. I'm twenty-three going on twenty-four. You're not my mother and you don't tell me who I can be friends with and can't. I make my own decisions. I always have."

"I know that. And that is the whole problem. Maybe if Stefan had controlled you more, you wouldn't have spun your life out of control and gotten yourself shot."

I nodded. "Yeah, you're all about the control. You even tell Grayson and the others what to do. Did you know he wants to be a PCU agent?"

"The whole family knows."

I looked to Asher, who had been silent. "And you're letting her tell your son what he can and cannot be? Why?"

"Because being a cop is dangerous." he said. "You being shot is proof of that."

"And you don't think the war won't be? God, Asher, he's a year older than me."

"The war will be different. My child won't be killed by some lunatic with a gun."

"No, just a lunatic with a sword." I snapped. "Are you really going to stand there and take Camille's side in this?"

Asher nodded. "Yes. Balian Ivanski isn't the man for you. He's dangerous and we don't mix our bloodlines. It just isn't done. Pursuing a relationship with him would be dishonoring the family."

"Get out." Nate spat. "Both of you. Get out. You have no right to stand there and tell Morgan who she can and cannot be with. You are only here out of show. Now get out before I throw you out."

Camille and Asher turned their fiery gazes to Stefan. "Are you really going to allow your offspring to talk to us like that?" Camille asked.

Stefan nodded. "Yeah, I am. In fact, if you don't leave, I might be tempted to throw you out myself."

Camille looked at me. "If we leave this room in this manner, you will no longer be allowed any contact with the family."

I laid there and wanted to scream. Why were they acting this way? "I guess you should send my best to Avery, Cristabel, and Grayson."

She gave a huff and then she and Asher stormed out of the room almost running into Elliott and Rafe as they were coming in.

Rafe smiled when he saw that I was awake. "Family feud?"

"Yeah, something like that." I said with my own smile.

Someone cleared their throat and we all turned our heads to see Dr. Stevens standing in the room pale faced. I'd forgotten about him. "Sorry to interrupt."

Stefan gave a small chuckle. I knew why and I smiled. A human had just witnessed a supernatural fight. I was sure he'd be drinking later. I was just glad no one had used any powers. "No need." Stefan said. "How is Morgan? When can we take her home?"

"Um . . . right. She's in top shape. The wound is fully healed and there isn't any scarring. She can go home tomorrow."

"Great. That's what I want to hear."

Dr. Stevens nodded. "Well, I'll be showing myself out." And then he practically ran out of the room.

I smiled and looked at Elliott and Rafe. "So, what did I miss?" I asked. I was curious to find out what had happened to Theophilius and his friends. I wanted to know the outcome of that horrible night that had almost cost me my life.

"Nothing much." Elliott said. "Four of the ten fairies were killed. Theophilius gave himself up and wrote out a complete confession and is waiting for transfer to Pandora State Prison. King Androcles is claiming he knew nothing about it."

I nodded. "So, what about Valentina? How is she?"

"Not sure. Last we heard; she was fine." Rafe said. "Her mate won't let us in to see her."

I wasn't really surprised that Constantine was up and about. He wasn't human. If he had, he'd have either died from the blood loss or lost his leg and been in the hospital for a long time. "Makes sense." I said hoping everything really was okay. "So now what?"

Elliott looked down. "I need to hear your side. We've talked to the others. Or at least the ones who would talk. Our side of it is pretty standard. Once Rafe and I arrived we were put on the back burner. That fairy started shooting at us. I didn't think we were ever going to get in there."

"They had to get a sniper to take him out." Rafe said, then smiled. "I was pretty sure Elliott was going to punch the head guy in charge."

Elliott shrugged. "Hey, one of my people were in that building." He smiled and I smiled back. "So, let's hear it."

"Okay." I said and went to telling him about what had happened. But I left out a few details about why I had been there. I told him I'd been there to check up on some things. That Balian had finally broke his silence about what he knew about the murders. Granted, he'd done that the night before, so I hadn't exactly lied. Just told him it was the night of the shooting. After I was done, I wrote out a report and signed it.

Part of me hoped if Balian had given his own statement that the part between us matched.

"Thanks." Elliott said. "Despite the outcome, I'm really glad I got the chance to work with you. I hope everything goes alright in Boston. And . . . without you, I'm not sure we would've solved this."

I smiled. "I was happy to help."

They stayed a bit longer and then left. I was sad to see them go. I didn't want this to be the last time I saw them. I'd liked working with them too. Elliott and Rafe were nice people and I hoped I'd get to see them again on better circumstances.

Stefan informed me that he'd talked to the head of the board. Since I'd been shot and was out for the count, I was given leave. But once I woke up and was released from the hospital, I was expected to be in Boston four days later.

The nurse came in soon after that and made everyone leave. I said my goodbyes and gave hugs and kisses to everyone. Nate was the last to leave. He sat in the chair by the bed and held my hand.

"You scared the shit out of me." he said. "I didn't think you were ever going to wake up. I thought I was never going to see your eyes again or hear your voice."

I gave him a small smile. "I'm sorry." This was a new and softer side of Nate I had to get used to. And once I was fired and moved back home, I'd have the time.

Nate shook his head. "Don't be. It wasn't your fault. These things happen. And if you hadn't done what you did . . . more innocent people would have died."

It was the truth and there was no denying it. If I hadn't started the fight with Theophilius, then he would've cut Valentina's baby out of her. If I hadn't jumped in front of Balian . . . well, that part didn't count seeing as he'd still caught a bullet.

"I know."

He brushed a hand over my hair. "Well, I guess I should go before the nurse comes back."

"Okay. See you in the morning."

Nate kissed me on the forehead. "See you tomorrow. Now get some rest."

I watched him leave and wondered how we'd gotten to this point. We had spent all that time as kids and as teenagers fighting over everything. He'd hated me, but now he didn't. I was his sister and I could tell that he was taking his big brother job very seriously.

My mind went to Balian. I hoped he was okay, that Kyriss had been telling me the truth. That he hadn't thought me too weak to handle the truth of how Balian really was. But I knew if he'd said that Balian was on his death bed, I wouldn't have stayed in this bed. I cared about him. My feelings for him were all scrambled, but I did care. That much was for sure. As for the other such as love? Well, I didn't know about that. We'd just met, it was too early for that.

I yawned. I was tired and I told myself I had all the time in the world to sort this out later. Right now, I just wanted to sleep. And sleep I did.

CHAPTER THIRTY-THREE

I woke up a few hours later with Balian firmly planted on my mind. I wondered how he was doing. Had Kyriss given me the truth? I thought so, but there was this part of me that wanted to see for myself. Granted, I'd heard him out in the hall of the hospital, but that didn't mean he was okay. That crash had indicated that he was weak.

I laid there in the somewhat darkened room and wondered if I was allowed to see him. I still had an IV in my arm and still wore the little hospital gown. And yes, I was still somewhat weak myself. But none of that mattered right now. I needed to see him. I needed to know that he was alright. And seeing it with my own eyes was what I needed. At least that was what I told myself.

I sat up slowly and slid my legs over the side of the bed. I tied the little strings of the gown closed so I wouldn't show off my backside. Then very slowly I stood and made my way out of the room and down the hall in the direction Kyriss had earlier that day. I put most of my weight on the IV poll as I walked. I wasn't sure what room Balian was in, so I looked in all the rooms.

I passed two rooms before I had to stop and lean on the wall by the third. I hadn't peeked in yet, but I hadn't needed to. Voices drifted out.

"What are you still doing here, Kyriss?" Balian asked in a quiet voice.

"I wanted to make sure you were okay. You seemed to almost lose your mind when you woke up. And earlier today. So, forgive me if I'm worried about my best friend." It was Kyriss

Best friend? Kyriss was Balian's best friend? I stood there and thought about that. Yeah, that made sense.

"I am fine."

"Are you? Because it seems to me that you're about two steps from losing it."

Balian sighed and I could hear sadness when he spoke. "I was so scared that I was going to lose her—that I had lost her. I cannot go through that again. I do not think I would survive it with my mind in tacked. I just . . . I needed to see her, to know that she was alive with my own eyes."

I knew the feeling.

"I know. And that's why I'm here. But man, I don't think that would have gone over very well. Hell, Stefan and Nate barely tolerated me checking in on her. I really doubt they would have been okay with you." There was a long pause. I frowned knowing that he was right. There would have been no way Stefan would have let Balian see me. "She's prettier than I thought she would be." Kyriss said after a long moment.

"Yes, that she is." Balian said. "Constantine is trying to find a way to take her away from me."

Kyriss gave a soft chuckle, no bitterness in his voice. "I know, but he's only worried about you. We all are. Just give him and the others some time. They'll come around."

"Will they? She saved Valentina and still, all I receive is coldness and hatred. Morgan has done nothing to them and still they hate her."

Well, guess that answered one question.

"Valentina is upset because Morgan got the upper hand of her mate. Constantine is pissed off because he got beaten up by a hot girl. And that he was accused of murder."

"And what is Zena's problem?" Balian asked.

"She's Valentina's best friend. You know how girls like to stick together."

"And you? Are you going to hold what she did to Gregory over her head? Are you going to hate her because she took up for an innocent girl who she looks at like a younger sister?"

"No. If I'd gotten there, I would have kicked his ass. I won't make excuses for him. I know what he did was wrong. And so, does he. He has to live with what he did for the rest of his life. I mean, I would like to say it was because he lost his mother, but hell, Balian, kids lose their parents every day. So no, I won't get mad at her over it. And besides, holding grudges isn't me. And it's hard staying mad at a hot girl." There was silence for a heartbeat. "Balian, are you . . . going to go through with it? With what you agreed?"

There was silence. Then Balian spoke. "I am not sure. There are so many things to consider now."

"Like what?"

Balian sighed. "I—she told me this in confidence, Kyriss. You cannot expect me to tell you."

"No, guess not. But whatever it is—"

"She is broken." Balian said cutting Kyriss off.

"And you're not?"

"My situation is different. I had people to care for me. Morgan . . . has no one. Not really. I think she believes she can deal with this on her own and because of that . . . it has left her broken."

"Well, as I see it." Kyriss said. "You're perfect for each other. You're both broken and damaged. And neither of you trust very many people and you keep your thoughts to yourself. Maybe together you can put your broken pieces together and make a whole."

Balian sighed and I could tell he was smiling. "Perhaps. But no matter what, I will not lose her. I will find a way to keep her."

"Yeah, I know." Kyriss said. "But the thing is, will she want you to keep her? I mean, you have to consider what she'll want too. She may not like you that much. You might have been bad in bed." Then he laughed.

There was more silence and I imagined a puzzled looking Balian in deep thought. Truth was, I did like him, and he was good in bed.

I wasn't sure what was on Balian's face, but it made Kyriss laugh a little harder. "Hey, I'm joking. She probably adores you and thinks you're a total Sex God."

Balian chuckled. "Perhaps. It is getting late. You should probably go home. Zena is waiting for you."

"Okay. But you have to promise me you'll think about what I said. About what she might want. It's not going to be just you in that relationship."

"I promise. Now go."

There was the sound of a chair being pushed back. "Just get some sleep and no sneaking off to the hot agent's room."

I straightened. I had to make a decision. I could either take that moment to go inside the room or just stand there and get caught eavesdropping. I didn't want Balian to know I'd been listening in on his private conversation. So, I slowly moved my feet forward and stepped in the doorway.

Balian and Kyriss turned their heads toward me. I was breathing a little hard and God only knew what I must have looked like.

"Morgan?" Balian said. "What are you doing up?"

"I...I needed to see you." I said. Yeah, and if Stefan found out that I was out of my hospital bed, he would go off the deep end. I'd get a good chew out. But what Stefan didn't know wouldn't kill him.

I leaned on the IV poll and took a deep breath. I was beginning to feel tired and a tad bit sore. "Are you alright?" Balian asked. "You should not be up walking around. You should be in bed resting."

Kyriss chuckled a bit at that. "Yeah and said vampire should take his own advice. Here," he said walking toward me. "You should probably sit before you fall over. You look like shit."

"Thanks." I said as he led me over to the chair he'd been sitting in only moments before. Kyriss put an arm around my shoulders and I regrettably leaned against him for support.

"Kyriss be nice." Balian chided.

"I am being nice. See. I'm helping her to a chair, and not once have I tried picturing her naked. Well, now I have, but that doesn't count. You should be proud of me. I'm making progress in becoming a gentleman."

I couldn't help it, I laughed. Kyriss reminded me of Julian. Always trying to make light of a situation. Always making me laugh.

Balian smiled. "Yes, I am proud. I know how much you want to be just like me."

I sat down as Kyriss smiled back. "Yeah, you're such an influence. Before you know it, I'll be wearing designer suits and speaking with profound punctuation of words. I might even adopt your Russian accent." Kyriss raised an eyebrow and very smoothly changed his voice to an impersonation of Balian's Russian accent. "I am Balian Ivanski, great lover of women. Come darling, let me enrapture you in desire."

"I do not talk like that. And I hardly believe myself to be a great lover of women." There was laughter in Balian's voice. "But perhaps I could become a great lover of one woman." He moved his dark blue eyes toward me, and they became very, very warm.

I suddenly wanted to get in next to him and get lost in his kiss and his touch. To just lay there in his arms and forget everything and everyone. But I couldn't. We didn't know each other that well. Granted, we'd slept together, but that didn't mean it was okay to snuggle up next to him. I didn't understand my feelings toward Balian, and until I did, there would be no snuggling.

Someone cleared their throat and I blinked, remembering that we weren't alone. Kyriss looked from me to Balian and grinned. "Um, guess I should be going. Zena's waiting. And uh, I can see you two need to be alone."

Balian nodded. "Yes. Thank you."

I smiled at Kyriss. "Yeah, thanks. And thanks for not holding a grudge against me."

Kyriss looked at me for a second, then gave me a look that said he knew I'd been listening. He gave a half-grin and shrugged. "No problem. I have a thing for hot tough chicks. And you, agent Morgan Montgomery, are a hot tough chick. And any woman who is willing to stand in a room full of men half naked and offer herself up to a psychopathic rapist, in order to save a room full of women she doesn't know, is badass. So, we're cool."

I realized then that I liked Kyriss. And if anything ever managed to work between me and Balian, and we somehow became a couple, Kyriss would become my friend too.

I smiled. "Yeah, that's me. Miss Badass."

Kyriss chuckled. "See you guys later." Then he left, leaving Balian and I alone in the room.

I scooted the chair up a bit. The room was dark, the only light was from the outside lights that were shining through the window. Seeing Balian gave me peace of mind that he was okay. I'd been so afraid that Kyriss had lied to me I suddenly realized.

"How are you feeling?" Balian asked.

"I'm feeling better. You?"

"Yes, the same. I have been awake for two days." He frowned. "No, that is not true. I awoke two days ago but was forced back to sleep. I have only been awake for maybe a day. I get to go home tomorrow if I behave and follow doctor's orders." Something passed through his eyes like he was remembering something unpleasant.

I offered him my hand and he took it. I watched as he raised his other hand and lightly brushed his fingers across my wrist. His touch sent sparks through my body and brought back memories of the night in his bed.

I swallowed hard. "Um, thanks for the lilies."

"You are welcome." he said, still brushing his fingers over my wrist. "So, when can you go home?"

"Tomorrow."

"That is excellent news."

I smiled. I stared at him and wondered who he really was. I knew almost nothing about him. I knew he was a demon/vampire and that he owned Illusions and Insidious. But I didn't know where he'd grown up or if he had any brothers or sisters. I mean, it was safe to assume he'd grew up in Russia, but I could be wrong.

"How old are you?" I asked without thinking.

Balian gave me a questioning look. "Why would you want to know that?"

I shrugged. "I'm just curious. I know nothing about you."

He smiled as he nodded. "I am not sure exactly on my age. I was created in the beginning with time itself."

I raised an eyebrow. "I'm not following. Are you saying—"

"I was created in heaven with all of the other angels." he said cutting me off.

My mouth almost dropped open. "So, you're a fallen angel."

"Yes. My wings were white at one time."

Wow, Balian was a fallen angel. Which explained his power. Why it had seemed so old and terrifying.

"You do not know how much I want you to climb into this bed with me and let me hold you right now."

I bit my lower lip. "Yeah, I do. But it would be a bad idea. There's too many wires."

"I could think of a work around." There was a hint of a suggestion in his voice that said that he wasn't just talking about me lying next to him.

I smiled but shook my head. "No, I don't think that would be wise. Besides, what if Kyriss came back in here or someone else. They might get the wrong idea."

"Or they might get the right one." he said with a devilish grin.

My cheeks warmed for a minute. What if Stefan came back to the hospital to check up on me and found that I wasn't in my room? What if he found me in here with Balian—laying next to him in bed, his arms around me? Or worse, what if Kaydan got past some stuff and stopped by and happened to see me in Balian's arms?

I shook my head. I didn't need that image stuck in it. I focused back to Balian. He brushed his thumb across my knuckles as his face fell. I could see he wanted to say something. "Balian, what's wrong?" I asked with a frown hoping that he hadn't sensed my sudden uneasiness.

He sighed. "You took a bullet for me." He closed his eyes and shook his head as if he could shake away whatever he was seeing.

I put my hand over his. "Hey, it's okay."

He opened his eyes. "No, it is not. I am a man. It is my job to save you. Not the other way around." He stopped and took a deep breath. "I am sorry. That sounded arrogant and sexist."

I bit back a smile. "Yeah, a little. But if it makes you feel better, you caught your own bullet. And you did save me. You killed that fairy, remember?"

Balian nodded. "I suppose I did."

Images of Balian ripping that fairy's throat out rushed through my brain. I needed to find a new topic before I was reliving that nightmare. "So, how's Valentina? I've been thinking about her and the baby."

"She is doing extremely well. Constantine took her and their son home a few days ago." He picked up a cell phone that was lying on the side table. He took his hand from mine and tapped on the screen a few times and did some scrolling. I wasn't surprised to hear that Constantine was out of the hospital. He was a supernatural and a werewolf on top of it. If he'd been human, he would have lost his leg and have been in the hospital for weeks. "Here." Balian said. "This is Felipe."

I looked at the picture on the phone and my heart melted. Felipe was probably the most adorable baby I'd ever seen. He had the same mocha skin as his parents. His lips were full, and he had a small nose that was just adorable. His eyes were dark brown like Valentina's but were Constantine all the way. I could tell just by looking at him, that he was going to grow up to be a heart throb.

"He's adorable." I said. "Tell Constantine and Valentina I said congratulations."

"I will." Balian said putting his phone back on the table. I yawned and winced as I stretched. "I see I am wearing you out. You should go back to your room and rest."

"No." I protested. "Not yet. I want to stay."

He eyed me with curiosity. "Is that what you want?"

I nodded. "Yes. It's what I want. I just want to stay for just a little while longer."

Balian nodded and I saw relief fill his eyes. He hadn't wanted me to leave either, but he was trying to be a gentleman about it. It was cute.

We talked for about a half hour after that about nothing in particular. Just random topics. I filled him in on how the case had ended with Theophilius giving a confession. I told him about how Stefan and Mariska were planning to have a baby and how I needed to apologize for my outburst. He listened the whole time and only spoke when he had something wise to say.

The whole time I wished there was a way for us—a future. I liked Balian and he seemed like he liked me too. It was a nice change from the past few months. But there was no way. If I got to keep my badge, I'd have to move away. And I wasn't cut out for long distance relationships. But if I got fired and moved back home . . . well, I hate saying this, but there still was no future for us. He was a demon and I was an angel.

At best we could be friends. But since we'd slept together, I didn't see that happening either.

Before Balian fell asleep I said. "I'm sorry about our date."

Balian brushed a finger over the skin of my wrist. "It is alright. There will be other dates. And for the record, I was planning on dining you."

I smiled. "Do you think we would have made it to the island to eat?"

He gave a soft chuckle. "Yes, darling, but I cannot say it would have been to eat." He brought my hand up to his lips and pressed them down on my skin. "Goodnight, little orchid."

"Goodnight Balian." I sat there in the dark and watched him sleep.

CHAPTER THIRTY-FOUR

I *stood in a meadow. There were* wildflowers of every color all around me. My long black hair whipped around as the wind blew hard. The bright blue sky turned dark as a dark cloud passed. The hair on the back of my neck stood up on end as the cloud grew closer.

I didn't know what was going on, but something told me it wasn't good. Maybe it was instinct, but I couldn't help but think it was time. But time for what?

In the distance I saw a figure walking toward me. It was a man by the looks of it. He was tall and had short black hair. He wore a dark grey suit, and the closer he came to me, the more I realized I knew him. It was the man from my visions. The man with eyes like mine. Samael.

He stopped in front of me and smiled. It was a nice smile, full of promise and something that looked like danger. He screamed bad boy and bad news. But there was also something intriguing about him too. I couldn't put my finger on it, but it was there. Something almost familiar about him other than the fact that he'd been in my visions. Some unwritten connection between us.

"Who are you?" I asked already knowing the answer but wanting to hear it from him.

He smiled even wider. "I am the man you've been looking for all your life." he said in an accent that sounded Italian. And now that I looked at him, I could see the Italian features. He wasn't bad looking. He was around twenty-five or thirty. But I didn't know what he meant about being the man I'd been looking for my whole life. I wasn't looking for a man.

"I don't understand." I said.

He stepped closer. "You will . . . in time." He leaned in and kissed both of my cheeks and the top of my forehead. "It will come to you." He pulled back and stared into my eyes. "You look so much like your mother, mia figlia bella."

Before I could ask him what he meant by that, he turned around and walked away and the dream faded.

"Morgan." A soft voice whispered as a hand shook my shoulder. "Morgan, wake up babe."

I opened my eyes and blinked, not sure where I was at first. Then it came back to me. I sat up slowly and winced when I saw Stefan and Nate. I was still in Balian's room. I must have fallen asleep. My head had been laying on Balian's hospital bed. I looked at Stefan and Nate and bit my lower lip as I saw suspicion in their eyes.

Great, I'd been caught after all.

I sat there and waited for the lecture, for Stefan to start ranting about how I was weak and still healing and in no condition to move around. It was true of course. And I was surprised when he just stayed quiet.

I looked over at Balian. He was still sleeping. I wondered if maybe I should wake him up.

I stretched out my hand and grabbed his and squeezed. I might as well get this over with. He opened his eyes and blinked a few times before they made contact with mine. He smiled sleepily. "Good morning." he said as he brought my hand up to his lips and pressed them down into a kiss. "Did you sleep well?"

I smiled. "Yes. You?"

"Yes, it was a wonderful sleep. I dreamt of you."

I laughed. "I wish I could say the same, but it would be a lie. But I'm happy you slept well."

Balian smiled at me and his gaze became warm. I knew that look. It was the look he'd given me the night we'd slept together. He wanted more than just to hold my hand. Balian had woken up in the mood. But his warm look disappeared when he saw Stefan and Nate standing in the room. "Hello Stefan. Nathaniel. What a surprise seeing you here."

Nate stayed quiet, but Stefan spoke. "We came to get Morgan, but she wasn't in her room."

"And you thought to look for her in here." Balian gave a smile that did not reach his eyes. "It must be hard on you Stefan, to know that she would . . . come to me even after you told her not to."

Stefan gave him a hard look and I was sure he was doing his best to keep his temper in check. Whatever was going on between them was making me feel uneasy. Balian had referred to Stefan by his name, as if he'd known him. Which made sense, since they seemed to be in the middle of a power struggle.

Balian chuckled when Stefan said nothing. "Do not worry old friend, my intentions are strictly honorable."

"Somehow I really doubt that."

I raised an eyebrow. "You two know each other?"

"Yes." Balian said with a nod. "A very long time ago, love."

I looked over at Stefan and he nodded. "Yeah, I know him. And trust me when I say, I try my best every day to forget it."

Balian's laugh was harsh. "Yes, I am sure."

Stefan ignored him and looked at me. "You need to come back to your room, Morgan. It's time to take you home."

I nodded. "Okay. Just give me a minute."

Stefan started to open his mouth, but Nate put a hand on his shoulder. "Go ahead dad and get Morgan discharged. I'll stay and help her to her room."

I could see that he wanted to say something, but he didn't. He just nodded and walked out.

Nate looked at me and smiled. "I'll just be right outside when you're ready."

I nodded and watched him leave. I turned back to Balian and smiled uneasily, not sure of what to say. Balian smiled back at me. "You know, it is a shame that I am in this hospital bed and you are hurt as well."

I smiled. Apparently, he didn't have any problems finding anything to say. "Yeah, a real bummer."

He brushed his fingers up and down my arm. "Maybe once we get out of here, we could make plans to see each other again."

I wanted to tell him no, that that wasn't a possibility, but I couldn't.

My throat closed up and I almost choked on the words. I don't know why, because there was no future for us. Agreeing to see him again would only make the inevitable harder. But what my brain was telling me and what my heart wanted, were two very different things. My mind was telling me to be reasonable and careful. I'd already broke one heart by refusing him what he wanted. But my heart was telling me to go for it. What was the worst that could happen?

I knew the answer to that. Heart break and anger toward me. Balian had been my rebound sex. It had been good. Really good. Probably the best sex I'd ever had. But I wasn't about to risk hurting him just because I wanted another...night with him. One more hit of...heroin. And that was exactly what he would be. I would tell myself that I needed one more night—one more hit, and that's how it would start. Balian would turn out to be a drug for me.

A very addicting and dangerous drug.

I started to open my mouth to tell him I didn't think it was a good idea, when Constantine walked into the room. He stopped in his tracks, and just stared at mine and Balian's clasped hands. I saw anger roll into his eyes like storm clouds. He leaned into his cane and just shook his head. "What the fuck are you doing in Balian's room? Don't you think you've caused enough pain?"

I opened my mouth to tell Constantine that it was none of his damn business, when Balian broke me off. He leveled his dark blue eyes at Constantine with his own storm of anger. "You will not speak to Morgan in that manner."

Constantine glared at Balian and growled. "I will speak to her however I damn well please. That bitch," He pointed a finger at me. "has done nothing but bring pain to all of us since the night she came back to Seattle. You're my friend and I will not sit back and watch you make the biggest fucking mistake of your life."

I couldn't handle it any longer. "I haven't brought anyone pain." I said. Well, there was Kaydan, but he didn't need to know about him.

Constantine turned his fiery gaze toward me. "I wasn't talking to you whore."

"And I'm not a whore either." I said, not allowing him to get to me. "I'm a woman. And I'm also a cop. Didn't your mother ever teach you any manners growing up?"

"And didn't yours ever teach you to not play with demons? Oh, that's right, she ran off. Guess she felt that you were ruining her life too."

His words cut me like a knife. I felt tears sting my eyes, but I choked them back. There was no way in hell I was letting him know that he'd gotten to me. I was stronger than most gave me credit for. Yeah, his words hurt, but I wouldn't let them bring me down to his level.

"Enough!" Balian practically yelled it. "Constantine for the last time, you will not speak to Morgan in that manner. Do not make me repeat it a third time. If I must, you will not like the outcome. Must I remind you of my old job?"

"You wouldn't." Constantine breathed.

"Oh, I would. The fact that you believe that our friendship would spare you my wrath in that way, is your downfall. I mean it Constantine, do not press me. I would not enjoy it, but I would do it."

I had no idea what Balian was talking about but had a feeling that I was better off not knowing.

Nate stuck his head in. "Is everything okay? I heard yelling."

Balian nodded. "Yes, everything is fine. But I believe it is time you escorted Morgan back to her room. Constantine and I have much to discuss in the way of manners."

A part of me didn't want to leave. I felt that if I stayed, it would save Constantine from whatever fate Balian had planned for him. Although, he was still weak from his injuries, so I didn't think he could do much. But by the expression on Constantine's face, I figured it didn't matter how weak or hurt Balian was. For a moment he seemed afraid of what was going to happen now or later. I slowly stood and bent down and pressed a kiss to Balian's cheek. "See you around." I said.

Balian gave me a longing look as he said. "Feel better little orchid. I . . . will be thinking about you."

I nodded then reluctantly pulled away and left the room with Nate's help.

"Do I even want to ask?" Nate asked me after we left Balian's room.

I shook my head. "Not if you don't want me to lie to you."

"Good point."

We got back to my hospital room and Nate helped me sit down on the bed. No farther than I'd walked had made me tired. This recovery stuff really sucked.

Nate stared at me and acted as if he wanted to say or maybe ask me something. But he didn't. Instead he picked up a duffle bag from the floor and set it on the bed. "I grabbed you some clothes." He started pulling out clothes; a pair of pink running shorts, a black tank top, and matching pink bra and panties. I felt my cheeks warm at the thought of Nate going through my drawers and looking at my undies. Nate caught me blushing and smiled. "Don't worry. I didn't look at anything. Not really. Just looked enough to make sure everything . . . matched."

My cheeks got hotter. "Right. That's a relief." I said and smiled.

Nate nodded. "Good. Now here's something to really make you worry. Julian, Dylan, and Alec went to Boston with a U-Haul to get your stuff. From what I understand from Julian, Daniel is going to be there, because he wants to make sure they take only 'your shit' and nothing else."

He was right, I did start to worry. I knew how much of an asshole Daniel was and probably was going to be. And I knew how protective Julian and the other two were when it came to me. Nate and I might not have gotten along when we were kids or teenagers, but his friends had always looked at me like their baby sister.

Once when I was sixteen and Kaydan and I were taking a break from our relationship, I had dated this guy from school. One-night things had gotten physical in a bad way. We'd gotten into a fight about something stupid and I found out he had a temper. Around the same time he hit me, Nate and his friends had come home to see it go down. And well, let's just say that was the last time we went out, because Julian and the other four took turns pounding their fists into his face and asking him how he liked it.

After I remember Julian saying, *"Next time you decide to beat some defenseless girl, you might want to make sure she doesn't have five brothers who are bigger and stronger than you."* The kid had left the house crying, but hey, he deserved it. And that had been the last time I'd dealt with some guy treating me badly, because the kid had spread the word that I had psychotic brothers.

Now I only hoped Daniel wouldn't say or do anything stupid, because he may not like how Julian and the others reply.

"That's a scary thought." I said. "I hope nothing bad happens."

"Yeah, Daniel getting the shit beat out of him would be tragic." Nate said with a laugh.

"I'm serious, Nate."

"Me too. I only wish I was there to help."

"Nate, this is not funny. I'm already in enough trouble as it is. Julian and the others beating the shit out of Daniel would be bad. It could be what costs me my job." I had no doubt Daniel would use it to fuel the fire that was already burning.

Nate's face sobered. "I'm sorry. Want me to text Julian and tell him to behave?"

I shook my head. "No."

A nurse came in and smiled. "I came to help you get dressed." She looked at Nate and pointed a finger at the door. "You need to leave young man."

Nate smiled at her. "Okay, I'll just wait outside."

The nurse helped me get into my clothes. It was a slow and painful experience. I might have been somewhat immortal and healed a hell of a lot faster than a human, but I was still in some pain. After my clothes were on, the nurse helped me back onto the bed so I could lay down. She smiled and left the room as Nate and Stefan came in.

Stefan was pushing a wheelchair and smiled. But I could still see a million questions running through his head. And I bet twenty bucks that most of them had to do with Balian. "Ready to go home?"

I nodded. "You have no idea."

Nate laughed. "Yeah, he does. Remember, it hasn't been that long since he was in here." He walked over to the bed and pulled out a pair of black ballet flats. "I thought these would be better than sneakers."

I smiled. "Thanks." I said as Nate slipped them on my feet and helped me out of the bed and into the wheelchair. I hissed a little at the pain it brought.

"Sorry." Nate said.

"No, it's fine."

"Okay," Stefan said turning the chair around. "Let's get you home so you can rest. Everyone will be there later."

I was seeing a repeat of the night I came home. "Everyone?"

"Yep. Everyone." Nate said grabbing the duffle from the bed and walking over and picking up the lilies from the window. "Dad pulled out all the stops. Steaks on the grill and cold beer. But not for you, you're on pain medication. But you can have a steak. I don't think it would be bad for the medication. Plus, there's going to be potato salad and bean salad. Which you have to cook, because dad and I can't cook worth shit."

"My God." I said. "I only got shot. Not coming home from war."

"Yeah dad, she's not coming home from war."

Stefan laughed out right. "Oh, my children. How I love you both. You two are my pride and joys."

"Now he's getting sappy." Nate said. "Good going, Morgan."

I turned my head back in time to see Stefan wrap his arm around Nate and plant a kiss on his cheek. "Even if you are two hundred, you will always be my baby boy."

Nate pulled away and stuck his tongue out. "Eck." But he was smiling.

I laughed. This was the Stefan I remembered, that Stefan from my childhood. Never afraid to embarrass his children in public. This was a fun Stefan who loved to joke. I hated fighting with him about anything, which was why I was going to wait until later to ask him about the one thing that was sure to cause a fight. Right now, I just wanted to enjoy this happy man who was having fun picking on his two grown children.

Later, much later, there would be time to fight. And I wasn't looking forward to it. But I had to know. I needed to know if I was right and why he'd kept it from me. I just hoped he wouldn't lie to me and would tell me the truth this time and that it wouldn't cause friction in our relationship. I didn't want to lose him over this. I loved Stefan too much for that. No matter what, he was my father even if he wasn't. But it was time that I knew the truth.

CHAPTER THRITY-FIVE

When *Stefan and Nate took me* home, I slowly made my way upstairs to my room, where I proceeded to kick off my shoes and climb into bed. The car ride home had worn me out and if I was going to have to see everyone and be in a good mood, then I was going to need a nap.

I crawled under the covers as there was a small knock on the door. It opened and Nate stuck his head in. "Hey, just wanted to make sure you didn't need anything."

"Just sleep." I said with a yawn. "Getting shot is a bitch, but recovery is a drag."

Nate smiled. "Give yourself a few more days. You'll be you soon."

"I know. I'm just whining."

He nodded. "I'm going to the store to get the stuff. Did you need anything while I'm there?"

I shook my head. "Nope, I'm good. I'm just going to sleep for a few hours."

"Okay. Dad's downstairs if you need him."

"Thanks." I said with a smile. "The only thing I may need is a wakeup call."

Nate laughed. "I'll tell him. Get some rest." Then he closed the door.

I laid there and it didn't take long for sleep to claim me. I was out and I highly doubted anything was going to be able to wake me anytime soon.

A few hours later I felt cool fingers brushing my cheek, pushing my hair out from my face and tucking it behind my ear. "Morgan, sweetie." Stefan's voice was soft and creasing. "Babe, it's six. Time to get up."

I stirred and groaned. "Ten more minutes." I mumbled.

Stefan chuckled. "That's what you use to do every time I got you up for school. It didn't work then and it's not going to work now."

I gave a sleepy smile and rolled over onto my back. "I know. The only time it did work was when I woke up with the flu."

He cringed. "Yeah, I hated it when you were sick."

He wasn't joking. The first time I got the flu after my mom had left, I remember Stefan saying, *"Damn you Lauren. Damn you to hell."* It had only gotten worse when Nate had gotten it too. Poor Stefan, he'd had his hands full that week. Luckily Sofia and Tamsin had helped him.

I'd gotten the flu three times that year and I could still hear Stefan and Nate fighting. *"What do you want me to do?"* Nate had snapped at his father.

"Help me!" Stefan had yelled back. *"Help me with Morgan. I can't do this on my own. I need to go out and make a paycheck."*

"Why not go get Sofia or Tamsin?"

"Nathaniel, I cannot always go running to them every time Morgan gets sick. You're here and it wouldn't hurt you to help me take care of her." Stefan's voice had cracked, and I knew he was two seconds from having a breakdown. The woman he'd loved had up and left in the middle of the night and left him her daughter. So, it was understandable.

After that, Nate had been a little nicer to me. He helped Stefan take care of me along with Julian and the gang. Julian had made a joke about playing doctor and the naughty patient. I hadn't really understood but I remember laughing.

And who would have known that only seven years later it would be me and Stefan fighting because I would turn into one of those uncontrollable teenagers with a high sexual drive.

I stared up at Stefan and smiled. "I'm sorry."

"For what?" he asked.

"For everything. All the shit I put you through."

"You weren't that bad."

"Yes, I was. And you know it." I sat up and winced at the pain.

"Are you okay? Where's the pain medication the doctor gave you?" Stefan asked.

I shook my head. "I don't need it. I'll be fine."

Stefan gave me one of those looks that only a parent can pull off. "Morgan." His voice was stern and a bit demanding.

I sighed. "In the drawer." I pointed at my nightstand.

He opened it and pulled out the bottle that was laying next to my gun and cell phone. He got up and went to the bathroom and came back with a glass of water. I took it and the pill he gave me.

"There. Happy now?" I asked.

"Yes." he said triumphantly.

I rolled my eyes and got out of bed. I went into the bathroom and did my business and brushed my teeth. When I was done, I made my way downstairs and into the kitchen. Stefan followed me all the way and sat down at the island and watched me as if I was going to fall or start screaming in pain. I ignored him best I could as I started peeling potatoes.

My mind wondered off as Balian's face popped into my head. That night at his apartment had been one of the best nights of my life. And last night . . . last night had been good too. But I knew it did me no good picturing a life with him in it. I was leaving for Boston in a few days and that was that. There was no future for us. But that didn't stop my brain from going there and forming a picture of a life with a man I could never have.

I shook my head and scolded myself for allowing the picture to form.

My mind changed subjects and I was suddenly thinking about the case I'd been helping Elliott and Rafe on. It might have been solved, but something about it still bothered me. Or well, two things still bothered me. The first I could do nothing about now and the second I could.

"Stefan." I said. "Can I ask you something?"

"Sure. Anything." he said.

"When I was at Illusions and Theophilius held me and everyone hostage, he said something strange. He told me that he met this group of angels that learned how to use Samael's mark against him. He called them rogue angels."

"Rogue angels?"

I nodded. "Yeah. He had this tattoo on his left forearm that was supposed to be the same thing only it was wings and a sword."

Stefan shook his head. "I find that very hard to believe."

"I don't. I saw it Stefan and I know it worked, because they knocked out a demon, I know bares the mark. I never saw it happen, but I saw him on the floor unconscious. So, my question is this, have you ever heard of rogue angels?"

"No. Never. This is something new. I've never heard of angels going rogue. I mean, what are they rebelling from? Other angels? Not likely. But if this group really does exist, then this is very bad."

"Hey, I have the steaks on." Nate said walking into the kitchen. He took one look at me and Stefan and frowned. "What's wrong?"

"Nothing good." Stefan said and began telling Nate everything I'd told him.

Nate sat at the island and his frowned deepened. "I don't like it. If there really are angels out there with their own version of the mark, then that means they could start killing demons who bare the original mark. And that's bad for everyone, because we all know Samael's just looking for any reason to start the war."

Yeah, and that was exactly the problem I was having with this. I saw the look that had crossed Samael's face when Theophilius had spilled the beans about the rogue angels and the mark. There was murder and something darker in his eyes. Nothing good was going to come from that knowledge.

And speaking of knowledge, I looked at Stefan and Nate and knew since we were having this great bonding moment, I should probably tell them about the baby and my job. I should tell them because they were my family more than anyone else in this world. I could tell them and make them promise not to say anything. And I knew they would because they both loved me enough to keep the secret.

But as I started to open my mouth to tell them, Cam and Sofia came into the kitchen followed by Mariska. I might have told them anyway with Cam and Sofia there, but I couldn't do it with Mariska in the room. I didn't know her enough to confide in her just yet.

They walked in with smiles and Sofia and Cam gave me hugs, while Mariska kept her distance. It was as well, seeing as I really didn't want her to hug me anyway. Stefan wrapped an arm around her waist and gave her a kiss and I resisted the urge to snap. Although my body language gave me away since I was now stiff, and my hands were in fists. It was silly I know. But to me there were only two women who had the right to be happy with Stefan.

And that was Charlotte and my mom. But one was dead and the other might as well have been since she wasn't here.

Stefan told them about the rogue angels. "That's very interesting." Cam said. "Scary, but interesting all the same. I've never heard of them, but I'll ask around. Someone has had to of heard something. Is there anything else that happened that night we need to know about?"

I faltered for a second, but that was all I needed to give myself away.

"What is it?" Stefan asked. "What aren't you saying?"

I turned around, my back to him. "Nothing." I said as I checked the potatoes. "I don't want to talk about it right now."

"Why?"

"Because it would only make us fight and I don't want to fight. I just want to enjoy my family."

"Why would we fight?" Stefan asked, voice low.

I sighed as I slumped my shoulders. "Because I know us, Stefan." I turned to face him and whatever was on my face then made him flinch and frown. "If I ask you this question that's in my head right now, we're going to fight, like we always do. And I don't want to do that. I'm leaving for Boston in what, two days? I don't want to leave here knowing that we've been fighting instead of enjoying what time we have."

"You make it sound like you're not coming back." Stefan said mournfully.

I smiled. "That's the whole problem, I don't know if I will. It all depends on what the board decides. Who knows, they may just let me keep my badge and send me to Alaska."

"Or Ohio." Nate said with a smile.

I shivered at the thought of both possible outcomes. "But most likely I'll be fired, and I'll be moving back home. So then—after I learn my fate, we will have the big talk."

And that was the end of it. No one else mentioned the case or the angels or anything about why I'd been suspended. I think they all knew I'd tell them when I was ready.

I finished dinner and Nate checked the steaks that were on the grill. It wasn't long until everyone showed up except a few. Julian, Alec, and Dylan wouldn't be there because they were on their way to Boston to retrieve my belongings. Alexi and Kaydan didn't show up because well, Kaydan was still hurt and Alexi being his best friend meant he was now pissed off at me.

"Hey." Piper said walking up to me and giving me a hug.

"Hey." I said hugging her back. "How's it going?"

"Okay. I guess."

"You guess? What happened?" I could tell that something was wrong by the sound of her voice.

She sighed. "Things didn't go as well with Luke and Natasha as I hoped it would."

"Is that why they're looking at you as if you're the devil or something?"

She nodded. "Yeah. Alexi and I told them, and they freaked. Started ranting about stupid stuff. Like marriage and grandchildren."

"I'm sorry, but you've lost me." I said.

"Natasha doesn't want her grandchildren to have red hair. And they're mad that we're having sex. I mean, okay, the sex thing I understand, my parents aren't exactly overjoyed that I'm having sex without being married. But my red hair? Seriously?"

I laughed. "Why does she care about the hair?"

"I haven't the slightest idea. But then again, this is Natasha. When does anything she gets pissed about make sense? Sometimes I think she and Daphne are in some kind of race or something to see who can be the bitchier."

I nodded. I understood my best friend's uneasiness all too well when it came to the Messer's. Only mine had been the Lewis's. There hadn't been one day during the time Kaydan and I had been together that they hadn't looked at me as 'the bad influence' in their mind. They'd never liked me and never hid the fact that they did. In some ways, it was probably best that Kaydan and I had ended it. Cause I wasn't so sure I would have liked them as my in-laws.

"Hey." Sabine said walking up and stopping to stand next to me. "Feel better?"

"Yeah, a little. I'm still tired, but all and all I feel fine." I said and smiled when I saw Matt coming toward us.

"Well, hello there ladies. Can I interest you in some pleasant small talk?" Matt said as he swung an arm around Sabine's shoulder. I saw her stiffen for a small second before regaining her composure. I suddenly remembered that she'd admitted to me that she liked Matt, maybe even loved him. She'd said that their souls were bonded.

"Are you drunk?" I asked already knowing the answer.

He shrugged. "Not that much. Only had like four beers." He raised up his other arm. In his hand was a beer bottle. "This makes five, but it doesn't count cause it's still half full."

"Not half empty?" asked Piper.

Matt shook his head. "Nah, I choose to look at it in a positive manner."

"Oh man." I said with a small laugh. "You are so trashed."

Matt just smiled. "Not yet."

I just shook my head. "I'm going to go mingle or something."

"Yeah, me too." Piper said. "I should probably go talk to someone who won't get me into trouble."

"Oh, come on." said Matt. "Where's your party spirit?"

"It left when I left home to become a cop. It made me responsible."

"Yeah, me too." Piper said. "You should try coming over to the adult side." She added as we both started walking away.

"Fine." Matt said and smiled wide at Sabine. "Their loss. Your gain. Now you have me all to yourself. Lucky you."

I never heard or saw Sabine's reply, I was too far away by that time, but I hoped it was in the positive. Sabine deserved to be happy and so did Piper. They both deserved to be happy with the men they loved.

But don't you? A small voice asked in the back of my head. *Don't you deserve to be happy too?*

I couldn't argue with that. I did deserve it. But that wasn't an option for me right now. Right now, I just needed to focus on the important things. And my love life and romance weren't at the top of the list. What was at the top was what I planned to do once I was relieved of my duties permanently. There was no time for romance.

I walked to the other side of the patio and found that Nate was laying down on one of the lawn chairs. He smiled up at me and patted the small place next to him. I smiled as I laid down next to him and laid my head on his chest and he wrapped an arm around me. His body felt strong and warm.

"So, what's going on with Matt and Sabine?" he asked.

"I don't know." I said. It wasn't a complete lie. I really didn't know. I only knew Sabine feelings not Matt's.

We laid there for a really long time after that and just watched as Matt and Sabine talked.

"Don't you two just look cozy." Cam said walking up with a smile.

"Actually, I am pretty cozy." I said.

"Me too." said Nate.

Cam turned to look at where Sabine and Matt were standing and talking. "Well shit." he said. "Julian's going to piss himself."

"You know about Sabine's feelings for Matt?" I asked.

Cam nodded. "Yeah, Sofia and I know about Sabine's feelings for Matt." He turned back to me and Nate and smiled. "A little piece of advice. Parents know almost everything about their children. Even the things they don't tell them. You are not as clever as you think you are."

"What are you talking about?" Nate asked.

Cam nodded toward where Stefan was standing with Mariska. He was watching me and Nate with a look of confusion. "Trust me, he knows. He may not understand what he knows and may even be telling himself that his brain is only seeing things—convince himself that it's just some brother sister affection fifteen years in the making that is long overdue. But he knows, even if he doesn't realize that he does."

"And what is that?" I asked.

Cam smiled as he said. "That you two are five seconds away from tearing each other's clothes off."

I stared at Cam and frowned. "Why would—oh." I pulled myself from Nate's arms and sat up. "But we're not."

Nate sat up too, then a beat later he started laughing. "Ew. Morgan is my sister. That's just gross."

Cam laughed. "That may be. But sooner or later he's going to ask. And you better have a damn good answer for why all of a sudden you're showing each other affection." Then he turned and walked away.

I just sat there bewildered.

"Do you think everyone thinks that . . . that we're like . . . you know?" Nate asked.

I looked around the patio and got the answer. "Yeah, I think they do."

Nate smiled. "Well that seals it. I'm going to go get a beer or four and pretend that this conversation never happened."

"Yeah, I'd love to join you, but I'm on pain meds. I think I'm just going to go to bed early."

"Okay." Nate said and leaned over and placed a kiss to my cheek. "Night. Love you."

I smiled as I rose from the chair. "Love you, too." My eyes flicked toward Stefan. He was still watching me and Nate. I walked over to him and smiled. "Hey, I'm going to turn in for the night."

Stefan frowned. "It's still early."

"I know, but I'm really tired."

Stefan raised a hand and placed it on my forehead. "Your head's a bit warm. Are you feeling okay? You don't need to go to the ER, do you?"

I smiled despite rolling my eyes. "I'm tired, not feeling faint." I kissed him on the cheek. "I'll see you in the morning."

"Okay. Love you." I could hear the worry in his voice. I had no doubts that he'd be checking in on me before going to bed himself later.

"Love you, too."

I went up to my room and didn't even bother turning the light on as I shut the door. I shuffled to my bed and crawled underneath the covers. I hadn't been lying about feeling tired. The recovery of being shot and the night's events of seeing everyone was too much too soon. I was worn out.

I closed my eyes and went to sleep. And barely noticed when Stefan came in to check on me.

CHAPTER THIRTY-SIX

I *stood in front of my bedroom* mirror making sure everything was in place. I wore a short jean skirt and a light blue silk top with a pair of black heels. My hair was down, and I quickly added a pair of silver earrings.

It was probably too much for just sitting around the house in, but for reasons beyond me, I just felt the need to look pretty today.

I headed downstairs where I found Stefan and Nate. They were sitting on the sofa looking over some papers and both looked up when I entered the sitting room.

"You look pretty." Nate said eyeing me.

"Thank you." I said with a smile. "If I become unemployed, I'll be wearing a lot of this around the house."

Nate smiled. "Good to know. Something for us males to look forward to."

Stefan chuckled. "Yes, and I've missed it actually."

"Well, you won't have too. So, what do you have planned for today?" I asked, already knowing. Stefan and Nate didn't look over papers just for the fun of it.

"Well, Nate and I were about to leave to go check out something on the P.I case we're working on." Stefan said. "Would you be okay being here alone?"

"Yeah, that's fine. I need to do some packing anyway." I said.

Stefan frowned. "I'm going to miss you."

"It's only for one day. I'll be back the day after tomorrow."

"I know." he said getting up. "But I liked having both of my children under the same roof." I stood and Stefan gave me a hug and a kiss on the cheek. "You're my baby girl and I worry about you."

I felt tears come to my eyes and I forced them back. Now was not the time for this.

Nate got up from the sofa and gave me a hug and kiss on the cheek too. "Just promise you'll come home no matter the outcome."

"I promise." I pulled back from Nate and saw a strange expression on Stefan's face. "What's wrong?" I asked.

Stefan shook his head. "Nothing."

"Obviously it's something or you wouldn't be looking at us like that. So, you might as well say whatever is on your mind."

"Are you two sleeping together?" He blurted out in a rush.

My mouth fell open. What was it with people thinking that just because Nate and I weren't fighting and were actually getting along, and showing each other affection, that it meant that we were sleeping together?

"No. Why would you think that?"

"Because . . . I don't know. I've just noticed you have been . . . touchy feely lately."

"And your first thought is that I'm boning Morgan?" Nate said, then smiled. "Sheesh dad, she's my sister."

Stefan grimaced. "I know, but I thought—"

I shook my head. "Stefan . . . Nate and I have come to an understanding. We've grown up."

"But I've never seen you show affection to each other before." His argument made sense. Nate and I had fought as kids and teenagers. Not once had we shown each other sibling love. So, I guess Stefan's assumption about me and Nate was understandable.

I wrapped my arms around Stefan. "Well, you better get used to it, cause there's going to be a lot of that going on for now on. You and Nate are my family and I love both of you."

Stefan hugged me to him. "Good. I'm glad that my children are finally getting along."

In the next instant Nate's arms went around both of us. "One big happy family. What I always wanted." We stayed like that for what seemed like a long time and I just relished in it. This was what I needed more than anything. To just be in the arms of my father and brother.

If these were the only people left in my life, I'd be okay with that. Because this was my family.

They left soon after that and I was now alone in the house. It was midday and I had nothing to do and nowhere to go. So, I settled for cleaning the house. It wasn't dirty by no means, but it helped to keep my mind from dangerous things like Balian. I still wasn't sure what I was going to do about him. He had seemed so hopeful about us back at the hospital.

And then there was that demon that had followed me that day after I had left Balian's apartment. I still didn't fully understand why Samael would have him follow me, but I was beginning to paint a picture. A picture that I didn't like that led to a million questions that I was sure Stefan would refuse to answer. But something had been revealed to me that night at Illusions and it scared me, because I couldn't understand why I had been lied to all these years.

I was in the kitchen cooking something to eat when the doorbell rang. I stirred the Pasta and headed for the front door. When I got to the door, I opened it and was surprised when I saw Balian. He stood there looking as sexy as ever in his black suit, those dark blue eyes of his that always reminded me of the sky at night shining with something scandalous and that smile. Yes, that smile that curved his lips said he was up to no good.

"Balian, what are you doing here?" I asked, trying not to sound as surprised as I was. My lower body tightened, and my heartbeat did a little thump, thump, thump, like I was some kind of silly teenager.

"Hello, Morgan." Balian said. His voice was like silk. "I wanted to see how you were doing."

"Thank you, and I'm doing okay. Um . . . would you like to come in?" I saw the surprise fill his eyes and I smiled. "Stefan and Nate aren't home. I'm here alone."

A twinkle flickered in his eyes as he said. "Yes, I would love too." And he slid passed me, his hand brushed against my arm and I thought I was going to faint. There was just something about this man and his touch that made me so weak in the knees.

I closed the door and followed him to the front room. "So, are you hungry? I was making something to eat and there's more than enough."

"Yes, that would be nice, thank you." And he smiled.

I smiled back and went to the kitchen and finished with the Pasta. There wasn't much that needed done, just draining it and mixing the green peppers and mushrooms in. When I had two plates fixed, I picked them up and headed back for the sitting room where I found Balian staring at the pictures of me that were on the mantel.

Balian turned and smiled. "You were cute as a child."

I laughed. "Yeah, that's what everyone tells me. Dinner is ready." I said as I set the plates on the coffee table. I ran back to the kitchen and grabbed two wine glasses and a bottle of white whine and took them to the sitting room. I set the glasses down and poured some in each glass.

I sat down on the sofa next to Balian, who had already taken a seat. "This looks wonderful." he said and took a bite. I smiled as I watched his eyes. "This . . . is probably the best thing I have eaten since ever."

I smiled. "Thank you." We ate for a while without talking and after we were done, I was the one who broke the silence. "Thanks for making sure I was okay."

"You are welcome, but why would I not check on you? You are important to me." Balian said. There it was again. That hopeful note in his voice that suggested that he was looking at a future for us. That made me frown, because I couldn't see it.

"Are you alright?" Balian asked sounding worried. "You look so sad all of a sudden."

I nodded. "I'm fine." I lied. I wasn't alright. How could I be alright when the man—no the demon/vampire sitting next to me seemed hopeful that we could ever become something more than what we already were? And even at that, I wasn't entirely sure what we were to begin with.

Before I knew what I was doing, I found myself moving toward Balian. I straddled his lap and he kissed me. I kissed him back as he wrapped his arms around me. I started to feel better. Not entirely, but I figured it was a work in progress. Being in his arms made all the hurt I'd felt for years go away. I felt complete somehow and I didn't understand why. After all, this man was a demon and demons weren't exactly the comforting type.

I pulled back and stared into those dark blue eyes that reminded me of the sky at night. This man was extraordinary. "What is it about you that makes me feel so damned safe?" I whispered.

"Perhaps it is my charm and intellect nature." he said with a half-smile.

"I'm serious."

"I am as well." I just gave him a look. "Alright, perhaps not the intellect part, but most definitely the charm. And besides, I believe there is a connection between us." He kissed me lightly on the lips and I pulled back. "What is wrong?"

I sat there, straddling his lap and promised myself never again. Never again would I go into a relationship without setting rules in place. "I can't do this."

"Do what?"

"This. Us. I broke my best friend's heart because he thought we were something we weren't. And I won't hurt you that way."

Balian seemed confused. "Why do you think you will hurt me? I know what I am getting into."

"Then you know we can't be together."

"Why can we not be together?"

"Balian," I began. "I'm leaving for Boston tomorrow and I may not be coming back."

He leaned forward and brushed his lips against my neck. "Then we should go back to my place so I can give you a proper send off. Or perhaps, upstairs?"

I pushed away from him. "That's the problem, Balian. If I leave and never come back, there will be no us. If I come home, there will be no us. Don't you understand? There is no future for us."

Balian stared at me and my heart broke, because there wasn't one piece of anger in his eyes. "Are you saying that because you mean it, or because you think that is what you should be saying?"

"Does it really matter?"

"Yes. If you say you really mean it, then I will leave you alone. If you say that you do not and that you want me just as much as I want you, then we will find a way to make it work."

"Balian, you're a demon and I'm an angel."

"And your point is?"

"It would never work. I mean, have you ever seen a demon and an angel couple before?"

"I have seen a lot of things before." he said and there was something in his voice that sounded bitter. "We will make it work if you say that you want me. I will go wherever I need to, to be with you. I will defy whoever I must to prove that what I feel is real."

"I . . ." I was kissing him. My soul was singing and for the first time in a very long time, I wasn't scared that the man almost professing his love for me was lying. But if I did this, I needed to be damn sure that it was what I wanted. I pulled back, my breathing heavy and my voice breathless. "I . . . I need to think."

"Let me take you upstairs and you can think there." Balian breathed.

I shook my head. "No. I need time . . . away from you to think."

Balian stared into my eyes. "You promise I will see you again regardless of the outcome of your job?"

I nodded. "Yes, I promise."

He kissed me. "Then I will wait for you."

Balian left soon after that and I was once again alone in the house. It was getting late and I went to my room and began packing a suitcase. I only needed one since I wasn't going to be in Boston for very long. I laid down on my bed and closed my eyes. It had been a very long and tiring day. I laid there and could still feel Balian's hands and lips on my body. Could still feel how happy my soul had been when he held me.

I laid there and sorted through my dilemma until I was sure that that was what I truly wanted. And then I asked myself one important question. Was this worth losing everything and everyone in my life? It was a good question and when I answered it, I knew I'd done the right thing. I only hoped my friends and family felt the same way.

CHAPTER THIRTY-SEVEN

I jerked awake as thunder boomed and lightning cracked, but that wasn't what woke me. There had been a noise coming from somewhere in the mansion. But as I laid there, I heard nothing. Had I been imagining things? I didn't think so.

I turned over and sighed at the time on my clock. 10:30 p.m. Great. I closed my eyes and the noise came again. A scraping sound like someone was scraping against the walls. I raised up and stared at my door. Maybe it was Nate and Stefan and maybe one of them—not if both, were hurt. I got out of bed and walked to my door and opened it.

I peered out into the hall not knowing what I might find. "Nate? Stefan?" I called out. There wasn't an answer. I walked down the hall and suddenly everything felt cold. "Nate? Stefan?" I called out again. Still there was no answer.

I walked past Nate's room and past the stairs and made it all the way down to Stefan's room before I heard the scraping again. It was coming from the hall, but I was in the hall. I slowly turned but saw nothing. So, I walked back down to my room. Only I didn't make it there before I saw a shadow of a silhouette standing at the end of the hall. I stopped in my tracks and silently cursed myself for not grabbing my gun. Someone had broken into the house. I needed to get to my room and call 911. No scratch that. I needed my gun. But the figure was blocking my way. It was almost like it was on purpose. I turned and started walking back the other way but stopped when another figure stepped out of the shadows. There were two—make that three, because out of the corner of my eye, I saw a third figure walking up the stairs.

I put my back against the wall and watched as the three . . . men—demons came toward me. They were all tall and each had their own weapons in their hands. The one coming from my left had an axe in one hand and a long pole with a round silver ball with sharp looking spikes at the end of it. The man coming from my right had long blades like knifes in his hands. But as I looked closer, I realized that the knives were actually claws and he had two horns coming from his head.

My eyes widened and my heart sped up. I had seen him before, or well, someone like him once when I was nine, the night my mom had left.

The man walking up the stairs made me look twice. He was tall with long blond hair and glowing red eyes. It was the man from the grocery store parking lot. The demon I knew bared Samael's mark. He'd been there the night Theophilius held me hostage. Granted he'd been unconscious, but he'd been there all the same.

"Who are you?" I whispered. "What do you want?"

The man smiled. "Who am I? It does not matter. What do I want? Well, the devil demands payment and I his faithful servant, am here to collect." he said spreading his arms out wide and stopping at the top. It was obvious that was blocking my way to the stairs on purpose. I didn't understand what was going on, but that didn't matter at the moment. What did was getting out of this alive and not leaving here is a body bag.

I looked around for an escape as panic set in. My eyes fell on Nate's door and I silently wondered if I could make it to his room before one of them made it to me. Well, there was only one way to find out. I ran for it, but I didn't make it. The man who had been standing in the way of my room, now blocked Nate's. His hand struck out and I ducked as I scrambled to my room, and barely got the door shut before the axe went through it.

I ran for my nightstand and opened it and pulled out my gun. I clicked off the safety and took aim just as my bedroom door burst open and the demon came inside. I fired and he stumbled back as the bullet hit him in the chest. He fell to the floor and I ran out of the room ready to shoot the next demon if he forced me.

But I never got the chance, because I was struck from the side and I fell as my gun slipped out of my hand and I went for it. But a black boot stepped on it and I looked up to see the red eyed man. He tsked at me. "No, no, no. That is not how the game works."

I got up from the floor and ran for it again. If I could get out of the house or get downstairs and to the room with all the weapons, I might have a shot at not getting killed. But I was stopped by the second demon and that's when I knew. I was trapped and there was no getting out of this without fighting.

I backed against the wall and looked at the two men blocking my way out. They were here for a reason and I was pretty sure the reason was me. Demons just didn't come into your house for no good reason. It was a rule.

The demon I had shot stood and seemed to be having difficulty breathing. I must have hit a lung. Good. Maybe it would slow him down.

The demon from the left attacked. I ducked as he swung the axe and it went through the wall. I scrambled to get out of the way as he pulled it out and came at me again. Before I knew it, the second demon was attacking me too. I took a deep breath and kicked out with my leg and there was a crack as his knee shattered. He screamed and went down to the floor.

I didn't have time for a breather, because the first demon came at me swinging his axe and spiky thing. I dodged and this time his weapons crashed into the small table that was in the hall. The table crashed onto the floor and the small vase that had been sitting on it was now in a million pieces.

I grabbed two of the table legs that had broken off. I stood up and gripped them in my hands as my heart pounded in my ears and my breathing came in pants. Now I had weapons.

Heat ran through my body in a rush of electricity and stopped at my fingertips. The next thing I knew, red sparks flew out from my fingers and ignited the table legs. Red sparks licked and danced across the wood and my hands like flames. It made the wood look like torches.

I didn't think, I just reacted. Although, fighting had always come easy for me. I slammed one of the legs into the side of the first demons head and slammed the other leg into his side. The third demon just stayed where he was and watched as I fought the other two.

The first demon was laying on the floor, trying to get up and the second was still on the attack. He slashed with his claws and even managed to cut my shirt. I stepped back and raised one of the table legs up. The end of it was sharp and pointy, like a wooden stake. He came at me and that's when

I pushed it into his chest, right through the heart. His eyes widened and I kicked him in the chest, and he stumbled backwards into the banister of the balcony. There was a crack as he went over, taking the banister with him. I ran to the end and watched as he fell and hit the floor with a slap.

He was dead.

Okay, one demon down, two to go.

I turned to see the first demon stand and I looked around for another weapon. My eyes fell on my gun and I ran for it. My hands reached the gun and I turned, took aim, and fired just as the demon came at me. I fired four rounds into his chest. He fell to the floor and didn't get up.

I stood, my gun now pointed at the third and last demon. "Who are you?"

He said nothing as he smiled and began clapping. "Bravo!" he said, as he continued to clap. "I must say, that was very entertaining. Tell me, Morgan, was that as good for you as it was for me?"

Okay, so he knew my name.

"Who are you?" I repeated. "And don't lie to me. I want your name."

He smiled. "My name is Grady." His voice had a slight Swedish accent. "And to answer your other question . . . I believe you already know why I am here and who sent me."

I did, but I wanted to hear it from him. "Why did he send you after me? What am I to him?"

Grady tilted his head to one side and very slowly, he laughed. "Oh, you are a peach. Really, your ignorance amuses me."

Actually, I wasn't as in the dark as he thought. But he didn't need to know that.

"Answer the damn question. What do you want?" I asked, my voice raising with each word.

"What would you do if I said to see if you are worthy to be called his offspring?"

"And whose offspring, am I?" Again, I already had a pretty good idea, but I wanted to hear it from him. If I was right, then someone had some explaining to do. But if I was wrong, then I didn't want to get all upset over nothing. This Grady guy could be making it up.

"I believe you already know the answer to that. But if not, then I do not want to be the one who let the cat out of the bag. Perhaps you should ask the man who raised you."

"Stefan?" I asked. I'd always known he knew who my real father was. This right here just confirmed it. "Why would Stefan know?"

He laughed. "Oh, lilla gnista, Stefan knows a hell of a lot he is not telling you. He has always known who your true blood was. What your true nature is."

"And what might that be?" My arm was starting to hurt holding the gun the way I was, but I forced my arm not to move. I didn't trust this guy. Not even long enough to allow my arm to rest.

"The truth of who you are. He has helped hide you from your true destiny. Why do you think he had him attacked? To prove who the true dominant is."

I was confused for only a half second, then I understood. "He was behind Stefan getting hurt?"

Grady nodded. "Yes. He has felt like he was robbed of your childhood. Of raising you and influencing your soul. The angels have tried so hard to make you pure, but he knows there is a darkness inside you that is begging to be let out."

"So, what, he wants a chance at my soul?"

He shook his head. "No, he wants a chance at releasing it." I so did not like the sound of that. The only way I knew to release a soul was through death.

"He wants to kill me?"

"No."

"Then how does he plan on releasing my soul?"

Grady smiled wide. "Through temptation."

He stepped forward and I stepped back. "Stop or I'll shoot."

"You will not shoot me. I am unarmed."

"You broke into my house. I'm home alone. I've just been attacked by two demons. Now stop or I will shoot you."

He didn't stop walking. He just smiled and pressed his chest against the barrel of the gun. "I do not believe you." He raised a hand and wrapped it around my wrist. I wanted to shoot him and probably should have, but I couldn't. It just didn't feel right. He squeezed my wrist and I dropped my gun. I gasped at the pain. He took that moment to make his move. He shoved me hard against the wall, penning my body between his and the wall.

At first, I thought he was going to rape me and I started to fight back, but he grabbed me by the wrists and penned them above my head. He leaned his body into mine and buried his face into the side of my neck. His breath was hot on my skin and when he spoke, chills ran up my back.

"I know he has had you, lilla gnista. One day I will have you too."

"I don't know what you're talking about." I said.

Grady laughed and stepped back, letting my wrists go as he stepped into the shadows. "You will." And he was gone.

I grabbed my gun from the floor and ran through the house checking every room. There was no one there. It was just me and the two demons. I went to my room and called Elliott. He answered on the third ring.

"Bronson?"

"Elliott, it's Morgan. I've got a situation."

C H A P T E R
THIRTY-EIGHT

The mansion was now a crime scene. I sat on the sofa as an EMT checked out the cut on my head and cleaned it. Bronson and Carlos stood to the side and watched. I winced as they brought down the body of the demon, I'd killed upstairs. His name was Mavis and his friends name was Meka. Both of their IDs claimed they were mid-twenties, but I was guessing they were lying.

The EMT was just finishing up when I saw Stefan and Nate run into the room, their eyes wide and frantic. They looked around the room and I knew they were thinking it was worse than what it was.

"What happened?" Stefan asked walking up.

"We had unwanted guests." I said. "But don't worry, I kicked them out."

Stefan and Nate both frowned and didn't laugh at my joke. "Who was it?" asked Nate.

I shrugged. "Three demons. But one was the leader, I guess. He said his name was Grady, and he brought two goons with him. Mavis and Meka. Which I killed."

"And Grady?"

"We had a very interesting talk and then he left." I leveled my gaze on Stefan and whatever he saw in it seemed to scare him, because he swallowed hard. I was angry and he knew it. He just didn't know why, not yet. I'd wait until Bronson and Carlos left first and the other police before I said anything.

Because if this turned into a screaming match, I didn't want anyone other than Nate to see it.

This was a family matter, not a police matter.

The EMT smiled at me. "All done. It wasn't as bad as I had originally thought. Just more blood. But you should be fine."

Detective Sanders walked over and gave me his best smile. "How's your head?"

"It's fine." I said smiling back. "Thanks for asking."

He shrugged. "No problem. Just wanted to let you know that everything's done. Everyone should be out of here in about thirty minutes." He gave me one of those appraising looks men give women when they like what they see and are trying to picture them naked. "I'm really glad you're okay. I would have hated if anything had happened to you. I hope I get to see you again. Actually . . ." He reached into his jacket and pulled out a pad of paper and a pen, and wrote something down, then tore out the piece of paper. "Here, this is my number. Call me if you ever need anything."

I took it reluctantly. "Thanks, Sanders." I said.

"Mark. Please, call me Mark."

"Um . . . thanks, Mark."

He smiled at me then and it was a good smile. I didn't have the heart to tell him I was sort of taken. "You're welcome . . . Morgan. I guess I'll be seeing you around." Then he turned and left.

Rafe burst out laughing. "Wow. Even with a bump on the head you still manage to make men fall all over you."

I rolled my eyes. "That's not funny."

"Sure, it is. And I think I've been wasting my time with human women."

I ignored him. "So how was your night?" I asked Stefan and Nate.

"Apparently better than yours." Nate said. "What did Grady want?"

"Nothing that's important right now." I said. I looked at Bronson. "Sorry if I ruined your night."

"Don't worry about it. I'm sure she understood. And if not, then there are other women out there. And besides, this is my job. Rafe and I will go have a talk with this Grady guy, see what story he gives us." Bronson said.

Thirty minutes later everyone left, and it was just me, Nate, and Stefan. I sat on the sofa and stared Stefan down. I could feel the anger coming back as I tried to find a way to ask my question. I knew he was going to lie to me, and I prepared myself for that. Stefan had never been honest with me in the past so why should he start now?

Stefan stood there and stared right back at me. There was a tension that had formed in his body. He knew there was something coming, and it was making him uneasy. "There's something you didn't tell the police, isn't there?" he said, voice hard. "So, let's have it. What did you and Grady talk about?"

I said nothing for a long moment. I didn't trust myself to speak, to not snap at him and accuse him of lying to me all these years. Stefan never made it a habit to lie to me or anyone else without reason that much I knew. So why had he lied about this? Why had he kept it from me?

"Samael's my father, isn't he?" I said, voice calmer than I thought it would be.

Nate jerked his head up and looked at Stefan with unsure eyes. "Dad? What's Morgan talking about?"

Stefan kept his gaze on me as he said. "No. I am your father."

"Stefan." I snapped. "Don't you fucking lie to me. I'm not in the mood. I want the truth. Is Samael my father?"

He sighed. "Yes, he fathered you, but I was the one who raised you. Not him. So that makes me your father. Because in this case, blood doesn't matter."

"Why . . . why didn't you tell me?"

"Because your mother asked me not to."

"Were you ever going to tell me?" I asked surprised that he actually admitted that Samael was my father. I had suspected the night Theophilius held me hostage, but I hadn't been sure. I had seen my eyes when I'd looked at him. And really, how many people have dark teal eyes?

"Yes, one day." Stefan said. He walked over and sat down in one of the chairs and rested his elbows on his knees as he put his face in his hands. "I was going to tell—I wanted to tell you so many times."

"But you didn't."

"No, I didn't." He pulled back and looked at me and seemed defeated somehow. "There were days I was scared he'd come and take you away from me. I could fight Camille, but there was no way I could have fought him."

I believed him. Samael was powerful and if he'd wanted me bad enough, I believe he would have just taken me. Even if he had to kill to do it. I began wondering how in the world my mom had gotten mixed up with him. Why would she willingly allow a man like Samael—a demon into her bed? It didn't make any sense. But other things did. Now I understood why Androcles had called me a hell-breed and why he'd gotten so mad about me being there. It also made sense why Theophilius said he could smell hell inside me.

I flicked my eyes to Nate, and he looked in shock. He shook his head. "I don't understand. How is that possible? Why would Lauren let him in her bed? Unless—"

"He didn't rape her." Stefan said cutting him off. "She claimed she didn't know it was him until after Morgan was born."

"But you don't sound like you believe her." I said. "Why?"

Stefan frowned and sat back in the chair. "Because something about it doesn't add up. I've had almost fifteen years to think about everything. And even Camille was told the same story and has the same thoughts."

"That she knew it was Samael and she willingly slept with him." I said figuring out what he was saying.

"I have no proof of that, Morgan. For all I know, she might have been raped or he just might have swept her off her feet. But yes, I have always wondered that." There was something in his voice that sounded sad. "She said that Samael was looking for her and for you. She was trying to keep you from him. She didn't want him tainting you. The night she disappeared; he sent a demon here. As soon as you said you saw a monster I knew, he found you. The next day she was gone. There have been nights when I lay awake and wonder if she went out to confront the demon, and he took her. But that's not possible since I know she took at least one duffle of her belongings with her."

"So, where is she?" I asked. "Where's my mom?"

Stefan's face fell. "I wish I knew. But the whereabouts of your mom is the least of our problems. There's something else I need to tell you."

What else could there be? I was the daughter of Samael and my mother was still nowhere to be seen. So, what could be worse?

"What is it?" I asked.

"After your mom left, I did some digging around. About a year ago, I ran into this demon—Kyriss. Balian had been in town for over a year and a half at that time and I found it strange."

"Why?"

"Because I knew him from a long time ago. And I knew he was one of Samael's men, which meant Samael wasn't far behind. I was curious about why Balian was in Seattle. So, I made a meeting with Kyriss and I persuaded him to talk."

"You mean you beat him." Nate said, not sounding happy.

"Yes, fine, I beat him. But he still told me everything." Stefan said.

"Which was?" I asked.

"My worst nightmare." Stefan went back to looking uneasy. "He told me that Samael had seduced an angel in hopes that she'd give him a child. A son, actually. He wanted a very powerful son. He planned for him to become part of his army."

"Does this mean I have a brother?"

Stefan shook his head. "No, Morgan, you are the child. Your mother was the angel he seduced and impregnated. But we know with you, he didn't get the son he wanted. Instead, he got a daughter."

I sat there and tried to take it all in. Samael was my father and he had seduced my mom in hopes of a great power. But he got me instead. So, what did that mean, that he was angry? "Okay, so what does this have to do with why Balian moved to Seattle?"

"Samael knew there was a chance that he could have a daughter, so he made . . . arrangements."

"Arrangements?"

"There's a reason why Balian has been around and why he's enchanted with you."

"What do you mean?" I asked. I wasn't liking where this was going.

"Samael promised him something." Stefan said and swallowed hard.

"What?"

He looked down. "You. Samael promised him you. You are to become Balian's mate." Stefan was silent for a moment before he continued. "Balian is to court and seduce you. And when he is ready . . . he will take you."

"You mean sex." I said as I felt a tear slide down my cheek.

"Yes." he said.

I nodded and just sat there feeling so stupid, used, and betrayed. How had I allowed myself to be used like that? Balian had lied to me. He hadn't been intrigued by me. He was out hunting, and I was his prey. And I had done exactly what he wanted. I gave into his charms.

Angry tears ran down my face as I realized that he hadn't been as sincere as I'd thought. I'd told him everything. I'd trusted him enough to break down and tell him about Daniel and my job and the baby I'd lost. He'd made me feel so warm and so safe in his arms, and I'd fell for it. So much so, that I'd given him my body for a night and was considering giving it to him again along with a piece of my heart. Stupid. So, fucking stupid. He didn't care about me. He'd only cared about getting me into his bed. And he'd succeeded. I bet he'd had one hell of a laugh after he'd left his apartment.

His apartment.

A memory flared in my brain about him saying that he'd only allow his mate in his home. Well, shit, that should have been my first clue that not everything was on the up and up with him. And then there was that conversation I'd overheard of him and Constantine arguing about me. Now I understand why Constantine was so angry about me and Balian, why he'd said I wasn't good enough for him.

"I'm sorry." Stefan said after about a minute of silence. "I didn't want you to find out like this. I really didn't. And there's something else. Kyriss said that when Balian takes you . . . he'll imprint. I don't know much about it. But from what I understand it's done through a bite and sex."

I closed my eyes and nodded.

I couldn't concentrate on that, so I focused on something that wasn't as scary. "My wings." I said. "Since I'm basically half demon and half angel, what does that mean for my wings?"

"I'm not sure." Stefan said. "Since you've never been able to summon them . . . I'm just not sure. You could be more one than the other or even in both. Which I would guess would mean they would be gray. But until we saw them . . ."

Right. Until we saw my wings we'd never know if I was more my father's daughter or my mother's. And with the way my life was going as of late, it was probably the ladder. Although, the good thing was, I didn't have to worry about there being a hit put out on me anymore. Samael didn't want me dead, he just wanted me shacking up with one of his men.

I looked over at Nate and he seemed to be in deep thought, so I didn't bother asking him his opinion about this. I knew once the shock wore off, he'd have an opinion. I stood up. "I need to think. I'm going to bed."

"Morgan." Stefan said. "We should talk about this."

I shook my head. "No. Not right now. This is . . . just too much. I need time to think about this."

Stefan seemed unsure but nodded. "Okay. I'll see you in the morning."

I said nothing as I went upstairs and went into one of the other rooms since my room was a wreck and no longer had a door. I crawled under the covers and curled my body into a ball as I began crying softly. I couldn't believe I had given in that easily. That I'd allowed Balian to take advantage of me like that. Stupid.

I laid there and made myself another vow. No matter what happened in Boston, I wasn't going to allow myself to be used like that again. If Balian wanted me bad enough, then he was going to learn how to work for it.

Because next time I wasn't going to be so easy.

CHAPTER THIRTY-NINE

The next morning, I woke up feeling hung over. I had cried myself to sleep and now I was paying for it by feeling like shit. I rolled over onto my back and stared up at the ceiling and wished I wasn't me. Wished I wasn't this damaged and screwed up person with too much baggage. I wished I had never met Balian.

I felt so used and so betrayed that it made that dark part of me, the dark beast that was down in my core so angry. I would like to say I hadn't any idea where my anger was coming from, but since I was Samael's child, well, that explained everything. Now I understood why I'd been so angry all these years. I was part demon. Part something dark and dangerous.

But as mad as I was about Balian lying to me, I was more upset that I'd allowed myself to confide in him. That I allowed myself to tell him stuff that was so private and so personal, stuff I hadn't even told my own family about.

It's time. My inner voice said. *It's time to tell him.*

I knew the voice inside my head was right. I had been putting this off for too long. It was time to tell Stefan about my job . . . and the baby.

I got out of bed and left the room. I padded down the hallway to Stefan's room and slowly opened the door and peered inside. He was laying on his back, the covers drawled up to his waist, the dark blue T-shirt he was wearing had ridden up just enough to reveal his hard-toned chest. I crept inside and closed the door behind me. I walked over to the bed and crawled underneath the covers, curling my body into him and laying my head on his chest.

Stefan stirred and moved a little, within seconds his arms went around me, pulling me closer to him. "You haven't done this since you were a little girl." he said still half asleep. "I've missed it."

I smiled a little. When I was a little girl, I used to sneak into Stefan and my mom's room and crawl in between them and go to sleep. After my mom had left, I still snuck into Stefan's room and curled into his arms to go to sleep. I'd done it for like two years, until I felt too old and Stefan had started dating again. I hadn't wanted to walk in on something that would scar me for life.

I took a deep breath as tears began to fill my eyes. This was so hard. But I had to do it. I had to tell Stefan everything, no matter how hard it was. "About five months ago, I found out I was pregnant, and a week later I miscarried." I said as I felt a sob threaten to escape.

Stefan stiffened, but only for a second, then he hugged me tighter to him. "Oh, sweetie. I am so sorry. Why didn't you call me?"

"Because I didn't want to inconvenience you."

"Morgan, I'm your father, you could never inconvenience me. I would have been there." His arms tightened around me and I felt safe.

"And what, beat the shit out of Daniel?"

"For starters. But I would have been there." And he would have taken me back to Seattle and hovered over me.

I smiled a little. "Yeah, I know. And that's part of why Daniel dumped me. Turns out, I made him sick and he didn't want the baby as much as I had thought."

I started crying and Stefan tightened his hold on me yet again and placed a kiss on top of my forehead. "I think I may kill him." he mumbled.

"I know now if I hadn't lost the baby, I would have come home alone and pregnant."

"You wouldn't have been alone. We would have dealt with it. I wouldn't have let you deal with it by yourself."

"I would have been a little over six months."

"Doesn't matter. I like babies. And I would have loved that one." I knew he was telling me the truth. I knew Stefan well enough to know if I'd come home pregnant, he'd been there for me and he would have spoiled the baby to death.

I took another deep breath. "I was suspended because I'm a supernatural."

"They can't do that." he said.

"Yeah, but they did. Stefan, they're going to take my badge away from me. I'm going to lose my job. Daniel is doing his best to spin it as if he didn't know I wasn't human."

"You were living with him. How could he not know?"

"He knew, but he's claiming he didn't. I'm being accused of lying about what I am." I pulled away from him and rolled over onto my back.

"What are you going to do?"

"Probably move back in and work at the firm." I sighed as my inner voice told me that I might as well finish my confession. "I slept with Balian."

"I know." Stefan said.

"You did?"

"Yep. I suspected he was the man you'd been with when you left for your date the night you got shot. And I knew for certain he was when I got to the hospital. Just tell me you used protection."

At the mention of protection, I stiffened. We had used condoms . . . that night, but not in the shower. We'd been careless and out of control with wanting and need. Oh, shit.

"Well, shit." Stefan said when I didn't say anything. "I may become a grandfather after all."

I sat up and shook my head. "No, no we used protection."

"But?"

"But not in the shower." I said. "And we only did it twice."

Stefan cringed at my over share. "Okay, now that I have that disturbing image in my head, how do you feel?"

"What do you mean?"

He sat up on the bed. "Well, when a supernatural conceives, she can tell that she's caring within weeks or even days without a test."

This was news to me. "How will I know?"

"You may feel tired more than usual or have morning sickness early. Sometimes you can feel faint."

"I haven't had any sickness and I'm no more tired than normal."

Stefan nodded. "Yes, and with the recent events of your state, you most likely would have lost it too. So, I'm going to guess that you're not pregnant."

That was a relief.

I sat there and wiped a hand over my face. "I can . . . I can still feel him inside of me. I can still feel his hands and his body. And it's not just the sex. I think I can feel him inside my soul."

Stefan blew out a breath and took my hand in his and squeezed. "I'm sorry. I know this has to be hard for you. Learning that your real father is a demon and he promised you to a demon."

"It is. But it's not just that. I told him, Stefan. I told him everything. I told him about my job and Daniel and about the baby. I went to his apartment and we talked. He was so nice and sweet, and he wanted me to tell him about what Daniel did to me so he could fix it. So, I thought why not? He wasn't my family or my friend. He was just some guy who confused me and . . . and he didn't know me. Not really and I liked that. He didn't know me enough to judge or be angry about it. So, I told him and then . . . and then I let him make love to me."

Stefan squeezed my hand. "I sort of figured that. Not the whole sharing thing, but the making love part. I knew you just needed someone who wasn't Kaydan. And really, I'm not surprised that you confided in him."

"So, you're not mad that I told him before you?"

Stefan shook his head. "Not even a little. I mean, was I upset that you were keeping everything from me? Yes. But I don't blame you for doing it. And now I understand why." I loved this man. It didn't matter that he wasn't my real father. Because as far as I was concerned Stefan Williams was my father. Samael's blood might run through my veins, but Stefan's love ran through my soul.

I got up from the bed and smiled at him. "Thanks for letting me tell you when I was ready."

He smiled back. "I know you enough to know when to pry and when to not. I just figured you needed some time."

I walked to the door and stopped and turned. "Oh, one more thing. Could you not say anything about this to the others?"

Stefan nodded. "Yeah, I can do that. But um . . . I need to say something on the whole Balian issue. I know you're upset right now, and I frankly don't like the idea about you being with him or any demon. But don't decide what you want right now. Give your anger some time. I know Balian, and I know what I saw at the hospital. And it wasn't a demon taking advantage of an angel. He was frantic. I thought he was going to lose it. If it hadn't been for

Kyriss being there . . . I honestly think Balian would have lost his mind." He paused for a moment, thinking. "I think he loves you, Morgan."

That took me aback. "Balian doesn't know me well enough for that. And he could have been faking it." I said.

Stefan shook his head. "No, I don't think so. I've seen the look that was in his eyes once. So, trust me, Balian wasn't faking anything."

"When? When have you ever seen a look like it? How do you know?"

His face fell and sadness filled it. "I know because it was the same expression I had when Charlotte and Elizabeth died."

I suddenly wished I hadn't asked. I knew how painful it still was to Stefan. I sighed. "Stefan, I'm sorry about me freaking about you and Mariska having a baby. And I think if that's what you really want, then you should have it."

Stefan shook his head. "No, not right now. I think after everything and with you just losing . . . I think we should wait. We have more than enough time."

"No, you shouldn't have to put what you want—you having a new family on hold, because you think I'm fragile and I can't handle it."

"New family? Morgan, if Mariska and I have a baby, they won't be my new family. They'll just be a part of my family. You and Nathaniel are my family. Mariska would just be joining it and the baby would be expanding it. I would never try and replace you and Nate. I love you."

I smiled. "I love you too . . . dad."

He smiled back. "I know."

I left and made my way downstairs and into the kitchen. I could smell bacon coming from inside the kitchen. I walked in to find Nate standing over the stove and he was cooking. His back was to me and he cursed when grease from the pan splashed up and hit his arm.

"Fuck!"

I giggled and he turned around and gave an embarrassed smile.

"Hey, I was cooking you breakfast, since you were leaving today. I thought you might like it. I'm not sure it's eatable . . . but I thought—"

I crossed the room and I hugged him. He stiffened for half a second, then he hugged me back, wrapping his arms around me. "I love you." I said pulling back. "And I'm sorry for not being here and keeping everything from you and Stefan and everyone else."

Nate stared at me. "Who are you and what have you done with Morgan?"

I smiled. "It's me. Don't worry. I've decided it's time you know everything."

"Everything? You mean Daniel and your job?"

I nodded. "And the baby."

Nate froze and looked down at my stomach. "Baby?" I could see him doing the math in his head. Since I wasn't showing, he probably thought I was only a few weeks, maybe a few months. "What baby? How . . . how far along are you?"

"I'm not. I found out about five months ago."

"And you lost it." Nate said guessing and I nodded. "And that's why that bastard refused to touch you, isn't it?"

"Turns out he didn't want the baby and me after all." I laid my head on his chest. "Do you know how close I came to come home pregnant? I would have been a single mother."

"No, you wouldn't have. Dad and I wouldn't have let you. We would have helped as much as possible. And so, would have everyone else. Especially Julian. I think he would have liked being called Uncle Julian."

I laughed. "There's a scary thought."

"Not as scary as him fathering a child." I pulled back and gave him a look. "I think he and Willow were making plans before they ended it. I'm pretty sure he went ring shopping."

I frowned. "Poor Julian. You know, I thought it was odd that I never got a wedding invitation in the mail or a phone call. I thought maybe they were mad and just didn't tell me."

Nate shook his head. "Nope. One minute they were talking marriage and I was being pulled into conversations about baby names. Then the next thing I know, it's over and she's moved away."

I started to say something when I smelled something burning. I looked around and saw smoke coming from the toaster. "Um, Nate, I think the toast is burning."

"What?" He looked toward the toaster. "Shit." He ran over and took out the two pieces of bread that was now black as night. "Shit. Ow! Damn it!"

I laughed. "Are you okay?"

"Yep. But the toast isn't." He turned and there was a serious expression on his face. He leveled his gaze on me and frowned. "I know you slept with Balian."

I hadn't been expecting that. I was speechless for a heartbeat. "Nate, I . . ."

"No, it's okay. Really. I mean, do I like the idea of my sister being with a demon? No. But I understand. You needed someone unfamiliar and unknowing of everything. And let's face it, Kaydan was even getting on my nerves and I wasn't the one he was trying to get with."

"So, you're not mad?" I asked. It was a stupid question.

"No. I just want you to be happy. So, if you want to be with him . . . then it's okay. No judging. Promise. As long as he treats you right."

"I'm not sure I want to be with him anymore. Not after that."

Nate nodded. "If that's what you want, then I'm on your side. Always. You are my sister. I love you Morgan and I don't want to lose you. Not ever."

I smiled as Stefan came in. He looked at Nate and then at me. "What's going on?"

"We were talking." I said hoping my face wouldn't give me away.

"I made breakfast." Nate said.

Stefan sniffed the air. "Is that what I smell?" He sat down at the island. "Oh, and by the way, I think the bacon is on fire." Nate and I turned around and sure enough, there were flames. Nate ran for the stove just as the fire alarm went off.

After that everything went back to normal. We ate our burnt food and I finished telling Nate about why I was suspended. He threatened to beat the shit out of Daniel if he ever saw him and he felt like it was wrong of them to fire me because of what I was. When breakfast was done, I went upstairs and took a shower and got dressed, then Nate and Stefan drove me to the airport.

At the airport Stefan and Nate took turns hugging and kissing me on the cheek and forehead and telling me that they'd miss me, even though I was only going to be gone for a day. Stefan looked like he wanted to cry, but thankfully he held his tears back.

"I'll be here to pick you up when you get back." Nate said hugging me for the hundredth time.

"Okay." I said hugging him back. Overhead, I could hear them call my flight. "I've got to go. They're calling my flight."

Nate hugged me tighter then let me go, only for Stefan to pull me into another tight squeeze. "I love you." he said. "Have a safe flight and call me when you land."

"Okay. I will." I pulled away. "I love you. Both of you." Then I turned and walked away and resisted the urge to look back. I knew what I'd see. Stefan was close to losing it and I was pretty sure Nate wasn't far off. If I turned around and saw that, I knew there would be no way in hell I would leave.

I got onto the plane knowing there was a good chance I was headed for my doom. I knew there was nothing I could do about saving my job, but I knew I had to try. This last case made me realize just how important supernatural agents were. If it hadn't been for me and my knowledge, then Elliott and Rafe would have either been killed or the case would have never been solved.

So, I got onto the plane with a plan. I might lose my job, but maybe I'd open the PCU's eyes and they'd hire new supernatural agents. It was worth a try anyway.

CHAPTER FORTY

Special Agent Tom Jameson wasn't a very nice man. He was of average height with dark greying hair and pale blue eyes. He was in his fifties and had been doing this job for a very long time. He'd started out in the FBI and when the PCU branch had been made, had been promoted to Director of the Paranormal Crime Unit.

He sat across from me now on the other side of the long cherry oak table and eyed me with a glare that said he didn't trust me, and I was below him for more than one reason. I disgusted him and he wasn't even going to hide it.

An hour earlier I had waited quietly outside while Daniel and the rest of the team gave their statements and opinions on what they thought should happen to me. I had no doubt they'd all told Jameson that I was a danger and I should be fired. I could tell by the looks he was giving me he felt the same way.

He cleared his throat. "So, agent Montgomery, what do you have to say for yourself?"

It was my turn to speak. I had been going over and over again on what I'd say. I had my speech all laid out. But now I felt my throat close up and my mind go blank. "Um, well, Sir I'm not sure what I should say." I said and wanted to run away. "I don't feel like I've done anything wrong."

He raised an eyebrow. "Oh, and lying about what you are isn't wrong?"

"I never lied. I thought everyone knew. I mean, it wasn't exactly hard to tell that I wasn't human. My eyes give me away."

Jameson narrowed his eyes and his nostrils flared. "There is no call for your smart mouth. You are here not just because your team didn't know you weren't human, but because the Paranormal Crime Unit was in the dark as well. I've been going over your file and I have yet to find where you reported to the board or your superiors of your inhuman nature."

I wanted to flinch, but I didn't. "I'm sorry Sir. I didn't know I was supposed to report it. When I signed up for the program, I was never asked about my mortality. I just assumed it wasn't a problem. And again, it goes back to every supernatural has a tell. Strength, speed, and their eyes. Mine is my eyes. Not very many people have eyes like mine. In fact, there is only one other person, and he is my father, Sir. And with all due respect, agent Fitzgerald knew."

He nodded, not looking happy. "Yes, I'm aware of your relationship with Special Agent Daniel Fitzgerald. But he has claimed that he was in the dark."

"Then he is lying."

"I am aware of that too. But he is not the one standing trial, you are. You are the one who failed to report what you are."

"What I am? There is a name for it agent Jameson. I'm an angel and a demon." I said, starting to feel angry.

"Demon?" he said, looking down at the papers in front of him. "I was not aware of the demon, only the angel."

I smiled sweetly at him. "That makes two of us. I have recently learned that I'm a hybrid. My mother is an angel and my father is a demon."

He ruffled through the papers until he found the one, he was looking for. "Yes, it says here that your mother's name is Lauren Montgomery and she went missing almost fifteen years ago."

"Yes."

"I have no name for your father. Could you fill that in?"

I nodded and took a deep breath. "My father's name is Samael."

The expression that crossed his face was priceless. Jameson swallowed hard. "Excuse me? Did you just say that your father is Samael—the most powerful demon on earth?"

Guess humans knew about him after all. "Yes. Yes, I did." I gave a small smile at his discomfort. "But don't worry. I'm not in contact with him. I only found out a few days ago."

Jameson eyed me with a hint of fear in his eyes and maybe some suspicion. "You realize you are being looked at as a danger to others, right?" I nodded. "And you do realize this changes things. You being the most feared demon's daughter doesn't do anything but make you more dangerous."

"I'm not dangerous."

"Yes, you are. And this proves it."

It was my turn to narrow my eyes. "You make it sound like I'm a monster. But I'm not. Supernaturals aren't monsters. Yes, sure, there are some out there who need to be policed, but really, they're no more monsters than a human serial killer. Or a woman who drowns her children or a cult leader who brainwashes his followers to commit mass murder or suicide. So, before you start accusing me and my kind of being monsters, why don't you take a hard look at your own damned species."

Jameson puffed up. "You are a monster, agent Montgomery. You are a problem and you are a potential endangerment to others. I do not see how you can continue to be a PCU agent."

So that was it. He was going to fire me. I'd seen it coming from the moment I'd been suspended. "Before you release me of my duties, I would like to say this. I think it may be wise if you and the board considered taking on other supernaturals as agents. This past case I worked on in Seattle proved that humans are not cut out for this."

He laughed at me. "And what do you suppose we do, agent Montgomery, hire a bunch of supernaturals to hunt down their own kind and fire all the humans?"

I shook my head. "No, I think there needs to be a new program started. Ten years ago, when the PCU branch was started, it was a good idea. I agree that there needs to be someone out there who knows how to police supernaturals. But I think there needs to be at least one or two agents who are not human on each team. The case in Seattle . . . well, we ran into some trouble with banshees and the agents and other police had no idea how to kill them or defend themselves."

"So, what, we just put a bunch of monsters on every team, because humans are stupid?"

"No, you train them."

"And how do we do that?"

I was beginning to get the feeling he was only humoring me. "You put them out in the field with a trained agent."

"Not the classroom?"

I rolled my eyes. "Honestly, no. Making them sit in a class for a year or two and teaching them about their own kind isn't going to do shit. Putting them in the field with a trained agent will." I could tell he was laughing at me with his eyes. "Look, the PCU is great, but the truth of it is, humans aren't cut out for this. I can't tell you how many times I saved my old teams asses. And when I was in Seattle . . . I met two great agents who seemed eager to learn what I knew. And honestly, I'm not sure their case would have been solved. And I'm positive that they all would have been killed. Just try it. Start with one or two and see what happens."

He stared at me and he wasn't smiling or laughing anymore. "Do you honestly believe that?"

"Yes."

"And who might I ask would train them. You?"

"Beg pardon?" I was confused.

"I got a phone call yesterday morning from agent Bronson. He gave you a very good recommendation. Told me that you were a great help to him and if I took away your badge, I'd be a damned fool." I smiled from the inside out. When I got back to Seattle, I would have to find Elliott and give him a kiss. "I also got a phone call from agent Carlos as well. You can guess what he said."

I bit my lower lip. "I'm sorry. I'm confused. I don't understand, I thought you were taking my badge."

Jameson nodded. "I was. But with the latest developments, I have changed my mind. I have spoken with agent Bronson and he has agreed to allow you on his team. We are transferring you to Seattle. And I will be running your idea by the board, and if they agree, would you be willing to train the participants?"

I nodded. "Yes."

"Remember, agent Montgomery, this was your idea. If it fails, you will be responsible for its failure."

Yeah, I had no doubt I'd be thrown under the bus.

"Thank you, Sir." I said.

Jameson gave a nod. "Just don't lie to us again. And frankly, if the new law had been past years ago, this would have never happened."

I raised an eyebrow. "New law? What new law?"

"The new law that says that every supernatural has to be branded."

I just stared at him. Was he for real? The look on his face said he wasn't joking, but he must be. Because if he wasn't, then this was bad. I didn't see any supernatural going for it.

"Branded?"

He nodded. "Yes. It has come to our attention that supernaturals are blending in too well with the human public. The brand will be a way for humans to know who they are dealing with. If the waitress waiting on them is a vampire or a werewolf."

"That is discrimination. You can't do that."

"We have done that. In a few months, the law will be put in motion and every supernatural will have to be branded."

I was floored and a tad bit angry. "Do you have any idea what will happen? Not every supernatural will be willing to go through with it."

"Then they will be killed. The law will be simple. Either they get branded or they get put down."

"And who will be putting them down? Me? Other PCU agents?"

"I do believe that is the job of the PCU."

"No, it's not." I said. "We're police, not assassins."

He narrowed his eyes at me with a look that didn't seem to care. "After the law becomes effective, it will be. If a supernatural refuses the brand, they will become rogue. Therefore, it will be your job and any other PCU agent's job to take them out. There will be no second chance. No trial. Just death."

"I don't agree with that."

He shrugged. "Doesn't matter if you agree with this or not. Soon it will be a part of your job."

I shook my head, not believing I was hearing this. "You're out of your damn mind. All of you. Do you really think the supernatural world will honor this? Hell, the fairy court has their own laws and don't abide by human laws as it is. Most supernaturals have their own laws. The only ones who might go along with it is the angels, but only because they are more about peace. Warlocks? Maybe. But that's a small maybe. But the other three groups? No. There is no way in hell they will go along with it. And the few that do, will only do it because they are doing their best to live in both worlds."

Jameson glared at me. "It will be the law whether they like it or not. And I expect you to be the first in line."

I would be. But I wasn't going to like it. "What about children?" I asked. "You can't expect children to be branded. They're still growing."

"We have thought of that. They will be expected to be branded on their eighteenth birthday."

A horrible thought formed in the back of my head. "What about those who bare the mark?"

"What mark?"

"Shit." I said. "This is why humans have no business doing this job." He gave me another glare. I ignored it. "Samael created this mark for his men. It's supposed to protect them from their enemies. If you have someone brand them that doesn't have the mark, then they'll be killed."

"Are you sure?"

I nodded. "Yeah. The tattoo will see it as an attack and your tattooist will be burned alive." I could just see it now. Someone with the mark sits down for the brand and when the tattoo Artist starts putting on the tattoo, he suddenly combusts. Yeah, that would start panic. The PCU would automatically think he was killed on purpose and would want the demon put down.

I could see he didn't like that. "I will keep that under consideration. Now, this meeting is over. Be sure to check in with agent Bronson. You may leave."

I wanted to say more, but I didn't. I just nodded, stood, and then left the room. I walked out the door and closed it behind me and turned to see my old team sitting outside in the small waiting room. Daniel was the first one I saw. He sat there with a cocky grin on his face that said he hoped I was hurting. I was hurting, but not in the way he thought.

Daniel had short brown hair and dark green eyes that at one time made me melt along with his smile. He had been charming and sexy, and I had fell for it. But I knew better now. He was just an asshole who broke my heart who looked to have a black eye that he hadn't had when I left.

Special Agent Troy Morrison sat beside him and his expression didn't seem any happier to see me. He was an older man in his mid-forties with short blond hair and bright blue eyes. He'd been married to the same woman since he was twenty-two, she'd been his high school sweetheart. They had two children—a boy and a girl. I'd been over to his house more than once for cookouts and I'd applied presser to his chest once when a vampire had tried to tear him to pieces. And this was how I was being repaid? A cold stare.

Looked at as if I were anything but trustworthy. As if I was going to just start ripping out their throats like some rapid animal.

I walked toward them slowly, not sure my presence would be welcome. Daniel and Troy both gave me unfriendly expressions.

"So, how did it go in there?" Daniel asked, not being careful of his eagerness to hear that I'd been fired.

"It was fine. I'm being transferred to Seattle." I said.

Daniel's cocky grin vanished. "Really?"

"Yep. Agent's Bronson and Carlos wants me on the team."

"Why?" Troy asked.

"Beats the hell out of me." I snapped. "But I was headed back to Seattle anyway."

Just then the door to the ladies room opened, and Special Agent Courtney McKenna stepped out. She was a few inches shorter than me with long brown hair and dark brown eyes. She was pretty in the girl next doorway, but right now she was looking a little green.

Daniel stood up and walked over to her. "Hey, how are you feeling?" he asked pulling her close to him in a way he used to me. What the hell was I missing?

"I'm okay. But I don't think I'm going to get use to that." Courtney said smiling at him the way I used to. "So, what was the verdict?"

"They're transferring her." Daniel replied.

She scrunched up her nose. "Why would they do that?"

I stood there and stared at him and her, trying to figure out if my eyes were deceiving me. But after a few blinks I soon realize they weren't. Daniel and Courtney . . . they were together. And by the looks of it, she was . . . "How far along are you?" I asked before I had time to think.

Daniel and Courtney turned and looked at me as if they'd just realized I was in the room. "What?" Daniel asked.

"How far into her pregnancy is she?" I repeated. "And I'm going on a limb here and assume that it's yours."

He swallowed hard. "Two months."

"And how long have you been sleeping with her?"

"Almost five months."

Right. Well, I guess that explained why he'd stopped sleeping with me and why every time we had a case outside of Boston he'd opted for his own room. Only now I knew he hadn't been sleeping in it alone. Courtney had been sleeping in it with him. They'd been having sex two or three rooms down from mine while I laid in bed and cried because he didn't want to touch me anymore. Now they were having a baby. A baby that by all rights should have been mine.

There was a lump in my throat, and I wasn't sure if I was going to cry or throw up first. Thankfully I did neither. I pushed back the tears, even though I knew they were visible. What made it worse and harder to control my emotions was the fact that neither of them looked sorry or guilty about it.

"A baby. Wow." I said, voice close to tears. "You moved on fast." Yeah, before we even broke up.

Troy stood and walked over to stand by Daniel and Courtney. I could see a hint of fear in his eyes, like he thought I was going to snap and hurt them. I wanted to, but not because I was part demon, but because Daniel had been cheating instead of taking care of me. I'd been grieving over the loss of my unborn child while he'd been out screwing someone, I thought was my friend.

"I'm not going to hurt them Troy." I said, feeling hurt that he'd even think I would.

"Then why do you look like you want to commit murder? And besides, I know what you are and what your kind is capable of."

Actually, he didn't. If he did, he'd probably pull out his gun and threaten to shoot me. I looked at Troy and saw hatred. "Do you really believe I'm a monster or are you just saying that because you think it's the right thing to say?"

Troy narrowed his eyes at me. "Yes, I really believe you're a monster. You are unnatural and have no business doing this job."

That's just what he thought. I had every right to do this job. "Yeah, well, that's a matter of opinion." I turned my gaze to Daniel. "Why? Why did you sleep with her?"

Daniel stepped away from Courtney and leveled his gaze on me. "What were you expecting, Morgan?"

I gave a harsh laugh. "What was I expecting? Really? What I expected was for you to be there for me and mourn over our baby, not go out and screw her." I pointed a finger at Courtney. I was feeling angry now and it was starting to show.

"I never wanted that baby." Daniel snapped. "So how was I supposed to mourn over it?"

"Yeah, I know. And you know what? You should have just said that the morning I told you I was pregnant. We would have just ended it then."

"What, the baby?"

I shook my head. "No, us. I would have moved out and moved back to Seattle sooner. Then maybe I'd still be pregnant. But no, you didn't do that. Instead you said you were happy and wanted a boy."

Yeah, things would have been a hell of a lot easier.

"And what, you would have just kept him or her away from me?" Daniel snapped.

"What would it have mattered to you? Since you didn't want your child to be a monster?" The first of the tears began to fall, but I wasn't sobbing. "So, I don't see where you would have had any say in it." And besides, I would have made sure he hadn't.

"Wow, you really are a heartless bitch."

"And you really are a dick." I said and kneed him in the groin before he had time to react. His eyes widened and he fell to the ground. "Have a nice life Daniel." And then I turned and walked away. If I stayed there any longer, I was going to do more damage than knee him and it'd be more permanent.

I walked away feeling a little better about myself. And I actually smiled. Kneeing Daniel in the groin felt good. I only wished I could do it again. Kelly Clarkson was right. What doesn't kill you does make you stronger and makes you stand a little taller. And right now, I was feeling pretty damn tall.

CHAPTER FORTY-ONE

Nate was waiting for me at the airport when my flight landed. I almost ran to him when I saw him, but instead just quickened my steps. He wrapped his arms around me and held me tight. I sighed in relief to finally be back in Seattle. Seeing Daniel today had been hard, but I'd pulled through. And now I was home with my family and friends and I had no regrets.

Nate pulled back and smiled. "I missed you."

"I was only gone for a day." I said.

He shrugged. "The house felt empty. And besides, dad did a lot of moping."

I smiled up at him. "Well, no one has to do anymore moping and the house won't feel empty either. I'm moving back in." My smiled widened. "I'm being transferred to Seattle. They didn't take my badge away."

Nate smiled wide and hugged me tight. "That is so great. What made them change their mind?"

I pulled back and smiled over at the two other men who were standing off to the side, quietly waiting for their turn to welcome me home. Elliott and Rafe both gave me knowing smiles. I walked over and hugged Elliott and gave him a kiss on the lips. He seemed startled.

"What was that for?" he asked.

"For taking up for me."

"You know," Rafe said with a smile. "I helped too." Then he wiggled his eyebrows.

I laughed and kissed him on the cheek.

"The cheek, huh? Cool, I'll take it."

Elliott just shook his head. "Welcome home and welcome to the team. I've already informed Livea that we're getting a replacement. She's eager to meet you."

I raised an eyebrow. "And she knows I'm not human?"

"Yep."

I was happy and a bit relieved. Elliott had said that Livea had been close to the agent killed and was having a hard time dealing with it. He'd suspected that there had been something romantic going on between them but had never asked. He'd said it was her business not his.

Nate picked up the suitcase I'd dropped on the floor and draped an arm around my shoulders. "We should get going. Traffic is crazy and I think dad's planning a welcome home thing. Oh, and Julian and the guys are back with your stuff."

I winced. "What sort of thing?"

"Don't know. But I think everyone is coming over again. Oh, and just a heads up, but Sabine is mad at you. You didn't tell her goodbye."

I knew she would be, but I could hardly handle the goodbyes from Stefan and Nate. So there had been no way I'd been able to say goodbye to Sabine without breaking.

"Okay, thanks for telling me. And um, I need to borrow your car when we get home. There's something I need to do before I go inside."

"Okay, what?"

I told him.

"Are you sure?" Elliott asked me.

I nodded. "Yes. I'm almost positive. But I have no proof."

"Need backup?" Rafe asked.

I shook my head. "No. I'm going in unarmed. No gun. No badge. Just as a supernatural. I think it would be better that way. He won't feel threatened and that's what I want. I just want him to know that I'm on to him and next time he won't get away with it."

Yeah, I knew if I just walked in with a badge and gun and an attitude, then he'd clamp up and give one right back.

"Oh, by the way." Elliott said. "Rafe and I had a talk with Grady. He claimed he had no idea what we were talking about."

"And don't leave out the fact that he was smiling smugly while he said it." said Rafe.

"Doesn't surprise me that he'd say that." I said. No, it sure as hell didn't. In fact, I'd expected it. A man like Grady wasn't going to just out himself. Not to mention, he was one of Samael's men. If he actually copped to it, then he'd have to give Samael away. And there was no way he'd do that.

"If you want, we could go back and pressure him." Elliott said.

I shook my head. "No, that's okay. This isn't really a PCU matter. More like a supernatural one." I looked down and decided if they were going to work with me, then they deserved to know before word got out from someone else. "You should probably know this before we start working together."

"Know what?"

I took a deep breath. "My father is Samael."

Elliott and Rafe's eyes widened. "You mean the all great and powerful, Samael?" Rafe asked.

I nodded. "I just found out a few days ago. That's why Grady was at my house. Daddy dearest sent him."

"Why?" asked Elliott.

"It's complicated. And I'm too tired to go into detail right now."

He smiled. "Okay, go home, get some rest, and enjoy your family. I'm sure there will be another case soon and you can tell me then."

"Deal."

Nate and I made our way to his car and got in. It was getting late and I knew I should probably just go home and enjoy my freedom for the next few days. But there were some things I needed to do first. Starting with something uncomfortable and possibly infuriating.

"Okay, I need to make a pit stop before going home." I said to Nate.

"Okay, where?"

I told him.

Nate just gave me a blank look then nodded. "Okay, but I'm going in with you."

Nate parked in front of Illusions and we got out of the car. I stared at the building and wanted to get back into the car. But I didn't. I needed to go inside and tell Balian to leave me alone. Or at least try. I had a feeling I could tell him all I wanted, but he wasn't going to listen.

There was no line to wait in, since there was a sign saying private party on the door. There was a new bouncer at the door, but he never stopped us from going inside. I found that kind of odd, but I guess since Balian knew I was coming home tonight, perhaps he thought I'd show up and had told his new bouncer to expect me.

The inside of Illusions was the same the night I'd been shot. The music was low and there were a few demons on the dance floor dancing to the beat. Samael and the woman with lavender eyes, sat on the long black sofa. Grady sat in one of the chairs, and Valentina sat in the other. She was holding her newborn son. Constantine, Kyriss, the dark-skinned girl, and Balian stood around her, their faces filled with awe.

Kyriss looked up and smiled as he saw me. He said something I couldn't hear and Balian looked up and smiled, but it disappeared when he saw Nate behind me. He stepped away from the chair and stopped maybe two steps away. I stopped about four steps away from him, not trusting myself to be any closer.

"Morgan, you showed up." Balian said, something shining in his eyes that almost looked like surprise. "I was worried you would not. What happened in Boston?"

"They didn't take my badge. I'm being transferred here." I said hesitantly.

He smiled. "That is great news."

He started to move forward but stopped when I put up a hand. "That's close enough. I didn't come here for a booty call."

"Then why did you?"

"I came here to tell you to stay the hell away from me."

Confusion filled his eyes. "I do not understand."

"Stefan told me everything. I know why you've been around and what you want from me."

Balian laughed. "Oh, did he now? And what may I ask do you think I want?"

"Me." I said. "Stefan said you made some deal with Samael to be my mate. And I'm here to tell you that's never going to happen. There's no way in hell."

Balian gave another bark of laughter. "Yes, but we are creatures of hell. And it has been known to be very persuasive at times."

"Doesn't matter. You're never going to get what you want."

"Brave words from such a delicate flower. Believe what you will, but I know the truth."

"And what might that be?"

Balian walked toward me and I resisted the urge to step back. I didn't know what he was going to do, but I didn't think he would hurt me. There were too many people around and if what I was told was true, then he wouldn't hurt me anyway.

He stopped in front of me and leaned in and whispered in my ear. "You may try to resist me, but when I am done with you, you will beg me to join you in your bed." And just like that, the mask he'd been wearing was gone. I saw right through him and his motives. He was cocky and arrogant and that was his downfall.

I swallowed hard. "You will never have me."

Balian chuckled and brushed his lips against my neck. "You see, that is where you are wrong, Morgan. I have already had you. Several times in fact." He lightly ran his tongue across my neck, and I shivered. "Do you want to know what you taste like?" His voice was like silk as he spoke. And this time I resisted the urge to moan. "You taste like honey and dark chocolate." I closed my eyes as he trailed his fingertips across the back of my neck and down my spine. "Sweet and bitter. Two of my favorite things."

I exhaled, but it sounded more like a moan. God, his voice. It was like his version of safe sex. I was almost in ecstasy just listening to it. I could still feel him inside of me and that scared me. I'd never felt that with anyone else. And with the vision of our naked bodies pressed together in my head, my body began screaming for him.

I cursed myself and shook my head. "Back up." I said breathlessly.

Balian didn't move.

"You heard her." Nate said, speaking for the first time. "Move back."

Balian pulled back to look at Nate and smiled. "Temper Nathaniel, people are watching. You would not want to make a scene, would you?"

"I could really care less about making a scene." Nate snapped. "Now move back, or I will do it for you."

"Well, haven't you become the great protector."

"I'm her friend and her brother. It's my job to protect her."

Around me I could hear small chuckles. Guess they all found that funny.

Balian tilted his head to the side. "Are you?" he asked.

"Yes." Nate snapped. "Morgan is my sister and it's my job to see that some jerkoff doesn't take advantage of her."

"Jerkoff, huh? Is that supposed to be an insult to my gentlemanly character?" Balian countered.

"If that's the conclusion you've come to, then perhaps you should rethink your life."

Balian laughed. "Yes, perhaps." His smile was mocking. "But after all, I am what I am. If I was not, then Morgan would not find me intriguing and I would not have gotten between her thighs when I had."

I moved to slap him, but Nate pulled me back before my hand could connect with Balian's face. "You bastard!" I yelled.

He shrugged. "I am. But it is what I excel at."

Anger boiled to the surface and I felt it start to seep out. I wanted to hurt him then. No, the darkness inside of me wanted to hurt him, but I forced it back. "Stay away from me."

"You know I cannot do that. You are my mate. You belong to me."

I narrowed my eyes at him. "I belong to no one but myself. Not you. Not Samael. No one. Whatever sick and twisted plans you made with him are over. I'm not going to fall for them or you again."

Balian smiled. "Like I said before little orchid, never say never."

I did a quick glance throughout the room and my eyes locked with Samael's. He looked between amused and angry. The expression that crossed his features said he knew I knew who he was and what he'd done to my mother. There was no remorse behind his dark teal eyes. No fatherly love either. That told me he hadn't wanted me because he loved children and wanted one for himself. It told me his motives were beyond sincere and if I made too much of a fuss, he'd gladly do something about it.

He'd hurt me and not think twice about it.

I moved my gaze to Grady, and he seemed smug and seemed to be enjoying the show. I looked over at the others. Constantine seemed disgusted and Valentina seemed angry, and I assumed it was at me since I was who they were looking at. Kyriss looked uneasy and somewhat shocked.

The dark-skinned girl seemed angry too. Guess these people were Balian's friends. Why else would they seem to loath me without even knowing me?

I thought back to the night in the hospital room when I'd overheard Balian and Kyriss talking. Balian had said something about Constantine and Valentina still hating me even though I saved their lives. Guess he'd been right.

I looked back at Balian as I pulled away from Nate. "Just stay away from me."

"No." Balian said and smiled. "I believe it is about time I stake my claim on you."

I froze and my body stiffened as a memory came back to me. A hallucination . . . or vision of Balian and I in my shower, water pouring over our naked bodies. His lips and hands and everything in between feeling so real. Him telling me the exact same thing. That he believed it was about time he staked his claim on me.

I had thought I had been seeing things, but as I stared at him and everything became clear, I began to feel sick as I realized that I hadn't been seeing things. Balian had really been there, in my shower, naked and pressed up against me.

I suddenly couldn't be here anymore. If I stood there any longer, I was either going to start screaming or I was going to throw up. I turned and almost ran out of the building. Behind me I could hear Balian laughing. I ignored it and just kept walking and didn't stop until I was outside and in Nate's car. Nate got in and just stared at me.

"Do I even want to know what that meant?" he asked.

I shook my head.

"Okay. Well, let's get home. I'm sure everyone's there by now."

"Okay. But I have to go see him before I go inside. If I don't do it tonight, I might chicken out."

Nate nodded. "That's fine. Let's just get out of here before I get the urge to go back in there and do some damage."

"Yeah, I second that."

Nate turned the key and we drove away. The whole car ride home I stared out the window and wondered just how deep in shit was I in. Had I done too much with Balian to just walk away and never look back? Or had I ended it just in time? Something told me walking away from him was going to be easier said than done. It would take a hell of a lot of will power.

I sighed, because I hoped I had enough will power. Because if I didn't, I was screwed. In more ways than one.

CHAPTER FORTY-TWO

I **sat in a black wooden chair** in front of a black wooden desk. The room matched the rest of the palace with soft purples and pale greens. I sat there and silently wondered what it was about those colors the fairies liked so much when the door to the office opened and Androcles walked in. He eyed me and did not smile. I half expected he knew why I was here and what I was about to say.

He crossed the room and took the chair behind the desk. "Special Agent Montgomery, what a pleasant surprise. What have I done to grant your presence?"

I smiled. "Not agent Montgomery. Just call me Morgan."

He raised an eyebrow. "Oh? So, this is not an official PCU matter?"

"Not tonight. Tonight, I'm just another supernatural."

He gave a bark of laughter. "Oh, somehow I really doubt that. You, Miss Montgomery, are anything but just another supernatural. And we both know why."

"My father has nothing to do with this. I'm here because I know you had Theophilius kill those people."

Androcles frowned. "First, they were demons—they deserved everything they got. Second, Theophilius acted on his own accord. I never ordered him to murder anyone. And third, where is your proof that I have done this?"

I had none, but only a feeling deep in my gut. I knew men like Andros, and men like him didn't just sit back and allow those who threatened or harmed his family to live. Stefan was one of them. I knew if I'd ever gotten raped, Stefan wouldn't sit back either. Only difference, he'd kill them himself.

"I know what happened to Ila and I'm sorry. But murder wasn't the answer. And how do I know you were behind it? Well, Andros, I'm a cop and I'm a supernatural. I understand how supernatural laws work. And I know that Theophilius would have never gone after who was responsible without there being an order. You are his king."

Androcles narrowed his eyes at me. "You know, Miss Montgomery, I know all about you. Your mother ran off when you were nine, and the man she was seeing at the time, Stefan Williams took you in and raised you as his own. But your true father is Samael, a powerful greater demon. A demon who takes his orders from Lucifer himself. When you were sixteen you gave your virginity to your best friend Kaydan Lewis, but somehow you managed to sleep around with other men on the side. At eighteen, you had a four-month relationship with Esten Harbin, a fairy boy that ended very badly."

"And your point is?" I asked trying to hide fear. How had he known all of that?

"My point is, be very careful who you make your enemy. You never know how much about you they may know. Or what they might do with said information."

"Are you threatening me? You know it's against the law to threaten a police officer."

He smiled as he tilted his head to the side. "I thought you were only a supernatural tonight?"

"Then I'm guessing it's against supernatural law to threaten the offspring of Samael."

That made him laugh. "Yes, I am sure. But let me ask you this, what would the man who raised you do if someone ruined his child?"

"Ila isn't ruined." I said. "She was raped, not ruined."

He frowned this time and almost seemed angry. "Oh, that is where you are wrong. My daughter is very much ruined. No male is ever going to want her. My only hope at heirs to continue this bloodline is from my son. Because I have one daughter that is dead and another that might as well be."

"And that's why you had them all killed." I said guessing. "Because you honestly believe that you only have one child left. How cruel is that?"

"It is not a matter of being cruel. It is a matter of honor. In some human cultures, if the female in the family gave herself before marriage, they killed her."

"But Ila didn't give herself. It was taken."

He shrugged. "The same difference. It does not matter if it was given or taken, Miss Montgomery, my daughter is still ruined. And the truth of it is, if Delisa would have come home . . . she would have died anyway, because she was ruined as well."

My stomach felt sick. I was so happy I wasn't a part of this whacked out family. I would have been killed at sixteen. But as sick as it was, Andros was right. That was how it was in some human cultures, so why not the supernatural?

"What about the child?"

"Child?"

I studied his face before I continued. Either he hadn't known Delisa had been pregnant or he was pretending not to know. "Delisa was pregnant when she was killed. Did you know?"

Andros gave a faint smile. "I was aware of the thing in her womb. But I don't see why it matters."

I just stared at him. "Are you saying that you would have still killed her knowing she was with a child?"

"Yes."

"But it was an innocent child. Your grandchild."

"It was an abomination. It did not deserve to live."

A lump formed in my throat. "How can you say that? How do you not know that she wasn't looking forward to becoming a mother?"

Andros tilted his head to the side. "I feel as if I have hit a nerve, Morgan. What am I missing?"

I looked down. Did I really want to tell my pain to a man who probably could care less? I raised my eyes up to meet his. "I lost a child five months ago. A miscarriage."

"Oh, I am sorry. Who was the father?"

"He was human."

He smiled then. "Yes, now I see why it hit a nerve. You were caring an abomination too."

I really needed to change the subject before I did something stupid. Like jump across the desk and pound my fist into his face. "So, what are you going to do with Ila?" I asked already knowing the answer and telling myself to hold back my anger.

"I have given her to my men. If they so desire to bed her, then she will oblige them. She has no choice in the matter."

"And what does your wife and son think about it?"

Andros looked heartbroken right then as he looked down at his desk. "My wife is not speaking with me and my son has threatened my men."

That was what I'd thought. I'd seen the way Zarek looked at his sister. He adored her, so it wasn't surprising that he'd been pissed at his father's order. I couldn't see him just sitting back and allowing his father's men to take advantage of his baby sister. Not without a fight.

Andros looked up. "You have not answered my question. What would Stefan do if someone would ever rape you?"

"He'd kill them." I said. "But he would still love me. He wouldn't think I was ruined."

"And that is the difference between the angels and the fairies." He studied me and smiled. "I know you were worried about coming here and why. But you need not worry about running into Esten. He is not here. Hasn't been for some time now."

I raised my eyebrows in confusion. "Um, okay. Actually, I wasn't. Not really. But um, why has he been gone?"

"Because I sent him away. I felt with what he was, it would not be appropriate."

"I don't understand."

"Have you not heard?" he asked, and I shook my head. "Esten was attacked by a vampire about a year ago. He is a hybrid now."

I stared at him dumbly. Esten, a hybrid? "Are you saying that he's a fairy/vampire hybrid?"

"Yes, that is what I am saying."

I wanted to accuse him of lying, but something told me he was telling the truth. But I didn't understand. Why would a vampire attack a fairy and turn him? They didn't do that. But then again, they didn't go around attacking angels either. Only I sort of understood that one. Now. Samael had been trying to send a message, and it had been received.

"Where is he now?" I asked.

He shrugged. "Not sure. Don't really care."

I had a bad feeling about this, but I didn't have time to decipher it right now. I could do that later. I stood, knowing it was time I left. "Well, Andros, I should leave. I just came here to tell you not to do it again. I might not have any proof, this time. But if something like this happens again, next time you won't be so lucky."

"We will see. Give my regards to your father."

"Which one?"

"Both." And then he laughed.

I left feeling uneasy and knowing I'd be back here. Maybe not tomorrow or next month or even next year. But I'd be back here, because Andros would do something stupid. Granted, he wouldn't do it himself, which would make it worse and harder to prove, but I'd find a way.

I pulled into the driveway of the mansion and sighed. It was dark and by the looks of it, everyone was here and inside. Personally, I just wanted to go to my room and sleep until the next case. Today had been a very hard day. From the knowledge of Daniel and Courtney's relationship and new baby, to Balian and his cockiness, and ending with Androcles admitting that he was pretty much making his daughter a whore just for his men.

That was sick on so many levels and I was grateful that no one saw me like that.

Looking at the front door I knew what was waiting for me inside. Family, friends, and foes. People who were eager to know if I was staying or leaving. Some would be overjoyed that I was staying, other's I wasn't so sure.

I knew I had to go in there and tell them about my job and the baby I'd lost. I had to come clean and tell all of them and I was scared. For the first time in a really long time, I was scared. I was scared that they'd all hate me or feel sorry for me. But what scared me most of all, was my feelings for Balian. I knew it was only a matter of time before he started coming around again and demanding that I see him. And I was scared that I'd give in. Or that I'd fall in love with him.

Actually, falling in love with anyone right now scared me. So that last one didn't just mean him.

I got out of the car and forced myself to go inside. I might as well get this over with. I walked into the house and was greeted with smiles. I took a deep breath.

Julian strolled over when I entered the room and smiled. "Hey, there you are. The girl of the hour. Thought you were going to stay hidden all night until we left." He wrapped an arm around me. "Not that it would have worked. I would have found you." I leaned my body into him and sighed. "So, how did it go?"

Everyone had been whispering and had stopped when Julian had began talking to me. I stood there and looked at all the eager expressions and I choked. I started to open my mouth to tell them about everything, but I choked. Instead I said. "It went okay. I'm being transferred here. Daniel was there and ... turns out he's already moved on with someone else. And they're having a baby." My voice cracked a little on the last part.

Julian pulled me into his arms and held me tight. "I am so sorry." he said. I smiled and sniffed.

Alec was the next one to grab and hug me. "Now I'm really not sorry that I punched him." There was a note in his voice that said he wished he'd done more.

I pulled back and raised an eyebrow as I remembered that Daniel had had a black eye. "You punched Daniel? Why?"

He smiled. "Why do you think? Because he's an asshole and doesn't deserve you. And when I was done, I might have left him with the impression that I was ... taking care of you."

"Oh, Alec, you didn't?"

"He did." Dylan said wrapping his arms around me. "He told him that he was sleeping with you. Even gave some details."

I flashed Alec a look and he laughed. "Hey, I've seen you naked, remember? So, it wasn't exactly hard to give details."

"Excuse me?" Stefan said. "When have you seen her naked?"

Julian laughed. "Stefan, every man in this room except you, my dad, Luke, Sheldon, and Donavon, has seen Morgan naked."

"When?" Stefan asked.

Nate sighed. "Remember when you were dating that girl ... Gloria and you took her to that bed and breakfast?"

Stefan nodded.

"Well, we all went to the beach and had this bonfire. And well, there was some drinking involved. Morgan was really drunk and decided that she wanted to go swimming. Naked."

"And I told Alec I'd give him a hundred bucks if he stripped down and went in after her and gave her a kiss." Julian said with a laugh. "And he did it."

Alec smiled. "That was one hell of a kiss too."

I had forgotten about that. But now that it had been mentioned, I remember that night perfectly. I remembered the bonfire, the drinking, the skinny dipping, the kiss and Alec's naked body pressed up against mine. I remember wanting more than just a kiss, but we'd never gone any further. There had been too many people around and if we'd gone off alone, everyone would have known. Plus, he was Nate's best friend and there was a rule.

Everyone stayed for a long time after that. They'd all seemed to take me being Samael's daughter pretty well. Everyone except the Messer's and the Lewis's. They'd gotten up and left, but not until they'd called me the devils seed and accused me of planning their deaths.

After everyone left, I went upstairs and went to bed. I was tired and just wanted the night to end.

The next day I got up and felt good about my move back to Seattle. Stefan had been so happy that I was moving back home, that I saw a few tears in his eyes. He and Mariska have talked about it and have decided that their baby making can wait for a while.

Stefan put his arms around me when I came into the kitchen. "I'm so glad you're home." he said.

"Me too." I said. "I promise this is only temporary. I'll get me a place as soon as I can."

"Nonsense. This is your home. You can stay however long you want."

I smiled. "I know." I knew that if I wanted to, I could live in this house for the rest of my life. But we both knew that that would never happen. I needed my own space and the only way I could get that was to have my own place.

There was the sound of the doorbell. I pulled back and went to go answer the door. I opened it to find a big square box in front of it. I frowned and picked it up. I carried the box to the sitting room and sat it down as Nate and Stefan walked in.

"What is it?" Stefan asked.

"I have no idea." I said and frowned as I heard the sound of scratching coming from inside. I examined the box and saw that there were small holes in the top of it.

I slowly opened the box and I gasped. Inside was a small long-haired kitten. It was completely black except for the white on its paws. I gave a quick look under the tail and found it was a girl. She looked up at me with big eyes. One blue and one green. And I fell in love.

"A kitten?" Nate said sounding puzzled. "Who would drop a kitten on our doorstep?"

"I don't know." I said.

"Well, maybe this will tell us." Stefan said holding a small white piece of paper in his hand. "It was inside the box."

I took the note and my heart fluttered. The handwriting was neat. A small tear fell from one eye as I read.

To help mend your broken heart. Love, Balian

Nate took the note and frowned. "Why would he do this?"

I shrugged as I looked adoringly at the kitten. "I need to name her."

Nate raised an eyebrow. "Seriously? You're actually going to keep that thing?" He pointed at the kitten in my arms.

I looked down at her and she looked right back. She purred and I was lost. This was so sweet. Probably the sweetest thing anyone had ever done for me. When I spoke, my voice was filled with love. "Yes. Yes, I am. And I'm naming her Balie."

Printed in the United States
By Bookmasters